Graham HURLEY

one under

This is Graham Hurley's seventh novel to feature DI Joe Faraday and DC Paul Winter. An award-winning TV documentary maker, Graham now writes full time. He lives with his wife, Lin, in the West Country. Visit his website at www.grahamhurley.co.uk.

By Graham Hurley

FEATURING DI JOE FARADAY

One Under
Blood and Honey
Cut to Black
Deadlight
Angels Passing
The Take
Turnstone

OTHER NOVELS

Permissible Limits
Nocturne
Heaven's Light
The Perfect Soldier
Sabbathman
Thunder in the Blood
The Devil's Breath
Reaper
Rules of Engagement

NON-FICTION

Airshow

ONE UNDER

Graham Hurley

An Orion paperback

First published in Great Britain in 2007
by Orion Gollancz
This paperback edition published in 2007
by Orion Books Ltd,
Orion House, 5 Upper St Martin's Lane,
London WC2H 9EA

An Hachette Livre UK company

3 5 7 9 10 8 6 4

A CIP catalogue record for this book is available
from the British Library

ISBN 978-0-7528-8173-7

Typeset by Deltatype Ltd, Birkenhead, Merseyside

Printed in Great Britain by Clays Ltd, St Ives plc

The Orion Publishing Group's policy is to use papers that
are natural, renewable and recyclable products and
made from wood grown in sustainable forests. The logging
and manufacturing processes are expected to conform to
the environmental regulations of the country of origin.

www.orionbooks.co.uk

For Kate and Tom
with love

I like the consistency of the dark. It keeps me safe
— *Don McCullin*

Acknowledgements

My thanks to the following for their time and advice: John Ashworth, Steve Beards, Derek Bish, Dorothy Bone, Martin Chudley, Roly Dumont, Andy Edwards, Norman Feeriat, Woody Fisher, Pat Forsyth, Diana Franklin, Jason Goodwin, Andy Harrington, David Horsley, Jack Hurley, Lisa John, Richard John, Bernard Knight, Barbara Large, Neil Maxwell, John Molyneux, Kevin Monks, Susan Newcombe, Ray Odell, Liz Oliver, Tim Pepper, Dave Sackman, Sally Spedding and Tara Walker. My editor, Simon Spanton, has piloted the series through occasionally rough waters while my wife, Lin, has remained the keeper of the charts. Thanks is too small a word.

Prelude

Every driver's nightmare.

Assigned to the first train out of Portsmouth, he'd checked in at the Fratton depot before dawn, double-locking his Suzuki 900, stowing his helmet in the crew room, and then making his way upstairs to glance through the emergency speed restrictions and confirm his station stops. This time in the morning, the five-car set would be virtually empty. A handful of staff hitching a ride to stations up the line, maybe a dozen or so City-bound commuters, plus occasionally a drunk or two, slumped in the corner of the carriage, unconscious after a night in the Southsea clubs.

He was two minutes late off Portsmouth Harbour, waiting for a lone punter from the Isle of Wight Fast Cat, but made up the time before the miles of trackside terraces began to thin and the train clattered over Portsbridge Creek, leaving the city silhouetted against the fierce spill of light to the east.

The station at Havant looked deserted. Coasting to a halt, he waited barely fifteen seconds before the guard closed the doors again. Picking up speed, heading north now, he wondered whether the promised thunder-storms would really happen, and whether his partner would remember to close the greenhouse door in case the wind got up.

Beyond the long curve of Rowland's Castle station, the gradient began to steepen. Ahead lay the dark swell of the South Downs. He added more power, watching the speedo needle creep round towards seventy. These new Desiros knocked spots off the old stock. German kit, he thought. Never fails.

Minutes later, deep in a cutting, came the sudden gape of the Buriton Tunnel. He slowed to 40 mph and sounded the horn, raising a flurry of wood pigeons from the surrounding trees. Then the world suddenly went black, the clatter of the train pulled tight around him, and he peered into the darkness, waiting for his eyes to adjust. Moments later, still enfolded by the tunnel, he had a sudden glimpse of something ahead on the line. In the dim throw of light from the front of the train, the oncoming shape resolved itself into a body spreadeagled on the nearside rail, then – for a split second – he was looking at a pair of legs, scissored open, and the unmistakable whiteness of naked flesh.

Instinctively, a single reflex movement, he took the speed off and pushed the brake handle fully forward, feeling his body tensing for the impact, the way he might on the bike, some dickhead stepping out onto the road. Then came a jolt, nothing major, and he knew with a terrible certainty that his eyes hadn't betrayed him, that what he'd seen, what he'd felt, was even now being shredded in the roaring darkness beneath the train.

The cab began to shudder under the bite of the brakes. The tunnel exit in sight, he pulled the train to a halt and reached for the cab-secure radio that would take him to the signalman back at Havant. When the signalman answered, he gave him the train code and location, asked for power isolation, declared an emergency.

'What's up then?' the man wanted to know.

The driver blinked, still staring ahead, aware of the guard repeating his question on the internal comms.

'One under,' he managed, reaching for the door.

One

This time, Faraday knew there'd be no escape.

He'd taken to the water an hour or so earlier, finning slowly out of the bay, scanning the reefs below, enjoying the lazy rise and fall of the incoming swell. An evening with a reference book he'd picked up in Bangkok let him put a name to the shapes that swam into view.

Beneath him, he could see yellow-ringed parrotfish, nosing for food amongst the coral; half a dozen milky white batfish, stately, taking their time, slowly unfurling like banners; even, for a glorious minute or two, the sight of a solitary clownfish drifting over the underwater meadows of softly waving fronds. The head of the clownfish was daubed with a startling shade of scarlet but it was the huge eyes, doleful, disconsolate, that had Faraday blasting water from his snorkel tube. The little fish reminded him of an Inspector he'd once served under in his uniformed days. The same sense of tribulation. The same air of unfathomable regret. Laughing underwater, Faraday discovered, wasn't a great idea.

Further out the colours changed, and with the blues and greens shading ever deeper, Faraday became aware of the schools of fish beginning to thin. He'd never been out this far, not by a long way, and a lift of his head told him that he must have covered nearly a mile since he'd slipped into the water. He could see the tiny wooden bungalow clinging to the rocks above the tideline. A line of washing on the veranda told him that Eadie must have finally surfaced. Shame.

Adjusting the mask and clearing the snorkel again, Faraday ducked his head. It was hard to judge distance underwater but twenty metres down, maybe more, he could just make out a tumble of boulders on the seabed. This, he imagined, would be the point where the coral shallows suddenly plunged away into something infinitely deeper. In the beachside bar, only yesterday, he'd heard a couple of French lads describing a dive they'd just made. Faraday was no linguist but his French was adequate enough to understand *profondeur* and *requin*. The latter word came with a repertoire of gestures and had raised an appreciative shiver in one of the listening women. *Requin* meant shark.

Floating on the surface, barely moving, Faraday was overwhelmed by a sense of sudden chill. A mile was a long way out. There were no lifeguards, no rescue boats. Trying to slow his pulse rate, he scanned the depths below him. A thin drizzle of tiny particles was drifting down through the dapple of surface sunlight, down towards the inky blue nothingness. Then, way off to the right, he caught a flicker of movement, the briefest glimpse of something much, much bigger than the carnival of cartoon fish he'd left in the shallows.

Faraday shut his eyes a moment, squeezed them very hard, fought the temptation to turn in the water, to kick hard, to strike for home. This is exactly what you shouldn't do, he told himself. In situations like these, panic was the shortest cut to disaster.

He opened his eyes again, watched his own pale hand wipe the toughened glass in the facemask. He'd been wrong. Not one of them. Not two. But half a dozen. At least. They were circling now, much closer, sleek, curious, terrifying.

All too aware of the quickening rasp of his own breath, Faraday watched the sharks. Every nerve end told him that something unimaginable was about to

4

happen. He hung in the water, his mouth suddenly dry, feeling utterly helpless. He'd never seen creatures like this, so perfectly evolved for the task in hand, so ready, so close. The water rippled over the gills behind their gaping mouths as they slipped through the shafts of dying sunlight, and as they circled closer and closer he became mesmerised by their eyes. The eyes told him everything. They were cold, unblinking, devoid of anything but the expectation of what would happen next. This was their territory. Their world. Trespass was a capital offence.

Faraday had a sudden vision of blood in the water, his own blood, of pinked strips of torn flesh, of jaws closing on his flailing limbs, of line after line of those savage teeth tearing at the rest of his body until nothing was left but a cloud of chemicals and splinters of white bone sinking slowly out of sight.

One of the biggest sharks made a sudden turn and then came at him, the pale body twisting as it lunged, and Faraday felt himself brace as the huge jaws filled his vision. This is death, he thought. This is what happens when you get it so badly wrong.

Another noise, piercing, insistent, familiar. The shark, he thought numbly. The shark.

His heart pounding, Faraday turned over and groped in the half darkness. The mobile was on the chair beside the bed. For a second or two, listening to the voice on the other end, he hadn't a clue where he was. Then, immeasurably relieved, he managed a response.

'Sure.' He fumbled for his watch. 'I'll be there in an hour.'

Buriton is a picturesque Hampshire village tucked beneath the wooded swell of the South Downs. A street of timbered cottages and a couple of pubs led to a twelfth-century church. There were 4×4s everywhere, most of them new, and Faraday slowed to let a harassed-looking mother load her kids into the back of

5

a Toyota Land Cruiser. Buriton, he thought wearily, is where you'd settle if you still believed in a certain version of England – peaceful, safe, white – and had the money to buy it.

He parked beside the pond at the heart of the village. Already, there was a scatter of other cars, most of them badged with the familiar chequerboard of the British Transport Police. Faraday was still eyeing a couple of BTP officers pulling on their wellington boots, wondering quite why a suicide had attracted so much police attention, when there came a tap at his passenger window.

'Boss . . . ?'

Surprised, Faraday got out of the Mondeo and shook the extended hand. DS Jerry Proctor was a Crime Scene Manager, a looming, heavyset individual with a reputation for teasing meticulously presented evidence out of the most chaotic situations. The last couple of years, he'd been seconded to the British effort in Iraq, teaching local police recruits how to become forensic investigators.

'How was the posting?'

'Bloody.'

'Glad to be back?'

'No.' Proctor nodded towards the parked Transport Police cars. 'These guys have been here a couple of hours now. They've got a DI with them and it needs someone to sort him out.'

Faraday looked away for a moment. Proctor had never seen the point of small talk.

'You're telling me the DI's a problem?'

'Not at all, sir. But they haven't got the bodies, not for something like this. You want to come up to the tunnel?'

Proctor was already wearing one of the grey one-piece discardable suits that came with the job. While Faraday pulled on the pair of hiking boots he kept in the back of the car, Proctor brought him up to date.

6

The driver of the first train out of Pompey had reported hitting a body in the nearby tunnel. The power had been switched off, and control rooms in London alerted. Calls from Transport Police HQ in St James's Park had roused the duty Rail Incident Officer, who'd driven over from his home in Eastleigh. By then, the batteries on the train were running out of juice and the twenty or so passengers aboard would soon be sitting in the dark.

'No one got them off?'

'No, sir.'

'Why not?'

'The driver didn't think it was appropriate. Young guy. Cluey.'

'Cluey how?'

'He'd taken a good look underneath the train, gone back with a torch, brave lad.'

'And?'

They were walking round the pond by now, following the narrow lane that wound up towards the railway line. Proctor glanced across at Faraday.

'He found the impact spot, or what he assumed was the impact spot. Bits of our man were all over the bottom of the train but the torso and legs were still in one piece.' Proctor touched his own belly. 'Chained to the line.'

'*Chained?*'

'Yeah.' Proctor nodded. 'We're talking serious chain, padlock, the works. Our driver friend thought that was a bit over the top, made another call.' He shot Faraday a bleak smile. 'So here we all are.'

'And the train's still in the tunnel?'

'Yes, sir.'

'Impact point?'

'About ninety metres in. That's from the southern end.'

'How long's the tunnel?'

'Five hundred metres. Transport Police are organising a generator and a lighting unit. Plus they've laid hands on half a dozen or so blokes to check out the tunnel. Don't get me wrong, sir. The DI knows what he's doing. It's just resources. Not his fault.'

Faraday was doing the sums, trying to imagine the size of the challenge that awaited them all. At worst, he'd assumed they were looking at some kind of complicated suicide. The fact that this body had been physically tied to the line changed everything.

'The DI's established a common path?'

'Yes, sir. Down this lane, under the railway bridge, along a little track, then up the embankment and into the tunnel. The train's maybe forty metres in.'

'And that's the way we get the passengers off?'

'Has to be. The Incident Officer tells me the rest of it's fenced miles back in both directions. We've got no option.'

Faraday pulled a face. In these situations, absolute priority lay in isolating the crime scene. If Proctor was right about access to the track, then whatever evidence awaited them was about to be trampled.

'We need Mr Barrie in on this.' Faraday fumbled for his mobile. Martin Barrie was the new Detective Superintendent in charge of the Major Crimes Team. If it came to any kind of turf war, then Barrie was the man with the ammunition.

Proctor watched while Faraday keyed in a number, then touched him lightly on the arm.

'That's another problem, sir.' He nodded towards the nearby embankment. 'This is a mobile black spot. Either end of the tunnel, there's no signal.'

The train was visible from the mouth of the tunnel. Faraday stood on the track, peering into the darkness, trying to imagine what five carriages would do to flesh, bone and blood. Like every policeman, he'd attended his share of traffic accidents, successful suicide bids and

8

other incidents when misjudgement or desperation had taken a life, but thankfully he'd never witnessed the cooling remains of a human body torn apart by a train.

Other men, less lucky, spoke of unrecognisable parcels of flesh, of entrails scattered beside the track, of the way that the impact – like the suck of high explosive – could rip the clothes from a man and toss them aside before dismembering him

The image made Faraday pause. Only days ago, three Tube trains had been ripped apart by terrorist bombs in London and some of the media coverage of the consequences had been unusually candid. Was this incident, in some strange way, a twist on that theme? He let the thought settle for a moment, then he was struck by another image, altogether more personal, and he found himself fighting a hot gust of nausea, remembering the oncoming shark of his nightmare and that moment before consciousness when he knew for certain that he, too, was a dead man.

'Sir?'

It was Proctor again. He'd fetched an Airwave radio to replace Faraday's mobile. The Transport Police DI wanted a meet as soon as possible. He was waiting back at the cars.

'Best not go in, sir.' Proctor nodded towards the tunnel. 'Not until we've had a sort-out, eh?'

Faraday favoured him with a thin smile, the taste of bile still in his mouth, then turned away.

The DI from the British Transport Police turned out to be an ex-Met copper with a realistic grasp of the shape of the coming days. Sure, his guys had jurisdiction on railway property but now wasn't the time to be throwing their toys out of the pram. There was a procedure here, boxes to be ticked, and – to be frank – he didn't care a toss who held the pencil.

He already had a bus on standby, ready to be called forward when the passengers were detrained. In the meantime came the business of putting a team together.

Getting the right people in the right places, properly briefed, would take hours. Amongst them would undoubtedly be the Home Office pathologist, who'd need a decent run at whatever remained of the body. Only after he'd finished would the search teams start trawling through the tunnel, on hands and knees, looking for every shred of evidence, human or otherwise. All that, he concluded, was best handled at county level.

'You've been inside yourself?' Faraday nodded in the direction of the tunnel.

The DI shook his head.

'The Incident Officer briefed me. Not pretty.'

'ID?'

'Nothing we've found yet. His clothing was in a pile at the side of the track. Jeans, trainers jacket, T-shirt – normal clobber.'

'You're telling me he was naked?'

'Apparently. Excuse me.'

He broke off to confer briefly with a colleague who'd just arrived, then threw a glance at Faraday and hurried away. Bit of a crisis with South West Trains. He'd be back as soon as he could.

The DI gone, Faraday settled down with the Airwave radio, sitting in his Mondeo with the door open, still thinking about the implications of a naked body in the tunnel. By now, nearly nine o'clock, the new Detective Superintendent should be at his desk in the Major Crimes Suite back in Portsmouth.

After Geoff Willard, who had moved on to become force Head of CID, Martin Barrie had come as something of a surprise. He had none of Willard's physical presence, none of his style, none of his bullish determination to steamroller any obstacle en route to court. On the contrary, Barrie was a slight man, thin to the point of emaciation, and seemed to have absolutely no interest in self-image. But the flat Essex accent and the nicotine stains from a lifetime of roll-ups masked an intelligence so acute and so subtle that it took someone in his own league to recognise it. From the start, Faraday had liked him a great deal.

On the Airwave radio, Faraday summarised progress to date. Thanks to the Transport Police DI, there were no turf issues. And thanks to Jerry Proctor, a decent team should have assembled by lunchtime. The search in the tunnel should be well under way by close of play and if Barrie was happy to carry the overtime, the lads could press on into the evening. With luck, a proper trawl would recover documentation and establish an ID, and if that didn't happen then there might be prints or DNA from the post-mortem that would raise a ping from the usual databases. As ever in these situations, it would be a name that turned the key in the investigative lock.

'You'll need to fire up the MIR.'

'Of course, sir.'

'Leave it to me. I'll get it organised.'

The MIR was the Major Incident Room, the beating heart of any enquiry, with plenty of space for the data-inputters and specialist officers who would drive the investigation forward. There was a long silence. Barrie was evidently deep in thought. When he came back on the line, he wanted to know who Faraday had in mind to head the Intelligence Cell – the officer who would try to tease an ID, a timeline and some shadowy first guess at a motive from the flood of incoming information.

Faraday was gazing down at the pond, watching a family of mallards emerging from the water.

'DC Winter,' he said at once. 'Please.'

Paul Winter was still in his pyjamas when the call came through. He'd been up for hours, circling the roomy apartment with mug after mug of tea, enjoying the sheer busyness of the scene that unfolded daily beyond the big picture windows. Just now, one of the huge P&O ferries was rumbling towards the harbour mouth. Purposeful and unlovely, it seemed to catch the essence of the city.

Winter bent to the phone. Conversations with Faraday were becoming a habit.

'Boss?'

Faraday apologised for intruding on a rest day but something had come up.

'Like what?' Winter's interest quickened at once. His attention had strayed to a woman on the promenade below, waving at someone on the fast-disappearing P&O.

Faraday explained briefly about the body chained to the line in the Buriton Tunnel. Barrie was throwing serious resources at what was obviously a suspicious death. Operation *Coppice* was going to need a beefed-up Intelligence Cell. Given Winter's new job on Major Crimes, Faraday wanted him involved from the start.

'No problem.' Winter took a sip of tea. The woman had turned round now. Nice figure.

'You're OK for today?'

Winter glanced at his watch. 'Give me half an hour,' he told Faraday, 'and I'll take a cab in.'

'No need. I've briefed Suttle already. He'll drop by and pick you up in fifteen minutes.'

'Sure, boss.'

Winter at last turned away from the window, enjoying the little tickle of anticipation that conversations like these had always stirred in him. As a detective on division for more years than he cared to remember, he'd lost count of the mornings he'd answered a phone call or eased into a conversation in a holding cell, and found himself up to his neck in the wreckage of someone else's life. These chance opportunities, cleverly exploited, had become meat and drink to him, the essence of his busy life, and it was only recently, after the diagnosis and everything else that had gone with it, that he'd recognised how much he relied on them. The limitless capacity of most of the human race to land themselves in the shit had never failed to delight him – and here, it seemed, was yet another example. Some bloke chained to a railway line? A sitting duck for the first train through? How promising was that?

He wandered into the bathroom and began to lather his face, warmed by the thought of the days and weeks to come. He'd been on Major Crimes for nearly three months now, occupying the empty desk in the Intelligence Cell. As a posting after lengthy convalescence, it had seemed a dream job. Normally, Occupational Health found you something cosy and safe, put you out to grass with the muppet statisticians or the Road Safety fascists, then hauled you in every week to make sure you hadn't blown a fuse with all the excitement, but for reasons Winter still didn't fully understand he'd managed to avoid all that. Given the seriousness of the brain operation, the DVLA were still withholding his driving licence, a measure which definitely cramped his investigative style, but so far he'd managed to cope by spending a small fortune on cab fares.

Newly shaved, he went through to the master bedroom, still thinking about the body in the tunnel. To be honest, he'd been slightly disappointed by the calibre of jobs that had so far crossed his desk. In three months he'd been involved in two murders, a linked series of rapes and a kidnapping. Both homicides were three-day events – the first a domestic, the second a Southsea club brawl that had got out of hand. The linked series of rapes had been binned after the woman admitted keeping open house for anyone her boyfriend owed, while the kidnapping had turned into an obscure generations-long feud between two branches of the same Kosovan family.

In every case Winter had done his level best to complicate the obvious, to impart some class to this dross, but one of the lessons he'd quickly learned was that the Major Crimes Team were as starved of decent jobs as every other bunch of detectives in the city. Now though, he told himself, it might be different. A body chained to a railway line sounded very promising indeed.

By the time DC Jimmy Suttle rang the entryphone, Winter was contemplating breakfast. Suttle took the lift to the third floor and pushed at the open door. The lad's transfer onto Major Crimes, nearly a year back, had come as no surprise to Winter. He'd worked with Suttle on a number of jobs on the Pompey Crime Squad, and had been impressed. Unlike most of the kids on the force these days, Suttle was prepared to take a risk or two. He shared Winter's hatred of paperwork yet he was never shy of making a stand when he thought the older man was going over the top. More important still, it had been Suttle who'd kept an eye on Winter when the brain tumour began to make life truly miserable. Marriage to Joannie had never blessed Winter with kids of his own but with a couple of Scotches inside him he occasionally viewed Suttle as a decent enough substitute.

Now, Suttle stood in the kitchen, staring at the pile of plates in the sink. Thanks to a training course in the West Midlands, he hadn't seen Winter for a couple of weeks.

'You're an old dosser,' he said. 'You see that thing next to the fridge? It's a dishwasher.'

Winter shrugged, rescuing his toast. It was true. He'd been in the apartment for the best part of six months and still hadn't bothered to sort out all the gadgets that went with the fitted kitchen. A couple of years ago, before the tumour, this would have been inconceivable. Now, it was just another chore that just didn't seem to matter.

'Slice of toast, son?'

'No thanks.' Suttle glanced up at the kitchen clock. 'We're out of here in three minutes.'

*

By mid-morning, with the help of Jerry Proctor, Faraday had managed to impose some order on the constant trickle of arriving vehicles that turned the long curve of gravel outside the village church into a car park.

A command post had been established at one corner of the nearby pond. A line of blue and white POLICE tape marked an outer cordon, with a local uniform on hand to explain crime scene etiquette to anxious villagers. Up the lane, beyond the railway bridge, a second line of tape barred access to anyone but essential personnel. Through here, an hour or so ago, had trooped the weary passengers from the train itself. Most had long abandoned any thoughts of a normal working day. One of them, meeting a reporter beside the pond, described his first sight of the masked and suited detectives as 'surreal'.

'You think you're off to London,' he'd said, 'and you end up in a film set.'

Now, the tunnel awaited the attentions of the search teams, the photographer and the woman whose job it was to transfer every scrap of recovered evidence onto a scale map of the area. Only when Faraday was satisfied with their work would he release the tunnel back to South West Trains, a decision that he already sensed was days away.

First, though, everything had to wait for the pathologist. Proctor had put the calls in after his initial meet with Faraday. Thanks to holiday and other commitments, only two on the regional Home Office list were available. The nearest lived in Bristol. Bristol to Buriton was a two-and-a-half-hour drive. God willing, the pathologist should be with them around midday.

With an hour to kill and Proctor available to take the pathologist into the tunnel, Faraday decided to scout the area, looking for access points to the railway, enlisting the help of the Transport Police Incident Officer with his sheaf of maps. They left the outer cordon, drove back through the village, and then turned south on a road that wound up the wooded face of the Down. At the top of the climb, the Incident Officer braked before hauling the Astra left. He'd already shared what little else he'd picked up from his brief visit to the tunnel. The train, he said, appeared to have sliced the body virtually in two. It was a sight he never wanted to see again.

Faraday sat back, following the route on the map, his finger tracing the narrowing track until the tarmac disappeared and they were bumping along a rutted path between fields of grass ready for mowing. Ahead, he could see a corn bunting perched on a strand of barbed wire and, for a moment, through the open window, he caught the signature call of this stout little creature. The *jangle-jangle* of keys, he thought, remembering hot summer days spent birding on the dusty Spanish steppes, his ear cupped for this same halting song.

'Empty, isn't it?' The Incident Officer gestured off to the right, where the ground dipped away. 'Can't make your job any the easier.'

Faraday nodded, forcing himself to concentrate. So far, on the way up from the village, they must have passed no more than half a dozen properties. All of these people, while memories were still fresh, would require a visit from the enquiry team. Did they have dogs or a CCTV camera? Had they heard anything suspicious last night? Headlights at two in the morning? Strange cars? Any other disturbance?

Faraday looked down at the map, aware of the familiar drumbeat of questions in his brain. Had the Detective Superintendent managed to lay hands on the small army of specialists that would make the Major Incident Room tick? Had he – Faraday – thought hard enough about a form of words to keep the press happy? Was it too early to draw up a specific set of Time and Scene Parameters?

The latter question deserved special attention. The

time frame seemed relatively straightforward. Already – on the basis of information from the Transport Police boys – he'd calculated a three-hour window between the last train through the tunnel on Sunday and next morning's London-bound service that had turned 500 metres of darkness into a crime scene. But the physical issue of Scene Parameters – quite how widely he should cast his investigative net – was partly dependent on the recce they were undertaking. Maps were always invaluable but nothing beat a first-hand feel for the shape of the terrain.

The car came to a sudden halt and Faraday glanced up to find himself looking at a locked gate barring a gap in the hedge. The Incident Officer got out and Faraday followed him as he clambered over the gate. Beyond, a track plunged down between encroaching hedgerows. At the end, explained the Incident Officer, was the deep cutting that funnelled into the southern mouth of the tunnel.

They walked down the path, single file, Faraday looking for signs of recent disturbance. Had the victim stumbled down this way, dragged by God knows who, maybe roped, maybe injured? Or was he already dead, killed by unknown hands? At the bottom, the path turned sharply right, offering a sudden view of a new-looking chain-link fence. Beyond the fence, on the bed of the cutting, lay two sets of railway tracks.

Faraday gazed down for a moment or two, aware of the gathering heat of the day. It was quiet on the edge of the embankment. Insects hummed and buzzed in the undergrowth. Far away, he could hear the lowing of cattle. Then came the sudden flap of disturbed wood pigeons and the cackle of a pheasant, before peace returned to the surrounding woodland.

The Incident Officer was explaining that the railway was fenced on both sides for miles north and south. From time to time there were bridges and level crossings, both of which gave access to the track. The only way of physically checking the fence itself was to walk the path beside the clinker.

Faraday nodded, adding another note to his checklist. The fence was substantial, at least six feet high, and as far as he could see looked intact, no sign of intruders; but the Incident Officer was right – every trackside metre had to be checked. Faraday found himself calculating the man hours involved in an exercise like this. Then he heard a distant purring noise that called attention to itself above the busy symphony of high summer. Turtle doves, he thought, with a sudden jolt of pleasure.

Minutes later, toiling back up the path towards the Astra, Faraday took a call on his Airwave. It was Proctor. The pathologist had arrived earlier than expected; he'd got himself kitted up and they were about to enter the tunnel. Was it safe to assume they could go ahead without Faraday?

Faraday found the transmit button.

'That's a yes,' he said.

Major Crimes occupied a suite of offices at the back of Kingston Crescent police station, a stone's throw from Portsmouth's Commercial Docks. On the second floor, Winter's perch commanded a fine view of the rooftops of nearby Stamshaw, framed in the distance by the chalk-gashed swell of Portsdown Hill. Out of breath after climbing the back stairs from the car park, Winter found DC Tracy Barber sitting at his desk.

Barber was a relatively recent addition to the Major Crimes team, a tall, handsome-looking woman with a big, square face, lesbian tastes in relationships and a fondness for tailored suits. Years of service in Special Branch had quickly drawn Winter's attention, and the fact that her sheer competence had won Faraday's confidence made her a doubly useful ally.

'Kicking off, isn't it?' Barber was already on her feet,

surrendering Winter's chair. Winter motioned her down again, squeezing his bulk behind the other desk.

'Dead right, love.' Winter grinned. Footsteps down the long central corridor. The non-stop ringing of phones. Shouted questions. Muttered answers. An occasional thump as someone kicked an office door shut. Winter loved all this: the buzz, the urgency, the sense of a machine – complex and voraciously demanding – shaking itself into gear.

'Where's the boss?'

'Barrie's in his office, preparing for the DCI interviews. Faraday's out at the tunnel. He called in a couple of minutes ago. Here . . . '

Winter took the proffered scrap of paper. The Major Crimes Detective Chief Inspector had recently left for pastures new. Normally, his replacement would be Senior Investigating Officer on a job like this. Except the hunt was still on for a suitable candidate.

'So who's in charge?'

'Faraday, as far as I can gather. Barrie's due for leave.'

'So Faraday runs it?'

Barber caught the inflection at once. 'Yes. You really don't like him, do you?'

'You're wrong, love. Believe it or not, we go back a long way. He's different, that's all.'

'You're telling me that's a crime?'

'Christ, no. It's just that I've never quite sussed what makes him tick. He's had some decent jobs; he's done well, but you'd never know it, not the way he behaves. Most bosses I've come across can't resist a little boast. They're in it for the medals, the glory, all that bollocks that comes with the rank. Faraday . . . ?' Winter shrugged, glancing down at the message. 'Most days you'd never take him for a copper.'

'He thinks you're extremely effective.' Barber was watching him closely. 'Did you know that?'

'No.'

19

'Well, he does.'

'I'm flattered.'

'And bloody dangerous, too. That's the bad news.'

'Really?' Winter dismissed the comment with a shrug. Dangerous, he thought, means nothing until you've lain on a hospital trolley, wondering whether you'll ever see the light of day again.

There was a brief silence while Winter tried to decipher Barber's scrawl. He seemed to be looking at a list of names. She helped him out.

'That's a first run at the Mispers. Faraday wants something on paper by tonight's meeting. Six o'clock, whole squad.' She gestured down the corridor in the direction of the Major Incident Room.

Winter nodded. Missing Persons were tallied on a national database. Anyone reasonably local fitting the victim's description was an obvious starting point in an enquiry like this. There were five names on Barber's list. Winter tucked the paper into his jacket pocket.

'What do we know so far?' he asked. 'Age? Sex? Colour?'

'White and probably male. That's about it. You know what happens with trains. They'll run out of bags. They always do. Faraday's pushing for a post-mortem late tonight.' She got to her feet and glanced at her watch. 'You can imagine what a treat that's going to be.'

Two

Faraday met the pathologist in the early afternoon. Tim Ewers had spent longer in the tunnel than he'd anticipated, chiefly because the impact scene was such a mess, and now he was glad to be back in civilian clothes after the clammy embrace of the forensic suit. Ewers was new to the regional list and Faraday was surprised at how young he looked. It was rare to meet a pathologist who turned up in jeans and a T-shirt.

They stood around the bonnet of Faraday's Mondeo in the bright sunshine as Ewers explained the state of the body and ventured a preliminary thought or two about what may have happened. Jerry Proctor was there as well, along with the Scenes of Crime photographer. Proctor was sweating in the heat.

'Here –' Ewers had drawn a rough diagram. '– The fella was chained lengthways along the rail closest to the tunnel wall. Let's call it the nearside rail. His feet were pointing towards the oncoming train. That must have been bloody uncomfortable for starters but I also got the sense that his feet must have been tied as well, keeping his legs apart.'

Faraday caught a grim nod from Proctor. He wanted to know more. Ewers got busy with the pencil again, drawing a dotted line up the middle of the cartoon body.

'In these situations, we're talking reflex. Just think about it. A train's coming at you. What do you do? It's instinct. You twist away, bring your legs up, try and protect yourself. Like I say, pure reflex.'

Faraday could imagine the scene all too well. It didn't bear contemplation. He tried to concentrate on the legs again, on the precise sequence of events to which flesh and bone held the key.

'You're telling me the legs would have been smashed?'

'Of course.'

'And they weren't?'

'No. They were damaged, of course, terrible lacerations, but not as bad a mess as you might expect.'

Faraday's eyes returned to the diagram on the bonnet. Then he felt a light tap on his elbow. The photographer was offering him a digital camera. Faraday took it, turning away from the brightness of the sunshine, and peered at the image on the tiny screen.

For a second or two he could make no sense of what he was seeing. Then he recognised the twisted remains of a human body. One leg was missing completely, the other hung over the clinker, oddly angled, attached by slivers of flesh and tendon. Above the leg, the naked torso had been split in two, navel to neck, not a neat, clean cut but a jagged tear that had ripped the body open. Faraday could see the glistening pit of the chest cavity, whitish blobs of what must have been lung tissue, and bulging loops of intestine, green and blue, trailing away into the darkness at the edges of the shot. There was no head.

The image was so bizarre, so macabre, so utterly unconnected with anything human, that Faraday found it curiously fascinating. Twelve hours ago this man would have had a life, a face, a tone of voice. Now, his remains belonged in one of the more cutting-edge London art galleries.

'Flange damage.' It was the pathologist. Faraday could feel Ewers' breath on the back of his neck. 'As I say, the legs were probably open, held apart somehow, and the flange on the wheel did the rest.'

22

'We can evidence that?'

'We found chain, certainly, and bits of rope, too. Here. You can just see . . .'

Ewers pointed at a detail on the camera screen but all Faraday could make out was a curl or two of something that could have been metallic. The chain, it seemed, had been secured around the man's waist.

'What kind of chain?' Faraday looked up.

'Old, galvanised iron, quite substantial.' It was Proctor this time. 'About this long.'

Faraday looked at the space between his outstretched hands. Four or five feet, at least.

'Padlocked?'

'Presumably. We're still looking.'

'And the rope?'

'Three separate lengths, all over the place. That would have been the train, of course. Chucked stuff everywhere.'

'But we're talking the same kind of rope?'

'Yeah. Looked like sash cord to me. Quite old, brittle. And something else, too.'

The photographer obliged with another shot. This time Faraday was looking at a length of metal somehow wedged beneath the rail. He peered harder.

'It's an angle iron, sir. The kind you might use for fencing, little holes drilled for wire, stands about so high.' The hands again, at the level of Proctor's belly.

Faraday's eyes were back on the screen. Then he glanced round at the pathologist.

'So what's the story?'

'Hard to say but my best guess says he probably had an ankle tied to each end of the angle iron.'

'Keeping the legs apart?'

'Precisely. Look . . .'

Ewers drew another diagram, two stick legs scissored open, the angle iron completing the triangle.

'The train's coming in this direction?' Faraday drew

23

a finger up through the triangle. 'And takes him in the groin?'

'That's what it looks like.'

'And he has maybe hours to think about it?'

'All too likely.'

Faraday nodded. It sounded inconceivably sadistic.

'But what if he was dead already? Is that something you'll be able to tell us? After the PM?'

'I doubt it.' Ewers shook his head. 'You've seen what the train did. We've got the torso, but most of what was inside is all over the place – on the track, under the train, even on the tunnel wall. Just think about the forces involved. Situations like these, the body explodes.'

'And the head?'

As soon as he'd asked the question, the photographer was busy with the camera again. The head, according to Ewers, had been severed by one of the wheels and then sucked along by the passage of the train. Proctor had finally spotted it a further fifteen metres into the tunnel, lying between the rails on the other track. Faraday studied the proffered image. The face had gone completely, as if a child had daubed it with finger paints. The only thing that Faraday could be sure of was the colour of the hair. Blond.

'Prints?' Faraday was looking at Ewers again.

'Unlikely. We might be able to recover a whorl or two but I wouldn't bet your life on it.'

'ID?'

Proctor shook his head. 'Nothing on him at all, sir. Nothing in his pockets. Nothing in his jacket. No mobile. No wallet. He didn't even have a bunch of keys.'

'Tattoos? Rings? Piercings? Birthmarks?'

'Birthmarks, we can't be sure, not yet, but no obvious tats or danglies. Mr Ewers here thinks we might be in with a chance with the teeth but we'll have to wait and see.'

'Sure.'

Faraday stepped back from the bonnet and rubbed his face. Every particle of evidence from the scene told him that they were looking at a homicide. The lie of the body. The presence of chains and rope. The business with the angle iron. The total absence of ID. Someone had settled a debt or two and that someone had gone to enormous trouble to send a particular kind of message. You didn't strip someone naked and then point his crotch at an oncoming train without good reason.

Faraday turned back to Ewers. Forensic procedure could be strangely comforting at moments like this. He nodded at the diagram on the bonnet.

'No problem with DNA, I take it?'

By mid-afternoon, DC Paul Winter had boiled down Tracy Barber's Misper list to just three names.

Missing Persons had become a bit of a pain over the last couple of years. With family ties loosening by the month and the city full of semi-feral kids, it was all too easy to attach undue importance to an anguished mum thrusting photos of little Connor at the Desk Officer, or a drunken twenty-five-year-old lurching in from the street to report the absence of her partner. In both cases, there was often layer after layer of subplot, and hard-pressed coppers were increasingly reluctant to enrol themselves in yet another drawn-out domestic. Far easier to fill out the forms, ping the names through to the duty Inspector, and get on with the next job.

Winter strolled down to the tiny kitchen at the end of the corridor and hunted for the biscuit tin while he waited for the kettle to boil. One of the names turned out to be an eighteen-year-old skate who'd allegedly jumped ship back in May. He'd been serving on HMS *Invincible* and had gone missing after a series of heavy mobile conversations with his girlfriend, up in Derby. The Naval Provost's office had drawn the obvious conclusions, posted him absent without leave, and alerted Derbyshire Police. Winter had pressed the Provost's office for more details and it turned out that the guy on the end of the phone had looked into the case personally. He'd seen a set of well-thumbed nude photos retrieved from the boy's shipboard locker and had no doubts about their implications. The girl, he'd told Winter, was a cracker, and gossip amongst his shipmates had convinced him that the lad was alive and well and having the time of his life. No way would he have ended up under a train.

The second Misper was foreign, a Saudi engineer on attachment to a defence-related firm in Southampton. Winter had put in a call but once again it seemed clear that there were no real doubts about the man's whereabouts. The engineer had been reported missing by his wife, who'd settled in a riverside maisonette in leafy Hamble. What she didn't know about was her husband's infatuation with an American divorcee he'd met on a training course in Massachusetts. According to the Human Resources executive, off the record, Mr Al-Ramedi was probably making quiet arrangements to smuggle the new love of his life back home to Riyadh.

Frustrated, Winter had turned to the third name. His name was Alan Givens and his employers – Portsmouth Hospitals NHS Trust – had supplied an address in North End. Givens, it seemed, had been employed as some kind of van driver, running medical samples around the city. He'd been at St Mary's Hospital for the best part of a year, given nobody any grief, then suddenly disappeared. Calls to his mobile had gone unanswered. A personal visit to the North End flat had found nothing but a locked door, drawn curtains and a mountain bike with flat tyres locked to a drainpipe round the side. The police had made further enquiries and circulated Givens' details, but seven weeks later, said the girl from Human Resources, the thing was still a complete mystery.

Intrigued, Winter had scribbled down the details. Givens was thirty-eight years old, unmarried, and had applied for the job from an address in Barnsley. From memory, she described him as medium height, thin, with a beaky nose and blond hair. His line manager, she added, had made a bit of an issue over the hair. Evidently Givens wore it longer than his employers would have liked. Meek as a lamb, he'd had it cut.

When the kettle began to boil, Winter decanted hot water onto a heap of Happy Shopper instant. He was still having trouble finding the biscuits when Tracy Barber appeared.

'Cupboard by the window,' she said. 'Down by your knee.'

Winter helped himself to a plateful of chocolate digestives. Since the operation, he'd put on two and a half stone. Barber wanted to know about the Misper list. Winter brushed the crumbs from his mouth.

'It's fine,' he said. 'Coming along nicely.'

'What does that mean?'

'It means I'm making calls. Has anyone seen this body yet?'

'Yeah, Mr Faraday.'

'And?'

'Exactly as we said. White, male. The blokes in the tunnel are still collecting bits.'

'Nothing else to go on?'

'Only the hair.'

'Colour?'

'Blond.'

Winter took a cab to North End. The area was a decent address, a grid of tree-lined streets that blunted the brutal impact of the rest of the city. Drive into Pompey this way, he thought, and you might even like the place.

Number 70 Meredith Road occupied the end of a 1930s terrace, a brick and pebbledash house with bay windows top and bottom, and a stained-glass fern

27

motif on the front door. A pair of bells beside the door looked a good deal newer than the rest of the property, evidence that the place had recently been converted into a couple of flats, and he could just make out a name scrawled beside the top one. Petchey.

The bottom bell must be Givens'. Winter pressed it, turning his face to the sun, waiting for the response he knew would never come. He hadn't felt so cheerful in months. It was almost like being a proper detective again. He gave the bell another poke, just in case, then took a step backwards.

The front bay windows, as the girl from Human Resources had indicated, were still curtained. Peering in through the crack in the middle Winter could just make out a table pushed against the back wall and a couple of chairs. There was some kind of vase on the table, or maybe a bowl, but it looked empty.

Winter wiped a smudge from the glass. He'd seen a thousand rooms like this in the city, temporary bolt-holes for solitary men. There'd be curdled milk in the fridge, abandoned plates in the washing-up bowl, grease marks down the kitchen walls, drip stains in the bathroom sink, maybe a poster or two on the bedroom wall. These were rooms that spoke of shipwreck and surrender, of lives abandoned to the daily struggle to make it through. Already, Winter could smell the place, the airless taint of cheap tobacco and unwashed bodies. He shook his head, easing back from the window.

Round the side of the house, the mountain bike was still U-locked to the drainpipe. Winter squatted for a moment, taking a careful look, then lifted the rear wheel and gave it half a forward turn. The pattern of rust on the chain argued for a long period of neglect. Givens hadn't been cycling for quite a while.

At the rear, a patch of untended garden stretched maybe twenty metres to a badly plastered back wall. Grass was growing up around a bird bath in the tiny square of lawn and someone had tried to grow vegetables in the beds beyond. Looking down at the riot of greenery, Winter began to have second thoughts about Givens. Amongst the weeds, he could see lettuces, spring onions, a fattish marrow, even a tomato plant or two. If this was Givens' work and not the upstairs tenant's, then maybe he was less of a stranger to self-respect and a spot of decent veg than he'd thought.

Back at the front door, Winter pressed the top bell. For a while nothing happened. Then he heard footsteps, very slow, very heavy, clumping down a flight of stairs. Finally the door opened. Blinking in the sunshine was a huge man, the wrong side of seventy, his cardigan crusted with soup, three days' stubble on his chin, a strand or two of greying hair combed sideways over his enormous skull.

'Mr Petchey?'

Winter produced his warrant card. The man studied it without much interest.

'Yeah?' he said finally.

Winter asked about the tenant downstairs. There were anxieties regarding his whereabouts. No one had seen him for a while.

'Who?'

'Mr Givens. Alan Givens. Your neighbour.' Winter nodded at the door behind him. 'The bloke in there.'

'What about him?'

Winter went through it again. Finally the man said that Givens hadn't been around for a while.

'Like how long?'

'God knows. Weeks? Months? It's hard these days. Dunno where the time goes.'

'Did you know him at all? Talk to him?'

'Yeah, a bit. I lives round the back, can't stand the sun. Some days I'd have the window open, natter to him like.'

'When he's in the garden, you mean?'

'Yeah. Always out there, he was. Veg and stuff.

Strange, isn't it, what some blokes get up to? That stupid bird bath was his idea. Bloody seagulls. Shitting everywhere.'

Winter was eyeing Givens' door. A single Yale. Easy.

'You want to get in there?' The question took Winter by surprise. He nodded. 'Ain't you got a key?'

'No.'

'You're not his mate, then? Alan's?'

'No. I told you. I'm a copper.'

'Why's that, then? In some kind of trouble, is he?'

'Dunno.' Winter gave him a smile. 'That's what I'm here to find out.'

The old man nodded, uncertain, then made his way upstairs again. Winter opened the blade of his penknife and slipped the lock to Givens' flat. The single overhead light revealed a tiny hall. An anorak hung beside an oval mirror. On the doormat, beneath the letter box, a stack of mail. Winter eyed it a moment. The man upstairs, he thought. Playing postman for his absent neighbour. Winter gazed round. From somewhere came a very bad smell.

A couple of steps took him into the living room at the front of the property. A stripe of bright sunshine lay across the carpet and Winter could see the bulk of a sofa angled towards a big, widescreen TV in the corner. There was a copy of the TV listings carefully folded open on the arm of the sofa and Winter made a note of the date. Sunday 22 May. Apart from the table against the back wall and a couple of chairs, the room was empty of any other furniture. It was a neat room, carefully organised, not at all the dump that Winter had been expecting.

Back in the hall, he followed his nose to a door at the end. The smell was stronger here, curdy, acid, and the moment he stepped into the kitchen he knew it had to come from the fridge. He opened the door. The contents of a carton of milk had jellied and yellowed with age, while the cling film over a Tupperware box, curling at one corner, hadn't managed to contain the stench of rotting mince. The mince formed part of some kind of risotto. Givens was clearly a man who never let the remains of a meal go to waste.

The big Zanussi was divided in two, freezer at the bottom, fridge at the top. In the freezer compartment Winter found an assortment of vegetables, all washed and wrapped, and shutting the freezer door he thought again about the carefully dug plot out the back. On a shelf beside the cooker Givens had been assembling a collection of recipe books. A list pinned to the nearby board reminded him to buy olive oil and fresh chillies. The bloke cared, Winter thought. He cared where his food came from and he was fussy about what happened to it afterwards.

Beneath the kitchen window was a swing bin for rubbish. Winter gave the lid a poke, stepping back as a gust from more rotting food billowed upward. Inside he glimpsed a slimy ball of what looked like lettuce and onions. On the evidence he'd seen so far, Givens was a man who tidied his life into neat little parcels. So how come he'd suddenly abandoned it all?

A visit to the adjoining bedroom offered few clues. A pile of magazines on the chair beside the single bed included four editions of *Digital Photographer* and a brochure for upmarket package deals to Venice. There was a line of shoes on the carpet beneath the window, while a swift riffle through the MFI wardrobe revealed a couple of suits, a leather jacket, a nice-looking overcoat and a fleece. At the back of the wardrobe, in one corner, Winter spotted a tripod, black, the legs secured with a Velcro strap. He looked at it for a moment, then used the chair by the bed to fetch down a couple of holdalls on top of the wardrobe. Both were empty. There was no sign of a camera.

Back in the hall Winter collected the post before turning on the light in the living room and settling himself in a chair at the table. The bulk of the post was rubbish, charity appeals from Save the Children, cut-price offers on insurance, but three items caught his eye. One was a letter with a Southsea postmark. Another, this time marked *Confidential*, had evidently come from Leeds. The third looked like a bank statement.

Winter hesitated a moment, then glanced at his watch. In less than an hour, ahead of the squad meet, Faraday would be expecting a report on the Misper list. Already Winter had eliminated two of the likeliest candidates. Givens, on the face of it, might well qualify as a possible but seven weeks was a long time to go missing and then suddenly turn up. Nonetheless, the abruptness of his disappearance definitely merited further investigation. One moment this man had been planning a menu, sorting out his evening's viewing, leading a life. The next he'd simply vanished.

The Southsea letter had come from Givens' landlord. Givens had evidently written to ask permission to build a lean-to round the side for his bike. The letter was friendly. Of course Mr Givens could go ahead. The landlord even offered to pay for the materials. Winter smiled, returning the letter to its envelope and making a note of the landlord's details. Were these the plans a man would make if he was plotting some kind of disappearance?

The Leeds letter carried the name and address of a firm of solicitors. The letter was brief. It acknowledged Givens' cheque in the matter of probate on his mother's estate and assured him of the firm's continuing support, should Mr Givens have need of their services. Once again Winter scribbled himself a note. Goldstein, Everey and Partners. 0113 2177762.

The last letter was indeed a bank statement. Winter flattened it on the table and studied it for a moment. Then came another smile, wider this time, and he tucked the statement inside his jacket pocket before checking his watch again and searching for his mobile.

Aqua answered his call on the third ring. A cab would be with him in minutes.

By late afternoon, still out at Buriton, Faraday was beginning to think about the first squad meeting. Tracy Barber had been on the Airwave to him several times, updating him on the individuals Barrie was putting in place, and to Faraday's satisfaction the Detective Superintendent appeared to be assembling a decent-sized squad. The priority at the moment was recovering evidence from the scene of crime, and Jerry Proctor was keeping a careful eye on the search team as they combed through the tunnel, inch by inch.

By now, the DS was happy that most of the victim had been bagged and tagged. The shortest straw, he told Faraday, had gone to a young uniform from Petersfield who'd spent the last hour or so carefully scraping flesh and miscellaneous gristle off the wheels of the first two carriages. In an aside to a nearby mate, he'd confessed to once fancying a life as a train driver. After this, he'd muttered, the romance of the railways would never be quite the same.

Faraday had some sympathy. His own walk-through at the scene would have to wait until the search team had got the tunnel plotted up, but already he'd seen enough physical evidence to shudder at the thought of what the last few moments of this man's life must have been like.

Unless he was already dead, the anticipation of what was to come would have been unbearable. Fear sharpened the nerve ends. He'd have heard the train miles away, felt the vibrations through the rail. Then would come the moment when the train entered the tunnel, a sudden blast of air, the thunder of the wheels on the track, the flare of lights from the oncoming cab. Did you scream in those final moments? Turn your head? Squeeze your eyes shut?

Faraday didn't know and told himself it was pointless to even speculate. At this point in time, Operation *Coppice* needed a name, a firm ID, friends, lovers, a life for Paul Winter's Intelligence Cell to sink its teeth into. DNA samples were already en route to the Forensic Science Service laboratories, an urgent submission that would make a £1000 dent in the investigation's budget, but it would be a full forty-eight hours before a readout emerged, and even then an ID would depend on a match in the national database. If the victim hadn't already come to police attention, then they'd be no closer to knowing who on earth this man was.

A glance at his watch told Faraday that he should be back on the road by now. Portsmouth was close – half an hour at the most – and he had a million issues to sort out before he'd feel confident enough to gather his team around him and point them in a sensible direction. But first he was curious to know what kind of prominence the *News*, the city's daily paper, was giving to the story.

A reporter had been on site for an hour over the lunch period, hanging around the queue at the Fire Brigade catering wagon, and although Proctor had told his blokes to zip their mouths pending a formal press conference, Faraday had learned that a wise copper never underestimated the power of the press to build a story on the tiniest fragment of overheard gossip. The reporter, a woman in her early twenties, was far from unattractive. Twice, to Faraday's certain knowledge, she'd been in conversation with blokes fresh from the tunnel.

He borrowed a paper from one of the gaggle of villagers that had lurked on the edges of the cordon all day. It was the midday edition and the story featured on the front page. Under the headline TUNNEL DRAMA TRIGGERS COMMUTER CHAOS was a spread of photographs: the southern mouth of the tunnel, a queue of relief buses waiting at Havant station and finally a shot of a smallish group of police officers in conference beside the Buriton pond.

To his amusement, amongst the familiar faces Faraday recognised himself. Beside the looming figure of Jerry Proctor, he looked smaller and older than he'd somehow assumed. The beard didn't help, the way it was visibly greying, but there was something in the stoop of his shoulders that spoke of a deep weariness. Maybe he needed another holiday, he thought. By himself, this time.

He returned to the paper, scanning the accompanying story. To his relief, no one appeared to have talked. There was mention of an 'incident' and the implication of a body on the line, but the thrust of the story – the meatiest quotes – came from disgruntled passengers. There was a grid of faces on page three. These were busy people. They had lives to lead. Schedules to keep. Deadlines to meet. Life, said one of them, should be a great deal simpler than this. Faraday read the quote twice, then found himself nodding in agreement. Too right, he thought.

'Sir?' It was Proctor. Faraday showed him the picture on the front page. Proctor barely spared it a glance. 'We've found a padlock. Thought you ought to know.'

Faraday looked up at him. He knew from the glint in his eye there was something else.

'And?'

'A key.'

Three

Faraday was in conference with the Crime Scene Co-ordinator when Winter tapped on his office door, back at the Major Crimes Suite. The CSC, a cheerful DI from the force training HQ at Netley, got up to shake Winter's hand and congratulate him on beating the odds.

'Odds?' Winter hadn't a clue what he was talking about.

'Brain job.' He tapped his own skull. 'The big C. Every article I've ever read says you're a gonner. Can't have been easy, operation like that.'

'Picnic,' Winter said drily. 'Recommend it to anyone.' He turned to Faraday, readying the Misper file he'd grabbed on the way out of his office. 'You belled me, boss.'

'That's right.' Faraday began to hunt amongst the papers on his desk. Finally he found what he was looking for. 'Here. It came out of the tunnel this afternoon. The key fits. We've tried it.'

Winter took the proffered colour photos. Four offered varying shots of a solid-looking padlock about the size of a packet of cigarettes. In the other two was a key attached to a simple ring. Faraday was assuming that the padlock had secured the length of chain because two lines of links were still attached. The impact of the train had shattered the fourth link on one side and the second on the other, and the padlock had been thrown free. The key had been recovered from the other side of the tunnel, about five metres from the body, a fact that was itself interesting.

'What do you mean, boss?' Winter was still leafing through the photos.

'The key may have been chucked away after our man was tied down. There were no other items on that side of the tunnel.'

'Prints?'

'Nothing recoverable.'

'What about the padlock?'

'They found it a couple of metres down the same track, along with bits of old rope. It looks brand new to me. We'll need a list of retail outlets asap. Talk to the manufacturers. Plot the distribution chain. You know the way it goes.'

Winter examined the shots of the padlock more closely. B&Q, he thought. Homebase. GA Day. Robert Dyas. Plus dozens of other local stores that might flog something like this. The list would go on for ever. Winter glanced up, wondering how wide to cast the net, but Faraday had already turned back to the CSC, querying the allocation of personnel for the second day's search in the tunnel. Winter lingered a moment longer, then slipped the photos into his file and returned to his office.

Already, he could hear footsteps in the long central corridor outside, and the rise and fall of conversation as people made their way to the Incident Room for the six o'clock squad meet. The fact that Faraday hadn't quizzed him about the Mispers list probably meant that he'd call on Winter for a summary during the meeting itself. Winter could handle that, no problem, but wondered how he could put a bit of a shine on his afternoon's work. He was still sprawled in his chair, minutes later, when Tracy Barber appeared at his door.

'The boss is making a start,' she warned him. 'Be nice if you could join us.'

They went down to the Incident Room together. A

DS by the door shot Winter a look as he appeared. Evidently the meeting had already begun.

Winter made himself comfortable on the edge of a desk. Faraday was going through the sequence of events that had ended with a call from the Netley control room first thing. Everyone here was aware of how tricky turf issues could be when another force was involved and there was a ripple of laughter around the room when Faraday blamed the London bombings for British Transport Police's early surrender of jurisdiction.

'These blokes are really stretched,' he said. 'They don't want to see another tunnel in their lives.'

Faraday picked up the timeline again, tracking backwards to the last train through the tunnel the previous evening. The Sunday schedule, he said, came to an end with the 00.50 from Waterloo, the so-called Matelot Special. That train would have cleared the tunnel by 01.55. According to Railtrack Operations HQ, there had been no freight movements on the line last night. That gave a clear three hours for a man to be tied to the track and readied for the 04.30 from Portsmouth Harbour, which would have entered the tunnel around five o'clock. Seconds later, our man was history.

The DS in charge of Outside Enquiries raised his hand. He wanted to know how certain they could be that the victim hadn't been dead already. It was a fair question but it seemed to irritate Faraday. He broke off for a moment, talked briefly about the state of the body, and then warned that – in all likelihood – the post-mortem would leave the issue undecided. In his own view, it was highly unlikely that the victim had already been killed. The pile of clothing beside the track suggested that he'd removed everything himself, presumably under pressure, whereas a dead man's kit would probably have been cut off. Likewise, the lie of the body argued for at least two other people in the

38

tunnel to restrain the victim while he was lashed to the rail. There was an element of theatre, he said, in the events they were trying to put together. Someone had thought long and hard about the impact they wanted this macabre tableau to make.

This conclusion naturally took Faraday into a detailed description of the probable position of the body in the tunnel and there was total silence in the room as his hands shaped the outspread legs, and the way they'd been tied to the angle iron secured beneath the single length of rail. The first set of wheels, he said, had effectively cut the man in half. There'd be a full set of photos available for anyone interested in the detail.

The DS in charge of Outside Enquiries lifted his hand again.

'The bloke's legs were pointing at the train?'

'That's right.'

'Tied open?'

'Exactly.'

'You think that might be significant? Some kind of revenge killing? Bloke had been helping himself? Messing with the wrong woman?'

'It's possible.' Faraday nodded. 'Extreme, but possible.'

This time there was no laughter. While the men remained stony-faced, one or two of the women exchanged glances. This, it seemed, might truly be a murder with a difference. You didn't have to see any photographs to picture the carnage that a speeding train would have left in its wake. Extreme, indeed.

Faraday was talking about strategy now, about the likely pathways that Operation *Coppice* was about to explore, and Winter watched him carefully as the DI outlined the limits to which he was prepared to cast the investigative net. He hadn't seen much of Faraday since the DI's return from Thailand and he was struck by how sombre he seemed to have become. His voice, never assertive, had become softer than ever. He still marshalled the facts in the right order, still held everyone's attention, commanded respect, but there was an edge of something else in his delivery, as if he'd got tired of picking up the investigative challenge of case after case. Winter had seen this in coppers before. It always seemed to affect the more sensitive ones. There must come a point, Winter thought, when people like these get to see one body too many. And after that it all starts to fall apart.

There was another question, this time about the issue of ID, and Faraday dealt with it deftly enough, but his voice had hardened, a definite edge of impatience this time, and Winter found himself trying to keep his thoughts about the DI in perspective.

He'd learned early on that you'd be wrong to underestimate Faraday. With all the man's oddness – the birdwatching, the solitary weekends, the deaf-mute son who'd fled the nest – he was still a very effective detective, shrewd in his hunches, stubborn as hell in fighting his corner, ruthless when it mattered. Winter knew that Willard rated him highly, and no one in his right mind would ignore Willard. In his new job as Head of CID, Major Crimes' ex-boss had already put the squeeze on some of the time-servers, and productive, reliable DIs like Faraday could only – in the end – cash in.

Nonetheless, at this moment in time there was definitely something not quite right about the man in charge of Operation *Coppice*, and when Winter tried to find the exact word to describe it, he knew he ought to keep it simple. Maybe, after all, it wasn't some midlife career crisis. Faraday, he finally decided, was simply pissed off.

The meeting went on. Faraday called for a summary from Winter on the strength of the Misper list, and Winter obliged. His thoughts on the marital welcome awaiting the missing Arab engineer raised a ripple of laughter but he left no one in any doubt that the list, as currently drawn up, was an investigative dead end. One bloke had looked promising – same colour hair – but he'd disappeared nearly two months back and Winter could see no obvious explanation that could put him in the tunnel.

Faraday, with a cursory nod of thanks, took the meeting onto other areas, chiefly housekeeping items like Incident Room staffing levels and the management of overtime claims, and as Winter's attention began to wander, he found himself gazing at the faces around him.

He knew most of these men intimately, especially the older ones. He knew who was sharp, who delivered, who you could trust if the wheels came off. He also knew who were the bullshitters, who had a bottle problem in dodgy situations and who was over the side with the prettiest of the five indexers who were sitting in a huddle by the window. He knew that Dawn Ellis, a recent recruit to the squad, was contemplating a new career in alternative therapy, and he knew that Bev Yates was still trying to figure out the exact chain of events that had got his wife pregnant for the third time.

Names, Winter thought. Lives. Reputations. But where had the real legends gone? The hard core of old thief-takers, hard-drinking, occasionally corrupt but immensely successful? The answer, he knew, was simple. Thanks to age, or alcohol, or simple despair at the prospect of retirement, they'd simply faded away, leaving behind them the blackest of holes that no amount of performance figures, or career development, or fancy policy statements could possibly fill.

Because the truth was that no one wanted to be a detective anymore. Today's policemen had lives and families to go home to. They wanted the reassurance of regular shift work. They hated the very idea of overtime. In fact, with the exception of gutsy kids like Jimmy Suttle, CID had become the posting from hell, and the situation had now got so dire that they had to draft in veterans, retired blokes for God's sake, just to keep the numbers up.

The squad meeting was coming to an end. Faraday was issuing the standard warnings about screwing down evidence, about grafting hard, about avoiding short cuts. Winter caught Dave Michaels' eye. Michaels was the DS who'd be acting as Statement Reader once the machine cranked into action.

'A fucking name,' he muttered, 'might be useful.'

Back in his office, Winter at last turned his attention to the padlock. Faraday had mentioned it twice in the squad meeting, telling the listening DCs that a great deal of legwork and a big slice of luck might be necessary to pin down its likely point of sale, but nothing at all could happen until the Intelligence Cell came up with a list of local outlets. Winter glanced at his watch, then slipped the photos back into his office drawer. Tomorrow, he thought. This time of night you'd be mad to start calling.

He sat back a moment, then reached in his pocket and fetched out the bank statement he'd lifted from Givens' flat. Givens had his money with HSBC. The statement was dated 5 July 2005. On 1 June Givens had £7,455.29 to his name. By four weeks later, after a £400 direct debit – presumably his rent – his balance had shrunk to a mere £214.70. Winter fetched a calendar from a neighbouring desk and set about doing the maths.

According to his employers, Givens had failed to turn up for work on Tuesday 24 May. This statement didn't cover the rest of May, but there was a clear pattern of debit card withdrawals in early June. On the first, second and third of the month, £700 had disappeared from the account each day, and in every case the name against the transaction appeared to be identical. Winter checked, then double-checked. No question about it. Portsmouth FC.

Winter lifted the phone. Dave Michaels was a mad Pompey fan. He answered on the first ring.

'Dave? Paul Winter. How much is a Pompey season ticket?'

'Why?'

'Nephew's birthday. Thought I'd buy him a little present.'

'You'd better start saving then.'

'How much?'

'For the best seats? Seven hundred quid.'

Winter, gleeful, told him it was cheap at the price, then hung up. Returning to Givens' bank statement, he traced the next week's withdrawals. This time, there were only two. On 6 June, £2100. A day later, £2800. Seven more season tickets. Simple. By now, 7 June, the account was nearly empty. No further transactions. Then, on 24 June, Givens' NHS salary cheque had been paid in, putting him £1857.29 in the black. Three days later, on Monday 27 June, another £1400 had gone up the road to the football club. After that, no one had touched Givens' money.

Winter went back over the sums, totalling the figures on his fingers. Nothing he'd seen in Givens' flat had even hinted at a passion for football. So what on earth would he want with a dozen season tickets?

Even now, he knew the answer. Somehow or other, someone had got hold of Givens' debit card. Maybe they'd rolled him. Maybe the violence had got out of hand. Maybe there was some other explanation. But whatever had happened, they were left with the key to Givens' bank account but no PIN number. Without the PIN they couldn't access ATMs or go for a shopping spree. And so they'd be looking for some other way of turning that little plastic wafer into hard cash.

A bunch of season tickets, early July, was the perfect answer. You wouldn't get seven hundred quid a pop for them but in a city as soccer-mad as Pompey, you could come close. Word would go round the estates.

Maybe there'd be bidding. £500? £600? £650? Who cares? Either way, the little scrote who'd dreamed up the scam would be laughing all the way to the offie. Six grand, minimum. How many Stellas was that?

Winter got to his feet and gazed out of the window. In a tiny back garden beyond the car park an elderly man in a pair of baggy shorts was enjoying the last of a decent day. His feet propped on an upturned crate, he was lying back in a deckchair, face to the sun. Winter watched him for a moment or two, still thinking about the Pompey scam. The figures, he knew, argued for themselves. But what was infinitely more promising was the fact that nothing had been heard from Givens himself. No block on his account. No sign that he'd ever tried to staunch the outflow of precious cash.

In theory, of course, he might not have noticed but you still needed a card to order tickets over the phone, and Winter had never heard of anyone whose card had gone missing for a month and hadn't made a fuss about it. No, every next piece of evidence – his non-appearance at work, the neglected garden, the state of the fridge and now the bank account – argued that Mr Givens was off the plot. Did that make him a likely candidate for the body in the tunnel? Winter still thought not. Back in May, in whatever circumstances, Givens had met his death. Soon afterwards someone had dreamed up a way of emptying his bank account. End of story.

Winter sat down again behind the desk. He had a picture of that bare, neat sitting room, so suddenly abandoned, in his head. Not one decent murder, he thought, but two. He contemplated the possibility, then retrieved his address book from his jacket pocket and lifted the phone again. What he needed now, what he always needed in this situation, was a great deal more information about the man himself. Givens had been at St Mary's Hospital for a while. A job like his, carting

44

medical specimens around, it was odds on he'd be in and out of the mortuary.

Winter dialled a mobile number. It took a while to answer. At last, a voice he recognised, gruff Pompey accent. Winter was on his feet again, peering out of the window. The smile was back on his face.

'Jake? It's Paul Winter. Fancy a pint?'

Faraday was back at his office, gazing at the Operation *Coppice* policy book. He'd lost count of the number of times he'd been through this little ritual, contemplating the bareness of that first page, wondering quite where all those entries he'd be making over the days to come would lead.

The policy book was his anchor, a detailed aide-memoire that would steady the investigation as the seas got rougher. Every decision he made, every tiny step he took along the path towards some kind of result, would go down on these pages. In months, maybe years, to come, a glance at a single entry would remind him why he'd authorised a particular action or convened yet another meeting.

At first, in his early days of heading complex enquiries, this fanatical exercise in record-keeping had seemed completely over the top, but experience had taught him that the policy book could prove invaluable. Defence solicitors could be ruthless picking holes in the conduct of a particular operation, and he'd seen fellow officers crucified in court for decisions that had long ago slipped their memories. The policy book, he'd learned, could be a shield as well as an anchor.

Reviewing the day's progress, he began to scribble a log of events. He'd got as far as removal of the body parts from the tunnel when he heard a knock at the door. It was Tracy Barber. She wanted a word.

'What time's the post-mortem, boss?'

'Half eight.'

'You want a lift?'

The offer surprised Faraday. Pending the construction of a new mortuary at the city's Queen Alexandra Hospital, Home Office post-mortems were being conducted at Winchester, half an hour away. On the motorway it was an easy drive. Why the concern?

Tracy muttered something about owing a girlfriend a drink. She could drop Faraday off and pick him up when the pathologist was through. Faraday knew it was bullshit.

'You want to chat?' He gestured at the empty chair. 'Help yourself.'

'It's not that.'

'What, then?'

Barber studied him a moment. She'd worked with Faraday for more than a year now and thought she knew him. Holidays, she told herself, were supposed to make you relax.

'You just seem ... ' She shrugged. ' ... Uptight, that's all.'

'Do I?'

'Yeah. It's not a crime, boss, no one's going to report you. But ... you know –' She nodded down at the policy book. '– It's still early days.'

Faraday nodded. Early days. She was right. He glanced at his watch, toyed with accepting her offer, then told himself it was unnecessary. The post-mortem could drag on for hours. A body this mangled would stretch the pathologist and the mortuary attendants to the limit.

Barber, uncomfortable now, was waiting for a decision. Faraday smiled up at her, then got to his feet.

'Kind of you.' He slipped on his jacket. 'But no, thanks.'

The motorway out of the city began at the end of Kingston Crescent. Faraday eased the Mondeo onto the slip road and joined the thin stream of northbound traffic. One or two French lorries were still rumbling

46

out of the commercial docks, last arrivals off the Le Havre ferry, and beyond them Faraday could see the darkening spaces of the upper harbour. The sun had gone now, buried behind threatening towers of cloud to the west.

Faraday reached for the radio, searching for a concert. He tuned to Radio Three and the haunting brass of Mahler's Fifth brought a smile to his face as he slipped the seat back a notch or two, making himself comfortable. Was he really as stressed as Barber seemed to think? And, if so, was it anyone's business but his own?

He thought about the proposition, knowing only too well where it led. For well over a year now Eadie Sykes had been living and working in Australia, and the relationship had survived on a drip feed of e-mails increasingly empty of anything but the bare facts of their working lives. He'd been lashed to the wheel of Major Crimes. She'd been making documentary films. The prospect of meeting her again after all this time had slightly alarmed Faraday, and on the long flight from Heathrow he'd begun to wonder whether this protracted, arm's-length affair of theirs could really survive the next three weeks.

The answer, of course, was no, and from the moment she'd met him at Bangkok airport, tanned and brimming with news, he'd known they were more than half a world apart. He represented a closed chapter in her busy, busy life. She'd done provincial England. She'd moved on. For someone with her talents – courage, looks, energy, plus an implacable determination to succeed – Australia was irresistible. She had an apartment on Manly Beach. She had the ear of a wealthy businessman happy to fund any film she wanted to make. The crews she used were the sassiest guys in the world. And, as the reviews she'd collated for Faraday's benefit so amply showed, she was making it. Big time. So why on earth would she ever want to come back to Portsmouth?

They'd taken a ferry to a diving island called Koh Tao. A contact of Eadie's in Sydney had pre-booked a sumptuous bungalow overlooking a secluded cove, and they'd settled in. The first couple of days, jet-lagged, Faraday had slept a lot. Whenever he'd woken, chilled by the powerful air conditioning, Eadie had been out somewhere, swimming or walking, or making new friends at the beachside bar on the other side of the bay. The second night, refreshed now, Faraday had proposed a meal at a recommended seafood place in the next bay. They'd ridden to the restaurant on a couple of rented Honda motorbikes. Even now, Faraday could still feel the sweet kiss of the night air on his burning face.

The meal had been a disaster. While Faraday sank a series of Chang beers, Eadie toyed with a glass of Perrier. She'd given up alcohol, she explained, because she'd found sobriety more of a turn-on. Glummer by the minute, Faraday had then listened to her brisk dissection of his life. He was in the wrong job. He had the wrong priorities. He'd settled, all the time she'd known him, for second best. He was a great copper, no question about it, but where on earth was the satisfaction in chasing a bunch of arsehole kids round a dump like Portsmouth? And as for birdwatching, how much fun was that?

Listening to her skating over the surface of his last three years, Faraday had managed to keep his temper. She'd always had a gift for the right phrase, a certain glibness that served her well professionally, but she didn't come close to the things that made him tick. She didn't understand how birdwatching was so much more than birdwatching, how the dawn chorus in the New Forest could open the door to the secret rustling world of water voles and stoats, of daubeton and pipistrelle bats. She had no inkling of the satisfactions of pausing in some forest glade, cupping an ear, filtering out the busy clamour of the wrens and the robins until there was nothing left but the trill of a wood warbler, high on a beech limb, singing its tiny heart out. To Eadie these kinds of pleasures were evidence of abnormality, of incipient depression, of a stubborn refusal to get stuck into real life.

With the latter phrase, Faraday could only agree. That's why he did it, he explained. Real life knocked on his office door every day of his working week, and without the birds, without the solitude, he really would be a headcase. At this point Eadie had leaned across the table and taken his hand. It was the first time since they met that she'd shown the faintest interest in physical affection. Yet her touch felt like the reassuring pat of a nurse or a doctor. He'd be fine, she seemed to be saying. Just fine.

Faraday remembered looking at her, surprised by the smallness of the truth on which he'd stumbled.

'You haven't a clue who I really am,' he said quietly. 'Have you?'

Next morning, alone, he'd gone snorkelling in the bay. By the time he got back to the bungalow, she'd packed and left. No note. No adieu. Just a sea urchin planted in the very middle of his pillow, still wet from the tiny cove beneath the terrace. The message it sent was all too obvious. Picturing it now, as the Mondeo sped north towards Winchester, Faraday wondered yet again if he was really that hard to get at.

By the time Faraday had found a parking spot, Ewers was ready for the post-mortem. Gowned and booted, he was on the phone to his wife in Bristol. Outside the office, Jerry Proctor was in conversation with the Scenes of Crime photographer.

Through the open doors beyond the line of stainless steel fridges Faraday could see the room where the post-mortem would take place. The head and two sections of torso occupied one of the tables and there were body parts heaped on a nearby trolley. Ignore the harsh glint of neon on the tiled walls, thought Faraday, and this could be a scene from a butcher's shop.

Ewers was off the phone now. He appeared at Faraday's elbow, snapping on a pair of surgical gloves. Given the circumstances, he looked remarkably cheerful.

'Shall we . . . ?'

He led the way into the post-mortem room. Braced for the smell, the sweet stench of death, Faraday caught Proctor's eye. Like Ewers, he seemed totally unmoved by the offal on the trolley and Faraday began to wonder how he coped. A couple of years before his recent spell in Iraq, Proctor had volunteered for a posting to Kosovo, disinterring bodies and subjecting them to forensic analysis ahead of a firm ID. Maybe the leftovers from a Balkan civil war armoured you against scenes like this, Faraday thought. Maybe that was the trick.

Ewers was already at work, assembling the body parts, addressing the overhead microphone as he inspected a smashed hand or a loop of viscera before carefully adding it to the growing jigsaw on the slab. To the head he paid special attention, inspecting the pulped flesh and sinew where the neck had been torn from the rest of the body, parting the matted hair to study the state of the scalp and running his fingers over what remained of the man's features. The nose had gone, one eye was missing completely, while the other hung down on a white thread of optic nerve, glistening and sightless. Faraday stared at it for a long moment, sickened.

Ewers handed the head to one of the mortuary technicians and muttered something else for the benefit of the microphone. Already, from the tone of his voice, Faraday could sense that little of real forensic value would come out of the post-mortem. The body was simply too damaged. There were certain physical observations that could be safely made – height, shoe size, hair colour, approximate weight – but the rest of the evidence had been utterly smashed by the impact. If you wanted to eradicate any trace of prior damage, thought Faraday, this is exactly what you'd do.

As Ewers moved on to the more intact of the two legs, Faraday's mobile began to trill. He stepped out into the fridge room. It was Willard.

'Sir?' Faraday was peering back through the open door. Ewers seemed to have found something on one of the legs.

Willard wanted to know how the post-mortem was going. Barrie had kept the new Head of CID briefed all day.

'Fine, sir. But don't hold your breath. The bloke's a mess.'

Willard grunted something Faraday didn't catch then asked him about his plans afterwards. Just now he was camping in a rented flat in Winchester. He needed a word or two with Faraday. Maybe a drink after the post-mortem?

Faraday was still watching Ewers. The invitation, he knew, had the force of an order.

'Of course, sir. I'll bell you when we're through.'

The Eldon Arms straddled the fault line between Portsmouth and Southsea. Within easy walking distance of the nearby law courts, it attracted a handful of barristers every lunchtime, offering a spread of real ales to go with a snatched lunch, but in the evenings it became a locals' pub, favoured by a noisy mix of builders, students, petty criminals and the odd lecturer from the university. The walls were clad with bookshelves and there was a house spaniel with three legs. The place was at once intimate, smoky and – if you had the need – deeply private. Winter loved it.

He'd already found a corner table by the time Jake

Tarrant arrived. Winter spotted him by the door, gelled blond hair, full lips, Madness T-shirt and jeans, giving someone he obviously knew a little wave. Seconds later, he was beside Winter, telling him to drink up.

'Stella top, son.' Winter was feeling better by the minute. 'And a packet of roasted peanuts.'

Tarrant returned with the drinks and nibbles, settled in the chair across the table. Although Winter had known him for at least ten years, he still hadn't a clue how old he was. Some days at St Mary's, rushed off his feet by a traffic jam of post-mortems, Tarrant could look almost middle-aged. Other times, afternoons especially when the pressure had eased, he might just have left college. Either way, with his boundless energy and easy wit, he'd always made trips to the mortuary a real pleasure, and Winter's affection for the boy had been shared by countless other detectives. Jake was also handy on the football field, a gifted defender, and for a couple of seasons he'd guested in the Pompey CID team, transforming their prospects in the local league. Coppers liked Jake Tarrant. Not only could he handle most centre forwards but he also held his own when it came to conversation at the bar.

'Mr Winter . . . ' He raised his glass. 'Good to know you're still with us.'

He wanted a proper account of what had happened. The way he'd heard it, Winter had looked death in the face. There'd been talk of cancer and all kinds of diagnostic bollocks, and some exotic operation that probably cost a fortune. Whatever the real story it must have worked because here he was, Jake Tarrant's favourite detective, fit as a butcher's dog. One DC, he said, had been running a book on Winter's chances of survival and Tarrant had corpsed when he'd heard the odds.

'What were they?' Winter was intrigued.

'Three to one.'

'On me dying?'

'Other way round. Most of the blokes didn't fancy death's chances.' Tarrant cackled with laughter. 'Me? I had a tenner. Pillock still owes me.' He leaned forward over the table. 'So talk me through it. Pretend I know nothing.'

Winter did his bidding. He was still trying to do justice to the crippling headaches that began it all when Tarrant interrupted again. 'There was some bird involved, wasn't there? Amazingly tasty piece? Funny name?'

'Yeah.' Winter nodded. 'Maddox.'

'Real looker? On the game in some fancy knocking shop down Old Portsmouth? Am I right?'

'You are, son. You are.'

'So what happened there, then? How come she fell for a fat bastard like you?'

'Class attracts class.' It was a question Winter had heard a thousand times. 'You wouldn't know it, but it's true.' He returned to his story, described the visits to the consultant up at the hospital, the CT scans and finally the news that a tumour was nesting in his brain. 'This size . . . ' He cupped his hand. 'Saw it myself on the screen. Big as a tennis ball. No wonder the codeine didn't touch it.'

The consultant had begun the search for a neurosurgeon. The operation would be complicated by the fact that the tumour had come through the sinus and was now growing on the nearby vein. Getting rid of it risked cutting the blood vessel.

'That's a litre of blood a minute.' Winter nodded. 'I remember writing it down. Anything goes wrong, they've got five minutes to sort you out before you're running on empty. Encouraging, eh?'

Tarrant nodded. He wanted to know where the story went next, more details, and Winter realised how easy it was to forget what this fresh-faced mortuary technician did for a living. He must have looked inside a thousand skulls, Winter thought. None of this would be remotely surprising.

He voiced the thought but Tarrant shook his head. The neurobod had been right. Unusual condition. Tricky bit of plumbing. Who'd been silly enough to pick up the challenge?

'American bloke. Phoenix, Arizona. Maddox did the legwork, bless her. Found him through a blog on the Internet. Another English guy who'd had the same problem.'

'I was right then. Must have cost a fortune.'

'It did.'

'How much?'

'Ninety-five thousand dollars. Plus another seven for fares and whatnot. Call it sixty grand in real money.'

'Shit.'

'Yeah?' Winter reached for his drink. 'You think I had a choice?'

'No, but –' Tarrant shrugged. '– That's a mortgage job. How many blokes do you know have got sixty grand to spare?'

'Doesn't matter, son. Situation like that, you're up against the wall. Some days, tell you the truth, I would have jacked it in. One morning I even asked Maddox to put a fucking pillow on my head. Yeah –' he nodded '– that bad. Other days, though, the drugs they give you do a good job. She'd drive me round, Maddox. We'd go places, just waiting for this American bloke to get back to us with a decision, and you'd stop, maybe down the coast somewhere, West Sussex, no one around, and the sun would be setting, and you'd get out of the car, right old state, wobbly as fuck, but then you'd smell the air, maybe even take your socks off and go for a little paddle, sand between your toes, the water not at all bad, and you'd think well, fuck it, there's a bit of me left yet and you're not having it.'

'You?'

'It. Death. God. Darth Vader. Whoever. Doesn't

54

matter. If there's a chance, you grab it. The price on the box doesn't matter. Sixty grand? A hundred? A million? It's just money, son. It doesn't count. You don't even think about it. It's what's *inside* the box that's going to float your boat.'

'And this woman? Maddox? She was with you the whole time?'

'Yeah. Never left me, not once. Tell you the truth, she was a headcase. She had this mad plan to take us both off to Africa. You ever heard of Arthur Rimbaud?'

'No.'

'Me neither. Not before I met her. But Rimbaud turned out to be a poet and she loved everything about him. He ended up in Ethiopia and we were going too but it all got too difficult in the end so we went to Phoenix instead.'

'For the op?'

'Yeah.'

'How was it?'

'Beautiful. The week before it happened I was shitting myself. If I didn't die on the table I thought I'd end up a basket case. Wheelchair. Towel to dribble in. Potty underneath. Crap television. The works. And you know what? I had cheeseburger and chips the night before, they gave me a couple of big fat pills to sleep on, and then it was six o'clock in the morning and the whole pantomime kicks off. Injection I never even felt, faces going all blurry, then it's four hours later and there isn't a bit of me that hasn't got a tube hanging out. Maddox loved it. Nearly died laughing.'

'She stayed with you afterwards?'

'For a bit, yeah, until I was on my feet.'

'And then?'

'She fucked off down to South America. I got a card just before Christmas. Load of Indians weaving carpets. Ecuador? Christ knows . . . '

Winter broke off and shrugged. He missed Maddox

more than he cared to admit but this wasn't the place to say so.

Tarrant was draining his pint. Winter reached for his empty glass.

'Same again, son?' He got to his feet and picked his way towards the bar, glad of the chance to get away for a moment or two. Not counting Maddox, he couldn't remember the last time he'd let his guard down like this. Tarrant was cannier than Winter had realised. If times got tough at the mortuary, the boy might consider a year or two with CID, guesting in the interview suite.

Back at the table, Tarrant wanted to pick up the threads again, talk about what life felt like when you'd been so close to losing it, but Winter wasn't interested. Life, he said briskly, was a big fat peach. What mattered now was making the most of it, something he fully intended to do. Had he changed at all? Of course he had. Were his priorities different? You bet. Was he about to take this conversation any further? No fucking way.

'There's a bloke called Givens.' He beckoned Tarrant closer. 'Something tells me you might know him.'

'Alan Givens?' Tarrant looked surprised. 'At work, you mean?'

'Yeah.'

'Sure I know him. He hasn't been around a bit lately but ... yeah ...'

'What's he like?'

'He's all right.' Tarrant was frowning. 'Why?'

'He seems to have disappeared.'

'*Disappeared*? How?'

'I've no idea. And neither do your bosses.' Winter took a swallow of Stella, then wiped his mouth with the back of his hand. 'How well do you know him?'

'So-so. He's a bit of a loner, really. Drives one of the delivery vans. Bimbles round the city with trays full of samples. Picks them up from QA, from our place, sometimes from GP surgeries, delivers them to the analysis labs. He used to drop by the mortuary when we had anything for him but, like I say, we haven't seen him for a while. Tell you the truth, I assumed he'd got another job.'

'Elsewhere, you mean? Outside the hospital?'

'Dunno.' Tarrant shrugged.

'Local, is he?'

'No. I can't place the accent but it's definitely from the north somewhere. I'm not sure what he really thinks of Pompey. The times we got to have a real chat I got the impression he wasn't that struck, but I may have been wrong.'

'You think he might have moved away completely?'

'Might have done, though I'm sure he would have mentioned it.'

'Is he married at all? Girlfriend? Anything like that?'

'Not that I know of. It's not that he wasn't friendly – don't get me wrong – but some blokes are just a bit shy, you know what I mean? Haven't got a lot to say.'

'Sure.' Winter's was picturing the bank statements. 'What about football?'

'Football? *Givens?*' Tarrant began to laugh. 'I think not, Mr W. That's one of the things that pisses him off about the town. He once told me he'd got away from home because everyone was soccer-mad. Then he finds himself down here. Blue Army. Pompey till I die. He hates all that. Thinks they're all hooligans. Can't begin to understand what all the fuss is about.'

'Not into season tickets, then?'

'Shit, no. Why do you ask?'

Winter didn't answer. Instead, he wanted to know whether Givens had any enemies.

Tarrant looked blank.

'*Enemies?* What would that be about?' He gazed at Winter a moment longer, then the penny appeared to drop. 'You think . . . ?'

Winter shrugged.

'I dunno. That's what it looks like. On the other hand, it might be down to something else. Maybe he's had a stroke, lost his memory. Maybe you're right. Maybe Pompey's got to him. Maybe he's gone home, back up north.' Winter nodded. 'Yeah, maybe that's it.'

Tarrant's eyes had strayed to the big screen on the far wall. A team in blue were running out of a tunnel. The roar of the crowd found an echo in the handful of drinkers who'd turned to watch.

'Pompey.' Tarrant was grinning. 'The Saints game at Fratton Park back in April. Four–one and it could have been a hatful. If this is like my local they'll be playing the DVD most nights. That's another thing that gets Alan going, all the bollocks about Scummers. He had a go at me once about it. We were having a brew in the office and I had a dig at the Scummers, the way you do, and he just couldn't understand it. So what's so bad about living in Southampton? he said. Southampton? *Scummerdom?* Can you believe that? A grown man? In this town? I had to be stern with the fella, told him to watch his mouth.' He smiled at the memory, still looking up at the screen. 'Didn't work, though, did it? Not according to you, Mr Winter . . .'

In the end, Faraday and Willard were too late for the pub, so Willard elected for a curry instead. The Midnight Tandoori lay towards the bottom of the town. As Willard had anticipated, it was virtually empty.

Willard edged his bulk behind the table and reached for the menu. Promotion, Faraday had already decided, sat rather well on the new Head of CID. The three-piece suit looked as expensive as ever and there was something in his manner that spoke of a deep sense of satisfaction.

On Major Crimes Willard had set a crippling pace, refusing to accept second best from anyone on the team, fighting battle after battle with his masters at

HQ. A DCI who knew him well had a theory that Willard couldn't function properly without someone to batter, and he was fearless when it came to choice of target. There were placemen way up the pecking order for whom the then-Detective Superintendent had nothing but contempt, and the fact that they outranked him simply added to his furious sense of injustice. There had been times in his office, back at Kingston Crescent, when Faraday had felt tempted to leave the room rather than endure another second of Willard's end of the phone call. 'Totally unacceptable' had been one favourite phrase. 'Pillock' another.

Now though, from the giddy heights of Detective Chief Superintendent, Willard appeared to have mellowed. He was the top detective in the force. What he said mattered. No one could spoil his day.

The waiter gone, he got straight to the point. 'It's about Winter,' he said. 'And this is in strictest confidence.'

'Of course, sir.' Faraday nodded.

'You're happy with him so far?'

'Yes.'

'No dramas?'

'None.'

'And he's doing the business?'

'Yes. There's been nothing to really stretch him so far but that's about to change. *Coppice* is a runner. Intelligence will be key.'

'Good.' Willard held Faraday's eyes. 'I want you to keep an eye on him, a real eye. How much do you know about POCA?'

POCA was police-speak for the Proceeds of Crime Act. Most working detectives had given up on the small print but in the right hands, according to colleagues whom Faraday respected, it could make life very tough indeed for major criminals.

'Confiscation orders? Tainted funds? Co-mingled assets?'

'That's it.' Willard nodded. 'This is the Exocet missile most lawyers think we can't even unpack. They've got a point. The legislation looks a nightmare but the principle couldn't be simpler. If a bloke's life is paid for by crime, we can have it off him, every last button, house, car, bank account, the lot. It's up to him to show the court how he legally got it all and if he can't do that, he's fucked. Beautiful piece of lawmaking. Should be the jewel in our crown.'

'But it isn't.'

'No, and one reason for that is no one really understands it. We all fight shy. We struggle through the act, all six million clauses, and then we give up and back to business as usual. It's got to change, Joe. And it will.'

Faraday nodded. He didn't doubt Willard for a moment. A while back, Operation *Tumbril* had tried to take down a drug baron called Bazza Mackenzie, Pompey's living proof that dealing in cocaine paved the way to serious wealth. *Tumbril* had been a covert operation, known to just a handful of officers, and both Willard and Faraday had been badly burned when it blew up in their faces. Two years later, from a desk in headquarters, Willard was clearly plotting his revenge.

Now he was talking about the need for a 'champion', a detective who could spend a year or so spreading the word about POCA, getting alongside fellow officers, putting their darkest fears to rest, explaining how the legislation worked. This missionary task, in Willard's opinion, needed an older man, someone with a record as a good thief-taker, someone indeed with an intimate knowledge of exactly what made criminals like Bazza Mackenzie tick.

'Someone like Winter,' Faraday murmured.

'Exactly.'

'A brave choice.'

'I'd call it controversial, Joe. And so will my colleagues.' He paused for the lagers to arrive. Then he bent closer. 'Naturally there's a procedure to be gone through. There'll be other applicants, an impartial selection process, but personally I've no doubt that Winter is the man for the job. We could argue all night about rights and wrongs but the fact is that the guy delivers. The only thing that bothers me is what's happened to him since that operation of his. As I understand it, he could have died. That concentrates a man's mind. People change. Different priorities. A different take on life. What do you think?'

'About Winter?'

'Yes.'

'I haven't a clue, sir.'

'But you'll keep an eye on him?'

'Of course.'

'And you get my drift?'

'Yes.' He looked up at Willard. 'The issue with Winter as I see it has always been motivation. With most of us it's pretty straightforward. We do the best job we can, we try not to get ourselves or anyone else in the shit, and if it all turns out OK, then we like to think it's a bit of a result. Winter's not like that at all, never has been. What drives him is the real issue. Some blokes will tell you vanity. Others that he's just plain bent. Me? I pass.'

A smile ghosted over Willard's face. He studied Faraday for a long moment.

'Passing isn't an option, Joe,' he said at last. 'Not in this case.'

'No.' Faraday reached for his lager. 'So I gather.'

Four

Faraday was up early next morning, patrolling the edges of one of the freshwater ponds on Milton Common. The ponds, barely half a mile north of the Bargemaster's House, were home to a variety of summer birdlife and Faraday spent a deeply contented hour or so keeping tabs on a family of little grebes.

The parents were shy, demure, slipping in and out of the reeds, fastidious in the care of their downy brood. Faraday had been watching them for months, ever since the emergence of the young, and this glimpse of parenthood gave him an oddly comforting sense of personal nourishment. The grebes, in common with most birds, faced a number of natural predators. Mere survival demanded constant vigilance. The young, with their rattling, slightly comical, high-pitched trills, were forever hungry. Yet the family seemed to flourish, bonded by the instinctive knowledge that their best chance in a hostile world lay in staying together. Life, thought Faraday, could be so simple.

By ten o'clock, after a brief visit to the crime scene out at Buriton, he was climbing the stairs to the Major Crimes Suite. Winter was at his desk in the Intelligence Cell when Faraday put his head round the door.

'You've got a moment?'

'Sure, boss.'

Winter began to get up to accompany Faraday to his own office but the DI had already helped himself to one of the two spare chairs. The sheaf of padlock photos lay beside Winter's phone. Faraday began to leaf through them. The padlock was chunky, solid-looking, a brass body with a steel hasp on top.

'So how are you getting on?'

Winter consulted his notes. So far, he said, he'd talked to two managers at B&Q, the area director at Homebase, and a helpful young totty at GA Day. Next, he'd be starting on the smaller hardware stores listed in Yellow Pages. As detective work, he confessed, it didn't hold a candle to busting high-class knocking shops or chasing drug dealers but fat old bastards like him were grateful for small mercies.

Faraday acknowledged the quip with a smile. On one side of the padlock was the make, Tri-Circle. Beneath, a figure, 266. He glanced through the rest of the photos. On the other side of the lock he could make out a company logo, three interlinked circles nesting in an oval.

'So who stocks them?'

'They all do. Homebase is your best bet. Six ninety-nine. That's a steal, believe me.'

'Why so popular?'

'They're Chinese. That's retail for cheap. The Chinkies knock 'em out, ten to a quid. Bloke at B&Q told me they buy them by the thousands. Says padlocks have become a hot item. Half the people in this city have something to their name. The other half can't wait to nick it. That's him talking, not me. Pompey? He thinks it's padlock heaven.'

'What about the paper trail? Do these people keep records of every transaction?'

'Yeah, the bigger stores do, but it only works for us if someone uses a card. Pay cash and there's obviously no name attached. Plus they're less than keen to sort through all the paperwork. Bloke at Homebase said he was ten understaffed as it was, could barely keep the bloody shelves stocked.'

'How many keys do they supply? With the padlock?'

'Two.'

'Always?'

'So they say.'

Faraday nodded. Maybe Winter would get a better result at one of the local hardware stores. Maybe a man behind his own counter might remember a specific transaction, or a face.

'Yeah, sure. But those blokes charge the earth. That's why they're going out of business. Who's going to be paying over the odds when you can go down the road and get one half the price?'

Faraday said it didn't matter. Detective work, as both men knew, was often a simple question of persistence. Dozens of phone calls, hours of getting nowhere. Then a sudden glimpse of something that could stop an enquiry in its tracks and point it in a totally different direction.

'What about the chain? And the bits and pieces of sash cord?'

'I was saving them for later,' Winter said drily. 'Have you seen the state of them?'

Faraday nodded. Both items were locked in the Crime Property Store down the corridor. The sash cord, brittle and frayed, could have been nineteenth century while the length of galvanised chain sheared by the train had definitely seen better days. Winter was right. Tracing them back would be a nightmare.

There was a brief silence. Then Winter wanted to know about the house-to-house. The Outside Enquiry Team had been at it since eight, going from door to door in Buriton. Any nibbles?

'None. I was up there just now. There's a little lane that leads to the railway. In all, we're looking at three properties. The bloke at the end's been done a couple of times – professional burglars, knew what they were after. Since Christmas he's had a new security system. Sensors, lights, all the bells and whistles. Plus he's got dogs. Anything that moves on that stretch of lane, he'd

know about it. Sunday night? Not a whisper. Quiet as
you like. Slept like a baby.'

'Wrong lane, then.'

'Obviously.'

Winter had an Ordnance Survey map tucked beneath
the still-wrapped sandwich he'd picked up on the way
in. Faraday flattened the map on the adjoining desk,
tracing the line of the railway as it snaked north from
the coast. Beyond Rowland's Castle, a pricey village
suddenly fashionable with executives from the likes of
IBM, the line passed through open country, largely
farmland dotted with occasional trackside hamlets,
until it began the long ascent towards the tunnel.
Faraday must have watched those passing fields a
thousand times from the London-bound train and had
always been surprised. For an area barely twenty
minutes' drive from a major conurbation, it felt almost
remote.

'I'm thinking we need to be looking down here, not
up at Buriton.' He tapped the area south of the tunnel.
'For one thing, there's nobody around. For another,
that's where we found the body. If you came in from
the north, you'd have to walk through most of the
tunnel until you got to the spot you wanted. Why do
that?'

'Sure.'

'So it's here we should be taking a proper look.'

Faraday began to indicate access points along the
line of the railway, drawing on yesterday's recce. Three
miles south of the tunnel, he said, there were limitless
opportunities to scale the low fence, scramble down
from a bridge or simply walk onto the bed of the
railway from one of the unmanned crossings, but the
closer you got to the tunnel, the more difficult access
became. For the last kilometre, the rising land west of
the track was covered with trees. The plantation was
commercially managed, and there was a forest track

that could take vehicles that wound down towards the railway.

'Here.' Faraday's finger rested on the point where the dotted lines collided with the railway. 'There's some kind of gate onto the track. Apparently it's a doddle.'

'Has anyone checked it out?'

'It's on the actions list. We're starting to look at houses along this road here, too.' He tracked back through the forest until his finger found the tiny country road, way up from the railway, that took local traffic south. 'We're talking a couple of properties at the most. It's a long shot, I know, but we're drawing a blank in the village.'

He began to fold up the map but Winter told him to leave it. This morning he was getting himself organised. He had Pentels for the whiteboard on the wall and as soon as he was through with the phone calls he'd be making a start on a timeline. By then, with luck, something might have come back from the house-to-house. If so, Faraday would naturally be the first to know.

Faraday was on his way out. Winter glanced round at him.

'What about the post-mortem? Any joy?'

'Yeah, I meant to say.' Faraday closed the door again. 'There's no way Ewers is going to risk any kind of clinical judgement on whether or not the guy was dead before the train got to him but he did find something.'

'Like what?'

'Old bruising.' Faraday ran his hands over his own body. 'Where there was undamaged flesh, we've got evidence of some kind of trauma maybe a week earlier, maybe longer than that. Could be an accident, maybe some kind of traffic incident, maybe a motorbike crash if he had one. On the other hand, it could be something more significant.'

'Someone had a go at him?'

66

'Ewers isn't ruling it out.'

'Some kind of warning?'

'More than possible.' Faraday offered Winter a bleak smile. 'Shame he didn't listen, eh?'

It was DC Jimmy Suttle who spotted the farmhouse first. The narrow country road had emerged from the tunnel of trees, and Suttle could see the upstairs windows and the steep pitch of the tiled roof behind the encircling brick wall. On the map, the L-shaped building was marked Gorecombe Lodge.

DC Dawn Ellis was waiting to overtake a tractor. Suttle told her not to bother.

'There,' he said. 'Look.'

They parked on the grass verge, a dozen metres short of the big double gates. Both the wall and the gates looked new. Ellis was studying the notes she'd made earlier. The DS dishing out the morning's actions had given her the name of the owners.

'Cleaver,' she said finally, reaching for her clipboard. 'Mr and Mrs. According to people in the village, they've been here less than a year.'

'Farmers?'

'We think not. He's a professional of some kind. Accountant, maybe. Or solicitor. The intelligence isn't clear.'

Suttle was already trying the gate. On his second attempt to push it open, a woman's voice came out of the entryphone set into one of the gateposts.

'Who is it?' she wanted to know.

Suttle gave his name. He was a police officer. He'd appreciate a moment or two of her time.

'Do you have ID?'

Suttle looked round for a camera, found it high on the adjoining wall. He fetched out his warrant card and held it up, shielding his eyes from the brightness of the sunshine.

'OK.'

He was able to push the gate open this time. Inside, he found a broad sweep of gravel flanked by lawn. The grass was newly mown – he could smell it – and there was a sprinkler down beyond the double garage sending a fine arc of water over the surrounding flower beds. The house itself looked centuries old, with its exposed beams and leaded windows, and someone had spent a great deal of money on ensuring that the recent extensions on either side were a perfect match. Suttle, who'd enjoyed a boisterous youth in a New Forest council house, had always aspired to something like this, and he was still pointing out the line of swallows' nests under the eaves when the front door opened.

Dawn Ellis took the lead, stepping round the parked BMW and introducing herself. The woman must have been in her forties. The blonde hair looked natural and she had the kind of fine-boned face that Suttle recognised from the magazines he sometimes browsed in his dentist's waiting room. *Tatler* or *Harper's*. This woman, he thought, had class.

She invited them in. Freshly ground coffee, another great smell. The big, open kitchen lay at the end of the flagstoned hall. Suttle could see a percolator bubbling on the Aga.

'How can I help you?' They were still standing in the hall.

Ellis mentioned the incident in the Buriton Tunnel. At once the woman said she'd read about it.

'In the *News*,' she said. 'Terrible business.'

'Quite. We were wondering, Mrs Cleaver, whether you were at home on Sunday night.'

'I was, of course I was.' She was frowning. 'How do you know my name?'

'Voters' register, Mrs Cleaver.' It was Suttle this time. 'It's just a routine call.'

'Of course, of course.' She tipped her head back a moment, the way that social smokers do, then turned her attention back to Ellis. 'My husband was here, too. We both were.'

'Do you sleep at the front of the house?'

'Yes.' The frown was back. 'Why do you ask?'

'I was wondering whether you might have heard anything.'

'In the middle of the night, you mean?'

'Yes.'

'What sort of time exactly?'

'That we don't know. Late, certainly.'

There was a long silence. She looked from one face to the other. Suttle had even forgotten about the coffee. This woman knows something, he thought. And what's more to the point, she's not sure whether to tell us or not.

'Around half one? Two o'clock?' Suttle ventured. 'Maybe a car?'

She stared at him, saying nothing. Ellis suggested they all sat down. Mrs Cleaver didn't move.

'What happened in the tunnel?' she asked at last.

'I'm afraid I can't tell you. Not at this point in time.'

'But someone died, didn't they?'

'Yes.'

'A man?

'I can't say.'

'Under the wheels of a train . . . Yuk.' She shuddered. 'On the local radio this morning they were talking about him being tied to the line. Who'd do a thing like that? Who'd even *think* about it?' She waited for an answer. Neither Ellis nor Suttle obliged. At length she folded her arms. She looked angry, as if this latest outrage had been designed for her personally. 'You know why we moved out here? To get away from all that ghastliness. The city's full of it. It doesn't matter where you live.'

'City, Mrs Cleaver?' Ellis was doing her best to sound sympathetic.

'Portsmouth. Actually Southsea, to be more precise.

It's probably meat and drink to people like you but I find it hard to put into words the kind of disgust . . . no, *despair* . . . ' She shook her head. 'It makes me so *angry*.'

'Disgust at what, Mrs Cleaver?'

'The way we've become. What we are. What we have to put up with. Out here in the sticks it was supposed to be better, more civilised, and now this.' There came another tilt of the head as she fought to compose herself. Then she looked again at Suttle. 'You're right. I did hear a car. That's rare, believe me, especially on Sunday nights at that kind of hour.'

'What kind of hour?'

'Ten to three. I was awake. I looked at the clock.'

'Did you see it at all? Go to the window?'

'No. By that time, it had gone.'

'In which direction? Towards the village? Or south? Back towards Pompey?'

'Well . . . ' she hesitated for a moment ' . . . that's the point, really. It went south. Definitely. Very fast, too. Very . . . you know, *aggressive*. But it didn't come from the village. No, it came from over there.' She nodded towards the front door. 'There's a lane that goes down to the plantation, becomes a track. That's where it came from. Not the village at all.'

Ellis and Suttle exchanged glances, then Ellis fumbled in her bag for a pen. While she began to fill out a form on her clipboard, Suttle asked to use the loo. Mrs Cleaver nodded, watching Ellis' racing pen. There was a problem, it seemed, with the lavatory along the hall. Suttle was welcome to use the one upstairs.

'What's this for?'

'It's routine, Mrs Cleaver. We call it a PDF, a Personal Descriptive Form. It won't take long. Just a handful of questions.'

Suttle disappeared. By the time he got back Ellis had finished.

'That's it?' Mrs Cleaver looked relieved.

'For now, yes. If we need to talk to you again, we'll phone.'

Ellis checked the number, then she and Suttle stepped towards the front door. Outside, in the sunshine, they paused for a moment before turning to say their goodbyes but it was too late. The door had closed.

The news was back with Faraday by lunchtime. The DS in charge of outside enquiries had conferenced with Jerry Proctor, and with the tunnel close to release, the Crime Scene Manager had dispatched members of his team to meet Ellis and Suttle beside the plantation. A call on the Airwave had also brought the Crime Scene Tracker racing back from her office at Cosham police station, delighted to be able to have a second crack at *Coppice*. Yesterday's search of the woodland path that accessed the railway at the northern end of the tunnel had yielded nothing more than a sackful of drinks cans, crisp packets and an assortment of discarded condoms. No broken vegetation. No footprints. Not the slightest sign that anyone might recently have scaled the fence and clambered up the embankment. Now, the prospects seemed infinitely brighter.

By the time the Scenes of Crime vans arrived, Suttle had managed to raise the local manager of the plantation. He confirmed that a gate at the end of the track would take you directly onto the railway and said he'd been doing his best to dissuade courting couples from using the wood after dark. A series of warnings about stiff fines for trespassing had been moderately effective, while planted rumours in the local pub about dog patrols had done the rest.

'These dogs exist?' queried Suttle.

'Christ, no. They cost the earth.'

Still laughing, Suttle left the Scenes of Crime team to get on with it. He'd already met the tracker from Cosham the previous day, a spirited redhead with a mischievous smile, and he blew her a kiss as he drove

Dawn Ellis away. Ellis was still preoccupied with Mrs Cleaver.

'You think she told us everything?'

'No. The way I see it, we were lucky to get as much as we did.'

'So why hold back?'

'Christ knows. What does the husband do for a living?'

'He's a property developer. In Pompey.'

'How do you know?'

'I phoned Paul Winter. He's in Intelligence. He knows everything.'

'And?'

'Cleaver's one of the bad guys. Money coming out of his ears. Bent as fuck.'

'Ah ... ' Suttle smiled. 'No wonder she sleeps by herself.'

'Who says?'

'Me. I had a look round when I went up there for a leak. The master bedroom's at the back. Like she said, she sleeps at the front. She's a slut, too.' Suttle grinned. 'The room was a tip.'

Winter stepped out for half an hour at lunchtime, glad of the sunshine on his face. There was a tiny park up the road from Kingston Crescent, a couple of benches and half an acre of grass, and he loosened his tie and sat down with his sandwich, wondering whether to wash it down with a pint at the nearby pub. Mention of Chris Cleaver in his conversation with Dawn Ellis had suddenly put all the other phone calls in perspective. *Coppice*, he thought, was beginning to look promising.

Ellis, to be fair, had been extremely cautious. The wife, she'd explained, was a bag of nerves. She'd hated them being there. Couldn't wait for them to leave. But the business in the tunnel had obviously got to her in some way and an outburst about her former life in

Southsea seemed to indicate she might have a great deal more to say.

At this, Winter had chuckled. Helen Cleaver, much as she resented it, was a Pompey girl. Six years at the High School, plus a couple of winters as an upmarket rep in a French ski resort, had raised her social game but in the end she'd married a local, admittedly a Grammar School boy, who even then was devoting his considerable talents to the property game.

Chris Cleaver, to Winter's certain knowledge, had cheerfully broken law after law en route to his first million. Hookey mortgages. Ruthless pressure on sitting tenants. Massive bungs to any individual, local authority or otherwise, who could conceivably influence the outcome of difficult planning decisions. By the time he and Helen celebrated his thirtieth birthday, young Chris was a major player amongst the several dozen Pompey businessmen who could afford to jet their friends en masse to Grenada without bothering to count the change.

Over the next decade the Cleavers continued to prosper. The purchase of an eight-bedroom spread in Craneswater Park brought them a swimming pool and a view of the Isle of Wight, as well as a whole new set of neighbours. Amongst the latter, equally new to Craneswater, was Bazza Mackenzie, by now controlling every last gram of the Pompey cocaine trade. Winter had never laid hands on the kind of proof that could stand up in court, but what he knew of Chris Cleaver made some kind of association with Mackenzie incontestable. Profit was Cleaver's middle name. The markups in cocaine were astronomical. A thousand quid spent in Venezuela would turn into ten grand on the streets of Portsmouth. No one with the nerve to call himself a businessman could resist that kind of arithmetic.

Winter chewed the last of the sandwich, still tempted by the prospect of a pint. At the end of his chat with

Dawn Ellis she'd sounded nervous about sparking more interest in the Cleavers than ten minutes of conversation could possibly warrant, but Winter knew that was bullshit. A working lifetime as a detective had taught him many lessons and one of them was that there was no such thing as coincidence. If someone as bent as Cleaver found himself within a mile or so of a body in a tunnel then somehow, somewhere, there'd be a connection. Cocaine? Winter didn't know. Some link to the ever-spreading tentacles of Bazza Mackenzie's empire? Pass. But these were early days. Pretty soon, one way or another, they'd have a name for the body. At that point *Coppice* would change gear. With a firm ID and a stir or two at the Pompey tea leaves, Winter could see immense possibilities in the weeks ahead.

He brushed the crumbs from his suit and got up, taking a short cut across the grass towards the pub, thinking again of last night's conversation with Jake about Alan Givens. Outside the pub were a couple of tables. He treated himself to a pint of chilled Stella and returned to the sunshine. People these days seemed not to drink at lunchtime, so he had the patio pretty much to himself. Before leaving the office he'd taken the precaution of jotting down the number of the Pompey FC ticket office. After a morning on the phone to every DIY outlet in the city, it would be a pleasure to get back to serious detective work.

Jerry Proctor phoned Faraday at two. Proctor seldom gave way to anything as unprofessional as excitement but on this occasion he let the mask slip.

'Recent tyre marks,' he said, 'down towards the railway. There's a kind of hollow where the rain gathers. It's a bit of a mess, lots of churn, but we've got the tracks at both ends, plus good sets of footprints.'

'All the same?'

'No. I'm guessing but I'd say a size nine, and maybe a seven.'

Faraday nodded, making a note of the time and scribbling down the details. It had rained on Saturday evening, a sudden downpour. He remembered the rainbow afterwards, an almost perfect arch over Langstone Harbour.

'Boss?' It was Proctor again. He was reminding Faraday that they'd recovered both trainers from the tunnel. 'They were Reeboks. The lads are taking a cast of the footprints here now.'

'Excellent. What else?'

'Too soon to say. The Tracker's doing her stuff on the fence. She's not one for jumping to conclusions but the last time I looked she was smiling.'

'But nothing obvious?'

'Aside from the bloke's credit card and address book? No, boss.'

It took a second for Faraday to realise that Proctor had made a joke. He couldn't remember the last time that had happened.

'Great,' he said. 'Stick them in the post.'

After telling Proctor to make sure he was back in time for the evening meet, he put the phone down. Faraday knew that the first forty-eight hours of any major enquiry were absolutely key. In this case *Coppice* was still handicapped by the lack of a positive ID on the body in the tunnel but Proctor and his boys were playing a blinder and it looked odds on that they were close to confirming an access point to the track. What mattered now was blanketing the local area with house-to-house teams. People's memories were short. One tiny detail could make all the difference. He sat back, pondering a call to the DS in charge of the Outside Enquiry Teams. Then came a knock at his door.

It was Winter. He was looking pleased with himself.

'May I?'

Faraday waved him into the spare chair. He could smell the alcohol on his breath. Winter beamed at him for a moment, then slipped the middle button on his suit.

'Anyone tell you about Chris Cleaver?' Winter enquired.

'No.'

'Ah . . . ' Winter's smile widened. ' . . . Then let me have the pleasure.'

DC Jimmy Suttle was back at Kingston Crescent by late afternoon. After checking in with the Incident Room, he found Paul Winter standing on a chair in his office, putting the finishing touches to the timeline on his wall board. The line began in the middle of the board. At 02.50, a car had driven away from the forest beside the railway track. Two hours later, at 04.58, train driver David Johns had reported hitting a body in the Buriton Tunnel. To the left and right of these two evidenced facts yawned the big white spaces that Faraday's team were charged to fill. Who was the body in the tunnel? Where had he been in the hours and days beforehand? What could a man possibly have done to warrant a death like that? And, most important of all, who had been at the wheel of the departing car?

Suttle wanted to know whether the casts had come down from the plantation.

'Yeah.' Winter nodded. 'The big one's a perfect match. Spot on. The bloke in the tunnel was definitely in that car. Faraday's creaming himself.'

'What else?'

'Not a lot. I'm sure there's a pile of actions in the Incident Room. If you fancy a couple of hours overtime round the DIY stores, be my guest.' Winter's morning on the phone had generated dozens of follow-up calls to individual hardware stores across the city.

Suttle shook his head. He was about to check out a bloke in Eastney who drove a timber truck to the trackside forest three or four times a week. Maybe the person in the car had been out to recce the location

76

prior to Sunday night's visit. Maybe there'd been a sighting, a lead to the car's colour or make.

'Eastney?' Winter glanced at his watch.

'Yeah.'

'Give me a lift?'

'Where to?'

'Fratton Park.'

'Why?' Winter had never expressed the slightest interest in football.

'Doesn't matter. It's on your way. Just drop me off, eh?'

Suttle knew Winter far too well not to press the issue. As they left the car park and joined the thickening traffic, he wanted to know what the football club could possibly have to do with *Coppice*.

'Who said it was *Coppice*?'

'Ah . . . ' Suttle was edging his way forwards towards the lights. 'You're telling me it's something else?'

'I'm telling you it's none of your business.'

'Some other job? Loose end? Statement check?' He glanced across at Winter. 'We *are* talking work here, I assume? Only you're a bit old for next season.'

Winter ignored the dig. He'd found a loose Werther's in his jacket pocket. Stripping off the paper, he popped it in his mouth.

'Traffic in this city is barmy.' He gazed out of the window. 'This rate, we'll all be buying fucking bikes.'

Suttle dropped Winter at the end of the cul-de-sac that led down to the football stadium and watched him stroll down towards the main entrance. He knew when Winter was happy. It showed in his body language, in the way he walked, in the way he dug his hands into his trouser pockets, in the way he made a tiny detour to sidefoot an empty Pepsi can towards the gutter. With the passenger window still down, he could even hear Winter's tuneless whistle. 'Bohemian Rhapsody', Suttle thought. Definitely something up.

The office that dealt with season ticket enquiries was

on the first floor. Winter went in without knocking, pinged the bell a couple of times for attention. He heard a muffled phone conversation coming to an end, then a blurred glimpse of someone standing up through the ribbed glass behind the counter.

She was young and extremely pretty, Pompey accent, big smile.

'Can I help you?'

Winter extended his warrant card. He'd already talked to someone on the phone about a bunch of season tickets that had been sold last month. There were twelve of them, different dates but all on the same debit card. Winter had details of the name on the card, the dates of the transactions and the number of the bank account. A Mr Givens. With an HSBC card.

'Ring any bells?'

The girl disappeared. Seconds later, Winter found himself talking to an older woman. She had a folded piece of paper in her hand, some kind of computer printout, but she looked worried.

'We don't usually give out these kinds of details,' she said. 'We have our customers to think about.'

'Of course.' Winter gave her a smile. 'I can go to court for a Production Order if you'd prefer.'

The woman's frown deepened. She sucked her teeth for a moment or two, then shrugged.

'Here,' she said, flattening the printout on the counter. 'Have you got a pen?'

Lines of pink highlighter ran through several entries. Winter could read anything upside down.

'That's a Somerstown address,' he said. 'Were all the tickets sent there?'

'Yes.'

'In the name of Alan Givens?'

'Yes.' She paused. 'What's the problem? Do you mind me asking? Only it might be nice to know.'

Winter scribbled down the address, then pocketed his warrant card. At this point, he told her, enquiries were strictly at the preliminary stage. Should anything dodgy have happened, he'd doubtless be back again.

He turned for the door, then paused. 'I take it all those transactions went through OK?' he said.

'Oh yes.' The woman nodded. 'But apparently there were a couple of other calls from Mr Givens. He wanted more season tickets.'

'And?'

'The card was rejected.'

'Why?'

'Insufficient funds.'

Faraday spent the late afternoon in the Coroner's office in the city's Guildhall, confirming that the events surrounding the death in the Buriton Tunnel were currently under criminal investigation. The Coroner, Martin Eckersley, listened carefully to Faraday's account of progress to date before declaring the inquest into the mystery death opened and adjourned. Should police enquiries lead to charges and a conviction in court, then a formal inquest would no longer be necessary. If, on the other hand, Faraday drew a blank then the inquest would be resumed at a later date.

On his way out of the Coroner's office, Eckersley called him back. He wanted to know how Eadie Sykes was getting on. Momentarily nonplussed, Faraday had forgotten Eadie's success in enrolling him in a project of hers a couple of years earlier. Eckersley had smoothed the path to certain sequences in a video she was making, an exploration of the circumstances leading to the death of a young local junkie, and some of this footage had even been screened at the lad's inquest. This official nod of approval from the city's Coroner had helped immeasurably when the contents of the video – shocking, graphic, immensely powerful – provoked a storm of controversy, and Eadie had afterwards made a point of adding Eckersley to her invite list of trophy professionals. Eckersley had come to a couple of her parties, enjoying the slightly raffish company Eadie liked to keep. Now he wanted Faraday to pass on his best. He hadn't seen Eadie for a while. She was a live wire, made things happen. Where on earth was she hiding?

'Australia,' Faraday told him. 'Sydney.'

'Holiday?'

'Work. She's making videos there, films, too. She loves it.'

It dawned on Eckersley that they were no longer together. He shook his head, said he was sorry to hear it. The city was poorer, he murmured, without people like Eadie.

'You think so?'

'Definitely.'

Now, crawling home through the traffic, Faraday resisted the temptation to brood about Eadie again. Their relationship was well and truly over. Of that he was certain. Yet there were moments, like now, when he'd have welcomed the chance to drive down to the seafront, let himself into her top-floor apartment, and let the often-volatile chemistry between them take care of the rest of the evening. The challenge with investigations as unusual and potentially complex as *Coppice* was the fact that they could so easily become all-consuming. You needed time out. You needed perspective. You needed a dig in the ribs, a reminder that there might be more to life than the consequences of flange damage and the overtime implications of running a thirty-strong squad. Eadie, he knew, would have provided all three.

Stuck behind a coachful of kids barely half a mile from home, he forced his mind back to the day's developments. Winter's news about the woman who'd heard the car roar by early on Monday morning sat nicely alongside the Scenes of Crime haul from the plantation, and while Faraday was keeping an open mind about the Cleavers – resisting Winter's conviction that a bent property developer must be somehow linked to the body in the tunnel – he'd quickly arranged for a couple of DCs to start trawling through footage from cameras covering the northern approaches to the city. The tapes were kept in the CCTV control room deep in the bowels of the Civic Centre, and most detectives loathed the hours they'd be spending in front of the tiny monitor screens.

Faraday had ordered every incoming car to be checked for driver and address details and as soon as some kind of decent list was available he'd set about organising house calls. Anyone heading into the city between three and four on Monday morning needed to account for their journey. If they couldn't, he'd want to know why. He nodded to himself, pleased by the progress they were beginning to make, at last easing the Mondeo into the cul-de-sac that would take him down to the water.

The Bargemaster's House was at its best this time of year. Faraday parked the car and pushed through the gate at the side. He'd made a big effort with the garden during the winter and all those back-breaking weekends with the spade and hoe had paid rich dividends. He paused beside a row of tomato plants, wondering whether one day he'd run out of recipes, then he walked on round the front of the house, casting his eye over the paintwork, hoping to God that he wouldn't have to redecorate for at least a year or two.

The house itself, brick-built with a timber-clad upper floor, sat four-square on a modest parcel of land beside Langstone Harbour. Down here, on the south-easterly tip of the island, Portsmouth was no more than a rumour, a low burble of traffic spiked by the occasional siren. Summer sunsets, if Faraday cared to stand in the garden at the rear of the house, etched the city's distant battlements – tower blocks, mainly – against the crimson flare of the western skyline, but the truth was that the Bargemaster's House had turned its back on Pompey and for that Faraday was grateful.

He loved the peace and quiet of this little area, peopled mainly by retired folk and weekend dinghy sailors from the club along the towpath. This time of year, he could wake early on summer mornings to the mirrored calm of the harbour. Up in his study, overlooking the water, he'd installed a tripod and a decent scope, and there was always a pencil and notepad readied for another set of sightings.

Faraday had been logging the harbour's birdlife for longer than he cared to remember, ever since he and the infant J-J had embarked on this collective adventure, and thousands of entries later – with J-J in his mid-twenties – he was still peering into that intricate web of relationships that gave the harbour its eternal fascination. The fussiness of a lone turnstone on the foreshore. That busy sequence of bright spring mornings when rafts of brent geese gathered in their hundreds for the long passage back to Siberia. The sudden glimpse of a low-flying shag, just feet above the water, arrowing seawards. Sights like these, however familiar, never failed to send a little jolt of pleasure through Faraday, and only last month, journeying through the lush green uplands of Thailand, he knew he'd never be able to live out of reach of the water.

He let himself into the house, realised he hadn't eaten since breakfast, checked the state of the fridge. He had courgettes, onions, a big bag of tomatoes, and a couple of plump heads of garlic. Ratatouille, he thought, with rice, grilled sardines and a chilled bottle of Chablis he'd been saving.

He helped himself to a stick of celery and a square of cheese, then keyed the messages waiting for him on the phone. There were a couple of work-related calls. Then came a pause and a click before he recognised J-J's cackle. His son was up in London now, working as a picture editor for a big video production house. The job, he knew, had been largely Eadie's doing. After she'd taken him into Ambrym, her own production outfit, the pair of them had become very close. In fact virtually everything J-J had picked up about the industry he'd learned from Eadie and Faraday knew he owed her a huge debt. How many other hard-pressed video producers would have spared the time to school a deaf-mute in the black arts of documentary-making?

Faraday listened to the tape again. For obvious reasons, father and son normally communicated by e-mail but when J-J was especially pleased with life he'd plant a cackle or two on his dad's answerphone to signal the presence of a waiting e-mail upstairs. Faraday was often lazy about electronic mail and if J-J had something important to say then he'd take no chances on his dad neglecting to check for incoming messages.

Faraday poured himself a beer and went upstairs. The bed was still unmade and he tidied the duvet before walking through to his study and settling at the PC. Most of the messages were bird-related – a reminder about his RSPB subscription, an exultant missive from an e-correspondent confirming that kites were back nesting in at least two Hampshire locations – and he scrolled quickly through the rest of the list until he found the electronic stone under which J-J had hidden his latest news. 'You'll never believe this,' his son had written, 'but these guys are sending me to RUSSIA. We're doing a big thing on ENERGY SUP-PLIES and we're doing the rough-cut in MOSCOW. So that means I've got to check out all the gear and make sure it WORKS. Cool, eh?'

Faraday read the message a second time, warming to the headlong, madcap prose. J-J's use of capitals echoed the way he communicated face to face, a wild frenzy of gesture, plucking meaning and nuance out of thin air, emphatic, urgent, most of it comprehensible even if you didn't know the first thing about sign language. Quite what the Russians would make of his windmill of a son was anyone's guess but this was a country that had produced the likes of Tchaikovsky and Rachmaninov, and in his own way Faraday suspected that J-J was no less romantic, no less theatrical. 'You'll love it,' he tapped back. 'And a big hug from your proud old dad.'

He sent the e-mail and scrolled through the rest of the messages. Nothing much caught his eye until he got to the very bottom of the list. He peered at the name, not recognising it. The message was tagged with an attachment. The suffix on the address, *fr*, meant France.

Puzzled, Faraday opened the message. It was long, maybe a couple of hundred words. '*Cher Joe . . .*' it began, '*vous m'avez dit que vous comprenez assez bien français. Donc, je devrais peut-être vous écrire dans ma langue maternelle. Ça ne vous embête pas?*' Faraday struggled on for a sentence or two, suddenly realising whose voice this was. Then he opened the first of the accompanying attachments and found a photograph of himself with a woman in her early thirties. They were standing on a thickly wooded hillside in northern Thailand. Faraday, in shorts and walking boots, was stripped to the waist. The woman was wearing a pair of baggy dark trousers and a plain white T-shirt. Her face was partly shadowed by the brim of a battered straw hat but her head was thrown back in helpless laughter and the photo had caught the whiteness of her teeth.

Faraday gazed at the image, instantly back on the jungle path amongst the bougainvillea and the wild orchids. He could feel the bubbles of heat rising from the red earth and the tickle of sweat on his bare chest. He could hear the deafening rise and fall of the cicadas in the thick green canopy overhead, and the faraway rumble of thunder as yet another storm tracked up the valley towards them.

On the eve of the wet season, with Eadie Sykes gone and Faraday travelling on his own, he'd met this woman on a country bus ten miles short of the Burmese border. Her name was Gabrielle and she was enjoying a brief holiday before returning to her native France. For the past year she'd been working with the hill tribes in the highlands that straddled the border between Laos and Vietnam. She was a qualified anthropologist with a PhD to her name, and European funding had made this expedition of hers possible. At some later date she'd be publishing a book. In the meantime, with the shrinking remnants of her research grant still in her pocket, she was making the most of Thailand.

They'd travelled together for a couple of days, shared meals, got to know a little of each other. Still bruised after the encounter with Eadie, Faraday wasn't really in the mood for company, but when Gabrielle had mentioned a riverside hotel back in the Kwai Valley, he'd made a mental note of the name and location. She'd be meeting a girlfriend there in ten days' time. This time of year, the huts overlooking the water were cheap. So maybe, *alors*, they might meet again.

Heading south after a week in Burma, Faraday noticed a roadside sign for the hotel and decided there'd be no harm in staying over for a couple of nights. Gabrielle was already in residence, sharing a room with her French girlfriend, a lecturer from one of the Bangkok universities. During the day the two women would hire mountain bikes and disappear into the maze of trails in the surrounding jungle. In the evening Faraday joined them in the hotel dining room, an airy terrace with a fine view of the river.

The Kwai Valley, with its memories of the death railway, fascinated him. He'd visited a nearby museum, walked several kilometres of surviving railbed, picked up a book or two, learned what disease, starvation and forced labour had done to tens of thousands of Allied prisoners of war. The last evening they were all together, out on the terrace, he'd talked about it, trying to explain what the surrender of Singapore had meant to a whole generation of Englishmen. Gabrielle's friend from Bangkok was regularly in Singapore and found it difficult to reconcile the gleaming tower blocks and booming economy with Faraday's account of the burning godowns and the desperate mobs of stranded white families. But Gabrielle, at the meal's end, had reached across the table and lightly touched his hand. 'My father,' she murmured in her broken English, 'was at Dien Bien Phu.'

Faraday, who knew very little about French military fortunes in the Orient, could only nod. Days later, passing through Bangkok en route to the airport, he'd made a point of finding a book on the subject. Dien Bien Phu, it turned out, was France's Singapore, a military defeat so catastrophic and so humiliating that it signalled the end of the French presence in South East Asia.

On the plane home, thinking about it, Faraday had meant to get in touch with Gabrielle. They'd exchanged e-mail addresses and he wanted to know more about her father's war. How come he'd survived the cauldron of Dien Bien Phu? And what had become of him afterwards, in the prison camp? But somehow, despite the best of intentions, the press of events on Major Crimes had swamped him almost at once, and his memories of that brief interlude, high above the Kwai River, had faded.

Now, he did his best with the rest of the e-mail. As far as he could judge, Gabrielle was back in her native Chartres. She'd picked up her dog and her ancient VW camper from her mother and was working on the book in her own apartment. Being back in the West, *bien sûr*, was a bit strange. She'd couldn't get over how busy everyone was, and how little time they had for each other, but she supposed it had always been this way and she'd simply forgotten. In closing, she wondered whether one day they might meet again. Joe was welcome in Chartres any time. There was an address and phone number, and she signed off with the hope that he'd enjoy the photos she'd sent him.

Faraday opened the other attachment. Gabrielle, it turned out, had been busy with the digital camera she always carried. None of the shots would win awards for focus or composition but Faraday knew only too well how hard it was to take decent photos of birdlife. He scanned them quickly, recognising a red-throated flycatcher, a river chat and a grey-faced buzzard. Then, touched by this totally unexpected gesture, he pictured again his days in her company.

What had struck him at the time, he remembered, was her sense of self-possession. Here was someone who knew exactly who they were. Travelling in the remoter parts of Thailand was seldom free of incident, yet whatever happened, however frequent the bus punctures or unscheduled detours, she never lost her fascination for the bustle of faces around her.

A greater contrast to Eadie Sykes – impatient, demanding, headstrong – Faraday couldn't imagine, and as he returned to the photo he'd first opened he tried to pin down exactly why Gabrielle's company had been so easy. It wasn't that he'd fancied her. It wasn't even that he'd ever thought of seeing her again. It was simply, he decided, the recognition of a fellow traveller, of someone for whom life offered a series of imperfectly locked boxes. She had a curiosity he understood, and a scientist's thirst for trying to make sense of the world. Every passing day seemed to bring her something new, and with her urchin haircut and wire-rimmed glasses she must have sensed the same in him. Hence, now, this e-mail.

Faraday got up from the PC, meaning to return to the kitchen and charge his glass, but beside the wall of books in his study he paused. The Michelin atlas of

Europe was on the bottom shelf. He turned the pages until he was looking at northern France. Chartres was half a day's drive from the Normandy coast. He studied the route for a moment, then tucked the atlas away again and headed downstairs.

Five

An Aqua cab dropped Winter in the heart of Somerstown. After a couple of sunny days, the weather was crap again, low cloud and a drop or two of rain, and the forecast on the radio was promising heavier stuff for the afternoon. Winter zipped up his anorak, standing amongst the swirl of chip wrappers and discarded burger boxes beside the battered parade of shops. Only in Somerstown, he thought, would the betting shop have a handwritten notice taped to the window. *Cash removed every night* went the note. *Save yourself the hassle.*

The address he was after was round the corner. He followed the line of cracked paving stones, stepping to one side to avoid colliding with a couple of teenage mums with buggies. Both had mobile phones pressed to their ears and for one lunatic moment Winter wondered if they were talking to each other. These days, he thought, you'd rule nothing out.

Hermiston House was an unlovely tower block with a bit of a reputation in the divisional CID office. Social Services had a habit of dumping single parents on the lower floors and some of the kids from families further up the building had long ago bailed out of full-time education. Despite periodic uniformed sweeps to satisfy the storm troopers from the Home Office Inspectorate, truancy was rife on the estate and Winter could cite case after case where kids had discovered that life outside the classroom could be immensely profitable, as well as fun. Shopkeepers round here, Asians especially, had been robbed blind. Drug dealing was frequently in the hands of fourteen-year-olds. Turn up pissed after dark, stray into the wrong areas, and you'd be lucky not to become a crime statistic.

Winter pushed in through the big double doors. The address was on the third floor. Number 34 was at the far end of the corridor. He knocked on the door. He could hear music inside, a girl band, loud. He knocked again, then a third time. Finally, someone turned the music down and the door opened. She looked tiny, barely a teenager. She was wearing a pink top and a pair of briefs and not very much else. There was a huge purple love bite on the side of her neck and and more than a hint of bruising under one eye.

Winter showed her his warrant card. He said he wanted to talk to a Mr Givens.

'Never heard of him.' Pompey accent. Wary expression.

'You live here?'

'Yeah. What's this about then? Only I'm busy. Me and Cher –' She jerked her head sideways. '– We gotta go down the doctor's. She's snotty again. My mum says she needs looking at.'

Winter made to step into the flat. The girl didn't move.

'You can't come in here.' She sounded indignant.

'Why not?'

'You could be anyone.'

'I've just showed you my warrant card.'

'Means nothing. Not round here it doesn't. We had someone said he was from the gas people the other day – fancy ID, all that shit. Friend of mine was stupid enough to let him in. Turned out to be a perve. Had to call the Old Bill.'

'I am the Old Bill.'

'Yeah?' She looked at him a moment longer, troubled, and Winter knew she was softening.

'Listen,' he said. 'This is going to take a couple of

minutes. Better we do it now than I come back mob-handed, eh?'

'Do what?'

'Let me in and I'll tell you.'

She frowned, trying to make up her mind. Then a baby started crying somewhere deep in the flat and Winter took advantage of the distraction, stepping round her and shutting the door behind him. The heat inside was overpowering. She must have the radiators turned up full, Winter thought. The baby was howling now, and he followed the girl down the tiny hall. Three steps took him into a bedroom. The baby was lying on a double mattress on the floor, naked, kicking its legs. There was a deckchair propped against the wall, nicked from the beach, and a collection of empty Kronenbourg bottles on a broken-backed chair beside a transistor radio. In the corner of the room was a brand new wide-screen television set, three grand at least, tuned to one of the morning chat shows. The sound had been muted in favour of the radio, and Winter wondered what the baby made of Fern Britton watching a black chef toss pancakes.

Winter bent to retrieve a pair of jeans. They obviously went with the scuffed Reeboks in the corner. He inspected the label on the jeans. Thirty-four leg.

'Who else lives here?'

'No one. Just me. And her.' The girl was doing her best to calm the baby.

'Whose are these then?'

The girl glanced round. Winter was still holding the jeans.

'My boyfriend.' She shrugged. 'He stays sometimes.'

'Yeah? What's his name?'

'It ain't Givens. I tell you that.' She picked up the baby and stepped past Winter at the door. Winter had found nothing in the jeans except a handful of change and a top-up card for an Orange mobile. He slipped the card into his pocket.

The girl was in the kitchen, trying to tempt the baby with a bottle she must have been warming up. The baby was watching Winter. Big blue eyes. Just like her mum.

'What's your name, love?'

'Ain't telling you.'

'Don't fuck around. I can go to Merefield House. You know I can.'

At the mention of Social Services, she turned her back on Winter, rocking the baby in her arms.

'Emma,' she said at last.

'Emma what?'

'Emma Cusden. Don't go grassing me up to that lot, will you? They've been well nice to me lately.'

'Why would I grass you up?'

'Dunno.' She glanced back at him and risked a smile. 'You ain't here for coffee, are you?'

Once the baby was settled, Winter took them both through to the living room. The room was bare, the fug even worse. A couple of chairs, scabbed with grease and crusty bits of food, were pushed back against the wall, and there was a beanbag as well, equally knackered. Someone must have been to the tip, Winter thought, and helped themselves.

'I'm interested in post for this Mr Givens,' he said. 'You'd have got some stuff through last month.'

'Not here.' She shook her head at once. 'Not me.'

'Someone else, then. Your boyfriend maybe.'

'Doubt it.'

'You're telling me you never saw any envelopes addressed to a Mr Givens?'

'Never.'

'You're sure about that?'

'Course I am.'

Winter nodded. He knew she was lying but that wasn't the point. In these situations you always took a hostage. Helped no end. He stepped across to her, tickled the baby under the chin.

'This boyfriend of yours. What does he get up to then?'

'Get up to? Like what do you mean?'

'Does he work? Has he got a job?'

'Yeah.' She sounded relieved. 'He's well busy.'

'Where?'

'All over.'

'Doing what?'

'Dunno. He never says.'

'How can I get hold of him?'

'You can't. He ain't got a mobile or nothing.'

'But he'll be back?'

'Yeah, I expect so, sooner or later.'

'Good.' Winter was looking at the baby again. 'Family man, is he? Helpful round the house? Takes his turn with the nappies?'

'What do you mean?'

'Little Cher here . . . I expect he misses her, being away all the time like that. Was she awake, incidentally? When he thumped you? Only there's all kinds of research these days – you know, the effect on toddlers when it all kicks off. Emotional abuse they call it. You ought to talk to someone. Merefield might be the place to start. They've got people there that think of nothing else.' He smiled down at her, a favourite uncle, someone with her very best interests at heart.

The girl was about to say something, then bit her lip. She was beginning to look seriously alarmed. Winter definitely worried her.

'I don't know what you're talking about,' she said at last.

'Yes, you do, love. You've heard of the At-Risk Register? All those kids taken into care?'

'Of course I have.'

'And you know how social workers hate to take chances anymore? Vulnerable little nippers like Cher? Their names all over the papers? All that publicity if they get it wrong?'

Winter strolled across to the window, gazed out, waiting. Everyone in life has something they can't bear to lose, he thought.

'Look . . . ' The girl was at his elbow. 'Them at the Social . . . Karl . . . you wouldn't, would you?'

'Wouldn't what, love?'

'Tell them. Only they might get funny again.'

'About Karl?'

'Yeah . . . I mean no— Oh shit.' She blinked, her eyes suddenly shiny with tears. 'I should never have let you in, should I?'

The call came through to Faraday himself. Alone in his office, he lifted the phone, stiffened a moment, then reached for a pen.

'You mind spelling that?'

He wrote down a name and a date of birth. Then he checked his watch. Nearly half past two.

'That's *less* than forty-eight hours. This must be a world record.'

The caller said something that made him laugh. Expressing his thanks, Faraday hung up.

The Intelligence Cell was housed in an office just down the corridor. Winter, yet to receive reinforcements, was still on his own, staring at his PC.

'Result.' Faraday closed the door. 'I've just had a woman from the FSS on. They've got a name for us.'

The Forensic Science Service had been processing DNA samples from the body in the tunnel. Evidently the readout had scored a hit on the database.

'He's got form?' Winter wanted a look at Faraday's piece of paper.

'Must have. I don't know the score yet but here's the name.'

Winter was having trouble deciphering Faraday's scrawl.

'Duley,' Faraday said. 'Mark Duley. DOB 17/11/1976. That makes him twenty-nine. Ping it across to

PNC. Let me know what they come up with. I'll be back by five.'

Faraday stepped out of the office. Winter found the PNC icon on-screen and clicked it open. Pass codes to the Police National Computer were strictly rationed but his current job gave him unlimited access.

He typed in the code. Moments later, he was into the site, transcribing Duley's name and date of birth. Up came the details. Winter scrolled down through a list of convictions. Over the past ten years, Duley had collected fines, plus a suspended prison sentence, for a number of offences, mainly riot, affray and criminal damage. Winter sped through the list, recognising a pattern in the arrest locations. Trafalgar Square. Edinburgh. Sellafield. Aldermaston. Newhaven Docks. In certain political circles this lot would read like a war record. Young Duley, it seemed, was a serial activist, never far from the action when a big demo turned violent and the ninja squads waded in.

He sat back a moment, gazing at the screen. Winter had never been the slightest bit interested in politics, especially the wilder extremes, happy to leave Special Branch to keep tabs on the hairies and assorted no-hopers that took their protests onto the streets. But even he knew enough about the lunatic fringe to have trouble coaxing a pattern from Duley's half-dozen court appearances. Here was a guy who plainly had strong feelings about more or less everything: globalisation, the Iraq War, animal rights, nuclear waste, asylum seekers, anti-personnel mines and the Trident missile programme. Was there any cause this man hadn't supported?

There was a custody photograph together with a physical description attached to the file. Duley was 5' 11", male, white, weighed sixty-four kilos, had brown eyes, blond hair cropped short, and – at the time of his last arrest – no identifying birthmarks or tattoos. The face in the photo seemed to have treated the arrest process as a kind of audition. The head was tilted back slightly, the eyes half closed, the stubbled chin thrust out. It was a shot, thought Winter, that any actor would have been proud of, and something told him that Duley might even have asked the Custody Sergeant for copies. This guy had no fear of the law. On the contrary, he probably papered his bedroom with copies of his various indictments.

Winter took a hard copy of the file and then closed it down. Duley's last known address was in south London. He made a note, then returned to the keyboard and clicked on the RMS icon. Hantspol's Records Management System was a treasure house of local criminality, and there was a chance that Duley might have attracted the attention of Pompey officers. Winter himself had never heard the name before but he'd been off the pitch for a while, and a year was a long time in this game.

To his delight, Duley appeared again. Last December he'd earned himself a caution for adding clusters of toy hand grenades to the Lord Mayor's official Christmas tree in the Guildhall Square – a protest, it seemed, against plans for an arms fair on Whale Island. Then, just two weeks ago, he'd been picked up by a marked area car after a passing motorist had reported a body lying on the pavement in Cosham, barely half a mile from the QA Hospital.

Winter read the details of the incident. The call from the motorist had come in at 02.45. The attending Traffic crew had summoned an ambulance and accompanied Duley to the nearby A & E department. After treatment they'd tried to interview him about what – in the opinion of the duty registrar – were plainly injuries inflicted during the course of a savage beating. Duley, in the dry prose of the attending officer, had declined to cooperate. Pressed for an address he'd been equally reticent, but an electricity bill retrieved by an A & E nurse from his torn jeans gave Flat 8, 74 Salisbury Road, Southsea.

Making another note, Winter checked for further traces of Duley but drew a blank. The incident that had led to A & E was an obvious lead, and already Winter was plotting ways of squeezing it harder. There were CCTV cameras in Cosham but a check on the map showed no coverage of the spot where Duley had been dumped. That in itself, though, was significant. These guys knew what they were doing, Winter thought. Definitely in Cleaver's league.

He glanced at his watch. Nearly three. Down the corridor, in the Major Incident Room, the news that the body in the tunnel now had a name had yet to break. Winter put the PNC printout on the desk of the DS running the Outside Enquiry Team.

'That's our bloke.' He tapped the photo. 'Before he lost his sense of humour.'

Very little impressed the DS. He spared the photo no more than a cursory glance.

'You've got an address?'

'Yeah.' Winter wrote it down for him.

'Does Faraday know about this?'

'The name, yes. His drum, no.'

'We're talking potential crime scene.' He was already reaching for the phone. 'I'll give him a bell.'

Faraday was in conference when the call from the Incident Room came through. He listened to the DS on the other end, warmed by the news that Winter had dug up a local address so quickly. Maybe things will really start to move, he thought. Maybe we're on the edge of some kind of breakthrough.

He told the DS to contact Jerry Proctor. He wanted a couple of DCs round to Salisbury Road to confirm the facts. If Flat 8 had really been Duley's address, then Proctor should put a full team in, comb every inch of the place. He ended the call, and turned back to the DI

97

across the table. The man headed the Financial Investigation Unit over at Netley. They'd been discussing the presentation of specialist evidence in an earlier case only days away from going to court. This case happened to revolve around laundered drug money.

Willard, Faraday said, was making all kinds of noises about the Proceeds of Crime Act. Faraday, like every other thicko detective, was still in the dark about the real scope of the legislation. Would it really make the kind of difference that Willard seemed to believe?

The DI nodded. 'It's the biggie,' he said. 'If we all get on top of this, the bad guys are going to hurt. Follow the money and you can't go wrong. We can strip them of everything. Just think about it.'

'So what does it need?'

'Someone to push it. Full time.'

'And that someone?'

'Should know some of these characters inside out.' He smiled. 'Willard's right. He mentioned Winter to me, too.'

For the second time that day Winter was out of the office. He'd phoned his contact at Merefield House but she was unhappy about discussing client cases from the big open office where she worked. If he cared to drive over, they could meet in a café across the road. She'd bring the file. It'd be a pleasure to see him again.

Carol Legge had become a legend in the Child Protection Team. She was a small, talkative Geordie barely weeks off celebrating her fiftieth birthday. There were mothers and fathers across the city who'd badly underestimated her ability to scent trouble, and if you had any family secrets you thought you could keep – domestic violence, child abuse – it was a mistake you only made once. Winter had seen Carol Legge in action and knew she how formidable she could be.

She was waiting in the café when he stepped in through the door. Winter's coffee was cooling beneath an upturned saucer. This time in the afternoon, only one other table was occupied.

Carol watched him sit down.

'Someone told me you were dead.'

'They were lying.'

'Good.' She patted his hand. 'You want a sticky, pet?'

She fetched him a doughnut from the counter. Winter was eyeing the file she'd left on the table. *Emma Cusden*, in heavy black Pentel.

'You mind if I help myself?' He was reaching for the file.

'Yes, I bloody do. Tell me what you're after. Then I'll decide.'

Winter explained the season ticket scam. Someone had been using young Emma's place as a delivery address. Six grand's worth of tickets had gone through her letterbox and she claimed to have seen nothing.

'Of course she didn't see anything. The girl's not stupid.'

'So who picked them up?'

'Could have been anyone. She's a popular lass.'

'She puts herself around?'

'Not the way you're thinking. No, she's got friends, that's all, and lots of them. Keeps open house, as far as I can see. No bad thing as far as the kiddie's concerned.'

'What about the boyfriend?'

'He's a headcase.' She patted the file. 'First time the girl came to our attention it was a call from a neighbour – anonymous, wouldn't give a name, scared to death young Karl would come looking.'

'Karl?'

'Karl Ewart. Emma says he's the father but you never really know. Either way, she dotes on him, poor lamb.'

'What's he like?'

'Horrible, says me. Violent, foul-mouthed, absolutely no self-control. He'd been battering poor Emma for days before the neighbour gave us a call. Said he couldn't stand the girl screaming anymore.'

'He lives there full time?'

'No way. If you're looking for someone who puts it around, you might start with him.' She took a sip of coffee and pulled a face. 'I take it he's back then?'

'Yeah.'

'How's the bairn?'

'Looked OK to me.'

'And young Emma?'

'Scared shitless I'd be talking to you lot.'

'Good. Then maybe she'll kick the bastard out. You need an address, don't you? Here . . . ' She pushed the file towards Winter. 'Help yourself.'

By the time Faraday emerged from his conference, detectives had confirmed Duley's link to the Salisbury Road flat. Number 8 was a bedsit on the third floor. The landlord lived with his wife in the basement, an elderly couple who'd once run a pub in the city centre. Duley had been renting the room for just over a year, money on the nail every month, never a hint of trouble. The last time they'd seen him was the end of last week. The wife said he must have been coming back from the beach because he had a towel with him and one of those roll-up mats. All the sunshine must have done him good because he was starting to look human again after the road accident. Said he'd been in a friend's car when it went off the road and rolled over. Nasty.

Upstairs, on the third floor, there were two other bedsits and a communal bathroom. One of the bedsits was rented to an Iranian student who no one ever saw, the other belonged to a middle-aged woman who worked night shifts in a local nursing home. Neither had answered to the detectives' knocks and they were now in the process of going through the rest of the house.

Proctor, meanwhile, had acquired the key to Duley's

room from the landlord. Winter had just briefed him on the dead man's background and he'd taken a preliminary look at the state of the bedsit. At first glance, he reported, the place was a doss: books and magazines and bits and pieces of computer gear everywhere, desk in the corner, piles of unwashed laundry, posters and photos all over the walls, total mess. If this was the best the far left could do, he told Faraday on the phone, then he was definitely going to stick with the Tories.

Back at Kingston Crescent, Faraday was looking for Winter. One of the management assistants thought they'd seen him going down the back stairs towards the car park. Someone else said he'd probably popped out for one of the Eccles cakes he liked to have with his afternoon cuppa. Faraday finally left a note on his desk. *Ring me*, it said.

Winter obliged nearly an hour later. Faraday wanted to know where he'd been.

'Salisbury Road. Thought I'd take a little look-see.'

'You're running the Intelligence Cell,' Faraday pointed out. 'I've got a dozen DCs to take care of Salisbury Road. You know the way all this works. We've all got our own boxes. Yours happens to have a door on it.'

'Sure, boss. Of course. My mistake.'

Winter wanted to bring this conversation to an end. Faraday wasn't having it. He bent to the phone.

'How did you get to Salisbury Road, as a matter of interest?'

'Cab.'

'Could get pricey, then? All this checking-up?'

'Is that what it was?' Winter sounded amused.

Faraday fought to keep his temper. He told himself that Winter was a real asset on the squad: effective, acute, extremely well connected. Detectives like that were increasingly rare.

'Listen, Paul,' he said heavily. 'I'm just saying we're a team. Teams help each other out. I need you behind your desk. I need to know where you are. Does that sound reasonable?'

'Sure.'

'Then bloody well stay put. You hear me?' He waited for a moment for some kind of reaction but Winter had hung up.

The regular squad meet that night was even better attended than the previous evening. Word had gone round about some kind of breakthrough and Willard – encouraged by the news from Kingston Crescent – had told Martin Barrie to throw more bodies at *Coppice*. In consequence, it was standing room only in the Incident Room as Faraday outlined progress to date.

The Detective Superintendent himself was there, folded invisibly into a corner by the door. He'd called Faraday into his office only minutes earlier, wanting an assurance that his DI was coping OK with the rising administrative pressure, and Faraday had assured Barrie that he'd be the first to know if the going got rough. Barrie had nodded, said he was pleased to hear it, but both men knew that this was a critical moment in *Coppice*'s brief history. Faraday, as Senior Investigating Officer, had to carry the enquiry forward. Ignore what might become a major lead, pile all your assets on the wrong square, and the consequences – way down the line – wouldn't bear contemplation.

Now, Faraday was reviewing the list of vehicles captured by the city's network of CCTV cameras. Analysis of tapes from the cameras covering Portsmouth's northern approaches between three and four on Monday morning had given the Outside Enquiry Team over a hundred addresses to visit. There was no guarantee, of course, that the car reported by Mrs Cleaver had gone anywhere near Portsmouth afterwards. But in situations like these you had to start somewhere, and every detective in the room was praying for a hit on the existing list. If not, then Faraday would doubtless extend the search parameters, widening the investigative net to other destinations along the coast.

After the CCTV actions, Faraday returned to the body in the tunnel. In the shape of young Mark Duley, they at last had a name for the victim. The man was busy on the political fringe. His views had nearly landed him in prison. Two weeks ago, on Sunday 26 June, someone had given him a beating. Whether or not that incident was linked to his death in the tunnel wasn't at all clear, but Jerry Proctor's team was combing through his Southsea bedsit and while there was so far nothing of forensic interest, Proctor was already talking about a rich harvest of personal stuff. Over the coming days it would be the job of the Intelligence Cell to build a picture of Mark Duley. Only that way – by getting to know the man – would *Coppice* be able to piece together the web of motivation and circumstance that had taken him into the Buriton Tunnel.

Faraday paused, glancing across at Winter to see whether the DC had anything to add, but Winter shook his head.

Minutes later, the meeting over, Faraday caught Winter before he returned to his office. Their exchange on the phone still rankled but he knew how important it was to keep the DC behind his desk. The key to *Coppice* was focus, especially now they had a name. He wanted no ambiguities here, nothing to shadow what had to become a close working relationship.

'We ought to have a drink one night,' Faraday suggested. 'What do you think?'

'Sure . . . ' Winter shrugged. 'Whatever.'

Back home in Gunwharf, a couple of hours later, Winter knew he had a decision to make. He circled the flat, tossing up between a can of Stella or a glass or two of Bell's. Finally, he settled for the Scotch, poured himself three fingers, then stepped out on the balcony. It was much colder than he'd expected, the wind gusting up from the harbour, and he went back for a pullover before returning to the chill night air.

A stone's throw from the gleaming café-bars and themed restaurants of Gunwharf lay Portsea, a nursery for the city's harder cases, and a mile beyond that you were back in the badlands of Somerstown. Winter had no time for socialism but you just had to look at the maze of terraced streets, at the crap post-war tower blocks, at the boarded-up chippies and rusting Transits, to realise just where the money ran out. Some of these people, he thought, have given up. For them, a lavish blowout in Gunwharf would never be more than a dream, a fantasy from the pages of one of Emma Cusden's *Heat* magazines. Others, on the other hand, saw absolutely no reason why they shouldn't help themselves. They could smell the money. They knew what it could buy. And one of them was doubtless Karl Ewart.

According to the Child Protection file, the boy had a basement flat in Southsea. Carol Legge had been there to talk to him about Emma and the baby. Ewart's place was a tip, she'd said, shared with some other lads. None of them seemed to have regular jobs and the afternoon she'd knocked on their door two of them were still in bed. Dormice, she'd called them, tucking the file back in her bag.

Winter sipped at the whisky. If he was serious about Alan Givens, if he thought the man really had come to grief, then there were certain investigative steps he had to take. So far, he'd freelanced the enquiry, stealing what time he could, clambering into the orchard that was Somerstown and giving Emma Cusden's tree a proper shake. To his delight, the apples had come tumbling down, but scrumping had its limitations and from this point on he had to be realistic. Pursuing the Givens enquiry was about to become complex and the truth was that he couldn't do it on his own.

He thought about it a moment longer, leaning on the rail, knowing in his heart that he had to have an ally. Finally, he drained the Scotch and went back inside. He found the number in his address book. It took an age to answer.

Winter sank onto the sofa, suddenly wondering if this was such a great idea.

'It's me, boss,' he said. 'Paul Winter. That drink you mentioned . . . OK if I come round now?'

Winter had been to the Bargemaster's House only once before, years back. His wife, Joannie, was in hospital, dying of cancer. He'd visited her on the ward most evenings and did his best to cope with the silence of the bungalow back home but this particular night Winter had lost his bearings completely. He had very few personal friends. Scotch could only blunt the pain. And so, very late, he'd driven down from Bedhampton and knocked at Faraday's door.

Like a handful of other detectives with his length of service, he knew that Faraday had been faced with exactly this situation years earlier. His own wife, whose name Winter could never remember, had died of breast cancer when their nipper was only a baby. On division, with Faraday behind the DI's desk, the two men had an arm's-length relationship. But away from the Job, Winter told himself that Faraday would understand.

And so it had proved. At the time Faraday had been besotted with a woman called Ruth. Seeing Winter at the door, the state of him, she'd made her excuses and left. Winter, already pissed, had tried to camouflage the real reason for his visit behind small talk about stuff at work but Faraday hadn't been fooled. After the second glass of Bell's he'd told his boss about Joannie, about the bastard consultant who'd drawn a line through her life, about the sheer depth of his rage and bewilderment. Faraday had listened, sympathised, fetched another bottle. And hours later, when he phoned for a cab, Winter had felt a whole lot better.

Now, he knocked once again at the door. Nothing much had changed, he thought, except the garden. The sight of all those tomatoes, oddly enough, reminded him again of Joannie.

'Come in.'

Faraday stepped back, closed the door, then led Winter through to the big living room at the back of the house. The last of the daylight was draining from the wide grey spaces of Langstone Harbour. It looked even chillier, Winter thought, than his own view.

Faraday had disappeared into the kitchen. When he returned he was carrying a bottle of wine and a couple of glasses.

'Yes?' He tipped a glass in Winter's direction.

Winter nodded. Turning back from the view, he noticed a magazine open on the sofa. *Model Aircraft Monthly*.

'I thought your game was birdwatching?'

'It is. My son bought me a subscription for Christmas. Tell you the truth, I've only just started reading them.'

'You going to take it up?' Winter was flicking through the magazine. 'Flying one of these things? Radio controls? All that?'

'It's a possibility. You can't watch birds all your life and not wonder how it's done.'

He poured a couple of glasses of red and settled in the chair across from the sofa. This was no-man's-land, neither work nor something less formal, and neither man knew quite where the conversation might go next.

'Cab again?' Faraday nodded out towards the road.

'Yeah. Five rides in any one day and you get a discount.' Winter stretched himself on the sofa. 'That's a joke, by the way.'

'Glad to hear it.' Faraday studied his glass for a moment. 'Must be strange being back in harness.'

'It is. Definitely. But then everything's a bit odd, you know, when you've had to think too hard about the alternative.'

'I bet.'

Faraday nodded. The last time he'd seen Winter before he fell into the hands of the surgeons was back last year. He'd been living with a startling-looking woman in his bungalow in Bedhampton, and Faraday – on a pastoral visit – had been impressed by his cheerfulness.

He mentioned it now. He thought the woman's name might have been Maddox.

'Spot on, boss. Lady played a blinder. Without her I'm not sure I'd have made it through. She was the one who found a bloke who'd sort me out but it was weeks and weeks before he could find me a slot and waiting for the phone to ring I wasn't the best company. You know something about dying you never suss when you're well? It's such a *business*, it just drains you, completely knackering. Me, I'd bought all the bollocks about bunches of flowers and net curtains at the window, and half a dozen angels waiting on the lawn outside, but when you get down to it it's not like that at all. Ask me what I remember and it's the bottom of a plastic bucket. It was grey if you're interested. Often with yellow bits floating around in it. Cheers. Here's to Maddox.' He shot Faraday a grin and raised his glass.

Faraday responded, wondering what else Winter needed to get off his chest.

'Is she still around?'

'Gone. Bless her.'

'Do you miss her?'

'Yeah. Big time. You cope though, don't you, situations like that?'

Faraday nodded, turning his head slightly to look out of the window. You do, he thought. You do.

Winter, to the best of Faraday's recollection, had flown back to the UK last summer. Someone had told him that the bungalow in Bedhampton had been on the market within weeks. By the time he'd been posted to Major Crimes, Winter was living in Gunwharf.

'Did the move help? Getting out of the old place?'

'Definitely. The moment I stepped back inside, it just felt wrong. It was like turning the clock back, like finding out the last month or whatever had never happened. I hadn't been to America. I hadn't had the operation. None of that stuff. No kidding, within a couple of hours I was getting the headaches again. Same bloody armchair. Same wonky door on the fridge. Same aggro from the neighbours about the state of the fence. In the end it got so bad I was looking up flights to Phoenix in case the bloke had left a bit inside. I'm not sure you can get a warranty with brain operations but I thought it was worth a try.'

Faraday laughed this time. Only Winter could turn the last year or so into a joke. He thought of the house again, the neat little bungalow on the slopes of Portsdown Hill.

'Easy sale?'

'Piece of piss. The agency put it on at two nine nine. Complete joke. Young bloke and his missus came along with a couple of babies, refugees from Wecock Farm. They'd had enough of living in a war zone and offered me two sixty. Two seven five, I said, and it was theirs. The agent gave me a right bollocking. Thought I'd lost my mind.' His fingers strayed to his hairline where the surgeon had made the first incision. 'Funny that.'

Wecock Farm was a newish housing estate up towards Waterlooville. Things had got so bad lately that some of the bus drivers were threatening strike action if they got another rock through the windscreen.

'And Gunwharf?' Faraday enquired.

'A steal. Belonged to a friend of a friend. No way was I getting it for two seven five or anything like, not with those kinds of views, but money feels different after you've been through what I went through and it turned out there were ways and means.' He grinned again. 'Undercroft parking? Video entryphones? Uniformed security to keep the inbreds out? Six months of that and you start wondering how you ever coped before. Yeah . . . ' He nodded. 'Definite result.'

Faraday studied him a moment, then reached for the bottle. *Money feels different*, he thought. What exactly did that mean?

'You phoned,' he said, changing the subject.

'Yeah.' Winter extended his glass. 'I thought we ought to talk.'

'About what?'

'About a bloke called Givens.'

'Who?'

'Givens. Alan Givens. He was on that Misper list of Tracy's. I've been making some enquiries. Like you do.'

He offered Faraday the bones of the story. The guy had a regular job, kept his nose clean, never got in anyone's hair. He lived alone, appeared to have fuck-all in the way of friends. Then, one day, he disappeared.

'It happens all the time,' Faraday pointed out. 'It's the way we live.'

'Sure. You want to hear the rest of it?'

Winter told him about the state of the bank account, the series of withdrawals, the blizzard of season tickets that had dropped through Emma Cusden's front door.

'How do you know all this?'

'I'm a detective. It's in the job description.'

'That's not what I asked.'

'I went round. Asked questions.'

'You went round to Givens' place?'

'Yes. I thought he might be a runner for the tunnel.'

'And that's where you got the bank details?'

'Last month's statement, yeah.'

'And this woman? Emma?'

'She's a girl, a tot, off the planet. The guy we should be looking at is the boyfriend.'

Winter told Faraday about Karl Ewart. The boy, he said, was on a nicking. Card theft at the very least. Possibly a great deal more.

'Like what?'

'Like homicide. Givens is a guy who's just lost seven grand from his account. It's nearly two months since he went missing yet no one's heard a dickie, least of all the bank.'

'You've checked?'

'Yes.' Winter took a swallow of wine. 'The account's still active.'

Faraday nodded. There was one major flaw in Winter's case.

'There's no body,' he pointed out.

'Sure. But Ewart's got a car. I've checked that too.'

'How?'

'Social worker at Merefield. She holds Emma's file. She had a run-in with Ewart over various issues, went round to where he lives, basement flat in Ashburton Road, clocked the Astra he drives.'

'That's a crime scene then. Or could be.'

'Exactly, boss. I thought you might like to take it further.'

Faraday stared at him a moment, amazed at how artful Winter could be. He was here, after all, to confess his sins. He'd strayed from the straight and narrow. He'd ignored all the careful instructions to stay behind his desk. He'd gone out there, probably on paid time, and turned his back on his *Coppice* duties. Yet now, when Faraday had every right to bollock him, even suspend him from Major Crimes, he could simply plead the imminence of yet another scalp. I found a moment to lift a stone or two, he'd doubtless say. And golly, just look what I've come up with.

Winter drained his second glass, then checked his watch. Faraday got up from the sofa and fetched another bottle from the kitchen. When he got back, Winter was struggling to his feet. Faraday told him to sit down again.

'Be honest,' he said. 'Why are you really here?'

Winter gave the question some thought, then leaned forward, his glass in his hand.

'Because it would be nice to sort two jobs, wouldn't it?'

'Together, you mean?'

'Of course.' He was beaming now. 'Be realistic, boss. How else could I ever do it?'

Six

Thursday, 14 July 2005, 08.30

Martin Barrie was seldom at his desk before nine, but this morning, after Faraday's request for an early meeting, he'd persuaded his wife to drop the kids off and left in time to miss the worst of the traffic. To Faraday, used to the bulk of Willard at the desk by the window, Barrie's was an almost spectral presence in the room. On a sunny day, in the words of one of the more disenchanted DCs, the man was thin enough to piss through.

Not that chain-smoking and a passion for cheese salads had taken the edge off his thinking.

'It won't work, Joe. There's no way.'

'With respect, sir—' Faraday had taken him through the intelligence on Givens. He wanted to launch another investigation with himself as Senior Investigating Officer.

'With respect, it's nonsense. You're pushed as it is on *Coppice*. I've got eyes, Joe. I'm not blind.'

'You think I'm not hacking it?'

'I think this Duley thing is open-ended. I think it's going to grow and grow. Whether you're hacking it or not gets us nowhere. SIO on Duley might be expecting a bit much without a deputy. Lead on both of them, and you'd be a headcase in days.' He frowned. 'There has to be another way.'

'Like what? There's still no DCI. Nick Hayder's off sick. Petersen's up to his eyes in the Titchfield job.'

Hayder and Petersen were fellow DIs on Major

Crimes. Normally, Alan Givens would have ended up in one of their in-trays.

Barrie was consulting his diary. Then he put a call through to his wife. When she answered, he asked Faraday to give him a moment's privacy. Faraday returned to his office. He was halfway through an overnight report from Jerry Proctor when the Detective Superintendent appeared at his open door.

'I had decorating leave booked,' he said briskly. 'You've given me the perfect excuse. Get the policy book up to date, then leave it on my desk. From now on, I'm heading up *Coppice* and the Givens job as well.'

'And me?' Faraday was astonished.

'Deputy on both. Think of the scope. You can get out at last, kick a few doors down. We're talking win–win, Joe. Except for my poor bloody wife.'

Faraday kept the news from Winter until lunchtime, a small act of revenge that Winter didn't find the least bit amusing. He was sitting behind his desk, looking glumly at a list of phone calls he hadn't made.

'Proctor's lads have nearly finished at Salisbury Road.' Faraday was carrying a handful of polythene evidence bags. 'I'm going for the walk-through this afternoon.'

'I'll come with you, boss.' Winter was already reaching for his jacket.

'No, you won't. I want this lot sorted by the time I get back. Should be around three.'

The evidence bags had been delivered this morning from Duley's bedsit, the first fruits of yesterday's search. Winter peered at the contents. He could see chequebooks, correspondence, photos, bills, a camera, a thick leather-bound book that looked like a diary of some kind, plus an assortment of other papers.

'Has this lot been DNA'd? Fingerprinted?'

'Yeah.'

'What about Givens?' Winter looked up at Faraday. 'Only I was thinking, you know . . . ' He shrugged. 'Me and Jimmy Suttle, the old team . . . Yeah?'

Faraday shook his head. Operation *Tartan*, he said, had been launched this morning with a squad of four DCs. He'd put a couple of the blokes into Ashburton Road, house-to-house. Already it was plain that Karl Ewart had done a runner, presumably warned off by his girlfriend, but with luck they'd scare up a lead on the details of the car he was driving. The other two guys were chasing the season tickets, making enquiries around Somerstown pubs. The tickets had all been issued in Givens' name but Ewart had doubtless offloaded them by now.

'Waste of time.' Winter was looking pained. 'You really think they're going to be talking to us?'

'It's a start.' Faraday nodded down at the phone. 'You'll be belling your own contacts too, no doubt.'

'Really?' Winter visibly brightened. 'So I *am* on the squad?'

'Of course. You'll be driving the intelligence. If you need help in here, I'll try and sort something out. It's like a two-for-one offer, you holding the fort on both *Coppice* and *Tartan*. That's the way I sold it to Barrie.'

'Do I get to leave the office?'

'I doubt you'll find the time. Barrie's one for regular updates. He likes to keep his finger on the pulse. You're part of the Management Group now, Paul. Top man. Terrific career opportunity. Just think of all those meetings.'

'You're kidding.'

'I'm afraid not. Like I said last night, intelligence is key to *Coppice*. The Givens job looks more straightfor-ward. TIE Karl Ewart, and we'll know where we are. Nice work, Paul. I told Barrie how well you've done.'

TIE meant trace, interview, eliminate. Faraday's thinking on *Tartan* couldn't have been plainer.

Winter was looking glum again. He'd always hated

meetings. 'I'm going to be crap at this,' he told Faraday. 'It's just not what I'm about.'

'Nonsense.' Faraday opened one of the evidence bags and emptied the contents onto Winter's desk. 'I'd make a start if I were you. Barrie wants us round the table at five and he'd hate it if you had nothing to say.' He paused, then nodded down at the exhibit label attached to the bag. 'And don't forget to sign the docket. Date and time. Yeah?'

The Scenes of Crime team were packing up their equipment by the time Faraday made it round to Salisbury Road. He passed one of them on the stairs, carrying a stepladder and a handful of lighting equipment back to the van outside. DS Jerry Proctor was standing in an open doorway on the top landing, talking to the photographer.

'Is this the one?'

Faraday was peering in at the room. Proctor's officers had removed a number of items but it still looked a mess. The spill of sunshine through the window betrayed years of staining on the threadbare carpet, and the walls, a vile shade of lavender, still carried traces of silver fingerprint powder. There was an MFI wardrobe in the corner, the door off its hinges, and more fingerprint powder on the surface of the table that served as a desk. The Dell PC was bagged, ready for dispatch to the specialist computer unit at Netley, and someone had made an effort to tidy the piles of paperbacks and magazines that lay against the skirting board. Faraday knelt briefly, flicking through the magazines. *New Statesman. Prospect.* Copies of something in French.

A poster over the single bed in the corner caught Faraday's eye. It showed a young protester struggling to escape the attentions of a couple of helmeted riot police. One had locked him in a choke hold while the other was steadying himself for a decent shot with his raised baton. There was a blur of flags and faces in the background and rags of drifting tear gas gave the photo an almost painterly feel. Across the bottom of the poster ran a couple of lines of text but Faraday's Italian was far from perfect. He gazed at it a moment longer. A window on a different world, he thought.

Faraday turned back to Proctor.

'Anything interesting?'

'Bugger all.' Proctor shook his head. 'The stuff I brought over this morning might be useful and there's bound to be something on the hard disk but there's no evidence that someone had a go at him in here. We found a T-shirt in the corner in a bit of a state but my money's on that kicking he got a couple of weeks back because he seems to have used it as a dishcloth since. Might have other DNA on it, of course, especially if he put up a bit of a fight. We'll make it a submission if you think it's important.'

'Prints?'

'About half a dozen lifts. We'll run them through AFIS but could be mates, old tenants, anyone.'

AFIS was the computerised fingerprinting ID system. In a matter of minutes it would tell Faraday whether anyone else with form had been in Duley's bedsit.

'Anything else?'

'Just this.'

Proctor retrieved another evidence bag from his briefcase. Inside was a handful of stubby roaches, retrieved – he said – from various corners of the room. They'd found a stash of cannabis too, and on the off chance that someone else may have been smoking apart from Duley, they might also be candidates for forensic submission.

Faraday nodded, postponing a decision. Given the human wreckage Proctor had found in the tunnel, he rather hoped that Duley had spent the evening in a warm haze of dope. God knows, he might have suffered rather less through the ordeal to come.

'May I?'

'Of course, sir. Like I said, we're through.'

Faraday stepped into the room. The herby bitter-sweet scent of cannabis seemed to have settled into the furnishings, into the curtains, into the untidy row of collarless shirts and denim jackets hanging in the wardrobe. He stood in the middle of the room, noted the view from the window, the glimpse of the sea at the end of the road opposite, tried to visualise the face from the PNC printout at home in this cluttered, intimate space.

On a hook on the back of the door hung an olive-coloured beret and a black scarf. There was a brown Buddha bag as well, and Faraday studied it a moment, sensing that this ensemble was something you might affect if you wanted the world to look at you in a particular way. It was an echo of the ID shot. It went with those hooded eyes and tilted chin – another hint of challenge, of proud apartness. Duley, he decided, was a man who took himself with some seriousness.

Faraday looked inside the bag. It was empty.

'Everything's with that stuff I left with you this morning.' Proctor had been watching him.

'Like what?'

'Notepad, Pens. Couple of *Guardian* articles from last week. Some flyer about a *Relate* meeting. Address book. Rizlas. More weed.'

'The notepad?'

'Nearly full. Crap writing, mind. Red ink.'

'Mobile?'

'Couldn't find one.'

Faraday walked over to the bed, lifted the duvet. The bottom sheet had gone. He glanced round at Proctor.

'Old semen stains, lots of them. Duley was either into big-time wrist shandy or he had a friend. We bagged the sheet in case we need it for analysis.'

Faraday was surprised. None of the statements so far gathered from other tenants had mentioned anything about regular visitors to Number 8. He made a mental note to quiz Winter. Amongst all those exhibits, there'd surely be a note or two, or at least a phone number. On the evidence of this room, Duley seemed to be a man who liked an audience.

Proctor was telling him now about a pile of type-script pages they'd found on the desk beside the PC. He'd only had time to flick through but it appeared to be a novel of some kind, fantasy fiction, lots of funny names. He'd seized it and had the lot sent over to the Intelligence Cell. When it came to stuff like this, he said, there were people better qualified than him to look for clues.

Faraday smiled, trying to imagine Winter's face when this latest haul of evidence appeared at his office door. Bank statements and address books were one thing; 50,000 words of Duley's fevered prose quite another.

'We found this too. It should have gone over to Major Crimes with the rest of the stuff but got left out. You mind taking it, sir?'

Faraday was looking at a postcard. It showed a turquoise bay beneath a tumble of tropical-looking cloud. The sand was bone white, with a scatter of rocks, and in the foreground an empty hammock hung invitingly between two palm trees. For a second he was back in Thailand. Then he turned the postcard over and discovered a Venezuelan stamp. According to the line of tiny typescript at the bottom, the bay evidently belonged to the Isla de Margarita.

Faraday peered at the writing. Red ink again.

'Same hand, sir. Put money on it.'

'Duley?'

'Has to be.'

The card was addressed to *Mia Querida, #8, 74 Salisbury Road, Southsea, Inglaterra*. On the left, instead of a message a single scarlet heart. Faraday tucked the card into his jacket pocket, perplexed. *Mia Querida?*

Back at Kingston Crescent, Faraday put his head round Winter's office door. Winter looked up at him, stony-faced. He had his jacket off and his tie was loosened. There were two empty mugs on the window sill and the borrowed transistor on the other desk was tuned to Radio Two.

'Well?'

Winter consulted the pad at his elbow. Duley, he said, was paying fifty quid a week, by cheque, for the bedsit. He was in trouble with British Gas over an unsettled account going back months and had probably fallen out with Southern Electric as well because there was correspondence about suspicious readings from the meter in his room. As far as earning money was concerned, he appeared to make a living from a variety of sources. A part-time job in Waterstone's as a shop assistant brought him in £174 a week. In addition to that, he did twice-weekly night shifts in a meat-packing factory in the north of the city and occasional freelance translation work for an agency based in Southampton. Add up a week's takings, said Winter, and you were looking at around £255 after tax.

'The night shift might be a cash job but on money like that he'd still be pushed.'

'Anything else job-wise?'

'Yeah. Here.' Winter extracted a payslip from the mountain of documentation on his desk. 'It's a local authority chitty. Portsmouth City Council. I phoned them up with the reference number. They were iffy, of course, but I got it out of them in the end.'

'Got what out of them?'

'Our man.' Winter nodded at the payslip. 'He's been doing a series of workshops on local history at the Buckland Community Centre. Every Wednesday morning. It's part of some regeneration scheme. They gave me a number for the woman who organises it. She says he's gone down a storm. It's mainly women in the class. They all think he's wonderful, her included. She can't wait for tomorrow.'

'You told her what's happened?'

'You have to be joking. Why would I ever do that?' Winter turned his head and gazed out of the window. 'Amazing, isn't it? Local history workshops in Buckland? Apparently some of them can even read.'

'Big class?'

'She said about a dozen. All ages. Mr Duley's got the knack, she told me. Really puts a new twist on things, really makes you think.'

He turned back, sorting through the pile of evidence, adding more and more bits to the jigsaw of Duley that Faraday was beginning to put together in his head. Tuesday evenings, said Winter, Duley reserved for Respect. He was on the committee and had evidently volunteered to edit the monthly newsletter.

'Respect? You mean the George Galloway lot?' Faraday was woolly when it came to politics. He'd joined Eadie for the anti-war marches a couple of years back but the way the far left was always regrouping had always baffled him.

Winter shot him a look, then opened a website on his PC. The Respect home page featured a scarlet masthead.

'Equality. Socialism. Peace. Environment. Community. Trade Unionism,' Winter read out. 'Does that help?'

'And you're telling me Duley's into all this?'

'Absolutely. And not just Respect, either. The rest of the week, except for his night shifts, he's at it with the stop-the-war lot. Or the anarchists. Or save the Kurds. We're talking commitment here, boss. Guy never knew when to stop.' Winter gazed at his notepad for a moment then pushed his chair back from the desk.

'Doesn't really help us though, does it, boss? How does any of all that put him in the tunnel?'

Faraday said he didn't know. Yet.

'What about the book he's supposed to be writing? Jerry Proctor mentioned he'd sent it over.'

'He did, bless him.' Winter indicated a brown evidence sack on the floor in the corner. 'I got to page 3. Didn't understand a word.'

'It's in English?'

'Allegedly. Starkis the Slayer of the Mighty Turk? The Perennial Goth? Biglet the Monster Fireman? Fair play to the man for all that typing but, believe me, I was pleading for mercy.' He hesitated a moment. 'You want to take the writing angle any further? Only you might be interested in this.'

He poked around in the pile of documents on the desk. This time Faraday found himself looking at a substantial-looking brochure for something that called itself The 25th Annual Writers' Conference. This year it had taken place at University College, Winchester.

'Page 8,' Winter grunted. 'Check out the photo.'

Faraday leafed through. Page 8 carried a list of workshops. A large red arrow drew his eye to a box announcing two sessions devoted to crime writing entitled 'Who Do You Think You Are?' The workshop was to be conducted by Sally Spedding.

'That was a couple of weeks back,' Winter pointed out. 'The Friday and the Sunday, last weekend in June. He must have gone because he's in the photo I found inside.'

'You're good at this, aren't you?'

'Fuck off, boss.'

Faraday smiled. The photo showed a group of a dozen or so, most of them middle-aged women. Duley was one of only two men. The group was mustered round what looked like a table in a bar, and Duley had wedged himself between a beaming forty-something with a wild fall of black hair and a much older woman, greying, stern-faced. He had an arm round each of the women and the slightly glazed expression on his face suggested he'd been in the bar for a while.

'Nothing to him, is there?'

Winter was right. Duley was thin, almost gaunt. Faraday turned the photo over. On the back were a couple of kisses and a scrawled signature that could have meant anything. This must be the woman with the camera, Faraday thought. Delivering the promised print.

'You think there's anything in it?'

'Dunno.' Faraday was writing down the contact number for the conference. 'It's recent, though, isn't it? And some of these conference things can be wild – bunch of strangers, bed and board, cheap booze from the student bar, all those women falling around . . . '

'Yeah?' Winter was eyeing the brochure with interest at last. 'You think it's too late to take up scribing?'

'Never.' Faraday pocketed the number, struck by another thought. 'Jerry gave me a postcard Duley must have sent. Does Venezuela tie in with anything you've got there?'

'Ah . . . ' Winter abandoned the brochure for an envelope at the very bottom of the pile on his desk. 'I meant to show you.'

He shook the contents out: a handful of Venezuelan banknotes, varying denominations.

'These were in the address book too. I make it a couple of thousand bolivars. He must have brought them back.'

'Any sign of a ticket? Invoice? Hotel details? Dates?'

'No, but we've got his passport here. Hang on.'

Winter found the passport and gave it to Faraday. The *entrada* stamp for Venezuela was on a page towards the end. *Aeropuerto de Isla de Margarita*, 14 May 2005. On the 17th, same page, Duley had left.

'Holiday?'

'No way, boss.' Winter was sparking now. 'Who in his right mind goes to the Caribbean for three days?'

Detective Superintendent Barrie convened the first of the *Coppice* Management Group meetings for five o'clock, ahead of the full evening squad brief. Faraday was there as Deputy SIO, along with six other members of the team. The faces round the table were responsible for every area of the ongoing investigation – from control of various crime scenes to the often tricky issues of family liaison – and it was an early clue to Barrie's leadership style that he insisted on full minutes, to be circulated within half a working day. He might look like a tramp, thought Faraday, but this is a man who leaves no administrative stone unturned.

Barrie began the meeting by confirming the transfer of the policy book to his own desk. There followed a careful summary of the operation's progress to date, together with an exploration of possible lines of enquiry. The Intelligence Cell, he announced, was sorting through a harvest of seized documentation from Duley's bedsit. Names and contacts from the victim's address book had already been passed to the DS in charge of the Outside Enquiry Team and appropriate actions were imminent. It was already clear that Duley was a political animal, an activist, with a finger in a number of far left pies. Special Branch would have their own contribution to make and Barrie had invited one of their DIs to attend the next Management Group meeting. Today was Thursday. By the weekend Barrie expected a firm timeline to have emerged, a sequence of events that would enable the squad to plot Duley's contacts and movements during the days and hours that led to his death.

Winter was sitting at the far end of the table and Faraday was watching him carefully. From the start his body language had made it clear that he didn't belong there. He was fidgety, bored, out of his natural habitat.

He contributed when called upon, confirming that the trawl through Salisbury Road had thrown up a number of useful leads, but he refused to share the stir of excitement around the table at the speed with which *Coppice* was beginning to motor.

Sure, a picture was starting to emerge of the kind of life that Duley must have led. Of course, there were conversations to be had with political contacts, with students of Duley's, with anyone else who'd stepped into his busy life. But the real crunch, the way Winter saw it, was motivation. No one took politics seriously anymore, least of all the people Winter knew who were capable of tying someone to a railway line. No, there had to be someone else Duley had upset – and from where Winter was sitting, the serious money had to be on the man's recent three-day visit to Venezuela. Crack that, he muttered, and we might be getting somewhere. Venezuela meant cocaine. Cocaine took *Coppice* to Bazza Mackenzie. And to a businessman mate of his, Chris Cleaver. And guess what? Cleaver turns out to be living in a big spread a stone's throw from the tunnel.

Challenged by Dave Michaels to produce hard evidence of this link, Winter said he couldn't, not yet, but one or two of the older hands, including Barrie, were scribbling themselves a note. The Detective Superintendent had spent his previous CID service elsewhere in the county, and by the time Winter had finally finished, he looked, if anything, amused. Martin Barrie had heard all kinds of rumours about Winter, about this dinosaur throwback to an earlier school of detection, but he'd never seen the man in action.

He signalled for Faraday to stay behind in the office once the meeting had broken up.

'He hates us, doesn't he?' He nodded at the empty conference table. 'He can't stand any of this.'

Daniel George was the moving force behind Respect in Portsmouth. Faraday got contact details from Duley's address book then returned to his own office. The call found him in seconds. George evidently helped his wife in the family business, an all-hours café in Southsea's Albert Road. On the phone he sounded guarded about Duley but said he'd followed the story in the *News* and agreed to meet at half seven. He had a bit of time free and Faraday was welcome to come to the café.

Faraday took DC Tracy Barber with him. The squad meeting had been shorter than usual and they'd had time to catch up over a snatched pint upstairs at the bar. At Faraday's prompting, Barber had phoned a contact in the force Special Branch office about George. It turned out that his SB file went back years. There was no way Barber's contact was going through the whole thing but he'd given her the essentials.

Sixty-three years old. Early career as a researcher at LSE, then a series of lecturer posts in various universities. Active on the far left – International Socialists and Socialist Workers Party – since 1968. Fought the rightward drift of New Labour and lent his weight to the stop-the-war campaign in Portsmouth.

'The guy sounds solid,' Barber had told Faraday. 'SB thinks we're talking root and branch socialism.'

One Minute To Midnight was a cheerfully bright café lodged between a second-hand book store and a sprawling antiques shop in Albert Road. According to Barber's Special Branch contact, the place was extremely popular with students and one look at the price list in the window told Faraday why. Corned beef hash with spring cabbage in fish sauce and garlic, £2.95. Moroccan-style fishcakes with couscous and a home-made chilli sauce, £3.65. At those kinds of prices, Faraday told Barber, he might start eating here himself.

Inside, there was barely room to edge between the tightly packed tables. The air was blue with smoke and there was a powerful smell of cannabis. At the counter at the back of the café, Faraday's enquiry about Daniel

George was greeted with a nod by the woman chopping onions beneath a line of posters advertising various upcoming music gigs. It seemed they were expected.

'He's up in his office.' She nodded at a flight of nearby stairs. 'Look for the light under the door.'

The stairs were in semi-darkness. Up on the top landing, Faraday found the office door and knocked. An answering grunt invited them in. George was sitting at a desk working through a list of figures. The window was curtained and a pool of light from the lamp at his elbow spilled across a litter of invoices. On the wall above the desk was a poster for a Rembrandt exhibition at the Rijksmuseum in Amsterdam, a brooding self-portrait that seemed to echo the weariness in George's face. In daylight, thought Faraday, this room would look a mess. There were books and magazines everywhere, piled on the threadbare carpet, and hundreds of photocopied flyers spilled out of a couple of cardboard boxes behind the door. In some respects it reminded Faraday of the busy chaos of Duley's bedsit. The same dismissal of orderliness. The same faith in the printed word.

George pushed his chair back from the desk and turned to greet them. He was a tall man, stooped, his eyes pouched with exhaustion behind the thick glasses. He was dressed for the allotment, old shirt, torn cardigan, but there was an additional echo of Martin Barrie in the steadiness of his gaze. This was someone you'd be foolish to underestimate.

'We'll have to get a move on, I'm afraid.' He glanced at his watch. 'I take it this is about Mr Duley.'

'That's right.' Faraday pocketed his warrant card. 'As I explained on the phone, we—'

George stepped past him, clumped down the landing and returned moments later with two chairs. Faraday and Barber sat down. George towered over them

'Normally, I wouldn't dream of talking to you,' he

said bluntly. 'But under the circumstances I imagine it might help.' He sank into his own chair. 'What exactly are you after?'

'Information on Duley.' It was Faraday again. 'We simply need to establish some facts. Is that OK with you?'

'We'll see. Try me.'

'Next of kin would be helpful. Was Duley married?'

'Not to my knowledge.'

'Parents?'

'He never mentioned them.'

'Someone special then? Partner? Girlfriend? Boyfriend?'

'No.' George shook his head. 'I can't help you with any of that either.'

Faraday nodded. Was this intransigence or was he telling them the truth? Barber took up the running.

'How well did you know Mr Duley?'

George glanced from one face to the other, then produced a packet of Rizlas and began to roll himself a cigarette. Something was troubling him here, Faraday could feel it.

'Listen,' George said at last. 'I've no idea what happened to Mark and naturally we're all a bit upset, but what is it you're really after? You want to know what kind of bloke he is? Who he'd pissed off? What might have taken him into that tunnel? Is that it?'

'Partly, yes.'

'Then you're talking to the wrong man. I'm not being difficult, I'm really not, but it's not my job to make life easier for you people.'

Barber exchanged glances with Faraday and then sat back in the chair. Faraday did his best to hide his irritation.

'We're dealing with a serious crime, Mr George,' he said softly. 'In all probability, Mr Duley was murdered. Not just killed but killed horribly. You knew him. You must have thought about him since the news broke. You can't tell me you haven't.'

'Of course not. But where does that take us?'

'I'm not sure yet. None of us are. All we know about Duley, all anyone knows, is that the man was politically active. The first entry we came across in his diary was Respect. That's you, Mr George. No one's saying it's a crime, being a politician. We're just keen to know what made Duley tick.'

'Good question.'

'You're telling me you don't know?'

There was a long silence. Then came the scrape of a match as George lit the roll-up. At length, picking a shred of tobacco from his lower lip, he asked which one of them was Special Branch.

'I am,' Barber said. 'Or was.'

'So you'd know about the kind of people we are, the kind of people we attract.'

'All sorts.'

'Exactly. I could take you out of this building right now and I could introduce you to maybe a dozen people I'm proud to call my political allies. Teachers, lecturers, tradespeople, blokes from the dockyard, students, the unwaged, one guy who happens to be an antiquarian bookseller. They all sign up, they all come along to the meetings, they all do their bit, but when I ask myself about motive, most of the time I haven't a clue. We're fellow travellers. We're sharing a journey. We agree on the essentials. But beyond that, it's often guesswork. Why do they do it? Why does anyone do anything? You tell me.'

'You didn't know Duley well?'

'No, but then that's not unusual. Respect isn't a social club.'

'So how long had he been around?'

'With us? A year at the most.'

'And you hadn't come across him before then?'

'No. He walked into a meeting we were having one

128

night, held his hand up when we needed bodies on the street, put himself about for us.'

'How?'

'By selling newspapers, by signing people up for various petitions, by canvassing back in the May election. I know you guys think it's all barricades and black flags, the left, but you're wrong. Democracy's bloody hard work. People like Duley are gold dust.'

'He was good at it?'

'He was conscientious.'

'What does that mean?'

'He got the stuff done. You could trust him. Some people thought . . . ' George broke off.

'Thought what?'

' . . . thought he talked too much. He certainly had a mouth on him and some days it could wear you out, the sheer energy of the man, but in our position you'd be mad to complain. Half a dozen Duleys and we could leaflet most of Southsea in a couple of evenings.'

Faraday nodded and made a note. He decided he liked this man, the way his mind worked, the way he so carefully parcelled out the information, the respect he was implicitly paying to his dead comrade. Everything he'd said so far keyed in exactly with the picture Faraday was beginning to put together. Duley the activist. Duley the volunteer. Total commitment laced with a hint or two of mania.

'He ran a workshop in Buckland,' Faraday began. 'What was that about?'

'I've no real idea except he managed to swing the funding somehow. Credit to him. These days that's not simple.'

'But what was it about? In broad terms?'

'Local history. We had a couple of posters up for a bit.'

'And he'd have taken –' Faraday paused. '– A particular line?'

'Of course.' George was smiling now. 'Spithead

Mutiny. Battle of Southsea Common. Patterns of outsourcing from the dockyard. Labour exploitation in the corset industry. It's all there if you look hard enough.'

'What's all there, Mr George?'

'The kind of role a city like this ends up playing. Pompey was founded on blood and treasure, Mr Faraday. We spill the blood; someone else gets the treasure. Sweet deal if you happen to be on the receiving end. Duley understood that. He was a bright man. And, like I say, he was good on his feet, had a way with words.'

'What about his other affiliations?' Faraday asked. 'The anarchists? Free the Kurds? Duley put himself about a bit, didn't he?'

'Of course he did. That's not uncommon. In fact we've got a phrase for it. No fixed abode.'

'So where was the middle of him? Where did it all hang together?'

'I'm not sure it did.'

'What does that mean?'

George shook his head, taking a deep lungful of smoke, refusing for the time being to go any further, and Faraday sensed at last that they'd arrived at some kind of bend in the road. He bent forward in the chair, his face in the pool of light from the desk lamp.

'Here's a man with a war record. He's been arrested umpteen times, he's got his name in the papers, a couple of times he's nearly found himself banged up. But when you analyse all that, try and join the dots together, what do you see? Mr Rent-a-Cause?'

'That's offensive.'

'Why?'

'Because the man had physical courage. And physical courage was something that mattered to him.'

'Mattered that other people recognised it? Mattered that he was out front, drawing a crowd, having a go? What does that say about him?'

'I've no idea.'

'But you must have, or at least you must have thought about it. For most of his political life Duley's head was way above the parapet. He's in there, mixing it. Like you say, he's brave, even reckless. Then he suddenly ends up tied to a railway line.'

'You're telling me there's a connection?'

'I'm asking.'

'Then you're wrong.'

'How can you be sure?'

'Because I know these people. Duley was a strange man, a loner, a solitary, but that's not uncommon. If you want the plod to the ballot box, the daily grind, the battle to win the public debate, you stick with people like me. If you want something a little more . . . ah . . . colourful, then maybe Duley's your man. But that's not what put him in the tunnel. Not the way I see it. You just don't make those kinds of enemies.'

'You said loner.' It was Barber this time.

'That's right.'

'In what sense?'

'In the sense that he didn't have a box, not full time, not a box he could call his own. He wasn't SWP, Old Labour. He hadn't come out of the CND tradition, the Aldermaston marches. He wasn't Green. He didn't spend his life blowing up vets' premises with the animal rights lot. He wasn't even an anarchist, not properly.'

'Just a bit of everything? Pick and mix?'

'That's glib.'

'But you take the point?'

'Of course I do.'

'So how come you just told us he was . . . ' Barber glanced down at her notes, ' . . . conscientious? Did his bit? Delivered all those leaflets?'

'Because he was serious, because he was committed.'

'To what, exactly?'

George rocked in his chair, sucked in another lungful of smoke, blew it out again.

'Oh, come on . . . ' he said at last. 'Do I have to spell it out? People like Duley regard themselves as free spirits. They don't like authority. They hate people telling them what to do. They think, in the end, they're only answerable to their own consciences. You ask me what these people are committed to, and I have to say I don't know. Which is why they always move on.'

'But he didn't,' Faraday pointed out. 'He stayed.'

George looked at him for a long moment, then pinched the end of his roll-up and buried the stub amongst the pencil shavings. At length, he consulted his watch and got to his feet.

'I'm out of time,' he said. 'I'm sorry.'

Faraday didn't move. He wanted to know whether George ever talked to Duley on the phone.

'Yeah, of course. Just like I talk to everyone else.'

'He had a mobile?'

'Yeah.' George frowned. 'Yeah, I think so.'

'You've got the number?'

'I must have, yeah, God knows where though.' He reached for the leather jacket behind the door. 'You want me to phone you later with it?'

Misty Gallagher had already ordered her first bottle of Moët by the time Winter made it to the American Bar. The Old Portsmouth pub was a ten-minute stroll from Gunwharf, and a recent change of ownership had filled the restaurant most nights. Late booking, Winter had been lucky to get the last table.

'Long time, no see.' Winter interposed his bulk between Misty and a tall, gelled youth half her age. 'How's tricks?'

'Fine.' She was peering over Winter's shoulder, trying to finish the previous conversation. 'I'd introduce you, love, but I didn't catch your name.'

'Kevin.'

'Ah. Kev. This is Paul Winter. We go back a while.'

Winter at last turned to acknowledge the new suitor.

'Nice to meet you, son.' Winter lifted the bottle and nodded towards the buzz of conversation through the open door. 'Shall we?'

Misty followed him into the restaurant. Only when they sat down did she tell Winter about the champagne.

'That's Kev's,' she said. 'He's picking up the tab.'

'Excellent.' Winter was already signalling for a glass. 'Known him long?'

'Twenty minutes.'

'The lad's due a toast then. Here's to a great conversation. Shame it was so brief.'

He checked around the nearby tables for familiar faces while the waitress poured the champagne.

'Packed,' he said approvingly. 'Must be making a fortune.'

Misty was still watching the bar. There came the slam of a door, then the roar of an engine outside. Evidently young Kevin had gone.

'Wimp,' she muttered, touching glasses with Winter. 'Back in the land of the living, eh?'

'Who told you about that?'

'Baz. You want to talk about it?'

'No.'

Winter seized the menu. For years Misty Gallagher had been Bazza Mackenzie's mistress, feasting off his chokehold on the Pompey cocaine trade. He'd set her up in a series of apartments, paid regular visits and given her a lifestyle to match. As far as Bazza was aware, she'd even had a daughter by him, a beautiful, truculent adolescent called Trudy.

Then came the news that Trudy's real father was Bazza's partner in crime, car dealer Mike Valentine, and Misty's goose was well and truly cooked when Bazza discovered that his mistress had never really lost her taste for Valentine's charms. Winter had naturally done his best to turn all this drama to good account but none of the parties involved was the least bit interested in grassing each other up, which was, on the face of it, a bit of a shame.

The last time Winter had seen Misty in the flesh was a couple of years back, after Special Ops had rigged Mike Valentine's cabin on the night Le Havre crossing. Winter and a handful of other detectives had settled down to watch Misty giving Valentine the blow job of his dreams when Bazza had burst in and tried to burn the cabin down. Winter's most cherished memory from that surreal evening had been the sight of Misty telling Bazza he'd got the wrong end of the stick. The startled friend with the flagging erection, she insisted, was nothing more than a travelling companion.

'So how is he? Valentine? Still got the place in Croatia?'

'Dunno.' Misty shrugged. 'We fell out after the first year. It rained a lot. In the end I couldn't stand it any longer so I came home. Mike always fancied Nice. Maybe that's where he is now.'

'You see Bazza at all?'

'Yeah.' Her fingers traced the line of the pendant necklace that disappeared into her ample cleavage. 'He's been very grown-up about it, especially where Trude's concerned. They've always got on really well. He's just written off all the other nonsense. Mike's out of his hair. That's all that matters. That and you tossers.'

'He thinks we've lost interest?'

'Definitely.' She nodded.

'He's right.'

'You want me to tell him that?'

'Yeah.' Winter nodded. 'Old times' sake, eh?'

Winter remembered the paternity certificate with Mike Valentine's name on it, the match he'd used to try and light the bonfire under Bazza Mackenzie. Winter had done his very best to put Pompey's drug king in front of a jury but Bazza seemed to have forgiven him too. Twice since he'd been back from the States, he'd run into Mackenzie, and both times Bazza had spared the time for a chat. Word on the street suggested that Bazza had tucked away his twenty million and washed his hands of the drugs biz, happy to prosper on the well-rinsed proceeds, and here was the living proof.

'Totally legit, mate, that's me,' he'd told Winter. 'Money coming out of my arse.'

Winter recounted the story. She nodded and reached for the Moët, laughing.

'So what's the matter with him, Mist?'

'I dunno, he's just changed. You seen him recently? He's got a sensible car, sensible haircut, nice suits, hasn't gone clubbing for months. Christ, he even shaves in the morning.'

'You'd know that?'

'Of course I'd know that. He's put a bit of weight on too. Nothing drastic but if you know where to look . . .' Her fingers curled round the stem of the glass and she smiled.

Winter wanted to know where she was living. Gunwharf had been the last love nest before Bazza threw her out of the waterside penthouse apartment and Winter knew first-hand just how addictive the views could become.

'Arethusa House again, is it?'

'No way.'

'Why not?'

'I fancied something out of town.'

'Like where?'

'Hayling Island.'

'You're kidding. You have to be ninety before they let you over the bridge.'

'Piss off. You know the bit down the bottom? Where all the money is?' Misty named a road that ran down beside Langstone Harbour. 'Baz has had a bit of land there for a while, planning permission, the lot. There's an old place on it at the moment but I've got this really great architect, Southsea bloke, and he's done the makeover.'

'Like how?'

'Like swimming pool, outdoor jacuzzi, huge conservatory round the back. You should see the views. Right on the water, it is.'

Winter was trying to picture the area. On a sunny day, he thought, she'd have a perfect view of Faraday's place.

'You're living there now?'

'Not yet. Baz reckons a couple of months. They're still finishing off. Place looks a tip at the moment. You know what his blokes are like.'

Winter nodded. Mackenzie had fuelled his empire on cocaine profits but like the rest of Pompey's business community he was busy turning every spare penny into bricks and mortar. He had a couple of building firms, staffed exclusively from the Sunday league football teams he still ran, and his blokes were as erratic with their timesheets as they were unforgiving on the pitch.

'So where are you at the moment?'

'Milton. Scuzzy fucking place I'm supposed to be doing up. You want the truth? I hate it.'

'So why stay?'

'Because it's free. Doesn't cost Baz a penny. Plus it gives him a conscience. Like he's going to owe me for a very long time.'

Winter was trying to imagine Misty getting herself involved in DIY but gave up. When he enquired further, she put him right. Baz had picked up the house, she said, as a business debt. Just now, he'd done some deal with a bunch of Buckland lads who fancied a modest stake in the property game.

'They'll come to grief because they're clueless,' she said 'But Baz just doesn't see it. Real blind spot. Tell you the truth, I've been surprised.'

'So why is he doing it?'

'Dunno. They're brain-dead, these kids, all mouth

and trousers and absolutely no fucking idea. With Baz, though, it's all arm's length. These days he has to be careful. You know what I mean? Strictly investment, nothing hands-on. Maybe that's where the kids come in. Where Baz has got to, he doesn't need any of that hassle. It's OK for him but I bloody live there and they're driving me mental.'

Winter, unusually, was lost.

'We're still talking property with these kids, Mist?'

It was Misty's turn to look pained. She extended a hand. Purple nail varnish. A ruby the size of a bird's egg.

'No, Paul.' She gave his hand a little squeeze. 'We're not.'

Seven

The trill of his mobile did nothing for Winter's bursting head. He rolled over, felt blindly on the floor, tried to focus on the clock beside the bed. Quarter to eight. More or less.

'Who is it?'

'Jimmy. Listen. Ewart's car.'

'Who?'

'Ewart. Karl Ewart . . . Paul?'

Winter had struggled out of bed. Groping his way into the bathroom, he was just in time to throw up in the loo. Sinking to his knees on the cold tiles, he tried to remember exactly who Ewart was. *Coppice? Tartan?* Fuck knows.

'Paul? What's going on there? You OK?'

'No.'

Winter shut his eyes a moment, tried to quieten his churning stomach, failed completely. He bent forward, vomited again, then felt a little bit better. He eyed the soupy remains of last night's meal before his hand found the flush. Scallops in white wine. What a waste.

'Paul? Speak to me. What the fuck's happened?'

Jimmy Suttle again. Winter got to his feet, steadied himself on the basin, reached for the toothbrush. The face that looked back at him from the mirror managed a weary smile.

'Jimmy?' he managed. 'I'm wrecked.'

Suttle was belling him on the entryphone within minutes. Winter checked the video screen in the hall, then let him in. He'd managed to find his dressing gown and had run a comb through his hair but for once he'd resisted the temptation to pull back the curtains on the view. All that daylight was more than he could cope with just now.

One glance at Suttle told him he was in for a bollocking. The young detective sat him down on the sofa, then found a box of Ibuprofen in the kitchen.

'Where, exactly?' Suttle was asking about the pain.

'Here.' Winter's fingers found the bony ridge above his eyes.

'And bad, you say?'

'Evil.'

'You've thrown up again?'

'No.' Winter winced with pain as he shook his head. 'Not yet I haven't.'

Suttle looked at him a moment longer, then disappeared into the bathroom. When he came back, he had a wet flannel. He sat beside Winter, sponging his forehead. Winter could feel the trickle of icy water down his chest. Suttle paused a moment, his other hand fumbling with his mobile.

Winter watched him, alarmed.

'What are you doing?'

'Phoning for an ambulance.'

'Why?'

'*Why?*' You've forgotten last year? The pains? Exactly the same place? Throwing up eight times a day? Shit, mate . . . ' He shook his head, thumbing 999.

Winter managed to wrestle the mobile from his grip. When a voice asked him which emergency service he was after, he grunted an apology. False alarm, love. Wrong number. Sorry. Then his hand found Suttle's knee and he gave it a reassuring pat.

'Self-abuse, son. My fault completely. How about some tea?'

Suttle, as Winter had anticipated, was angry. The medics had warned him off too much booze and yet here he was, tying on a big one with absolutely no fucking thought for the consequences. Most people with half a brain would listen to advice like that, but not Paul Winter.

'What was it did the damage, as a matter of interest?'

'Bacardi. Neat.'

'*Bacardi*? Since when did you start necking Bacardi?'

'Misty had a bottle she'd been saving. We ended up round her place.'

Mention of Misty Gallagher brought Suttle to a halt. He'd been pouring the tea in the kitchen, shouting at Winter through the open door. Now he stepped into the lounge, astonished. Winter, full length on the sofa, gestured at the line of drips from the kitchen.

'Mind my carpet,' he said.

'Why Misty?'

'Just fancied it.'

'Bollocks, you fancied it. She's back with Mackenzie. Did you know that?'

'Yeah.' Winter had closed his eyes, the flannel still clamped to his forehead. 'She told me.'

'So what's your game? You get blind drunk. You end up with Bazza's bird. Are you after a slapping? Or are you just stupid?'

The question pained Winter. He struggled up onto one elbow. Jimmy Suttle, a couple of years ago, had been foolish enough to mess around with Misty's Trude for a couple of months. Winter had tried to warn him off but Suttle hadn't listened. Days later, a couple of Bazza's mates had put him in hospital.

'A slapping? You should know, son.'

'Exactly. So why risk it?'

'Because . . . ' Winter frowned, remembering the pair of them falling out of the cab last night. After the American Bar, they'd gone to a couple of other pubs. Bacardi at Misty's place sounded like a nice nightcap. Wrong. 'Listen—'

'No, *you* listen. Some people in this job think you're a pillock for even coming back. They tell me you've got

140

the perfect ticket out. Early retirement. Disability allowance. Pension. Cushty. So why screw all that up by working for a living? Me? I know they're wrong. Or at least I thought I did. Are you listening to me?'

Sobered, Winter had managed to get to his feet. He was grateful for all the attention but he was better now so maybe they could start all over again.

'Tea first,' he said. 'Then you can tell me about Ewart.'

Karl Ewart, it turned out, was driving an X-reg. Astra. House-to-house enquiries in Ashburton Road had unearthed a retired district nurse who'd seen him backing into her brand new Renault. She'd had it out with him on the street, got a mouthful in return, but taken the registration number and reported it to the police. Nothing much had happened but she still had the number and nursed a powerful grievance against the hooligan in the basement flat across the road.

'So what happened to the car?'

'Someone torched it last night. Ewart probably. Disused quarry round the back of the hill. Dickhead left the plates on.'

'Any sign of Ewart himself?'

'None. Word round the pubs says he's into small-time drug deals – delivery boy, dial-a-snort.'

'Using the car?'

'Presumably. He's not popular, our Mr Ewart. A lot of blokes can't wait to grass him up.'

Winter wanted another cup of tea. Jimmy Suttle was part of the four-man squad that Barrie had put together to get a fix on Givens' disappearance. So far they hadn't traced any of the season tickets but knew that Ewart had been flogging them. At this rate, said Suttle, they'd be waiting until the start of the new season to name-check bums on seats.

'That's September, son.'

'August.'

'Still a month away. What does Mr Faraday think?'

'He thinks Ewart's on a nicking, like we all do. Sooner or later he's convinced the arsehole will turn up at that doss of his again. We've put a camera in across the road. Nice old boy on the second floor. Me?' He glanced at his watch. 'I've got the day shift. Nine till whenever.'

Winter's brain was beginning to work again. He picked up the flannel and disappeared into the bedroom. When he came back, he was carrying a slip of paper. He gave it to Suttle.

'What's this?'

'Ewart's mobile number. I lifted his top-up card and talked to Orange. He bought a new card a couple of days ago so the phone's still active.' He managed a grin at last. 'Might turn out handy, eh?'

Mid-morning, feeling almost normal, Winter rapped on Faraday's door. He'd gone to his own office only to find an overweight DC called Babs sitting behind the spare desk. He wanted to know why.

'Reinforcements.' Faraday had barely looked up. 'Mr Barrie thinks you could do with some help.'

'He's not happy with what's he's getting?'

'On the contrary, he's very impressed. Just thinks you might need a hand with the paperwork.'

Winter frowned, looking for a trap. Hangovers always made him paranoid but in these situations you never took anyone at their word. Spare bodies were thin on the ground. How come Babs had been plucked from her other duties?

Faraday tidied the report he'd been studying and slipped it back into an envelope.

'Sit down.' He nodded at the spare chair. 'We ought to talk.'

'About *Tartan*? Jimmy Suttle briefed me this morning. Said you've put surveillance into Ashburton Road.'

'That's right. My feeling is that Ewart may be

drawing benefit. I want you to action that, find out whether it's true or not. If it is, he might have to go back home to pick up his giro.' He paused. 'What about Givens' bank account? We'll need statements going back beyond the last one.'

'I've applied for a production order. Should get the details out of HSBC within a week or two.'

'Good. Did Suttle tell you about the car?'

'Yeah.'

'So what do you think?'

'I think it's well dodgy. If he's been running coke round the city, he'd need wheels. That means there has to be a very good reason for trashing the Astra.'

'Givens?'

'Exactly. You roll the bloke, give him a hiding, overdo it a bit, and you've got a body on your hands. What then? You fetch the motor, stuff him in the back and wonder what the fuck to do next. Either way, he's leaking all over the boot. That's serious DNA. Even Ewart would work that out.'

'But we still haven't got a body.'

'Sure, boss. And now we haven't got a car.'

Faraday was toying with a pencil. The logic, he knew, was beyond argument. Everything in this city, he thought, goes back to the swamp where youths like Ewart screw themselves a living. Petty theft, assault, even murder, it made no difference. Time and again, the same shaven heads, the same pinched faces, the same cold eyes. He pushed the pencil away then sat back in his chair, his hands behind his head, staring out of the window. Thank God for Mark Duley, he thought. At last a hint of something new.

'Let's talk about *Coppice*,' he said. 'What's your feeling?'

Winter hesitated a moment. He'd been anticipating this conversation for the best part of an hour and wasn't quite sure how to handle it.

'I had a drink or two last night,' he said carefully. 'With an old mate.'

'And?'

'Bazza Mackenzie's at it again, arm's length, putting together investment syndicates.'

'Did he ever stop?'

'Yes, it seems he did, just for a while, but you know the way it is, boss. He goes into legit business, looks at the profit margins and then pisses himself laughing. The powder makes him more in a week than most blokes see in a year. Local businessmen stick money in the hat, rich arseholes like Chris Cleaver, ten grand a time. Bazza adds his own stake, then the pot goes to some little scrote down the pecking order who fancies becoming a drug baron. He buys wholesale, sorts out the distribution, takes his profit, then returns the stake and a fucking great divvy at the end. Money for nothing.'

'So who was this mate of yours? And how come he knows so much?'

'She, boss.'

'She?' Faraday raised an eyebrow, waiting for a name, but Winter shook his head.

'This is kosher. I swear it. That's all you need to know.'

'And *Coppice*? Mr Duley?'

'The kid Bazza is staking at the moment probably sources from the Caribbean, like they all do. You want the details?'

'Don't fuck around, Paul. Just tell me.'

'Odds on, he's using an island off Venezuela. Isla de Margarita.'

'Where Duley went?'

'Exactly.'

Faraday reached for a pen. Like Winter, he wasn't a great believer in coincidences.

'You mentioned a kid. Who is he?'

'I haven't got a name. Even pissed, she wouldn't tell me. But I know where to start looking.'

'Where?'

'In that class Duley was teaching. Apparently Bazza's little helper is a Buckland boy.'

'You're telling me this kid goes to local history workshops once a week?'

'No chance. But I bet he has a friend who does.' He got to his feet. 'Think about it, boss. Say the lad's buying from the locals in Margarita. He can barely manage his own language, let alone Spanish. He needs someone along with him, and that someone must have been Duley.'

'We're sure Duley speaks Spanish?'

'Positive. I talked to the translation agency in Southampton. Spanish and French. He was fluent in both.'

Suttle and DC Dawn Ellis had been sitting in the stake-out for nearly two hours by the time the hooded figure with the brand new Nikes appeared at the corner of the street. Ellis readied the camera then reached for the binoculars. Standing well back in the old man's living room, shadowed by the fall of curtain, she was invisible from below.

Suttle stood behind her. The face beneath the hood looked unshaven. Beyond that, it was impossible to pick up any real detail.

Even with the binos, Ellis was equally unsure. Might be. Might not. Suttle dug in his pocket, found his mobile, produced a scrap of paper with a line of figures.

'I think he's slowing,' Ellis said.

'What's happening now?'

'He's stopped. He's looking for something. He's got a mobile. Someone must have belled him.'

'Me.' Suttle was holding his own mobe at arm's length. Genius, he thought. Pure genius.

'He's going down the stairs into the flat.' Ellis was back behind the curtain. 'He's inside now. I've lost him.'

'Right.' Suttle was using the Airwave radio this time, talking to the DS on the *Coppice* Outside Enquiry Team. They'd worked out the details earlier. Suttle had done the recce. All he needed was a couple of blokes round the back.

'Skip? It's Jimmy. Ewart's in the flat. Repeat, the flat. Yeah –' He nodded. '– Soon as you like.'

The DS called back within a couple of minutes. Two uniforms were in position, same frequency. He wished Suttle the very best of luck.

'You kidding?' Suttle couldn't take his eyes off the basement flat across the road. 'The guy's toast.'

Dawn Ellis was already down in the street in case Ewart chose not to hang around. Suttle joined her. They crossed the road, pushed in at the sagging gate, stepped around a fold of sodden mattress, descended the stairs to the basement. There were recent splinter marks around the rotting wooden frame where the Yale lock engaged. Someone had already been at the door. These tossers prey on each other, Suttle thought, pressing the bell push.

There was no answer. He did it again. A third time. Then came the slightest movement in the blanket that hung behind the adjoining window and Suttle knew they had to get on with it.

'We've been clocked,' he told Ellis.

He took a step back, then kicked hard at the point where the lock met the door. First time it held. Another kick and he was in. The place was in semi-darkness. There was a smell Suttle recognised only too well. Somewhere out the back, he heard the crash of breaking glass.

'Check for gas,' he yelled over his shoulder. 'Little fucker's trying to make life hard for us.'

Suttle was in a narrow hall now. Ahead, he could see

the grey spill of daylight from an open door. The panel of glass in the middle of the door had been shattered. Suttle pulled at the handle. The door was locked.

'Ewart!'

He could see him now, out in the tiny oblong of back garden, scrambling over the wall. Suttle kicked hard at the door but it didn't budge. Shards of glass still in the frame tore at his clothing as he clambered through. Ewart was over the wall, gone.

Suttle jumped for a handhold, saw blood on the roughly plastered brickwork, realised that it was probably his own. At the top of the wall, wondering what had happened to the uniforms, he searched in vain for Ewart. Then he saw him. The basement flat next door must have been open. Still hooded, Ewart had taken a hostage. She was in her seventies at least, frail, bent, pale with shock. Ewart was standing behind her, one arm locked around her neck. In his other hand he had a knife.

Suttle dropped to the ground, wiped the worst of the blood on his trousers, approached the open back door. Ewart's hand was over the old woman's mouth. Her milky eyes were huge in her bony face. She looked terrified.

'Steady, mate.' Suttle was only feet from the back door now, his hands well away from his body, no threat. 'I'm a police officer. You haven't thought this through at all, have you?'

Ewart didn't answer. He was still panting from the climb, his face grey with exhaustion. He's been at the merchandise again, Suttle thought. Tosspot.

He inched closer, talking all the time, telling the old woman that it was going to be OK, no problem, that the lad was a bit upset about one or two things, that he'd come to his senses in just a minute, that soon it would all be over.

'Isn't that right, Karl?'

At the mention of his name, Ewart blinked. His head

went down for a moment and he seemed to waver. Stepping forward, Suttle seized this one opportunity, grabbed for the knife hand, twisted as hard as he could. The old woman began to scream and then Suttle was sideways on as the woman fell towards him. He tried to catch her, to protect her, and then he felt the blade in his own flesh, driving hard through the fold of muscle beneath his ribcage. It was a hot feeling, strange, not that painful, not at once, and he had time to register the old woman collapsing in a heap in the doorway and a blur of black uniform as someone large stepped over him, and then another figure, a face, bending over, very close, and a voice that seemed to get fainter and fainter, telling him to hang on, to get a grip, to stay conscious, telling him that everything was going to be OK.

Winter was reminiscing with his new colleague in the office. It turned out that Babs was a recent addition to the Intelligence team up at Havant, posted down to Major Crimes for the duration of both *Coppice* and *Tartan*. She'd come to police work relatively late, after a lengthy stint as a social worker in Leigh Park, and her brisk explanation of this unusual career move had made Winter laugh. After seven years running around after teenage mums and skagged-out junkies, wiping their arses and listening to how stressed they all were, she'd come to the conclusion that most of them needed locking up. Winter loved this kind of repartee, and they were busy swopping horror stories when the phone rang. Winter recognised the voice at once.

'Boss?'

Faraday was across at the Buckland Community Centre. He'd talked at length to the woman who had organised Duley's history workshop, and she'd given him a name.

'Kearns,' he said, 'Mickey Kearns.'

The name rang no bells with Winter.

'Who is he?'

'He seems to be tied up with one of the girls in the class. The woman says he picks her up sometimes from the Community Centre. Apparently he knew Duley, too. She'd seen them talking together, out in the street.'

'You want me to run a check?'

'Please.'

'Now?'

'Yes.'

Winter hit the PNC icon on his computer screen, typed in his pass code, and waited a few seconds before getting into the right field. Kearns raised several hits but none of them registered with the Christian name Michael.

'Could be a nickname,' Faraday said. 'What kind of ages are we talking?'

Winter scrolled quickly through. There wasn't a Kearns under thirty, and none lived closer than Gloucester.

'Try RMS then.'

Winter did his bidding. Babs had struggled to her feet and was standing at his shoulder. Seconds later, Winter had accessed the Records Management System. He typed in the name, sat back.

'Bingo, boss. Mickey Kearns. DOB 1979. That makes him twenty-five.'

'Perfect.'

'Buckland address too.' Winter read it out.

'What's he in there for?'

'Couple of cautions for suspected football violence . . . ' Winter was squinting at the screen ' . . . plus query narcotics.'

'Possession or supply?'

'Both. Amphetamine and cannabis but nothing nailed down.'

'Excellent. What are you doing at the moment?'

'Chatting Babs up.'

'I'll pick you up in five minutes. Be out the front, will you?'

Faraday had been parked up a while by the time Winter made it down to the forecourt. A single glance at the DC's face and Faraday killed the engine.

'What's the matter?'

'Ewart's done Jimmy Suttle, boss. Knifed him. They've taken Jimmy to QA. Ewart's down the Bridewell. Cunt.'

Faraday was out of the car. He tossed Winter the keys, told him to park it round the back. Then he was gone, running up the stairs to the big double doors and disappearing inside.

Winter got behind the wheel. At first he hadn't believed the news about Jimmy. Then, as it sank in, he felt chilled to the bone, swamped by a deep sense of impending doom. Not Jimmy, he thought. Not the cheerful face at his apartment door. Not the lad who bothered to concern himself with an overweight old bastard who'd necked too much Bacardi. Not the boy he'd come to think of as some kind of son. News, he thought numbly, couldn't get worse than this.

He started the car and began to back towards the entrance that led into the car park. Then he had second thoughts. By car, this time of day, the hospital was fifteen minutes away. Faraday would understand and even if he didn't, Winter didn't really care. He hadn't driven for over a year but he adjusted the rear-view mirror, found first gear, signalled right to filter into the traffic, amazed at how quickly it all came back. The lights, mercifully, were green. Turning left, he headed north.

The Incident Room was buzzing when Faraday made it to the second floor. The Outside Enquiries DS stood up when he walked in and drew Faraday aside.

'I've just had one of the uniforms on, sir,' he said. 'One of the guys we sent to Ashburton Road. They arrested Ewart in the house next door, took him down to the Bridewell. He's still—'

'What about Suttle?' Faraday cut in.

'The guy isn't sure. He managed to stop the blood loss but the paramedics were talking internal injuries.' The DS nodded down at his desk. 'I'm expecting a call from the hospital any time.'

'Do we have anyone up there with him?'

'No, sir. Not yet.'

'Organise it.'

Faraday left. Barrie's office, at the far end of the corridor, was empty. Faraday stuck his head round the door that belonged to the Management Assistants.

'Seen the boss?'

'He's up at Winchester, sir. Budget review.'

'When's he back?'

'He said five, earliest.'

'Shit.'

Faraday returned to the Incident Room. He wanted two DCs and a Tactical Interview Adviser standing by within the hour. He also wanted a full SOC team into Ewart's basement flat. In the meantime, if anyone needed him, he'd be at the hospital.

Faraday headed for the stairs, then had second thoughts. Winter, he knew, was close to Suttle. Better, he thought, to take him along as well. He put his head round Winter's door, finding Babs alone at her desk.

'Winter?' he queried.

'Haven't seen him, boss. Not since he went down to meet you.'

'Hasn't been back with any keys?'

'Afraid not.'

Faraday nodded, glanced at his watch, took the stairs to the back car park. Minutes later, still hunting for his Mondeo, he finally realised what must have happened.

'Shit,' he said again.

Winter left the Mondeo on a double yellow line within sight of the A & E entrance. He hurried up the slope towards the big glass doors, stepping round a mother with two squalling kids. At the reception desk he jumped the queue, thrusting his warrant card at the woman behind the PC.

'DC Winter,' he said. 'I'm after a lad called Jimmy Suttle.'

The woman nodded towards a pair of doors. 'Through there,' she said. 'Ask for Sister Barr.'

Winter pushed through the double doors. The first nurse he stopped went away to find the sister in charge. Minutes later, fearing the worst, Winter found himself in the cubbyhole she called her office.

Jimmy Suttle had been admitted over an hour ago. He'd briefly regained consciousness in the ambulance and been transfused with a plasma expander before arrival. By now, she said, he'd be on the operating table.

'But how is he?'

'Impossible to say, I'm afraid.'

'How did he look?'

'Poorly. I understand he'd been stabbed.'

'That's right. That's what they told us.'

'Then,' she tried to sound sympathetic, 'it's a question of where and how deep and whether or not anything really important got in the way. I simply can't help you, I'm afraid.' She got up, shepherding Winter back towards the waiting area. 'You're welcome to stay, of course. In fact you could give next-of-kin details to the front desk if you're a close friend. There's coffee from the machine by the door. Someone will come through for you once he's out of theatre.'

Winter nodded, mumbled his thanks. Back at the reception desk he scribbled down a contact in Major Crimes for a number for Suttle's mum, then found himself a seat tucked away in an area reserved for teenagers. This corner of the waiting room was empty. He settled himself beneath a poster warning of the dangers of cocaine abuse and stared at the wall opposite. He hated hospitals, loathed waiting about, but just now he was beyond getting angry. He sat for a while, his head back, his eyes closed, trying not to think of this morning, of Jimmy with his wet flannel and his wagging finger, of other times they'd shared together – jobs they'd done, corners they'd cut, the look on the lad's face when an especially cheeky move had taken a decent scalp. The boy was strong, he told himself. No God in his right mind would let him die. But then he thought about Joannie and this same hospital, these same smells, and the terrifying straightness of the line that led from admission to the worst news any man could ever hear. Would it be the same with Jimmy? Would there even be the time, the opportunity, to say goodbye?

Winter swallowed hard, fumbled blindly in his pocket for a Kleenex, felt tears welling behind his eyelids. Then came a voice he knew, very close, very soft.

'Paul? You OK?'

He opened his eyes. Faraday's face was a blur.

'Boss . . . ' he muttered. ' . . . What the fuck's going on?'

An hour and a half later, Winter got a cab home. He'd stayed long enough to hear the outcome from the operating theatre. Jimmy Suttle was still alive, but only just. His blood pressure was giving cause for concern and the next twenty-four hours would be critical. Ewart's thrust had sliced through the sheath of stomach muscle, missed his liver by millimetres, but wreaked havoc amongst the densely coiled loops of intestine below his belly. The surgeons had excised the worst of the damage, stitched the intact bits back together again, and given him a powerful dose of antibiotics to try and minimise the inevitable infection. With luck, the registrar had told Winter, the lad might survive, but it would be a while yet before he'd be in any kind of state to receive visitors.

Back at his apartment Winter sank onto the sofa. The sight of the teapot where Suttle had left it in the kitchen reduced him to tears again and he stared blankly at the darkening spaces of the harbour, knowing that there wasn't enough Scotch in the world to soften the news he was dreading. Would they phone if he died in the night? And would Winter be able to cope if they did?

He shook his head, knowing that this was the last place he wanted to be, alone with his misery. He studied the phone for a moment or two. The list of people he could call was pathetically short. He thought of Dawn Ellis, then shook his head. They'd been close in the past, and she was a nice kid, but he felt uneasy about bothering her, especially since she'd been part of the same incident. He thought, too, of Faraday. Up at the hospital, he hadn't even mentioned the Mondeo, even though Winter's parking had attracted the attention of the clampers. But no, he realised it couldn't be Faraday. For one thing the DI would be busy at the Bridewell, sorting Ewart out. And for another there was a limit to just how intimate you could be with your boss.

Winter got to his feet, utterly bereft. He wandered up and down the big living room for a while, toying with a handful of sleeping pills and an early night, but that – too – was less than perfect. He'd be awake by three, thinking too hard, listening for the phone, worrying himself to death. No, there had to be another solution, someone who'd pour beer down him, someone who knew a thing or two about how resilient the human body could be, someone he could trust to cheer him up. A name came to him and he paused, studying his own reflection in the big picture window. Of course, he thought.

Eight

The city's Bridewell, which also served as the central police station, was a low, unlovely brick-built establishment connected by an underground corridor to the nearby magistrates' courts. Holding cells housed newly arrested shoplifters, stroppy drunks on disorderly charges, and various other sweepings from the city's streets. Karl Ewart occupied Cell 6.

The Custody Sergeant was manning the desk when Faraday arrived. He confirmed that Ewart had been processed, fingerprinted, photographed and given access to the duty solicitor. He'd no visible injuries and an examination by the police surgeon had found nothing else amiss.

'Who's duty?'

'Michelle.' The Custody Sergeant nodded towards an office door. 'She's waiting for you now.'

Faraday nodded. Michelle Brinton was a plump, freckle-faced solicitor in her late thirties. Portsmouth had come as a bit of a shock after five years practising in her native Tavistock but she'd coped well with the ceaseless drumbeat of big-city crime, and won respect amongst the detectives who'd dealt with her.

She was on the phone when Faraday went into the office. She brought the conversation to a close. She knew Jimmy Suttle well.

'How is he?'

'Rough.'

'But he's going to pull through?'

155

'We hope so.' Faraday helped himself to the spare seat. 'You've talked to Ewart?'

'I have.'

'This thing is complicated. There's more to it than Jimmy. We've arrested him on suspicion of fraud as well as attempted murder. I've no idea whether he's discussed any of that with you.'

'He hasn't.'

'Well, maybe he should have done. There are implications we need to explore.'

'I'm sure.' She reached for a pen, scribbled herself a note. 'Fraud in connection with what, exactly?'

Faraday hesitated. He liked this woman but he owed Karl Ewart no favours.

'Pompey season tickets,' he said briskly. 'Bought on a nicked debit card. Face value, we're talking about a sum in excess of eight thousand. We think that's down to Ewart.'

'Would you care to tell me why?'

'I'm afraid not. Ewart is clearly a violent individual. He has some serious questions to answer.' Faraday checked his watch. 'I'll leave the rest to the interview team, if you don't mind.'

Winter's third call at last brought someone to the phone. A woman's voice, Pompey accent.

'Is Jake there?'

'He's in the shower. Just finished.'

'Tell him it's Paul.'

Winter hung onto the phone. In the background he could hear a television and the more distant yelling of kids. *EastEnders*, he thought.

'Mr W.?' It was Tarrant.

Winter was trying to visualise the scene. He knew nothing of Jake Tarrant's private life except the trio of faces in the small gold-framed photo he kept on his office desk. The kids must be nearly school age, Winter thought. His wife looked gorgeous.

'Jake. Listen, I know this is a bit sudden but I could really use another drink. On me, son. Or a meal, if you fancy it.'

'I've just eaten,' Tarrant said at once.

'Drink then?'

There was a pause. Tarrant clearly wasn't keen. Then he came back on the phone.

'What's this about?'

'Nothing, son. Me, if you want the truth.'

'You? How does that work?'

'It's complicated. Let's just say today's been a bummer. You know those days? Everything stacking up against you? Then something truly fucking horrible happening?' Winter paused. He realised he was sweating. 'Just a drink, son. I'd be grateful.'

'Sure. Hang on a moment.'

Winter heard a muffled conversation, a hint of raised voices, then Jake back on the phone again. This time he was laughing.

'Great idea, Mr W.' He named a pub. 'I could use a pint or two myself.'

By eight o'clock Faraday's interview team were ready for their first session with Karl Ewart. Both Dawn Ellis and Bev Yates had been on the *Tartan* squad from the start of the operation, and an hour with the Tactical Interview Adviser back at Kingston Crescent had given them a shape for their dealings with Ewart over the coming days. PACE legislation only permitted suspects to be held for twenty-four hours, but given the seriousness of the attack on Suttle, Faraday anticipated no problems with obtaining an extension, if he had to. Ewart, everyone seemed to agree, was a nutter.

The turnkey brought him along to the interview suite. A little under six feet, thin-faced, unshaven, he was wearing a pair of second-hand tracksuit bottoms and an oversized T-shirt supplied by the Custody Sergeant. The jeans, trainers and grey hoodie in which he'd been arrested, all splashed with fresh blood, had already been bagged up and sent away for forensic examination.

Faraday retired to a nearby room. A video feed supplied him with live pictures from the interview, and he settled at the desk with his pad and pencil, his eyes glued to the monitor on the wall. Both uniforms acting as backup in Ashburton Road had seen Ewart stab Suttle, and Dawn Ellis had managed to coax a supporting statement from the woman whom Ewart had so briefly taken hostage. On this evidence alone, Ewart was in deep, deep trouble.

The preliminaries were over. Time, date and attending personnel had been recorded by Yates at the head of the audio and video tapes, and Michelle Brinton had signalled her willingness to begin the interview. Ewart sat beside her, slumped in the chair, head down, picking his fingers. He might, thought Faraday, have been waiting for a bus.

Yates was asking Ewart to account for his movements over the course of the day. Ewart mumbled something about kipping at a mate's place.

'Where was that?'

Ewart shrugged. 'Can't remember.'

'You *can't remember*?'

'Up Stamshaw way. Only had it a couple of months.'

'Who only had it a couple of months?'

'Bloke that owns it.'

'Has he got a name?'

'Yeah, I expect so.'

'What is it?'

'Dunno.'

Faraday could see Yates gazing at the ceiling. He was losing his temper already. Not a good sign.

Dawn Ellis stepped in. She'd obviously sensed it too, and she took a different line, treating Ewart with cold indifference.

'Why weren't you staying at your own place, Mr Ewart?'

'I was pissed.'

'Too pissed to get a cab back?'

'No money. Skint, wasn't I?'

Ewart began a rambling account of people he had to catch up with, people who owed him money, people he could never find. Come the middle of the afternoon, knackered, he'd decided to go home for a kip.

'And then what?'

'I got back there. I told you, I wanted to get my head down. Then some geezer started knocking on the door. Wouldn't go away.'

'Who did you think he was?'

'Could have been anyone. How the fuck was I supposed to know?'

Ellis nodded. For obvious reasons, neither she nor Suttle had announced themselves. In retrospect, this might have been a mistake.

'Why didn't you answer the door?'

'Because you don't, do you? Not round where I live. There's all kinds of low life.'

'You're suggesting these people might want to do you harm?'

'Of course.'

'Why?'

For the first time his head came up and Faraday had a glimpse of the defence he was going to run. Obvious, he thought. But still shrewd.

'There's people out there I don't really want to see.'

'Why not?'

'Loads of reasons. Money, mostly.'

'You mean debts?'

'Yeah.'

'What kind of debts?'

'For stuff I've sold, like.'

'Stuff?'

'Drugs. Blow. Speed. These people can be crazy. You

don't want to fuck with them. Tear your head off as soon as look at you. Just think about it, yeah? I get some bloke banging at the door, next thing I know he's kicking it in. What would you do?'

'So what happened?'

'I grabbed a knife from the kitchen and got out the back.'

'Did you turn the gas on first?'

'I . . . ' He hesitated, looked away.

'Did you?'

'Yeah, I did.'

'Why?'

'Because . . . like I said . . . anything to put these animals off.'

'And the knife?'

'Same thing. These blokes can be a nightmare, really heavy. They come after you. And he did. Scared me shitless, if you really want to know. Over the wall I was, and away. Yeah?' He looked to his solicitor for confirmation, for approval of the sensible steps he'd taken. Michelle was making notes.

'You were in the next-door garden,' Ellis prompted. 'What happened next?'

Ewart faltered a moment, ducked his head. Then he described Suttle appearing at the top of the wall. Like he'd said, the geezer was coming after him.

'I panicked,' he said. 'Tell you the truth I hadn't a fucking clue what to do. The door was open. There was an old dear in there, an old lady . . . '

'And?'

'I grabbed her. I didn't know what I was doing. Like I said, I was bricking it. All I had was the old lady and the knife. Bloke could have done anything.'

Faraday, watching, shook his head. At this rate, they'd be awarding Ewart a medal for gallantry.

Ellis pointed out that Suttle had identified himself as a policeman.

'Yeah?'

'You don't remember?'

'I don't remember anything. He might have said it, might not, but what difference does it make? He didn't have a uniform on. Any cunt can say he's a policeman. It means fuck all.'

Yates was stirring again. He wanted to get this over, Faraday thought. He wants to dispense with the questions, with the lies, with this whole unfolding pantomime. He wants to lean across, grab Ewart by the throat and batter him senseless.

The interview went on. When Ellis mentioned the two uniforms who had appeared in the back garden, he said he hadn't seen them. By that time, he insisted, Suttle was trying to attack him and he'd simply been defending himself. Stabbing the bloke had been a reflex, blind panic, him or me, nothing else. Of course he was sorry about what happened, anyone would be, but it wasn't his fault, he hadn't started it.

There was a long silence. Yates stirred.

'So that's it then? Self-defence?'

'Yeah.'

'You'd no idea this bloke was a copper?'

'No.'

'Even though he told you he was, identified himself?'

Ewart shrugged then smothered a yawn. At length, Ellis changed tack.

'There's a girl called Emma Cusden. She lives in Somerstown. She's got a flat in a block called Hermiston House. We understand you know her.'

'Who told you that?'

'Social Services. One of their people came round to see you.'

'Yeah? What of it?'

'This person wanted to talk to you about young Cher. Your daughter.'

'Yeah?'

'She *is* your daughter?'

Ewart held her gaze for a moment, then looked

sideways at Michelle. The solicitor murmured something in his ear.

'That's right,' he agreed at last. 'She's my little girl.'

'And you're round there a lot, at Emma's place?'

'A bit.'

'A bit then.'

'Yeah.'

Ellis glanced across at Yates. Yates produced a copy of Givens' bank statement, went through the transactions one by one, piling up the season tickets until the account was nearly empty.

'That's over eight grand,' he said. 'On someone else's debit card. Most juries would call that theft.'

'What's that got to do with me?'

'All those tickets went to Emma's address. Someone was picking them up to flog on. And now, guess what, we find a couple in your place. In the name of Givens. With your prints all over them. We've also found nearly fifteen hundred quid in notes. How do you account for all that? When you're supposed to be so skint?'

'It's not mine. It's got fuck all to do with me.'

'Someone else's, then?'

'Yeah, must be.'

'One of your flatmates?'

'Dunno.'

'They say not.'

'Surprise, surprise.'

'You're telling me they're lying?'

Ewart was picking his fingers again. When Yates put the question a second time, he simply shrugged.

'Dunno,' he said. 'Haven't a clue.'

Ellis muttered something in Yates' ear. Yates ignored her. Watching, Faraday was aware that this interview was going far too fast. The challenge phase, finger-pointing, should come later, once Ewart had been given the chance to make his case.

Yates didn't take his eyes off Ewart.

'We've got guys in your flat are gonna tear the place apart,' he said at length. 'What happens when they find Givens' debit card? With more of your prints? What will you say then?'

Again, Ewart had no answer. He looked helplessly at his solicitor. She began to protest that this was pure speculation, that no debit card had yet been found, but Yates was angrier than ever. He was leaning forward now, inches from Ewart's face.

'That card came from a bloke we can't find,' he said softly. 'He's just disappeared, vanished, gone. People don't do that, Mr Ewart, not in the real world. Something has to happen to them. Someone has to take them out.'

Ewart was starting to put it together. 'Fuck off, mate.' He sounded indignant. 'You think I did that?'

'Did what?'

'Rolled this bloke, whoever he is? Gave him a slapping?'

'Yes.' Yates nodded. 'We do. In fact we think you killed him.'

'*Killed* him? You have to be joking. You really think I'd do a thing like that?'

'We know you would, Karl.' It was Ellis. 'We saw what you did to DC Suttle.'

Michelle was on her feet now. She wanted to bring this interview to an end. Her client had been arrested on suspicion of attempted murder and fraud. He was denying the fraud and claiming self-defence with respect to the stabbing. No way should these accusations extend to killing someone else. She reached down for Ewart's arm but he shook her off. This was personal. Him and Yates. He sounded genuinely outraged.

'Yeah, but . . . but that was different. I just told you . . . He came after me . . . I didn't know him from fuck. Listen . . . *killed* him? This other bloke? You have to be out of your mind. What the fuck would I do with him for starters?'

'You'd put him in that car of yours,' Yates said. 'Then you'd get rid of him. Only that would be a bit of a problem afterwards, wouldn't it? All that blood in the boot? Other stuff we might find . . . ?'

He let the thought dangle a moment. Michelle, with some reluctance, had resumed her seat. When she leant towards Ewart and told him that he didn't have to answer any of these questions, he dismissed her advice with a terse shake of the head. Faraday, watching, bent towards the screen. Michelle was right. There could be repercussions here. Without a formal caution over Givens' disappearance, any admissions on Ewart's part would be inadmissible in court.

'The motor's history,' Ewart said at last. 'Some fucker . . . '

'Some fucker what?'

'Nicked it.'

'Oh yeah?' Yates was grinning at him now. 'Not you then? Not you with half a gallon of four star and a box of matches?'

Ewart was in trouble, and he knew it.

'Listen –' He was beginning to sweat. '– This is well out of order. So yeah, I'm a bad boy. I do drugs. I get about a bit. I buy and sell. And yeah, you're gonna do me for the copper. OK, fair play, but killing some bloke I've never heard of? You're out of your head.'

'What about the season tickets?'

Ewart stared at Yates, then his head went down again and he finally beckoned Michelle closer, whispering in her ear. She muttered something in return, then turned her attention back to the DCs across the table.

'This is completely irregular,' she said. 'If you want to talk to my client about this so-called missing person, then you must caution him in that regard. Otherwise, I must insist that you limit this interview to the matter in hand.' She stared at Yates, colour flooding into her face. Then she got up again. 'I and my client would like a break. Can we all cope with that?'

Winter was pissed again. He'd taken a cab out to the Copnor pub that Tarrant had named for their get-together, and he'd swallowed a couple of Stellas and two whisky chasers by the time Tarrant finally turned up. Tarrant apologised for the delay. Mate of his on the phone. Long time no hear.

Now, nearly two hours later, Winter had abandoned any hope of making it to the bar. Instead, he pushed a ten-pound note towards Tarrant and told him to sort another round. Peanuts would be good too. Winter was famished.

Tarrant did his bidding. He was drinking halves of shandy, blaming a course of antibiotics he'd just started, but he'd been more than happy to listen to Winter's account of what had happened down in Southsea and to sympathise. These days, he said, there were bits of the city you'd be mad to risk after dark. Even in broad daylight, like with Suttle, you could knock on the wrong door and find yourself looking at a knife.

'But it wasn't the wrong door, mate. It was the *right* fucking door. That's the whole point. There was a time when it would all have been sweet. You do your homework, you box a guy off, he knows he's potted, and there he is, fetching his coat, nice as pie. You know what that was about? Respect. Rules. That's all gone though. Fucking history. Scrotes like Ewart are vermin. There's nothing to them. They'd stick you as soon as look at you. And for what? *Season* tickets? For *Pompey*?'

'I thought you said he was down for Givens too?'

'I did, son.' Winter reached for his brimming glass, and missed. 'You're right.'

'So what's the strength?'

'One hundred fucking per cent. Has to be.' Winter

began to tally the counts against Ewart on his fingers. 'Number one, he did the bloke's bank account. Clean as a whistle. Number two, he's been fencing all those tickets, stands to reason. Number three, he's torched his own fucking car to bury the evidence. And number four . . . ' He frowned, staring at his hand. ' . . . He's a murdering cunt.'

'How do you figure that, Mr W.?'

'Because he's just done Jimmy.' He peered at Tarrant. 'Haven't you listened to a single fucking word I've said, son? Jimmy's dead, or near on. Jimmy, my mate Jimmy. Name mean nothing to you?' He gestured vaguely at the empty glasses on the table. 'Or has your memory gone?'

Tarrant leaned forward, put his hand on Winter's.

'Mr W., Paul . . . I'm really, really sorry. I know him too. He used to come round the mortuary sometimes when we were doing the business. He's a good lad – funny, made us all laugh. Listen. He's in good hands. I know the blokes up at QA. If anyone's going to sort him out, they will. Trust me. Believe me. He'll pull through.'

Winter leaned into the table. He wanted desperately to believe this man. His spare hand closed over Tarrant's.

'No bullshit?' His eyes were glassy. 'You think Jimmy'll make it?'

'I know he will.'

'You promise?'

'Scout's honour.'

'You're a good lad.' He gave Tarrant's hand a little squeeze. 'A good mate. What's that wife of yours think, me dragging you out like this?'

'She wasn't best pleased if you want the truth, Mr W.'

'Call me Paul.'

'Paul.'

'Bit difficult is it? Young kids? All that broken sleep? Not enough . . . you know . . . action?'

Tarrant gazed at him a moment, then laughed.

'Yeah. Spot on, Mr W. Action pretty much covers it. Maybe I should tell her that. More action. What do you think?'

'Me? What do *I* think? I think you're bloody lucky. She's a looker, isn't she? What's her name?'

'Rachel.'

'Rachel.' Winter was peering round, as if she might be sitting at a nearby table. 'Rachel. You known her long, young Rachel?'

'I'm married to her.'

'Of course you are, son. Of course you are. Makes sense now. That photo on your desk. Blonde hair. Nice lips. Am I right?'

'Yeah.' Tarrant nodded. 'And funny too, when she's in the mood.'

'Mood. That's it, isn't it? Gotta catch 'em. Gotta recognise it. Gotta be there. Yeah . . . ' he nodded ' . . . when they're in the mood.'

Winter reached for the peanuts, tried to open the packet with his teeth, failed. Tarrant did it for him, emptying a handful onto the table. Winter peered at them for a moment.

'You happy then?' He looked up. 'With your Rachel?'

'Most of the time, yeah.'

'And what about her? She happy with you? Only you know what it is about these things . . . ' He waved a limp hand, scattering the nuts. 'When you're married.'

'Yeah, I do. You've been there, Mr W. You'd know about it, too.'

'Paul.'

'Paul.'

'Yeah, too right. You wanna word of advice? About Rachel? Look after her, son. Be nice to her. A good woman is worth more than anything else in the world. Doesn't matter what you have to do, what it costs, any of that bollocks. If she's as nice as she looks, you'd do anything, wouldn't you?'

'Yeah.' Tarrant was smiling again. 'I would.'

'Good lad.' Winter tried to retrieve a peanut from the carpet. Tarrant rescued the table as he struggled upright again. Winter found another peanut, his lap this time, and held it between his finger and his thumb. 'Dinnertime,' he mumbled, popping it in his mouth.

He looked round. The pub was beginning to empty. Tarrant had already volunteered to get him safely home.

'What's that?' Winter wanted to know.

'It's a mobile, Mr W. I'm calling a cab.'

The interview at the Bridewell began again. Michelle Brinton, tight-lipped, announced that her client was now prepared to admit fraudulent use of the debit card in addition to stabbing DC Suttle in self-defence, but still insisted that he'd had nothing to do with whatever had happened to the owner of the card. If they wanted to extend their area of interest to the Missing Person, there were procedures to go through. Yates, who'd conferenced with Faraday during the break, now rearrested Ewart on suspicion of murder and read him the formal caution. Watching the video feed from the adjoining room, Faraday anticipated the interview hitting the buffers. Ewart would go No Comment. Bound to. He was wrong.

'You say you had nothing to do with the owner of this debit card.' Yates was looking across the table at Ewart. 'How do we know that?'

'Because it's fucking true,' he mumbled.

'Prove it.'

'Yeah? What if it means grassing someone else up?'

'Someone who did the owner?'

'Someone who sold me the card.'

'And who might that be?'

Ewart looked from one face to the other. His choice couldn't have been plainer, Faraday thought. Either he comes up with a name or he's facing a potential murder charge.

'A kid found a wallet,' Ewart said at last.

'Where?'

'The newsagent in Somerstown. It was on the floor, he said. Down by the magazines.'

'Whose wallet was it?'

'Same bloke. This Givens. Apparently there was sixty quid in cash in it, plus some other stuff, including the card. The kid had the notes away but couldn't do anything with the card.'

'No PIN?'

'No.'

'So what happened?'

'I got the card off him. Ten quid.'

'And what's his name, this kid?'

There was a long silence. Ewart summoned the grace to look troubled but Faraday hadn't got the slightest doubt that he'd already made the decision.

'You going to tell me or what?' Yates was getting impatient again.

'This is fucking suicide,' Ewart said. 'You know that?'

'Yeah.' Yates nodded. 'Here's hoping.'

'Wanker.'

Yates, enraged, was getting to his feet. Ellis restrained him.

'The name,' she said wearily. 'Just give us the bloody name.'

Jake Tarrant rode back to Gunwharf with Winter. The cab dropped them both at Blake House and Tarrant told the driver to wait while he took Winter upstairs. Winter was weaving towards the harbourside walkway that skirted the front of the residential area. Tarrant had to run to catch up with him.

'The view . . . ' Winter wanted to share it.

Tarrant hooked an arm under his, steered him gently round, headed back towards the looming apartment block.

'You've got a key, Mr W.?'

Winter didn't seem to understand the question. He wanted Jake to be sweet with Rachel. He wanted everything to be sweet.

Tarrant found the keys in Winter's jacket pocket. The biggest one opened the doors to the lobby.

'Which floor?'

'Up.' Winter waved vaguely at the recessed lights in the ceiling.

Tarrant wrestled him into the lift, his finger hovering over the buttons by the door.

'First? Second? Third? Top?'

'Whatever.' Winter was looking troubled. 'Did I tell you about Jimmy?'

'Yeah, Mr W. Real shame, eh?'

The last time they'd met, Winter had been banging on about the best view in the building so Tarrant gambled on the top floor. Coming out of the lift, he propped Winter against the wall, then went from door to door, trying the key in each. In the last door the key turned. Inside, fumbling for the light, he could smell the familiar aftershave.

Back beside Winter, he managed to manoeuvre him down the tiny hall and into the lounge. The sight of his own four walls appeared to take Winter by surprise. He looked round, said he wanted a drink.

'Bacardi,' he mumbled. 'Try the fridge.'

Tarrant had found the master bedroom. He put on the lights, pulled the curtains, helped a protesting Winter towards the big double bed. Winter gazed down at it a moment, then slowly folded onto the floor.

Tarrant stood over him. Next week, he told Winter,

he'd be back at work. It was important he had it right about Alan Givens. People should know. People should be told.

'Told what, son?'

'Told that he's dead.'

'Yeah, of course.'

'So he *is* dead? You're sure about that? Only he was a mate of mine, sort of. We worked together. St Mary's. The hospital. You remember all that, Mr W.?'

Winter peered up at him.

'You're a good lad, son.'

'We're talking about Givens.'

'We are?'

'That's right.' Tarrant was kneeling now, slipping a pillow beneath Winter's head. 'And you told me that Givens had been killed. By this Ewart bloke. Am I right?'

Winter nodded, his eyes beginning to close. Then he reached up and found Tarrant's hand.

'Yeah,' he murmured peaceably. 'Dead fucking right.'

Faraday drove Dawn Ellis back to Kingston Crescent. It was nearly midnight. Karl Ewart had been formally charged with attempted murder and credit card fraud and would be appearing in front of the magistrates first thing Monday morning.

'What do you think?'

'I think the man's a complete arsehole. I think I need a shower.'

'About this Dale Cummings?'

'Don't know, boss. Don't even know if it makes any difference. He's going down anyway, isn't he?'

Faraday was still waiting for the lights to change. They not only had Dale Cummings' name but his Somerstown address as well. At nine years old, young Dale was still living with his mum.

'But you believe him?' He glanced across at Ellis. 'You think it happened the way Ewart described?'

Ellis didn't answer. She'd been with Jimmy Suttle only hours ago. Like everyone else on Major Crimes, she had a soft spot for the lad. He had prospects, no question, but he was a lovely bloke as well. Ellis turned her head away, stared out at the parade of darkened shops that led to Kingston Crescent. A drunk was pissing against a window full of prams. He gave her a little wave as they drove by.

'Well?' Faraday still wanted an answer.

Ellis was about to say something sensible about waiting for further evidence, about getting alongside the lad and his mum, about testing Ewart's story the way she knew they had to, but then she shook her head.

'You know what I really think, boss?' She closed her eyes. 'I think I really don't care.'

Nine

'Suttle?'

It was Martin Barrie's first question. The Detective Superintendent, much to his wife's annoyance, had been at his desk since before eight. Saturdays, as she'd acidly pointed out, used to be family time.

'He came through the op, sir. But I still get the impression it's touch and go. He's in Critical Care at the moment. Liable to be there some time.'

Faraday had been onto the hospital first thing. Suttle was still gravely ill but in one sense it seemed he'd been extremely lucky. Had the knife penetrated a millimetre or two deeper, Ewart would already be facing a murder charge.

'Card? Flowers? Anyone organising anything?'

'A card went round last night, sir. We'll get it up to the hospital today.'

'Hmm . . . ' Barrie frowned. 'What about Ewart?'

Faraday talked Barrie through the interview at the Bridewell. He was outlining the steps he'd need to take to interview Dale Cummings when Barrie interrupted. The news about Suttle had clearly shaken him.

'There's a problem, isn't there Joe?'

'I'm sorry, sir?'

'With Suttle. The way I see it, he's chasing this man Ewart. Ewart takes a hostage. He has a knife. The situation can kick off in any direction. There are procedures here. Suttle should have been aware of that.'

'I'm sure DC Suttle did what he thought best at the

173

time, sir,' Faraday said woodenly. 'He saw a direct threat to the woman's life and moved to intervene.'

'But it could have been her, Joe. Once it all kicked off, she could have been the one who was stabbed.'

'But it wasn't, sir. It was Jimmy. And he's lucky to be alive.'

'Of course.' Barrie waved a hand over the paperwork on his desk. 'You know that, I know that. Whether the Chief will see it the same way remains to be seen. Suttle's come very close to getting himself killed and our friends at headquarters will want to know why. You know how these things go. The lad could end up with a commendation or a kick up the arse. For my money, given the circumstances, he'll probably give the boy his rightful due. What do you think?'

'About the Chief?'

'About Suttle. About what he did. About the decision he took.'

'I applaud it.'

'Really?'

'Yes, sir. He took the responsibility. I'm not sure we could have asked more of him.'

'Would you call that good judgement?'

'I'd call it courage –' He paused. '– Sir.'

Faraday was fighting to contain his anger. Barrie was right, of course. In the inevitable debrief there'd be issues about risk assessment, about recklessness, about the needless hazarding of life and limb. Play it by the book, and Suttle should have backed off, called for assistance, summoned the cavalry. A minute's chase would have turned into a full-blown siege. TV would have arrived. For a brief moment of time Ashburton Road would have entertained the entire nation.

'So what do you want me to do, sir,' Faraday asked quietly, 'after I give Jimmy our best?'

'Nothing, Joe. The case file should give us all the facts, and once that's complete we have to leave it to the Chief's review. This is just a heads-up, that's all.

You're right. Suttle was a brave lad. He took a split-second decision and paid the price. But we want him coming out of this with a commendation, not a disciplinary hearing. Suttle will obviously be making a statement, God willing. Just let me know when it's available. Eh?'

'Of course, sir.'

Faraday nodded, still seething. He knew he shouldn't be the least surprised at the games they were obliged to play these days but he was still a working copper and he resented the time he wasted feeding the monster that the last decade of policing seemed to have created. Nicking the bad guys wasn't enough anymore. The buzzword that earned you the real brownie points was accountability. Every decision had to be justified and re-justified. Everything had to be transparent. The general public, even toerags like Ewart, had – by some strange political sleight of hand – become customers. Maybe Jimmy Suttle should have stayed on the other side of the wall, thought Faraday grimly. Maybe he'd been rash to even knock on Ewart's door.

Barrie had already moved on. *Tartan*, in his view, could be safely left to bubble on the stove. Karl Ewart would doubtless be remanded by the magistrates, giving Faraday's team plenty of time to explore his connections with the disappearance of Alan Givens. Operation *Coppice*, on the other hand, was going to need a hefty stir or two. Over the weekend Barrie had reduced the staffing but Monday would see a new start.

'Mr Willard's coming over this morning. Did you know that?'

'No, sir.'

'It seems there's media interest in Mr Duley. We need to be on top of the game.' He reached for his Rizlas. 'So what do we tell him?'

Faraday summarised progress to date. In the shape of Duley, they had a name and a focus. They also had evidence that put him in the plantation beside the railway line. The tread pattern on the tyre imprints had been identified but the makers sold hundreds of thousands of these things a year and the casts were of little use until they had a vehicle. Mrs Cleaver, at the top of the track from the plantation, had heard a car leaving in the middle of the night, heading south. Faraday's presumption had the vehicle returning to Portsmouth, but enquiries thrown up by the CCTV footage had produced no hits so far. Intelligence was still trying to source the padlock, chain and bits of rope but all three items were far too common to offer the prospect of a speedy result.

'Which leaves us with Mr Duley.'

'Exactly, sir.'

'Motivation?'

'Winter thinks we should be looking hard at Venezuela.'

'So I gather. You agree?'

'Yes. To be frank, sir, we haven't got much else. The man was a loner. Politically, he seems to have put himself around a bit, in fact a lot, but I get the sense that he never hung around for very long.'

'No friends? No one close?'

'Not really. Winter's been going through his address book. The man attracted a lot of attention but we haven't been able to find anyone really special, not so far anyway.'

'Mobile?'

'We haven't found one so far but we've got a number for Duley from a couple of sources. Winter's put it through the TIU. We haven't had a response yet.'

The Telephone Intelligence Unit was the force's single point of contact with the phone companies. Billing and cell site enquiries could take weeks to process.

'What about the postcard you showed me? *Querida*?'

'That's still a bit of a mystery. *Querida* is Spanish. It

means lover or loved one. It's female, not male. But why is he sending it to his own address?'

'Because someone would pick it up.'

'But they didn't. And no one in the rest of the place seems to have seen anyone.'

'Did you fingerprint it?'

'Yes, sir. One set. His own.'

Barrie nodded. 'So you think he might have sent it to himself? Is that what you're saying?'

'Yes. Either that or it's part of some game. We just don't know.'

'You think that's odd?'

'I think it's unusual but in a way, sir, it might fit. Odd's a good word.'

'You think Duley was odd?'

'Yes.'

'In what sense?'

'I think he was reckless. I think he was a bit of an exhibitionist. And I think he had a lot to get off his chest. This is a man who moved at the speed of light, complete dervish, blink twice and you've lost him. Like I say, odd. Definitely a one-off.'

Barrie studied Faraday for a moment.

'Why reckless? How does that work?'

'Well, sir, physically reckless to begin with. It's there in his record. The big demos. The arrests for affray. Nothing seemed to frighten him, certainly not the likes of us. Then there's something else too. The way I see it, Duley was a kind of all-or-nothing guy. When he went for something – a cause, say – he went for it one thousand per cent, nothing withheld, nothing in reserve. You know what I mean?'

'Carpet bombing.'

'Exactly. We were talking to the guy who organises Respect. He said that Duley had tremendous energy but he also had a mouth on him. He'd wear you out. If you're running some kind of political campaign, that can obviously be useful, but there's a downside, too.

Like I said, Duley didn't seem to win himself many friends.'

'Sure.' Barrie nodded. 'So how does all of that link to Venezuela?'

'I'm not sure. He led a local history workshop down the road in Buckland. I went down there yesterday, talked to the woman who runs it. It turns out that Duley had become a bit of a star. He speaks a couple of languages and she thinks he might have got himself tied up with a local lad who needed someone who spoke Spanish. She wasn't sure about the details but she gave me another name, a girl in the class who might know more. It's down as an action. We'll be onto it.'

'This lad ... ' Barrie was interested now. ' ... You've got a name?'

'Kearns. Mickey Kearns. He's known to us already. Football violence and suss supply.'

'So who's chasing it?'

'It's with the Outside Enquiry Team. They went to his address this morning but no luck. His mum said he was off somewhere.'

'Like where?'

'She said she didn't know. He comes and goes. Par for the course, apparently.'

'You think he really lives there?'

'I doubt it. We're asking around.'

'Hmm ... ' Barrie glanced at his watch. 'You know what I think?'

'What, sir?'

'I think we should put Winter onto it.' He smiled. 'Cut him loose.'

Winter followed the instructions from the pretty receptionist on the front desk, hurrying down the wide central corridor, keeping his eye on the overhead signs. Mr Suttle, she said, was in the Department of Critical Care, up on the third floor.

The lift to the third floor was a squeeze. An elderly

woman was lying on a trolley with her eyes closed. She had a drip in her arm and her thin, white-shrouded body told Winter she was half-dead already. The hospital porter standing beside her was staring into nowhere as the lift groaned upward and Winter was glad when the doors finally opened again and he could slip away. His memory of last night was far from perfect but he was mildly surprised he didn't feel a great deal worse.

The Department of Critical Care turned out to be two open wards with side rooms for solo occupancy. Winter recognised the woman sitting outside in the corridor at first glance. The same reddish curls. The same light blue eyes. Even the same frown lines when she looked puzzled.

'Mrs Suttle?'

She was gazing up at the outstretched hand. Winter introduced himself, said he was a good friend of young Jimmy's, tried not to breathe last night's Stella all over her.

'You've seen the boy?' She nodded. 'How is he?'

'Terrible.' Her lips began to pucker. 'They're keeping him under sedation. He's got tubes coming out of everywhere, drips. I'm sure they're doing their best but . . . ' She shook her head.

Winter looked around. There were eight beds in the nearest ward.

'Is he in there?'

'Yes. It's the second bed in on the left. You'd never recognise him.'

Winter peered in. She was right. All he could see was the outline of a body in the bed, the upper half hidden by a thicket of tubes. Winter asked about getting into the ward. Could he just walk in? Would anyone mind?

'I don't know. I think the doctor's coming back in a minute. Maybe you should see what he says first.'

With some reluctance, Winter agreed. While he waited, he wandered along the corridor, back towards the lift. Trying to take his mind off the implications of the impending conversation, he sent Jake Tarrant a text. 'FOB says thanks for getting me home,' he wrote. Minutes later, a reply arrived: 'FOB?' Winter looked down at it. 'Fat old bastard,' he messaged back. Jake countered within seconds. 'No problem, mate,' he wrote. 'Any time, U FOB.'

Winter gazed at the text. Good lad, he thought. Thank Christ someone's got a sense of humour.

There was still no sign of the doctor. Winter pocketed the mobile, muttered something about being up against the clock and stepped into the ward. Suttle's name was on the sheaf of charts clipped to the foot of the bed. The sheet was tented over his lower body, only his head, shoulders and arms visible against the whiteness of the pillow. A tube taped to his mouth fed him air from a ventilator at the bedside and Winter counted four drips into his neck and upper arm. He was very pale. All the colour seemed to have drained from his face, even the freckles, and there was a hint of swelling under one eye. His eyes were shut, and as Winter watched he thought he caught a tiny tremble of movement under one eyelid. The boy's dreaming, he thought. There must be hope.

At length, a nurse appeared. Startled to find a visitor at Suttle's bedside, she asked Winter what he was up to.

'I just wanted to see him, make sure he was still with us.' Winter spared her a glance. 'Is that OK?'

'Are you family?'

'Close friend.'

'Does his mum know you're here?'

'Yes.' Winter was still staring down at Suttle. 'Gonna be all right, is he?'

'Once we sort his blood pressure out, he should be fine. It's just time, really. Time and rest.'

'What's this lot then?' Winter gestured at the drips.

'Blood and fluids to keep him hydrated.'

'And these two?'

'Analgesic. Plus a sedative for the ventilator.'

'Is that why he's out for the count?'

'Yes. If you're after a conversation, I'm afraid it could be a bit of a wait.'

Winter nodded. Suttle's hand felt warm beneath his.

'You're not bullshitting me, are you?' he said softly, his eyes never leaving Suttle's face.

The nurse took his hand away, then smoothed a rumple on the sheet.

'Are you talking to me or him?' she enquired drily.

Back outside the ward, Winter rejoined Suttle's mum in the waiting room. She'd been watching Winter from the corridor. An audience of stuffed toys on the table in the corner gave the conversation a slightly unreal air.

'What did that nurse say to you?'

'She said the boy was going to be fine. He's just a bit knackered at the moment.'

'She said that?' Her eyes were moist.

'More or less.' Winter wanted to put an arm round her. 'But he'll be OK, I know it.'

'Says who?'

'Me.'

'But how can you be so sure?'

'Because he just has to be. That's all.'

She nodded, trying to digest this latest piece of news, then she fumbled for a Kleenex.

'You know something? I never wanted him to be a policeman.'

'I'm not surprised.'

'And you know something else? Nothing I'd say would make a blind bit of difference.'

'I know how you feel.' Winter's mobile began to trill. 'He never listens to me either.' Winter smiled at her, then stepped outside to take the call.

'Paul?' It was Faraday. 'Where are you? We need to meet.'

At Winter's suggestion, Faraday came to Gunwharf. From the apartment, Winter watched him emerge from the big underground car park and make his way across the ribbon of water that separated the residents from the riff-raff who crowded the nearby shopping malls at the weekend. The weather was beautiful, almost too hot for Winter's comfort, and Faraday had hooked his jacket over his shoulder as he strolled across towards the apartment block.

Over the last twenty-four hours, with Jimmy close to death, Winter had begun to warm to Faraday. He'd never had any doubts about the man's effectiveness as a detective. Unlike many DIs Winter had worked with, Faraday knew his business and held his ground. But there'd always been an apartness about him, a sense that something walled him off, and Winter – who knew a great deal about the solitary life – had always found Faraday a bit of a frustration.

Once, not so long ago, a newish DC had described him as a space cadet. That had been completely out of order because the detective in question would never hold a candle to Faraday, but at the same time Winter knew exactly what the spotty youth had meant. Faraday, with his beard and his bird books, wasn't quite there. You saw the label on the box, you opened it up, but what you got wasn't a detective at all, not in the usual sense. No, what you got was a real loner, a man much like Winter himself – no real friends, no real appetite for all that chummy bollocks – but a man who somehow lacked the buccaneering spark of mischief that made life in the job so bearable.

As a result, Faraday could often seem detached, humourless, even cold, but yesterday up at the hospital he'd been a real brick. Most blokes Winter knew would have gone ballistic at the sight of a hefty bill to get their clamped motor back, but Faraday hadn't even mentioned it. Not only that, but he seemed equally oblivious of the fact that Winter had been driving the Mondeo without even a valid licence.

'Coffee, boss?' Winter had the pot on.

Faraday grunted a yes, still touring the apartment at Winter's invitation.

'Bloody palace,' he said, stepping back into the big lounge. 'Bit of a change from Bedhampton, eh?'

Winter nodded. The longer he stayed in Gunwharf, he told Faraday, the more he began to wonder about the rest of his life. Why hadn't he moved earlier? What was so bloody special about net curtains and a 120-foot garden he could never keep under bloody control?

'Habit.' Faraday was standing at the window, enjoying the view. 'Truth is, we're all bone idle.'

Winter came in with the coffee. Faraday wanted to know more about Suttle. Winter put a smile on his face and told him the boy was going to be fine. Faraday saw through the fiction at once.

'How is he really?'

'Dodgy. Tell you the truth, boss, he looks half dead already. It has to get better than this. Has to.'

'Did you talk to anyone?'

'Yeah. But they're all born liars, aren't they?'

'But they know, Paul. They do. Give the lad a couple of months and he'll be back at Kingston Crescent with a war story for the girlies and a big fat cheque from the Criminal Injuries Board. You know the way it goes.'

'I do?'

'Of course you do. And a damn sight better than most. He could have been facing brain surgery. Ever think of it that way?'

'Christ, no. Brain surgery was a doddle compared to what Jimmy's going through. What happened to Ewart last night?'

'Held his hands up.'

'I'm not surprised. Three witnesses and you try and do a copper? The bloke should be put down. What about Givens? Did he cop to doing him too?'

'No.' Faraday shook his head. 'He says he bought the card off a Somerstown lad. Even gave us a name.'

'Really?' Winter reached for the coffee pot. 'And we believe him?'

'Don't know. I've asked Dawn Ellis to do the business. He's nine years old. Don't hold your breath.'

Winter nodded, shaking his head. Whichever direction this conversation took, he couldn't rid himself of the image of Jimmy Suttle's pale chest rising and falling in time with the ventilator at his bedside. A flick of a switch, Winter thought, and the boy would drift away.

'*Coppice*,' Faraday began. 'Barrie's got the wind in his sails. A couple of the London tabloids have picked up on Duley, and Willard's after a headline or two.'

'Meaning what?' Winter tried his best to concentrate.

'Meaning Barrie wants to escalate the operation. *Tartan*'s on hold for the time being until Ellis sorts out the Somerstown lad. As far as *Coppice* is concerned, we're talking a bigger enquiry team. You'll be pleased to know that includes you.'

'I get to leave the office?'

'On specific actions, yes.'

'Like?'

'Mickey Kearns. The address on file turns out to belong to his mother. She says she hasn't seen him for a while but there's a young lady in Duley's history workshop who might be able to help us. I got her details yesterday. Apparently she's close to Kearns. She also thought the world of Duley so she might take us somewhere useful. It's certainly worth a try.'

'And that's down to me?'

'Yeah.' Faraday smiled. 'I'd love to tell you all this is my idea but I'd be lying. Blame Mr Barrie.'

With Faraday gone, Winter pondered the implications of this latest development. Under normal circumstances he'd have been over the moon at the prospect of getting out and about again, but these weren't normal circumstances. However hard he tried, this morning's visit to the hospital lay like a cloud over everything. Jimmy could still die. Easily. That kind of injury could wreck your plumbing, send all kinds of shit swilling round your insides, and even a gallon of antibiotics might not keep the resulting infection in check. Your temperature would nudge upwards, then gallop away, and before anyone could raise a finger to help, Jimmy would be spark out, an empty sack of bones connected to the bellows at his bedside.

Winter contemplated the prospect, then shook his head in disgust. Last night's gutful, he decided, hadn't done him any good at all. What he owed Jimmy was a bit of optimism, a bit of faith. Over the last couple of years he'd made a decent start on teaching the lad everything he knew about nicking the bad guys and just now was no time to chuck the towel in. If Jimmy was here, he thought, he'd want me out there, belling a few contacts, cupping an ear, listening to the Pompey tom-toms. It was Saturday night, for God's sake, the perfect opportunity to wade back into the swamp, and as he contemplated the prospect, he began to cheer up.

He thought for a moment about the woman in Duley's history workshop. Her name was Donna Werbinski, and Faraday had made it plain that he wanted some kind of result by tomorrow. That wouldn't be a problem but Winter knew that these conversations always profited from a little prior know-ledge. Personally, Winter had never heard of Mickey Kearns and before he talked to young Donna he really ought to rectify that.

His first call, he thought, would go to a serial grass called Sammy Lewington. Lewington knew everyone who had a serious finger in the drugs pie, even the apprentices, and if there was anyone in the city who could give him the SP on Kearns, it would be Sammy.

Winter padded through to the bedroom and retrieved his address book. There were two mobile numbers for Lewington. The first didn't work at all; the second made a connection. A voice dissolved into a prolonged fit of coughing.

Winter smiled. Lewington had always smoked so many fags he couldn't get through a sentence without hoisting a grolly or two. Clearly nothing had changed.

'Paul Winter,' he announced. 'Thought we might have a beer.'

Lewington, it was clear at once, didn't want to know. He'd been off the scene for a while. He hadn't got a clue what was going on.

Winter didn't believe a word.

'Me, too,' he said. 'That's exactly why we need a little chat. Bloke called Mickey Kearns might be a good place to start.'

Winter named a bar in Fratton, the Anson, and told Lewington to be there at half five. Then he hung up.

Outside on the balcony a sea breeze had made the heat more bearable. Winter fetched his new lounger, fixed himself a restorative glass of ice-cold Stella, and settled down with the *Daily Telegraph*, determined to put Jimmy Suttle to the very back of his mind. An hour later, he was woken by the familiar trill of his mobile.

Shading his eyes from the sun, he peered at the tiny screen for caller ID. No clues. He put the mobile to his ear.

'Winter? That you?'

Winter stiffened, recognising the gruff Pompey vowels. The man was angry. He wanted a meet.

'My pleasure.' Winter was on his feet now, turning away from the sunshine, stepping into the silence of his apartment. 'Where, exactly?'

'You know the Water Margin? You bloody should do, that new pad of yours.'

'Here, you mean? In Gunwharf?'

'Yeah. Table by the window. Ten minutes. Old times, eh?'

The Water Margin was an upmarket Chinese restaurant with a fine view of the foot of the Spinnaker Tower. It opened all day at the weekends but this time in the afternoon the clientele was limited to a handful of exhausted shoppers, sampling the last of the lunchtime specials.

Bazza Mackenzie was sitting alone, picking shreds of beef from a bowl of soup. He was wearing a smart-looking pair of tan chinos and a monogrammed burgundy shirt. He'd spent a fortune on his haircut and probably a lot more on the Ralph Lauren shades that lay folded on the tablecloth. To any of his mates from the old 6.57 crew, shock troops for Pompey away games, he'd have been unrecognisable. Misty was right, Winter thought. With twenty million quid in the bank and a tan that had never seen the inside of a bottle, Bazza wants the world to know he's gone legit.

'Fancy anything?' Mackenzie pushed a menu towards the DC. Winter thought he might like a plate of tiger prawns.

'Number forty-seven,' he said. 'Easy on the ginger.'

Mackenzie signalled the waiter, ordering a couple of beers as well. Then he turned back to Winter. He'd never had a talent for small talk.

'Misty seems to think you've got an interest in Mickey Kearns,' he said. 'Why's that?'

Winter took his time. The last thing you did in these situations was let Mackenzie batter you. When it was in his interests, he could be as charming and attentive as you like, but his normal style was altogether more direct, a blend of subtle menace and outright threats that normally worked a treat.

'Misty?' Winter said mildly. 'Keeping well, is she?'

'You should know, mush. You were all over her a couple of nights ago.'

'How's that then?'

'How's *that*? You drag her round half the bars in fucking Southsea and you don't think word'll get back?

What did they do to that brain of yours? Leave it in the operating theatre?'

'We had a couple of beers.'

'Sure. And I'm Marco fucking Polo. Misty says you were after a name. She also swears blind she didn't help you out. But being the devious bastard you are, you've come up with Mickey Kearns. Fuck knows why.'

'Really?'

'Yeah, really. Except you can't stick anything on the boy. And so now, like always, you think you're going to get a cough out of Sammy Lewington. But it ain't gonna work like that because Sammy phoned me first. Why? Because he doesn't fancy it. And you know what? That makes him a whole lot cleverer than you might think.'

Winter looked pained.

'You're right, Baz. Bad move.'

'Mickey, you mean?'

'Sammy Lewington. And he was always so reliable.'

'Well, he ain't anymore. So do us all a favour and leave it out, yeah? Don't go bothering the man. Just give him a bit of respect for a change.'

'Respect? Sammy?' Winter was laughing now. 'You have to be joking. Things might have changed in this town but you're not telling me Lewington's one of them. That man was born frightened.'

'And you think I don't know that?'

'I'm sure you do but there's more than one way of putting the shits up him. It's a free world, Baz. We all take our chances, Sammy Lewington included. Shame, though. I quite like the Anson.'

'I'm not surprised. It's an arsehole pub.'

The lagers arrived. Winter raised his glass. 'To Mickey Kearns,' he said. 'So why all the drama?'

'You don't want to know.'

'But I do, Baz, I do. And, one way or another, I'm going to find out. As you've probably sussed.'

'That would be silly. In fact that would be a real mistake.'

'Yeah? Why's that then? You used to be subtler than this, Baz. Maybe it's the clobber. Maybe you're feeling, you know, a bit insecure. Take a tip, mate. Dress the way you really are. Be true to yourself. Stick to the Burberry. You're having a laugh, aren't you? All this gear?'

When Mackenzie got really angry, he had a habit of biting his lower lip. Any minute now, Winter thought, he's going to draw blood.

The waiter returned with a plate of tiger prawns. He enquired whether Winter wanted chopsticks. Winter looked at the prawns a moment, then glanced up at Mackenzie.

'Are you going to be sensible? Or do I take this lot home?'

'Sensible?'

'About our Mr Kearns? The way I see it, Baz, you're staking him. I don't know how much, and I don't know who else is chucking money in the pot, and if you want a little something for free then you ought to know that my bosses have no real interest just now in finding out. But you know what? That's because they never suss how everything fits. Life's a puzzle, Baz. It's all dots. Join them up in the right order, and guess whose pretty face we're looking at?'

Mackenzie reached for his shades but Winter got there first, covering them with his hand.

'You want to talk about Mickey Kearns or not, Baz? Only there are ways we can sort this thing out.'

'Fuck off, Winter.'

'It's a serious offer.'

'You're off your head, mush. I'm not one of your fucking grasses. This kind of shit, I could—'

'What, Baz? What could you do? You going to tell me? Spell it out? Only my gang's a lot bigger than yours, even now.'

Winter at last let go of the sunglasses. Mackenzie didn't touch them. He began to say something, then had second thoughts. Winter was beaming at him. The waiter was at his elbow, still wanting to know what to do.

Winter nodded down at the bowl of glistening prawns.

'Bag that lot for me, will you?' He pushed his chair back. 'Mr Mackenzie's paying.'

Willard waited until the meeting with Martin Barrie was over before beckoning Faraday aside.

'Somewhere private?'

Faraday led Willard back to his office. To Barrie's relief, Willard appeared happy with the thrust of *Coppice*. A death this bizarre, as he'd told a reporter only a couple of hours ago, merited detailed and meticulous investigation. Buried amongst the hundreds of individual enquiries already actioned were the key leads that would finally resolve themselves into a pattern. Only when that pattern was secure – properly evidenced, 100 per cent lawyer proof – would Detective Superintendent Barrie and his team be in a position to contemplate arrests.

Faraday shut the door and offered Willard a seat. The new Head of CID was dressed for a weekend on the water. He'd recently made a sizeable investment in a twenty-seven-foot yacht, and was still fine-tuning a brand new set of sails ahead of Cowes Week. The yacht had a berth across the harbour. With the tide still on the ebb, Willard needed to be away sharpish.

'Winter,' he said. 'What do you think so far?'

The question took Faraday by surprise. Winter was the last thing on his mind.

'He's been fine,' he said carefully. 'Just fine.'

'What does that mean, Joe?'

'It means that he's driven the Intelligence Cell exactly

the way we wanted. Good analysis. Good work rate. And single-handed, too, until yesterday.'

'He's ticking the right boxes then?'

'Definitely.'

'No complaints at all?'

'Not complaints, no . . . '

'What then? Surprises?'

'Yes.' Faraday frowned, trying to frame the thought. 'Let's say he's more complex than I'd realised.'

'Did we ever think otherwise?'

'No, sir. But there's something extra there, something I hadn't seen before. He seems to have sorted something out in his head. I don't mean the tumour, it's something else. He seems –' he shrugged '– different.'

'And you think that's about the illness? What he's been through?'

'Yes, I do. In one sense, he seems more at ease with himself. There's still plenty of the old DC Winter. Management meetings, for instance. He'll never be a team player. He's still got no time for all that sitting around. But he makes it less obvious than he used to. And he's still sharp as a tack, no question about that.'

'But?'

'But . . . nothing, really. Except he's really vulnerable.'

'*Vulnerable?* Winter?'

'Yes, sir. Take what happened to DC Suttle. I always knew they were close. In fact Suttle's the only bloke recently that Winter's really had time for. But I never realised how much he cared about the lad.'

Faraday described finding Winter at the hospital.

'He'd lost it. He was gone. Totally distraught. I think Suttle brought something to his life that wasn't there before.'

'Like a son, you mean?'

'Yes.' Winter nodded. 'Exactly.'

'Hmm . . . ' Willard was gazing out of the window. Faraday wondered whether he was checking the wind.

'What about this new place of his?'

'You mean Gunwharf?'

'Yes. Have you been there?'

Faraday nodded. It was big, he said. Impressive. Fabulous views.

'Not cheap then.'

'I wouldn't have thought so.'

'How much do you think?'

'I've no idea, sir.' He frowned. 'Why?'

Willard was on his feet now, glancing at his watch.

'Call it insurance, Joe,' he said at last. 'My time of life, the last thing you need are surprises. I'll be back in the office first thing Monday. Talk to some estate agents and get me a figure.' He paused by the door, glancing back. 'Yeah?'

Willard drove out of Kingston Crescent and headed back into the city. He'd phoned earlier, fixing a time and a place, and there were still a couple of spaces in the seafront car park beside the funfair. Locking his Saab, he spared a moment or two for the view. One of the Isle of Wight car ferries was nosing out of the harbour, buoyed by the last of the ebb tide, and a scatter of yachts were bearing away under a decent sea breeze. Nice, he thought.

Covert Operations favoured the new Skodas. He'd spotted the car at once. There were two figures sitting in the front, both plain clothes, and one of them leaned back and unlocked the door as Willard approached. They'd never seen him in jeans and a T-shirt before.

Willard slid his bulk onto the rear seat, shut the door.

'Well?'

The undercover officer in the passenger seat had been nursing a camera. He passed it back to Willard.

'It's all set up, sir. Screen's on the back.'

Willard tried to shield the tiny screen from the spill of sunshine through the side window. The young DC behind the wheel was describing the way they'd handled the assignment, one of them covering the apartment block itself, the other in the car on the approach road outside Gunwharf. Whether he left on foot or by cab, they'd had the target nicely boxed off.

Willard nodded. He'd made sense of the image, the two men at the restaurant table, heads together, deep in conversation. The guy with the camera must have been working at a distance but the telephoto lens removed any ambiguities about the target's choice of company.

'Bazza Mackenzie,' Willard said thoughtfully.

Ten

Buckland lay immediately south of Kingston Crescent, at the very heart of Portsmouth. The Luftwaffe, overflying the nearby naval dockyard, had razed entire streets and the post-war planners did the rest, replacing acre after acre of Victorian terraces with their vision of a more wholesome future. Decades later, the area figured prominently on most of the poverty indices, and CID files were full of no-hopers who'd launched their criminal careers in the shadows of the surrounding tower blocks. Winter, who had no time for wank theories about social deprivation, rather liked the area. It was authentically rough. It looked you in the eye. If Buckland was a haircut, he thought, you'd be talking a serious grade one.

The address Faraday had given him lay in one of the streets off the long central road that threaded through the middle of the estate. The taxi driver, concentrating on the speed bumps, missed the turn. Winter told him to stop, paid the fare, got out.

Number 33 was halfway down on the left-hand side. Winter hadn't bothered to phone ahead, telling himself there was no point. All he had was a name.

An enormous woman in her fifties answered his knock. She was wearing pink slippers and an extra large jogging suit. Her bare arms were coated with flour and there were splash marks down the front of her apron. Behind her, Winter could see the light on in a tiny kitchen.

'What's this?' The woman wiped her hands on the

apron and took the proffered ID. She had a broad Pompey accent underscored with a hint of something foreign.

'It's a warrant card, love. My name's Winter. CID.'

'Old Bill then?' She looked at him, neither hostile nor defensive. A first, Winter thought.

He said he was looking for Donna Werbinski. It wasn't a drama or anything, he just wanted a chat.

'She's my daughter.'

'Is she in?'

'Yeah, she's upstairs with the baby. Is that your car out there?'

'No, I walked.'

'OK. You'd better come in.'

She stepped aside, checking along the street before shutting the door and yelling Donna's name up the stairs. Winter found himself in the adjoining lounge that ran the depth of the house. He'd never had a taste for squirly carpets or oversized aubergine sofas but the room was spotless. On the mantelpiece, flanking the repro carriage clock, was a line of tiny silver trophies. Winter peered at them. The most recent date was 2002.

The woman was back, asking him if he wanted tea.

'Yours, are they?' Winter was still looking at the trophies.

'No, love, they were Roman's. He played regular in one of the local darts team. He was always good at darts, my hubby.'

Winter said yes to tea, then sank into the sofa. The widescreen TV was tuned to *Casualty* but the sound was off and Winter had to guess at the plot. A bunch of medics hurrying a trolley through a pair of swing doors made him think of Suttle again, and he was still fighting the temptation to give Critical Care a ring when he heard footsteps on the stairs.

'Donna?' He looked up.

She was standing in the open doorway. The baby couldn't have been more than a couple of months old.

She held him on her shoulder, patting him gently on the back.

'What's this about? Mum says you're the Old Bill.'

'Mum's right. Paul Winter's the name. Good to meet you, Donna.'

She hesitated a moment, uncertain what to do next, then the baby nuzzled the side of her neck, gurgling with delight. Winter stepped towards it, hand outstretched.

'He'll spew next. I'd keep your distance, if I were you.'

She was right. Mum appeared with a length of kitchen roll, mopped up the damage, then took the baby. She'd bring Winter's tea when she'd got the cake in the oven. Winter watched the door shut behind her, then turned back to Donna. She was barely out of adolescence – slim, freckled, nice eyes. Like her mum, she wore slippers on her bare feet.

'You live here, do you?'

'Yeah.'

'What's his name then? The baby?'

'Justin.' She reached down for the remote control and switched the TV off. 'D'you mind telling me what this is about? Only I'm supposed to be getting myself ready to go out.'

'Of course. You want to sit down?'

She shook her head, then changed her mind and perched herself on the edge of the armchair next to the sofa.

Winter explained about Mark Duley. Donna might know that he'd been found dead. There was a criminal investigation into the circumstances and Donna's name had surfaced in connection with the history workshop Duley had been running. Winter had simply come to check the facts.

'About Mr Duley?' Donna seemed to relax.

'Yeah.'

'He was terrific. In fact he was brilliant. Me, I've

always been crap at all that history stuff but Mark made it really interesting. He was cool too. We liked him. We all used to chat loads afterwards. Real shame he ... You know ... '

'How long had you been doing the workshop?'

'All year. Since September last.'

'Was this to do with college or something?'

'No, I never bothered with college.'

'Why then? Why were you doing it?'

'Because ... ' She began to pick at a nail. 'Why do you want to know all this?'

'Because I'm nosy, Donna. You get a case like this, and you want to know everything about everybody.'

'But how can all this stuff help? Why aren't you talking to someone else in the class?'

'Maybe I am.'

'Yeah? Like who?'

The door opened. Winter's tea had arrived. Donna's mum, sensing the atmosphere, asked her daughter if everything was OK. Donna was about to shake her head but Winter got there first.

'I'm interested to know why your daughter was going to the history workshop, Mrs Werbinski.'

'Oh?' She turned to her daughter. 'Tell him, Don. Go on. You should be proud of yourself.'

'I just fancied it.' Donna shrugged.

'No, you didn't. Tell him about your dad.'

'Yeah? But what's that got to do with him?' She nodded at Winter.

'Doesn't matter, Don. There's no harm in it.' She turned back to Winter. 'My Roman passed away a couple of years back. He was Polish, like me. He always told Donna that your birthplace is precious. You should get to know as much as you can about it, and you know why? Because one day it might be too late. I don't know whether Don took any notice of her dad at the time but when this workshop thing happened I told Don all about it. So off she goes because

I'm always on at her, and then what happens? She loves it. Not just that, but it turns out that this Mr Duley can teach her Spanish. Donna's got her heart set on the travel business. She wants to work local first, then maybe be a rep when the little one's a bit older. Doing the Spanish would have helped no end. Except the poor man's dead.'

Winter nodded. So far, so good. Now, he thought. Before Mum disappears again.

'Is there a Mickey Kearns in the class?' he enquired.

'Mickey?' Mum was hooting with laughter. 'You have to be joking.'

'Why's that?'

'He wouldn't go near a teacher if you paid him. He hated school. Every minute of it. Not that it's spoiled his chances, mind. Doing OK, our Mickey. Let's just hope Donna sees some of it.'

'Mum . . . ' Donna didn't want this to go on.

'No, but it's true, isn't it, love? Mickey's doing OK, better than OK. You seen that motor he's driving? Big black thing? Most kids round here are pushed to afford a bike. Not Mickey.'

'Mum . . . just shut it, eh?'

'Don, you've got to stand up for yourself. The gentleman's interested. You're bettering yourself. Just like Mickey. You're trying to get out of this shithole. That's nothing to be ashamed of.'

In the kitchen the baby had started crying. Donna was out of the door in seconds.

Winter sipped at his tea, enjoying the conversation.

'Mickey's baby?' he asked.

'Yeah. Shame it didn't last but then nothing does these days, does it? They still see each other, like, just for a drink sometimes, and I think he bungs her a few quid though she never says anything.'

'So how do I get to find the lad?'

'No idea. He's all over the place.'

'You don't have an address? Mobile number?'

'No. Donna's probably got his mobile. Ask her.'

'I will.' He smiled. 'Do you happen to know whether Mickey ever met Mark Duley?'

'Yeah, he did. Definitely.'

'When?'

'Months ago. In fact it was here, in this room. Mickey was after someone who spoke Spanish, something to do with some business phone calls he was making, and Don told him about their teacher, this Mr Duley. He came round like, skinny bloke, nothing to him – nice though, real live wire.'

'And he helped Mickey out?'

'Must have done.'

'Why?'

'Cos him and Mickey went off together somewhere, West Indies, I think – the Caribbean, somewhere like that. Got on like a house on fire, Don said.'

'What were they doing there?'

'Dunno. You'd have to ask Mickey. He hasn't been around for a bit. Don might know where to find him.'

'Was this recent though? This trip of theirs?'

'Oh yeah, yeah. Where are we now? July? Must have been the month before last, round May time. They didn't hang around at all, just a couple of days, quick in and out, according to Don. She got a postcard from Mickey. Showing off he was. Wrote it in bloody Spanish.' She hooted with laughter again, then reached for Winter's empty cup.

'You want another one, love? Only I made a pot.'

Winter shook his head, aware of the low murmur of Donna's voice next door. She must be on the phone, he thought. Moments later, Donna reappeared from the kitchen. She had the baby on her shoulder again, swaddled in a blanket this time.

'I need to talk to Mickey Kearns.' Winter gave the baby a tickle under his chin. 'Your mum says you've got a number.'

'She's wrong.'

'Really?'

'Yeah. I had it once but God knows where it is now. Plus he's always changing phones.'

'Why's that?'

'Dunno.' She shrugged. 'You'd have to ask him.'

'So where does Mickey live?'

'With his mum.' She named the road.

'You're sure about that? Only we had blokes round there last night and there wasn't any sign of him.'

'So?'

'So something tells me he's dossing somewhere else.' Winter smiled at her. 'Do us a favour, Donna. Are you going to help me with Mickey Kearns or not?'

'I can't,' she said woodenly. 'Because I don't know anything.'

Winter held her gaze until she turned her head away. Her face had begun to redden. Guilt, thought Winter. Or anger.

'Listen, love. This is a murder enquiry. Someone killed Mark Duley and we're going to find out who. This kind of attitude can put you in court.'

'Attitude?' She was rocking the baby now. 'What's that about?'

'Obstructing the course of justice. Sweet phrase. Think about it, eh?'

'I gave you an address.'

'You did, Donna, you did. And it's useless.' He produced his wallet and slipped a card into a fold of the baby's blanket. 'Obstructing the course of justice carries a decent sentence these days. Prison's no place for young mums. Give me a bell when you've had a bit of a think, eh?'

He glanced across at Mrs Werbinksi, thanked her for the tea and made his way out of the room. At the front door, aware of Donna behind him, he hesitated a moment, giving her a chance to restart the conversation. When nothing happened, he opened the door.

'Nice to meet you, love.' Winter stepped into the gathering darkness. 'Give Mickey our best.'

Faraday spent the evening at his PC, composing a long e-mail to Gabrielle. He'd attended a French conversation class years ago and maintained a basic feel for the language. France had always intrigued him, and the more he saw of it, the more fascinated he became. How could a country so physically close be so fundamentally different? How come the French had ended up with a thirty-five-hour week and the best food in Europe? Why did they seem to cherish the good things in life so much? He thought of Gabrielle in Thailand, with her urchin grin and her ceaseless curiosity, and when he looked again at the photos she'd sent it occurred to him that this might be a conversation worth having.

Hours later, with the big Collins dictionary open on his lap, he was still trying to put some of his thoughts into half-decent French when his mobile began to trill.

Caller ID said it was Winter. Curious, Faraday lifted the mobile to his ear.

'Paul?' Nothing. 'Paul? Is that you?' Silence.

Winter changed his mind, pocketing his mobile. He was still in Buckland, walking south towards the short cut that would take him to the top of Commercial Road. Three calls to taxi firms had failed to raise a cab. This time of night, on a Saturday, he probably had no chance. He quickened his step, telling himself that he was seeing things, that the big black 4x4 that had passed him a minute or so ago was just some tosser with nothing better to do, that he'd been going that slowly because of the speed bumps, that he was as brainless as everyone else on this estate. Whatever.

Winter tried not to brood on the mistakes he knew he'd made. Trusting his luck in Buckland, no backup, was madness. The girl, Donna, might turn out to be genuine enough, a New Labour advert for self-betterment, but she knew exactly what Mickey Kearns was up to, even though she seemingly hadn't shared this knowledge with her mum. Either way, she'd probably been on the phone from the kitchen to summon help. I've got the Filth next door, asking a load of questions. Come and give us a hand.

Up ahead lay the turn that would take Winter into the short cut to the roundabout. Out amongst the traffic, there wouldn't be a problem. He'd walk up through the busy shopping precinct. There was always a line of cabs waiting at the station. This rate, he'd be home by half nine. Sweet.

He thought about calling Faraday again, apologising for the earlier false alarm. He'd make a joke of it, put it down to loss of bottle, tell him he was getting paranoid in his old age, but in the end he didn't bother. Faraday had better things to do on a Saturday night than listen to some fat old bastard dribbling on about a bunch of inbreds.

The short cut led into what little remained of the old Commercial Road. This had once been Pompey's backbone, a busy stretch of cobblestones feeding traffic north towards the mainland, but the city had long moved on, leaving this little cul-de-sac empty and silent in the gathering dusk. Winter eyed the big shadowed Georgian houses set back from the road. Charles Dickens had been born in one of them and the place now served as a museum. Dickens, as far as Winter knew, had left the city as a babe-in-arms. Wise man.

Ahead, Winter could see the loom of the big orange street lights beyond the tiny cut at the end of the cul-de-sac. He crossed the road, aware for the first time of footsteps behind him. Someone else, he thought. Heading out on a Saturday night.

Seconds later, no warning, a chokehold closed round his throat. Then came the black plastic bag over his head, pulled down tight. He tried to struggle, kicking out, flailing with his arms, outraged at the liberties these tossers were taking, but they were far too strong for him.

Somebody kicked his legs away, then he was being dragged backwards, struggling for air, his heels clump-clumping across the cobbles. The sharpness of the kerbstone on his ankles took him by surprise and he roared with pain. Dimly he thought he caught the rumble of an approaching motor. Next came a squeal of brakes. Someone mentioned his name. Someone else laughed. He tried to struggle again but the fight had gone out of him. Then, as the darkness thickened, everything seemed to slip away.

He surfaced minutes later. They must have loosened the plastic bag. Fresh air tasted of engine fumes and reefer. He was lying on his side in the back of a van. Someone had taken his shoes off and his hands and ankles were tied. The van was grinding along, probably still in the city, and every time it swung left or right he could feel the metal ribs of the floor against his hip. There was music too, loud, interminable lyrics, worse than toothache.

'Turn that fucking noise down,' he managed.

There was laughter. He was aware of the stir of someone's boot in the pit of his belly, someone here in the back of the van with him. A warning. Behave yourself.

'Cunts,' he muttered to himself, feeling instantly better.

No one said a word. Winter piled on the abuse. Twats. Retards. Numpties. Anything to spark a riposte, to launch a conversation, to get a fix on an accent, to recognise – if he was really lucky – a voice. But these guys had thought this thing through, recognised the kind of risks they were running. Kidnapping a police officer would put you inside for a very long time, and they didn't need Winter to remind them where this joyride of theirs might lead.

Nonetheless, he persevered.

'What's the game then? Only you've got one big fucking problem, haven't you?'

More laughter, this time from the front of the van. Then something wet and papery between his lips. His tongue explored it. He took an exploratory drag, a tiny sip of air, then spat the spliff out. Somebody very close was creasing himself. I'm the performing fucking bear, Winter thought. What next?

The van was going faster now, the growl of surrounding traffic left behind. The city's only motorway tracked north towards the mainland, and Winter tried to estimate speed and time as the tick-tock of the indicator signalled a change of lane. The van lurched to the right. East, he thought.

Minutes later, they began to slow, the driver grinding down through the gears until the van had come to a halt. Then, within seconds, they were off again, pulling hard to the left, and Winter visualised the roundabout that funnelled traffic from the motorway into Havant. Soon there'd come a succession of traffic lights, then another roundabout before the brief stretch of dual carriageway that bordered Leigh Park.

Leigh Park was an enormous post-war housing estate, a refuge for countless families as blitzed Pompey made way for the bulldozers. For a while it had been the dream address – fresh air, a bit of countryside, familiar neighbours, handy pubs and schools – but successive generations of kids had put the boot into the planners' fantasy, and by the time Winter stepped into the job, the badlands of Leigh Park were every copper's nightmare.

The van was slowing again. A couple of sharp turns, heavy braking for some kind of obstacle, and then they rolled to a stop. With the engine off, Winter could hear shouting outside, the drunken shriek of some fourteen-year-old bint, then the answering taunt of blokes nearby. She's off her head, Winter thought. Pink handbag. Platform heels. Tats. Belly hanging out. A couple more vodka ices and she won't remember a thing.

There was a clink of coins and then someone opened the van door at the front and Winter felt the chill of the night air. He was stiff now, his lower legs beginning to cramp, and he toyed for a moment or two with yelling for help but managed to resist the temptation. If he was right about Leigh Park, the last thing he needed was a bigger audience.

'Bazza in on this, is he?'

Nothing. No response. Then someone tweaked the volume on the music, but amplified rap was too much even for these tossers and there came a brief moment of silence before they were listening to Robbie Williams.

Winter shut his eyes. There were parts of him that associated Leigh Park on a Saturday night with the wilder headlines from Baghdad, and now he began to wonder how blokes taken hostage ever survived. Did you simply switch off? Plunge into zombie mode? Adopt the foetal position and hope to fuck that someone would wake you up? Or was it best to try and get on top of these animals, extract a little respect? He contemplated the prospect for a moment or two then, for some inexplicable reason, he was back in the hospital, back at Jimmy Suttle's bedside. I'm as helpless as he is, he thought grimly. And twice as uncomfortable.

The van lurched on its springs as someone got in. The front door banged shut and they were off again. Winter could smell vinegar and freshly battered fish, and as they took the next corner at speed, his body rolling back against the wheel arch, he realised how hungry he was. He tried to struggle upright, easing the pain in his legs. In the sitting position, he nudged his body backwards until his bound hands found the side of the van. The effort left him breathless and he could hear the rustle of the black plastic bag as he sucked air into his lungs.

Then came a mutter of conversation, very low, and a giggle from somewhere close. Seconds later he felt the brush of knuckles against his chin as a hand found his mouth inside the bag, and he tasted the saltiness of the chip. Bloody hot, he thought. And not quite enough vinegar.

More chips, presumably from the same hand. Then, unannounced, a flake or two of fish before a brief explosion of light. They're taking pictures, Winter thought. They've put the monkey in the cage and now they want a souvenir or two. He felt the nudge of the hand again, another titbit, but he turned his head away.

'Just fuck off,' he said quietly.

More laughter. They drove around for a while, the driver grinding up and down through the gearbox, then the van began to slow and finally stopped. For a moment there was total silence. Winter stirred.

'What now then?'

As if in response there came a squeak as someone wound one of the front windows down. Then, very distantly, Winter heard the clatter of an approaching train. He stiffened, asked the question again, tried to imagine just where they might have parked up. Then the train was on top of them, very close, a deafening roar in the chilly darkness, receding as quickly as it had appeared, taking with it a little of his bravado and his courage. In the space of a minute or two a Pompey jape had become something infinitely more sinister.

They must have stayed beside the railway track for a couple of hours. Trains came and went, each one – Winter assumed – trailing the same message. This wasn't subtle, far from it, but by the time the van's engine stirred back into life and they began to bump away, Winter's sense of humour was exhausted. He was cold, extremely uncomfortable and not a little frightened. The last thing he wanted to concede was any hint of anxiety, but he, like everyone else on the *Coppice* squad, had taken a good look at the thick sheaf of photos from the Buriton Tunnel. Dying under the surgeon's knife was one thing, Winter thought. Being torn apart by several hundred tons of speeding train quite another.

'Cunts,' he muttered again. And meant it.

This time the journey was shorter. Towards the end the van was grinding uphill. At length they slowed, pulled left off the road, and bumped down over rough ground. The driver killed the engine, and there was a stir of movement in the back of the van. Winter was aware of his numbed body being pulled forward. Someone rolled him over. Flat on his face on the floor of the van, he felt the coldness of a knife against his bare wrists, sawing back and forth, then his hands were suddenly free. He rubbed them together, winced at the hot scald of blood flooding back into his fingers, wondered what on earth was coming next.

Someone was pulling at his ankles. Moments later they too were free. Winter flexed his legs, making sure, then tried to roll over and tear the plastic bag off his head. But he barely had time to register a flicker of light and the shape of someone bending over him before the hands were back again, pulling him into a sitting position, winding a rough blindfold around his head. The blindfold was very tight, the knot biting into the back of his neck, and he bellowed with pain as these same hands finally pushed him back against the side of the van. He felt the belt of his trousers loosening, then a grunt as someone pulled hard on his trouser bottoms. Instinctively, he brought his knees up, protecting himself, then he felt the kiss of cold steel again and relaxed, a gesture of hopeless surrender as the knife sliced through his favourite kaks. Naked below the waist, aware of the hands again, tugging at his shirt, Winter knew what was coming next.

'Leave it out, will you?' he grunted. 'I'll do it myself.'

He struggled out of his jacket, then undid the buttons on his shirt and peeled it off. Naked, still wearing the blindfold, he felt someone arranging him before a series of flashes signalled more photos. Winter drew up his knees, covering himself, but knew it was too late. Moments later, he was being dragged towards the back of the van. Then came the briefest pause and the touch of something light across his back, before a hefty push rolled him out of the van. Face down again, arse in the air, struggling to get to his feet, he could feel dew on the grass. The van's engine was already stirring into life. As it accelerated away, Winter did his best to get rid of the blindfold, his fingers tearing at the tightness of the knot, but by the time he'd managed to undo the thing, the van was a distant pair of red lights, back up on the road, hundreds of metres away.

Winter began to shiver – partly from the cold, partly shock, partly a sense of overwhelming relief that he'd managed to survive more or less intact. They'd dumped him just beneath the top of Portsdown Hill, maybe a hundred metres from the road that ran along the crest of the long fold of chalk. Beyond the road lay one of the Victorian forts that straddled the hill, a looming wall of red brick. Below, when he turned to look, lay the long tongue of Portsmouth, necklaced with street lights, licking out into the blackness of the Solent.

Winter sank onto his haunches, unable to control his bowels, letting the tension spill out of him. Happiness, he thought grimly, has a smell you wouldn't want to take with you. Immediately below, the grass and scrub was dotted with bushes. He made his way down to them, tearing at the longer clumps of grass around the bushes, doing his best to clean himself up.

Already, he'd dismissed the option of calling for official help. This time of night, he could make his way back to the road, try and flag down the next passing motorist. No way would they stop for some naked stranger but the sight alone would warrant a 999 call on the mobile, and Winter could visualise only too well the arrival of a couple of uniforms and the eternity of wind-ups that would follow. For twenty years Winter had successfully resisted attempts to bring him down. He'd courted controversy, had several near-disasters, but nothing that would hand his many enemies this kind of ammunition. No, there had to be another way.

The nearest public phone box, to Winter's knowledge, lay amongst the grid of residential avenues on the southern slopes of the hill. Without a mobile or watch, Winter had no real idea of time but the lack of traffic told him it was late, certainly gone midnight. This time in the morning the roads below him should be quiet, most of the residents hopefully asleep in bed.

He began to make his way down the hill. A footpath took him into the first of the avenues. Hugging whatever shadows he could find, he trotted down the hill, stark naked, trying to navigate his way towards the phone box. After a quarter of a mile or so he realised he'd gone wrong. Cursing, breathless, one of his feet already bleeding from a cut, he retraced his steps, took a left, then another left, began to climb again. At the next corner, flattened against a privet hedge, he peered round. The phone box, horribly overlit, was less than fifty metres away.

He checked behind him, looking for somewhere to hide when the time came. Halfway down the street was a bungalow with a fenced front garden. He counted the gates, made a mental note of the address, stole round the corner, and bolted for the phone box. The Response Desk at the Netley Control Room was manned twenty-four hours a day. Calls from public boxes were free.

Winter hopped from one foot to the other, waiting for someone to pick up. To his relief, the heat from his sweating body clouded the glass, masking him from the street, but he was rapidly cooling in the chilly night air.

At last, he found himself talking to the Response Desk. He confirmed his ID and said he wanted a mobile number. She'd find it on the Major Crimes' database. Name of Jake Tarrant. On call-out for the mortuary at St Mary's Hospital, Portsmouth.

There was a pause. When the controller came back, there was no way she'd give Winter the number. Instead, she'd ask Tarrant to call Winter.

'379008,' he said, peering at the line of figures above the console.

'That's a public box.'

'I know, love.' Winter was shivering now. 'Just do it, yeah? And tell him it's bloody urgent.'

'I'll have to log this. You know that, don't you?'

'Whatever.'

She told him to hang up. Winter began to jog up and down in the tightness of the space, trying to coax some warmth back into his body. Condensation was running down the glass, little rivulets of moisture, and Winter was beginning to shiver again when the phone rang. It was very loud in the silence. He grabbed for the receiver.

'Jake?'

'Yeah, me. You know what time it is? What the fuck's going on?'

Winter gave him the name of the street and the number of the bungalow round the corner.

'You got that?'

'Yeah.'

'Just pick me up, OK?'

'*Now?*'

'Sooner. You'll be coming up from the Eastern Road. You know the New Inn? Drayton? Take the first right. Straight up the hill. You with me?' He frowned. 'Jake?'

The connection had gone dead. Winter stared at the phone a moment, then smashed it against the cradle in frustration. Seconds later, through the blurry glass, he saw an upstairs light in the house across the road flick on. Backing out of the phone box, he hurried back towards the corner, glad to be on the move again. Thank Christ he'd given himself somewhere to hide.

The area car swept up the hill minutes later, blues but no siren. Crouching behind the bungalow's fence, Winter could feel the damp softness of the earth between his toes. His naked bulk would be white against the black creosote. If the punters indoors wake up, he thought, I'm dead.

Round the corner, he heard a car door slam. Then footsteps. They'll be talking to the caller, he thought. The householder will be waiting for them, slippers and dressing gown, still not quite believing what they'd seen across the road. Winter hugged himself, rocking on his heels, praying that they hadn't clocked him leaving the box. Next thing for the area car was a cursory search. If they drove the other way, he still had a fighting chance. The car door again. Then the purr of the engine, slowly receding as they drove away. Brilliant.

Jake arrived a minute or so later, easing slowly up the hill, checking the numbers on the gates. As soon as his Fiat had come to a halt outside the bungalow, Winter was out of the front garden, limping across the thin strip of grass beside the pavement, reaching for the handle on the back door. He clambered in, then folded himself into the floor space between the seats.

'Drive, son,' he said.

'Where to?'

'Pompey.'

Jake twisted backwards in the seat. Winter was aware of his face above him. He wanted to know what was going on, why he'd been phoned by some policewoman at two in the morning, what Winter was doing bollock naked in someone else's front garden. Winter shook his head. He wasn't interested in a conversation.

'Just go, son. Just do it.'

Jake shrugged. A three-point turn took him back

down the road towards the parade of shops at the bottom. Still wedged between the seats, Winter had his eyes closed. The area guys would be driving a grid, widening the search area with every street turn. With luck, they'd have stopped a couple of times already, investigating a movement in the shadows, taking a torch to the darker corners. If they found him now – if they pulled the Fiat and did a stop search – their list of questions wouldn't bear contemplation.

At the bottom of the road Jake swung the car left. From here it was less than a mile to the intersection that would take them south, back to the safety of the city. Winter shifted his bulk until he was lying on his back, staring up at the roof, counting the orange street lights as they rolled by. Finally, Jake was slowing again.

'Are these the traffic lights?'

'Yeah.'

'Red?'

'Green.'

'Thank fuck for that.' Winter began to struggle upright, bracing himself for the turn. 'Brilliant, son. You've done brilliant.'

Jake was eyeing him in the rear-view mirror. Finally, he began to laugh.

'Am I taking you home or what?'

'Your place, I'm afraid. Bastards nicked everything. Keys. Mobile. The lot. We can sort it tomorrow.'

'We?'

'Yeah, son. You and me.'

Jake nodded, said nothing for a moment. Then he told Winter there was a blanket in the space behind the rear seat. They used it for picnics. Winter fumbled around in the back of the car. Beneath a litter of property details from various estate agents, he found the blanket. It was old and threadbare but big enough to drape around himself.

Jake was still watching him.

'Just one question,' he said at last.

'Anything, son.'

'What's that terrible smell?'

Jake Tarrant lived in a brand new estate tucked into the north-east corner of the island. The cul-de-sac of starter homes looked like sentry boxes under the sodium street lamps. As the Fiat rolled to a stop on the tiny apron of hardstanding, Winter noticed a light in the window above the door.

'Shit.' Tarrant had seen it too.

'The missus?'

'Yeah.'

Tarrant helped Winter out of the back of the car, then retrieved his keys. Winter wrapped himself in the blanket and padded across the damp concrete. Tarrant was already at the front door, slipping the key into the lock.

'In here,' he said. 'Follow me.'

Winter found himself in a tiny hall. There was a line of kiddies' boots beneath the hanging anoraks and a glimpse of a neat kitchen through the nearby open door. After the chill of the night air, it felt suddenly warm again.

'Up there, mate.' Tarrant was pointing at the narrow stairs. 'Bathroom's first right. I'll sort you a towel in a moment.'

Winter crept up the stairs. There were photographs on the walls, all of them featuring two young kids. He paused beside the biggest. The kids must have been in the back garden. There was an inflatable pool and a miniature swing, and not much room for anything else. The smaller of the two kids, a girl, was beaming up at the camera while her brother emptied a bucketful of water over her head. The kids looked happy and guileless, a moment of innocence caught forever. Sweet, Winter thought, heading upward again.

The bathroom was the size of a cupboard with just

enough length for a tub but the tiling looked spotless and there were half a dozen shower gel samplers neatly flanking the imitation gold taps. In a blue plastic box beneath the window lay an assortment of toys.

Winter mustered a grin in the mirror over the tiny sink. Half an hour ago he'd been looking at an awkward conversation with his bosses and a lifetime of wind-ups in the squad room. Now, all he had to worry about was a choice between Forest Mist and Hawaii Coconut. He abandoned the blanket and juggled with the shower controls until he couldn't bear it any hotter. Underneath the falling water, he emptied a sampler of Coconut over his balding head and began to soap himself, working slowly downwards, letting the heat seep into every corner of his body. Minutes later, the bathroom full of steam, it occurred to him that he had company. Dimly, he could make out a figure by the door. Must be Jake.

'Result or what, son?' he murmured, turning his back.

Wrapped in a dressing gown he'd found behind the door, Winter made his way back downstairs. He could hear raised voices now, one of them Jake's. It wasn't my fault, he was saying. The phone goes, the bloke's in trouble, he's a mate of mine, *what else do you do?* He said it twice, as if for emphasis, then another voice, a woman's, told him he was a fool. They had kids for Chrissakes, neighbours, responsibilities. What were people supposed to think? At this time in the morning?

Winter stood in the hall, wondering idly whether to intervene. The voices were coming from the living room. At length, his cough brought a woman to the door. She was wearing a scarlet towelling robe pulled tight around her and a pair of blue slippers. In the photo on Jake's office desk, this wife of his had turned a succession of heads. Now her face was dark with anger.

'Rachel . . . ?' Winter extended a hand.

She looked at him a moment, then pushed past. Halfway up the stairs, she paused. 'Show him your back,' she said.

Mystified, Winter stepped into the living room. Jake was standing in front of the gas fire. He had a armful of bedding and there were a couple of pillows at his feet.

'She saw you in the shower,' he said. 'Told me to look for myself.'

'Look at what?'

'Your back.'

There was a long mirror over the mantelpiece with yet more kiddie photos tucked into the frame. Winter unbelted the dressing gown and dropped it to waist level. Half turning, he caught sight of something scrawled across his back. Red felt tip. Obviously waterproof.

'47?' Tarrant was looking too.

Winter twisted his body and stared at himself in the mirror. He remembered his last moments in the van, those light touches across his back. They must have done it then, he thought. They must have addressed me, like a parcel, or left a clue or two in case I ever got curious. 47? For a second or two the message made no sense. Then, quite suddenly, he was back in the Water Margin, consulting the menu, hunting for something tasty to sustain him. Tiger prawns with ginger in oyster sauce. Number 47.

'Fucking Bazza,' he murmured, pulling the dressing gown tightly around him.

Eleven

The locksmith was still at work when Faraday stepped out of the lift at Blake House. Winter's call had found him at his desk in the Major Crimes Suite, drawing up a full review of progress on Operation *Coppice*. The new Head of CID wanted something in his locker in the event of further press enquiries first thing Monday morning, and Martin Barrie had passed on the request. Willard's hunger for publicity, they both agreed, might be turned to *Coppice*'s advantage. If you wanted to flush out fresh leads, nothing beat the telly or a decent spread in a national tabloid.

Faraday paused in the hall outside Winter's apartment. The old lock lay on a sheet of newspaper and the locksmith was having trouble making the new Chubb fit. The door was open, and Faraday could hear Winter on the phone. He sounded angry.

By the time Faraday made it into the living room, Winter had hung up. He was wearing a pair of black tracksuit bottoms that looked too small for him and a blue Pompey football top. He spared Faraday a nod, then turned to retrieve a notepad he'd left beside the phone. On the back of the football shirt, in white letters, a player's name: *LuaLua*.

'Can you believe this?' Winter poked a finger at the pad. 'Last night I lose my mobile. One of those things that happen. Bad karma. Too many Stellas. Whatever. This morning I bell Orange, tell them to put a block on it. And you know what? Some scrote's only dialled the Melbourne speaking clock.'

'How much?'

'Three figures. Fucking unbelievable. From now on, I'm going top-up.'

'You lost your keys as well?' Faraday nodded back towards the front door.

'Yeah.' Winter tore a sheet from the notepad and crumpled it in his fist. 'Had to spend the night at a mate's place. Couldn't even get back in.'

Faraday was still thinking about the mobile. 'You had numbers stored on it?'

'Of course.'

'How many?'

'Couple of dozen. Tops.'

'Job numbers?'

'Yeah. It's what you do, isn't it?'

'But you've no idea who might have picked it up?'

'None. I was across the way there . . . ' He nodded towards the Gunwharf commercial centre. 'Couple of pints, left my anorak on the chair while I went for a piss. The keys and the mobe were in one of the pockets. Plus my wallet, cards, the lot. Must have happened then.'

'They took the anorak as well?'

'Yeah, of course.'

'Bit rash, wasn't it? Leaving that lot lying around?'

'Yeah, dimlo me.' Winter shook his head. 'You wouldn't believe how many calls you have to make. Visa. Abbey National. All sorts. And on a *Sunday*?'

He offered Faraday coffee. Faraday shook his head. He wanted to know about Suttle. Had Winter been in touch with the hospital this morning?

'An hour ago.'

'And?'

'Apparently he's off the ventilator, breathing for himself again.'

'But that's good news, isn't it?'

'Yeah.' Winter nodded. 'As long as they're not winding me up.'

217

Faraday looked at him a moment, then shook his head.

'You're getting paranoid,' he said. 'Why would they do that?'

'Because . . .' Winter threw the ball of notepaper at the waste basket and missed. 'God knows. Listen, boss. I've got a meet fixed for this afternoon. I thought you might like to come along.'

'Why?'

'Because I need a motor. And because it would be handy to have a witness. This is a bloke who won't want to talk to me. I can't nick him because he hasn't done anything wrong. But he knows what I know, or at least what I think I know, and I want you to be the one to hear it first.' He stared at Faraday, still angry. 'Does that make sense, boss? Or am I completely out of my fucking mind?'

The Druid's Arms was a corner pub in the heart of Buckland, webbed by the surrounding terraced streets. On a cloudless summer Sunday, with the temperature nudging 25°C, the walled garden at the back was full of local families tucking into five-quid weekend specials. Parked across the road, his window down, Faraday could hear shrieks of laughter from the kids playing on the bouncy castle.

Winter had already been inside. Sammy Lewington, he said, was up the far end of the bar. Better still, he was well pissed.

'In company?'

'No.' Winter had bought himself a copy of the *Sunday Telegraph*. 'Sammy doesn't do company.'

It was gone three by the time he emerged, a tall, thin figure in knock-off jeans and a faded Pink Floyd T-shirt. Faraday watched as he consulted his watch, rubbed his face, then set off uncertainly in the direction of Buckland. Winter was right. Sammy was out of it.

Faraday waited until he was well clear of the pub,

then he started the Mondeo and went after him. Cars were double-parked the length of the street, leaving just enough room to get through. This will have to be quick, he told Winter.

'No problem, boss.'

Sammy was weaving now, one arm out, fumbling with the zip of his fly and heading for the comfort of a nearby wall. Faraday drew up beside him, watching Winter as he stepped from the car, bodychecked past a builder's van and confronted Sammy on the pavement. Seconds later, he was helping the man into the back of the Mondeo. Thirties? Forties? With his lank hair and bony face, Faraday couldn't be sure.

'Got a friend I want you to meet, Sammy,' Winter was saying. 'Think you can handle that?'

They drove out of the city and took the road that wound up to the top of Portsdown Hill. Faraday took his time, watching developments in the rear-view mirror. Winter was sitting beside Sammy, immensely pleased with himself, patting him on the arm from time to time, making nonsense small talk the way you might with a favourite uncle on trips out on Sunday afternoons. When it dawned on Sammy that all was not well, that he wanted the car to stop, that he wanted to get out and find his own way home, Winter told him everything would be sweet.

'Just relax, Sammy, eh?'

The car park on top of Portsdown Hill was full. Kids were mobbing an ice cream van parked in one corner while dozens of families picnicked on the acres of grass that rolled down towards the tiled rooftops of Drayton. The car park had been Winter's idea. Nice views, he'd said. And a cornet for Sammy if he behaves himself.

Sammy was trying to get out of the car. Winter leaned across, grinned at him.

'Childproof locks, Sammy. Nice touch, don't you think?'

Sammy muttered something about needing a piss. Winter patted his thigh.

'A time and a place for everything, son. Get this lot boxed off, and you can be on your way.'

'What lot's that?'

'Just a couple of questions, Sammy. I got your message, by the way, and I wasn't impressed.'

'I don't know what you're talking about.'

'Yes, you do, son. We were going to meet last night. The Anson. Remember? Only you belled a mutual friend of ours, didn't you?'

'I never.'

'Yes, you did, Sammy. And when I turned up, you never showed.'

'You went?' He looked startled. 'You went to the Anson?'

'Of course I did.'

'But he told me—'

'Who, Sammy? Who told you?'

Sammy's eyes flicked towards Faraday. He was frightened to even mention the name.

'That friend of ours . . . ' he muttered. 'He swore blind you wouldn't be there.'

'Well, I was. Which just goes to show what bad company you've started to keep. Does the word "disappointment" ring any bells with you, Sammy? Or are you just stupid?'

Sammy ducked his head. He definitely needed a piss. He said he was getting desperate.

'Of course you are, mate. Six pints at lunchtime? Knackered old bladder like yours? I'm surprised it hasn't exploded. Listen . . . ' He beckoned Sammy closer until their heads were nearly touching. 'You want some advice? Whatever you do, don't piss yourself in here. You know why? Because this car belongs to Mr Faraday and Mr Faraday's my boss and he has a thing about strangers wetting themselves all over his upholstery. So get a grip, yeah?' Winter's hand found the top of Sammy's thigh, and he gave it a little squeeze. 'Deal?'

'Yeah.' Sammy nodded, crossing his legs. 'Whatever you say.'

'And another thing.'

'What's that?'

'Forget about finding somewhere out there to take a leak. There are kids everywhere, Sammy, and Mr Faraday and me take our responsibilities very seriously. Are you with me?'

'No.'

'Indecent exposure, Sammy. Magistrates hate it.'

'So where am I supposed to go?'

'You stay with us. Help me out, Sammy, and I'll find you a nice little pisser down the hill. Mr Faraday'll drive you. Take no time at all. Now how's that?'

Sammy had given up. His eyes were closed and his head was back against the top of the seat.

'What you after?'

'It's about Mickey Kearns, Sammy. As you well know.'

'I don't know nothing about Kearns.'

'That's bollocks, Sammy. Try again.'

'I've told you, Mr Winter, I'm out of touch. I wouldn't know Mickey Kearns from a hole in the road. I'm too old for this game. It's kids now. Fucking infants running around in four-by-fours. What would I know about them?'

'Is Kearns running around in a four-by-four?'

Sammy's eyes were open now, staring out at the view. Winter asked the question again. Then a third time. At length, Sammy nodded.

'Is that a yes, Sammy?'

'Yeah.'

'And what colour is it?'

'Black.'

'A black Beemer? Is that what you meant to say?'

'I dunno. It's just black. Brand new. Kid must have a death wish.'

'Why?'

Another long silence. Sammy was sweating. Faraday could smell it. Winter changed tack.

'Kearns took himself off to the Caribbean, didn't he, Sammy? Him and another bloke, Duley? Just nod. That's all you have to do.'

Sammy swallowed hard, then nodded.

'Good.' Winter was pleased. 'That's good. And Kearns had himself this little holiday with a pocketful of other people's money, people like that nice Chris Cleaver, didn't he? Sort of *working* holiday. Am I right?'

Another nod.

'So what happened then, Sammy? Only it's here that you're going to have to help me out. Me and Mr Faraday, of course.'

Sammy appeared to have gone into a trance. The pressure of his bursting bladder had locked the muscles of his face. He even had trouble getting the words out.

'Little fucker came back,' he managed at last, ' . . . without it.'

'Without what, Sammy? The shit that he'd gone to buy?'

'Yeah.' Sammy winced. 'And without the money too.'

This news put a smile on Winter's face. No wonder Kearns had made himself scarce. His smile grew and grew. He patted Sammy's thigh again. He was extremely pleased.

'So what do we think, Sammy? Or, let's put it another way, what do all those investors think? No, better still, what does *our mutual friend* think?'

'He copped for it. Big time.'

'I bet he did. And there's Mickey Kearns running around in his new four-by-four. Bazza wouldn't have seen the joke, would he? His dosh buying Mickey's wheels?'

Sammy groaned.

'Mr Winter . . . ' he began.

Winter ignored him. He wanted to know more about Bazza. Had he given Kearns a slapping? Only the details might be important.

Sammy shook his head.

'Someone grassed Kearns up,' he muttered.

'Where? How?'

'Out there. Wherever they went.'

'But who'd do that?'

'The other bloke.'

'Duley? The bloke he went with? This Duley grassed Kearns up and Bazza lost his stake? Is that the story?'

'Yeah.'

'So what happened to Duley?'

'They talked to him, Mr Winter. Oh shit . . . '

'When, Sammy? When did they talk to him?'

Winter was on top of him now, his face inches from Sammy's. He told him they were nearly through. In a moment or two, he said, they'd be off down the hill. They'd find Sammy a nice little khazi, somewhere decent, and then he could have the piss of his dreams. Only first he wanted to know when they'd sorted Duley.

'Couple of weeks ago. I don't know the date.'

'Long chat, was it? Somewhere nice and quiet?'

'I dunno, Mr Winter.'

'You do, Sammy, you do. You always say you don't, but you do. Come on, son. One last big effort. Where did they talk to Duley?'

'A caravan. I dunno. Oh, fuck . . . '

'A *caravan*? In the city, you mean?'

'No. Somewhere else.'

'Somewhere of Bazza's?'

'I dunno.'

'Somewhere like Hayling?'

Sammy shrugged. His head was back against the seat and the muscles of his thin face were rigid with effort. Winter studied him a moment, then patted him on the shoulder.

'Good lad,' he said. 'Much better than I expected.'

He leaned forward and muttered something to Faraday. Then came a click as Faraday released the child locks, and Winter reached for the door beside Sammy, kicking it open. Outside in the sunshine a bunch of kids were trying to fly a kite.

'It's fuck-off time, Sammy.' Winter gave him a little push. 'And tell our mutual friend where I dropped you, yeah?'

Faraday drove to Hayling Island, following Winter's directions. To Faraday's surprise, he didn't want to dwell on the exchange with Sammy Lewington, to glory in the information he'd squeezed out of the man, even to claim a scalp. This is a very different Winter, he thought, and he's still extremely angry.

Traffic was heavy onto the island, long queues of cars packed with families desperate to spend the rest of the day on the beach, and Faraday took a couple of short cuts to avoid the worst of the jams. Twenty minutes later, he was down in the south of the island, turning into North Shore Road. Beyond the row of big, detached properties on the left lay the gleaming blue spaces of Langstone Harbour. Faraday smiled to himself. He swept this same line of plump waterfront villas every morning with his binos from the upstairs study at the Bargemaster's House. Ironic to think that one of them might hold the key to Duley's death.

'You've got an address?'

'Last one on the left, boss. It's a dead end after that.'

The last property looked like a building site. The house had been scaffolded and an area near the gate was piled high with bricks on wooden pallets. Heavy vehicles had turned the lawn into a parking lot, deeply rutted, and a sizeable mound of sand had spilled into a once-decent display of roses. Beyond the roses was a cement mixer and an assortment of timber.

'There, boss. Has to be.'

Faraday followed Winter's pointing finger. The property was thickly hedged on both sides. In the furthest corner, before the road petered out altogether, stood a white caravan.

Faraday parked beside the bricks and got out. Winter followed him round the side of the house and down the long stretch of ornamental garden until they were standing on the front wall at the water's edge. As far as Faraday could judge, it was high tide. There was a strip of pebble beach and a wooden pier that sagged in the middle. A noisy group of Mediterranean gulls were sunning themselves on the end of the pier and Faraday caught a glimpse of a solitary shag further out on the water. Perfect, he thought.

He turned back to look at the house again. A new conservatory had been added to the rear of the property and excavation was under way for what must soon become a swimming pool. Faraday gazed at the yellow digger perched on the edge of the hole, trying to visualise what this place would be like in a year's time. With the swimming pool would doubtless come underwater lighting, an outside jacuzzi, non-stop cocktails and a huge sound system. The inhabitants of North Shore Road, he concluded, were in for a treat.

'You're telling me this is Mackenzie's?'

'He owns it, yeah. But it's a present really.'

'Who for?'

'Misty.'

'*Misty?* Last time I looked she was banged up with Mike Valentine. What happened to that?'

'She dumped him. Ten quid says she's back with Baz. This time he's taking no chances. As you can see.'

They began to walk again. The caravan was locked, the curtains pulled on every window. Without a key

225

and a Scenes of Crime search there'd be nothing to connect it to the beating that had put Duley in the A & E unit but its very isolation argued strongly in favour of Winter's theory.

Duley's name had gone in the frame for the loss of Kearns' stake money. He'd been out on Margarita Island with the Buckland boy. He spoke the language, would have talked to the locals, might have done some deal to give himself a slice of the action in return for grassing Kearns. Given the pattern of recent investments, you were talking a substantial sum, tens of thousands of pounds. Losing that kind of money would hurt a great deal, offering every incentive – back in Pompey – for a serious conversation. The most creative of Bazza's heavies was rumoured to favour a couple of Stanley knives taped together. That way, the slash wounds were said to be unstitchable. Where better to practise his skills than here?

Winter strolled away, leaving Faraday to plot the steps he knew he'd need to take next. Jerry Proctor's team could bosh the caravan in a day, max. DNA that linked to Duley would explain the beating he'd taken. But that, alone, didn't necessarily tie Mackenzie or his associates to the incident in the tunnel. For that to happen, there had to be additional evidence.

'Boss . . . ?'

Winter was up by the house. Faraday found him standing beside a pile of discarded interior fitments, unwanted relics that still had to be skipped and disposed of. For a moment Faraday didn't recognise the length of rope in Winter's hand.

'What's that?'

'Sash cord. It must have come out of one of these.' Winter nodded at the wooden sash frames stacked against the wall. 'Mist hates all this stuff. She's into UPVC, big time. Always has been.'

Faraday was still looking at the sash cord. To the naked eye Winter was right. It looked a perfect match for the lengths of rope recovered from the tunnel. Lab analysis, Faraday thought. Just to make sure.

Winter was on the move again, picking his way through piles of rubbish, making for the cement mixer. The grin on his face told Faraday that *Coppice* was about to turn another important corner.

'Here, boss. Look . . . '

Faraday knelt to inspect the length of chain that secured the mixer to a cemented eyebolt nearby. Again, he couldn't be sure, not without forensic examination, but experience told him to discount coincidence. Duley had been bound to the railway line with something very similar. Odds on, they'd find more anti-theft chain elsewhere on the site.

'What's left then?' Winter was trying to tally the items recovered from the tunnel.

'An angle iron.' Faraday could see it in his mind's eye, the length of steel that had kept Duley's legs scissored open. 'About this long.'

Winter gauged the space between his outstretched hands, then nodded.

'Fence post,' he said briskly. 'Has to be.'

He frowned, eyeing the wreckage around him. Then he was off again.

Faraday followed him back towards the road. Wooden gateposts flanked the entrance to the property but the gate itself had obviously succumbed to one of Bazza's many delivery trucks. As a makeshift solution, someone had wired together a series of iron stakes. Winter found them rolled up beneath the nearby hedge. Every night, he told Faraday, someone would be along to drag them out and secure the property.

Faraday bent to examine the stakes. Winter was right. They were angle irons, with punched holes for the wire, exactly the same pattern as the stake recovered from the tunnel. In a moment or two he'd have to set about organising search warrants for the caravan and an overnight guard for the property as a whole, but for now he couldn't resist the obvious question.

He glanced up at Winter.

'Couldn't manage a padlock, could you?'

Twelve

Martin Barrie, to Faraday's surprise, was openly sceptical. He wrapped up a phone call and joined them at the conference table. Winter had been at his desk since half past seven, preparing a brief report for the Scenes of Crime team. Uniforms had been guarding Mackenzie's property all night.

'I thought this guy was supposed to be smart?'

'Arrogant, boss.' Winter was a man transformed – eager, attentive. 'Smart took him to the big time. Now he doesn't bother.'

'So he just leaves this stuff lying around? Knowing what we'll have retrieved from the tunnel? He's had a week to get rid of it, hasn't he? That's not arrogance, that's just dumb.'

'Happens, boss. Believe me. This is Pompey, remember. And Bazza couldn't give a shit.'

Faraday ducked his head. The Detective Superintendent had a point. The same questions had occurred to him. One step at a time, he thought.

'We need a good look at the caravan, sir,' he said to Barrie. 'We're sorting the warrant at the moment.'

'And Mackenzie?'

'He's not taking calls. I just talked to his solicitor. She says she'll get back to me within the hour.'

'No need to be hasty though, eh? Not yet. Not until we've got something to attack him with.'

Faraday nodded his agreement. Only when SOC came up with hard evidence to link the caravan with

Duley would there be any point in pulling Mackenzie in.

Winter was looking aggrieved. He abandoned his notes and leaned towards Barrie.

'Begging your pardon, boss, but this is wake-up time, isn't it? Mackenzie's taking the piss. He thinks he's home free. He thinks he's been home free for years. We need to give him a shake, remind him who's in charge. By holding off, we're sending exactly the wrong message. Yeah, of course we put a search team into his caravan, upset the neighbours, all of that. But the longer we leave him, the longer he's got to sort himself a decent alibi. Mackenzie's got favours coming out of his ears. Half this town owes him. A couple of days, and he'll be interview-proof. I guarantee it.'

This, for Winter, was a major speech. Faraday, watching the blood pinking his face, wondered why it had become so personal.

Barrie remained unconvinced. He wanted to know about Mickey Kearns.

'Him too,' Winter said at once. 'We need to lean on the boy, pull him in, ask him some serious questions. The way I hear it, he owes Mackenzie and a whole lot of other guys over the Margarita trip. Bazza will be telling him he has to work the debt off. That's a lot of graft. The right kind of pressure, and he might be really silly and dob Mackenzie in it.'

'You think he took part in the beating? Supposing it happened in the caravan?'

'More than possible. Kearns has just been grassed up. He's lost a ton of someone else's money. The way he sees it, it has to be down to Duley. He's trusted the bloke, had a few beers, made him part of the team. Then, bingo, it's all turned to rat shit. So Duley, number one, is on a severe slapping. And young Mickey can't wait to lend a hand.' Winter had a smile on his face. 'Does that sound kosher or am I missing something here?'

'What if it was Kearns who took the money?'

'Then it works even better, doesn't it? In fact, it's game, set and match. Duley gets whacked. Denies everything. Knows it wasn't him. Bazza starts having thoughts about young Mickey. At this point young Mickey wants Duley off the plot entirely. He also needs to score a few points of his own. You know the way it is round here. Violence-wise, the tariff's going through the roof. The younger you are, the more psycho you have to be. Blame it on the movies, the video games, whatever, but a serious kicking doesn't cut it anymore.' Winter was looking at Barrie. 'You with me, boss?'

'You're telling me that Kearns might have put Duley in the tunnel?'

'I'm telling you that sticking a grass on the railway track with his legs apart would have them creaming themselves in Buckland. That's ultra-violence. Serious cred. Plus, like I say, it gets Kearns out of one fucking big hole.'

There was a moment of silence. Then Faraday stirred. Already, he'd briefed the detectives studying CCTV vehicle footage to look for a black BMW 4×4. But supposing Winter was right about Kearns, where would that leave Mackenzie? Winter had seen the question coming.

'With a load of questions to answer,' he said. 'It's Bazza's caravan. Bazza's rope. Bazza's fucking apprentice. No one can tell me he wasn't in on it. Kearns is the monkey, boss. Why ignore the organ grinder?'

Bazza Mackenzie turned up at Kingston Crescent an hour later. He had his new solicitor in tow, a trim, ferociously aggressive Hong Kong Chinese with an Oxford degree and an accent to match. Passers-by paused to watch as she slid from Mackenzie's Mercedes SL500, adjusted her skirt, bent to retrieve her calfskin briefcase and headed for the front door. Mackenzie, in a dark business suit, followed her. He'd left the car on double yellow lines in the station forecourt, the windows still down.

Faraday took the call from the front desk. A Nelly Tien wanted a word. Said it was urgent. Faraday thanked the desk officer, then put the phone down. Two years ago he'd led an undercover bid to entrap Mackenzie. Operation *Tumbril* had swallowed months of Faraday's working life and he'd ended up with a painfully detailed understanding of the kind of power and influence that large-scale dealings in cocaine could buy. Mackenzie's reach extended into every corner of the city and when *Tumbril* collapsed amidst a welter of recrimination, Faraday had made a mental note to learn the lesson. This man's very success had given him everything to lose. He was clever. He could afford to buy the best professional advice. And when a threat materialised, like now, he confronted it at once.

After a precautionary call to Martin Barrie, Faraday headed for the stairs. Halfway down, he had second thoughts, returning to the Major Crimes Suite. Winter was bent over the filing cabinet in the Intelligence Cell.

'Mackenzie's at the front desk,' Faraday said. 'I gather he's come for a chat.'

They met in an empty office downstairs. Mackenzie had put a little weight on since Faraday had last seen him, but he looked tanned and fit, and whatever he was using on his hair had taken years off him. The blond Pompey businessman with a finger in so many pies.

Winter was the last to sit down. Faraday noticed the smile on Mackenzie's face.

'All right, Paul? Life treating you OK?'

'Never better, Baz. You?'

'Cushy, mate. This is Nelly, my brief. Can't believe the rubbish restaurants in this city. Wants me to sort out a decent Chinky. Any ideas?'

Winter held his gaze for a moment or two, then glanced at Faraday and sat down. Nelly Tien had already produced a yellow legal pad and a Mont Blanc fountain pen. She was interested in nobody but Faraday.

'You phoned this morning. My client was unable to take your calls at the time but is happy to help you in any way he can. So . . . ' She offered Faraday a cold smile. ' . . . What seems to be the problem?'

'We wanted a key, Ms Tien.'

'To what?'

'A caravan.'

'But what's that got to do with Mr Mackenzie?'

'I understand it belongs to him. At least, it's on his premises.'

Winter was watching Mackenzie. For the first time it occurred to him that he might be unaware of the search team descending on Hayling Island.

Just a flicker of curiosity. Or more likely irritation. 'Where's that?'

'North Shore Road, Mr Mackenzie. The officer in charge has a search warrant.'

'On what grounds?' It was the solicitor again. The sharp sideways flash of her eyes warned Mackenzie to leave it to her.

'We're pursuing enquiries in connection with a recent death. The magistrate was satisfied that a search of the caravan might be pertinent to those enquiries.'

'On what grounds?' she repeated.

'I'm afraid I can't give you that information. At least, not yet.'

'My client has a right to know. It's his property.'

'Your client will be given the appropriate information at the appropriate time. All you need to know for now is that we shall complete the search as expeditiously as we can. And that we shall, of course, be arranging for a replacement lock. In the meantime it might be useful if Mr Mackenzie could furnish us with a list of workmen with access to the caravan. As you say, it's his property.'

'Big deal,' Mackenzie murmured. 'This is about Duley, isn't it? Little fucker in the tunnel?'

There was a long silence. Winter was grinning. Nelly Tien had folded her arms. She looked extremely angry.

At length, Faraday glanced at his watch.

'I'm going to have to make this formal,' he said. 'Ms Tien, we'll be conducting the rest of this interview at the Bridewell. Under caution.'

'What if I don't want to come?' Mackenzie wanted to know.

'I'll arrest you. Your choice.'

Faraday got to his feet. Nelly Tien was staring up at him.

'Arrest Mr Mackenzie for what?'

'Suspicion of murder.'

'*Murder?*' Mackenzie was laughing now, leaning forward over the table, eyeballing Winter. 'When? How?'

'Are you coming to the Bridewell or not?'

Faraday had got to the door. Mackenzie ignored him.

'Duley got himself killed on Sunday, right? That's what they've been saying all week in the *News*. So why don't you ask me where I was Sunday night? Isn't that what you blokes do? Check it all out? Draw your little diagrams? Lay yer little traps? Go on then. Ask me. Put the question. You think I got this tan in fucking *Petersfield?*'

Winter gave the question some thought. Then brought his face very close to Mackenzie's.

'Big mistake, Baz, leaving Misty like that.' He patted his hand. 'She gets lonely, you know. Misses it.'

Faraday detailed Winter and another DC to accompany Mackenzie and his solicitor to the interview suite at the Bridewell. Returning to his office, he picked up the phone. DS Brian Imber, to his knowledge, was still operating from the Intelligence set-up at Havant police station. As a key part of *Tumbril*, he too had been badly burned by the collapse of the operation and had kept the file open ever since. Winter was the only other officer in the city with in-depth knowledge of the shape and spread of Mackenzie's empire, and after the last fifteen minutes Faraday badly needed a second opinion.

'Brian? It's Joe.'

Quickly, Faraday summarised the case against Mackenzie. At the Bridewell he'd doubtless be running a cast-iron alibi. What Faraday wanted was a steer to other names.

'Like who, Joe?'

'Heavies. Blokes on the payroll who'd be happy to put the boot in.'

'Strap someone to a railway line, you mean?' Already, Faraday knew how fanciful it sounded. Imber had another word. 'It's rubbish, Joe. There's no way Mackenzie would sanction anything like that. This guy didn't get rich by pulling stunts. It's cartoon stuff. You're away with the fairies.'

'Names, Brian. Just give me names.'

Imber obliged. There was an ex-matelot called Jamie Frensham who occasionally knocked people around for a lot of money. There was another bloke, much younger, who specialised in terrifying sitting tenants out of properties Bazza wanted to acquire. Then there was a new guy, Brummie hardman, to whom Bazza had recently taken quite a shine.

'What's his name?'

'Brett West. They call him Chalky. He's black. First met Mackenzie through the football. Useful player. Once had trials for Villa.'

'And you say he's violent?'

'He's whatever Bazza wants. Man for all seasons, Brett. Good with a drill if you want a kneecapping. Babysits, too, the way I hear it. Very keen on the laughing powder though, so he can be a bit of a liability.'

Faraday added his name to the list. Duley had been beaten up a couple of weeks ago. West sounded a definite runner and was maybe in the frame for the tunnel job as well. He put the possibility to Imber.

'No chance, Joe. Absolutely none.'

'Why's that?'

'Chalky's been inside since May. Possession with intent to supply. Didn't even bother to go No Comment. No, Joe. Based on what you just told me, I'd be amazed if Mackenzie had anything to do with this Duley. It's just not his MO. He'd be off his trolley even thinking about it.'

'You're sure?'

'Positive. The slapping in the caravan, if there was one? Maybe. Pompey's full of nippers who can't wait to be Bazza, and if this Kearns blew a load of stake money, then Mackenzie would definitely want a word or two. Duley sounds like a handy target and Kearns would have to be brain-dead if he didn't take advantage of that. But the Buriton job? That's unnecessary, completely over the top. You can stick a lot on Mackenzie, and personally I'd love to, but I've never had him down as theatrical.'

Theatrical. Faraday paused. He'd used the term himself. Imber, as ever, was right. The carefully composed tableau in the tunnel, torn apart by the train then painstakingly reassembled in the chill of a Winchester post-mortem room.

Theatrical.

'I'm grateful, Brian.' Faraday was already on his feet. 'I'll be in touch.'

The interview at the Bridewell dead-ended after the first ten minutes. En route from Kingston Crescent, Faraday had checked with Jerry Proctor about progress on the search of Mackenzie's caravan. Proctor had confirmed bloodstains on a mattress and on an area of lino under a table but it would be forty-eight hours at least before he could establish any DNA link with Mark Duley. His team, he said, would probably be through by close of play. The caravan was largely empty, its use evidently confined to blokes on site who wanted to use the Calor gas stove to make themselves a brew. As far as fingerprints were concerned, they'd so far gathered more than a dozen lifts, and were still counting. They'd also be looking for tyre marks around the property that might offer a match to the casts recovered from the plantation next to the railway line.

Faraday shared the interview with Paul Winter. Under normal circumstances he'd have devoted a couple of hours to careful preparation but, as the Detective Superintendent had already pointed out, this exchange with Mackenzie was hopelessly premature. As ever, Pompey's premier drug baron had forced his hand.

The formal caution did nothing for Mackenzie's temper. Ignoring his solicitor, he challenged Faraday to pin down his movements over the previous weekend.

'The guy Duley's in the tunnel on Sunday night, right?'

'That's correct.'

'OK, so ask me. Go on, fucking ask me.'

'Mr Mackenzie—'

'Mr Mackenzie, bollocks. Ask me where I was. Ask me what I was doing. Ask me how I can prove it. Is all that a bit straightforward for you? OK, here's where I help you out. Wednesday the week before last, I go to Heathrow. I take an Emirates flight to Dubai. Naturally I go first class because that's the way that successful people like me travel. You want proof of that? I have a ticket. I have a boarding card. I have a nice little stamp in my passport. Plus I have a trillion extra air miles because I'm the ragheads' favourite passenger. OK, that puts me three thousand miles from Pompey. What do I do then? Well, things being the way they are, I fancy getting my head down. So it's off to the Burj Al Arab hotel, and seconds later I'm spark out. Over the next week I'm shopping. And getting nice and bronzy. And having a little punt on the horses. And guess what, Mr Detective, on Sunday, I pull a winner at – wait for it – twenty to one. That's more money in five minutes than you clowns earn in a couple of months. And you want more bad news? I've still got the winning slip *and* one of those nice digital photos with the date and time on it. Mate of mine took the photo that night. We were back at the hotel having a bevvy or two. That's the Burj again, butler service for every suite, enough Krug to fill the bath, three in the fucking morning, Monday the eleventh. So how come bad Bazza's supposed to be in some khazi of a tunnel? Three thousand miles away?'

'You obviously know Duley.' It was Winter.

'Who said?'

'You know his name. Back in our nick you called him a "little fucker". You're right, too. He's a streak of piss. Or was. But how did you know?'

'I don't. I never did. Where I come from, "little fucker"'s a phrase. It's someone who causes umpteen people all kinds of grief.'

'Grief? What kind of grief?'

'This for starters. I don't know about you guys, but I've got better things to do with my time than listen to bollocks about caravans. Whatever happened to the guy, he probably deserved it. But don't even begin to think you can put me in the frame.'

There was a brief silence. Before the interview started Faraday had mentioned the discovery of certain items from North Shore Road to Mackenzie's solicitor. Now he wanted to discuss this matter in greater depth. Mackenzie wasn't having it.

'Sash cord? Some poxy chain? Bit of angle iron? You guys are off the wall, totally out of order, and, more to the point, you know it. Stuff goes missing from building sites every minute of the day. That's why we have to chain it up. Any more of this pantomime and I'll tell the Dragon Queen here to do you for harassment. You fancy that? Only believe me, she's awesome when she really gets going.'

At that point, led back to his chair after heading for the door, Mackenzie had gone No Comment. The interview, as far as he was concerned, was over.

Faraday drove Winter back to Kingston Crescent. Winter was looking glum. True, they could nick Mackenzie any time they liked and drag him back to the Bridewell but, without evidence, it would simply provoke another mouthful.

'Some of that felt personal.' Faraday was waiting for the lights to change in Fratton Road.

'I'm not with you, boss.'

'You and Mackenzie. The dig about Misty. What was all that about?'

'I was winding him up. Normally works, too.'

'I don't buy it. There's something else, isn't there?' He glanced across at Winter. 'When did you last see Mackenzie, as a matter of interest?'

'Can't remember,' he said at last. 'Must have been a while ago.'

'Really?'

'Yeah.' Winter forced a smile. 'Weeks ago probably. I'm crap at dates.'

'OK.' Faraday nodded. 'So what did you make of the interview? Still convinced that Mackenzie was involved?'

'In the slapping, definitely.'

'And the tunnel?'

The lights went green. Winter turned away.

'No fucking comment,' he muttered.

Back in his office, Faraday brooded. Brian Imber was a good copper, one of the best. Winter, too. Between them, these two men could probably muster fifty years of CID experience. Both knew the city backwards. And

both of them, despite Winter's obvious disappointment, had virtually ruled out any direct link between
Mackenzie and what was left of Mark Duley once the
train had torn him apart.

The Detective Superintendent was due back in an
hour or so. Ahead of this evening's squad meeting,
Faraday had to come up with new lines of enquiry that
somehow took account of yesterday's finds at North
Shore Road. All three items recovered from the
property had been dispatched for detailed forensic
examination and Faraday himself was in no doubt that
they would supply a perfect match for the articles
recovered from the tunnel. Workers on site with access
to the caravan had been pulled in for detailed question-
ing. But where, without a breakthrough, would that
take *Coppice*?

Faraday lifted the phone. He wanted an update on
the billing enquiries on Duley's mobile plus a full list of
cars caught on CCTV returning to Portsmouth in the
early hours of Monday 11 July. Maybe they've already
managed to trace a black BMW, he thought. Or maybe
the time's come to widen the CCTV search parameters.
Southampton. Chichester. Brighton. Wherever.

Babs answered Faraday's call to the Intelligence Cell.
As far as she knew, they were still waiting on billing
and cell site data from Vodaphone but she'd give the
TIU a ring and see if they could exert any extra
pressure. Regarding the CCTV logs, she had a list that
she was pretty certain was up to date.

'Is there a black BMW 4×4 on there?'

'Wait one, sir. I'll check.'

She was back on the line within a minute. DCs
working down at the CCTV control room, she said,
had logged 127 cars between 03.00 and 04.00. After
registration checks, they'd so far done house calls on
eighty-four owners.

'What about the rest?'

'Most of them were out, sir. They're still doing call-backs. I'm sure DC Winter will keep you posted.'

'Is he there?'

'No, sir. He's popped out for some air.'

Paul Winter sat in the café, glad of the swirl of fag smoke and conversation that thickened the brutal heat of the street outside. When he was really low, he had a habit of adding an extra spoonful of sugar to his mug of tea. This afternoon he'd seriously thought of emptying the entire bowl into the thin brown liquid that passed, in this place, for a cuppa.

Life, to Winter, had always been about coming out on top. Year after year, the city had delivered his share of trophy convictions, small-time or quality criminals who, one way or another, had underestimated the matey quip and easy smile and found themselves paying the price in court.

In this ceaseless hunt for battle honours Winter had won himself a reputation that he cherished. Many of his colleagues viewed him with alarm. A handful, when pressed or legless, acknowledged that he had a kind of genius, an instinct for human weakness that he deployed with great charm and equal ruthlessness. Winter, they confessed, was unmatched as a thief-taker, a talent they put down to the way he'd been made. Had he not, through some accident of circumstance, gone into the job, then he'd doubtless have been a career criminal, and a good one. Big spread in Malaga. Nice motor. Plus a reputation around the city for staying several laps ahead of the Filth.

Winter cherished this reputation of his. Until very recently he hadn't wanted, or needed, friends. Neither was he especially fussed about accumulating a stack of money, or any of the other consumer goodies that seemed to badge everyone else's tiny lives. No, what fuelled him, what roused him every morning with a smile on his face, was respect. People knew his name.

People took notice. People talked about him. And when they did so, they never took him lightly.

Saturday night and Sunday morning had changed all that, and he knew from the expression on Mackenzie's face that word would have gone round. They'd lifted him before it was even bloody dark. They'd stuffed him in the back of some twat builder's van, they'd driven him around for a while, played with him, and been clever enough for once not to let slip a single clue. For all he knew, Mackenzie himself may have been in the van. Alternatively, on top of the photos they'd snapped, he may have bunged them a video camera, demanded a tape, struck copies, sent them round to selected friends. A little present, he'd have said. Pull up an armchair. Switch on the telly, Pour yourself a drink. Enjoy. He'd even let them feed him a couple of chips, for fuck's sake. And when they'd finally pushed him into the night – bollock naked – they'd scribbled the world a little message for luck. Winter the tame monkey. Number 47. What kind of reputation could he expect after that? Criminals he could handle; humiliation was something else.

They had his mobile too, and Winter's heart sank still further at the thought of what they could do with it. As Faraday had pointed out, there were countless numbers on the SIM card. Thankfully, he'd always kept a separate mobile for informants, but here, now, he could list two dozen officers – from Detective Superintendents downward – who would be obvious candidates for a wind-up call or two. I expect you're wondering how we got your number, the voice would say. And I expect you're wondering just who the fuck I am. So why don't you talk to that nice DC Winter? And while you're at it, maybe you should ask him about the tiger prawns . . . eh?

Winter shuddered at the prospect, surprised that it hadn't happened already. By facing Mackenzie down in the interview he'd done his best to win back the merest hint of self-respect, but he knew that this brief truce couldn't last. Sooner or later, Mackenzie or one of his trusties would cash in on all those numbers, and at that point Winter would be history.

All his life he'd been a fan of black-and-white World War Two movies. His all-time favourite was *The Cruel Sea*. Just now, he thought, I'm in mid-Atlantic, it's blowing a gale, and some clown up on the bridge has just spotted the torpedo tracks off the starboard bow. Send a pipe, Bosun. All hands to action stations.

Brilliant. But what the fuck could he do? He took a sip of the tea, then pushed it away. Last year the tumour in his brain had – for once – robbed him of the initiative. For months he'd been vulnerable, helpless, his very life in someone else's hands. It had been an experience he'd never wanted to repeat yet here he was again, equally vulnerable, equally helpless. Not his life, this time, but his living. Could he really survive in the job without his precious self-respect?

He got up, picked his way amongst the crowded tables, knowing already the answer.

Faraday sat at his desk, waiting for the number to pick up. A woman's voice answered on the third ring, a warm Canadian accent. Faraday asked for Barbara Large.

'This is she.'

'I'm looking at a brochure for something called the Annual Writers' Conference. Am I talking to the right person?'

'You should be. I run it. But I'm afraid you're a bit late. It's been and gone.'

Faraday said he understood that. He was a police officer, CID. He was pursuing an enquiry in relation to a Mr Mark Duley.

'I know that name,' she said at once. 'He was here last month, a delegate of ours.'

'You met him?'

'I shook him by the hand.'

'May I ask why?'

'Because he won one of our prizes. The first 500 words of a thriller, I think. I'll have to check.'

Faraday felt a faint quickening of his pulse, the merest tremor of excitement; after the door that Mackenzie had slammed in their faces, the faintest scrape of another handle beginning to turn.

Barbara Large was talking about someone else, a published writer who'd run a workshop at the conference. Her name was Sally.

'Sally Spedding?' Faraday had the brochure open in front of him, the workshop circled in scarlet biro. 'Page eight? "Who Do You Think You Are?"'

'That's her. That's who you should be talking to. Mark was in her workshop. That's four hours on a Friday night, and another session on Sunday. They're pretty intense, these workshops. You can get to find out all kinds of stuff.' She paused. 'You mind me asking something?'

'Not at all.'

'Why the call? Is Mr Duley in some kind of trouble?'

'I'm afraid he's dead.'

'Really?' There was a long silence. 'Dead, how?'

For a moment Faraday hesitated. Then he realised there was no point withholding the information. Duley's death had been all over the local paper. For days.

'He got hit by a train,' he said. 'In a tunnel north of Portsmouth. There's evidence that he was chained to the line.'

Another silence, even longer. When she finally came back on the phone, she sounded shocked.

'Maybe you ought to read the piece he wrote,' she said. 'I remember it now. Gifted, sure. But kinda spooky, too.'

*

244

Two hours on the phone took Winter no closer to Mickey Kearns. Whoever he talked to, whatever pressure he applied, the answer was always the same. Haven't seen him for a while. Must be out of town. Even his mother, when she finally answered the phone, still seemed clueless about her boy.

'The last time I saw him was a couple of weeks ago.' She said cheerfully, 'He could be anywhere.'

Invited by Faraday to share this news with the full squad meeting, Winter simply shrugged. There was a possible chain of events, he said, that could put Kearns in the tunnel with Duley. Intelligence indicated a massive drug debt and it would have been in Kearns' interest to have Duley off the plot. On the other hand, this was speculation rather than hard fact, and guesswork never cut much ice with a jury.

Faraday, for once, was impatient. 'What do you think? Has Kearns legged it? Is he on holiday? Or has somebody nobbled him?'

'Dunno, boss,' Winter had confessed wearily. 'You tell me.'

Now, with dusk falling over Gunwharf, Winter decided to draw the curtains on his day. The fact was he'd done his best to trip Mackenzie up, to goad him into the kind of disclosure that might transform *Coppice*, to settle accounts after the weekend's abduction, but a couple of stiff Scotches told Winter he was way off the mark. Bazza might well have ordered someone to give Duley a slapping but there'd be no mileage in going any further. Even a nice quiet murder was bad for business. Why risk something as high profile as the job in the tunnel?

Winter was asleep on the sofa when his entryphone began to buzz. Groggy, he checked his watch: 10.45. The video screen was in the hall. Three floors down, a small, blond figure turned his face towards the security camera. Winter rubbed his eyes, peered at it. Bazza Mackenzie.

'What do you want?' Winter wasn't in the mood for more wind-ups.

'A chat.'

'What about?'

'Mickey Kearns.'

'*Kearns?* Are you by yourself?'

'Yeah.'

Winter released the lock on the main entrance, opened his own front door, waited for the soft pad of footsteps from the lift along the hall. Mackenzie was wearing jeans and a denim shirt, and carried a bottle of Bacardi loosely wrapped in tissue paper.

'Present from Mist.' He thrust the bottle at Winter. 'No hard feelings, eh, mush?'

He stepped past Winter and sauntered into the lounge. Misty herself had once had a similar apartment, different floor plan but comparable view, a present from Bazza before he realised that Mike Valentine was giving her a regular knobbing.

'Nice.' Mackenzie was looking round. 'Better fucking taste than Mist. You remember all them stuffed animals? Place looked like a zoo. You never knew whether to take a bottle of decent wine or a bunch of bananas. Listen . . . ' He turned back to Winter. 'Why don't we sit down?'

Mackenzie parked himself on the sofa, body bent forward, elbows on his knees. A business meeting, Winter thought.

'Kearns?' he queried woodenly.

'That's right. You're still trying to find him. I admire that. You don't fucking give up, do you? Eh?'

Winter shook his head.

'No,' he said. 'We don't.'

'Good. Except you're wasting your time.'

'Why's that?'

'Because Kearns had fuck all to do with what happened in that tunnel, and that's God's truth. The kid fancies himself as a player, a face – of course he

246

does – but there's no way he'd go to all that trouble. He ain't got the imagination, for a start. Plus Duley gave him everything he wanted.'

'He did?' Winter felt his interest quicken.

'Yeah. This is off the record, right? I'm here to spare you lot a great deal of running around. You're going to owe me, big time.'

'How's that then?'

'You're right about the caravan. Duley had been out of order, upset some important people. The way they saw it, he had a couple of questions to answer. He'd been with young Mickey in Margarita. Mickey said he'd been talking to all sorts over there, in Spanish obviously. One of these blokes must have grassed Mickey up.'

'For what?'

'For a lot of money. So Mickey wants a name, doesn't he? He wants to know where the money went and he wants to know who to go after. It's down to Duley to give him that name and after a while he's yelling fit to bust.'

'In the caravan?'

'Yeah. I wasn't there, mush. It's got fuck all to do with me, any of this. I'm just marking your card so you lot get off my back.'

'So what was the name?'

'Querida. Micky got him to write it down. Señor Querida. Some smart spick bastard Duley must have run into. Worst mistake he ever made, talking to Duley.'

'Why's that then?'

'Because Mickey and a couple of mates are out there now, back in Margarita, looking for him. And you know something else? A lot of money says they'll find him.'

Winter nodded. Querida was the addressee on the postcard Duley had mailed from Margarita. Winter could see it now, red ink, big letters. *Mia Querida.*

Faraday, who knew a bit of Spanish, had translated this as "my loved one", though no one had a clue why Duley should have sent it to his own address. There'd been a big fat heart, too, where you normally wrote a message.

'Señor Querida.' Winter was smiling. 'You wouldn't be him for the world, would you, Baz?'

'No, mush, I fucking wouldn't.' Mackenzie was eyeing the Bacardi. 'Are we going to do that bottle or what?'

Winter looked at him a moment, trying to weigh up the direction that this unexpected conversation was about to take. Mackenzie had an obvious interest in staying well clear of *Coppice* and had been blunt enough to say so. At the same time, to Winter's surprise, he hadn't even tried to play the other cards in his hand. No little digs about builders' vans. No mention of Chinese meals. Nonetheless, it still rankled.

'There's something that's bothering me, Baz.'

'What's that?'

'The other night, in the van.'

'Yeah?'

'Why did they park up by the railway line?'

'Because they were pissed off, mush. Because you were out of order with Donna and her mum. Because you took *advantage*.'

'But why the railway line? If they'd got nothing to do with the job in the tunnel?'

'Because they were trying to put the shits up you. It wasn't just a laugh, they were angry. Everyone in this city knows about that tunnel and they wanted to teach you a bit of a lesson. Worked too, didn't it?' He leaned across and slapped Winter on the knee. 'Listen, mush, that's history now. Like I said, no hard feelings.' He nodded at the Bacardi again. 'Ever tried it with Coke and lemon? Only there are a couple of other things I'd like to discuss.'

'Like what?'

'Like how much this place cost, for starters.'

'Six hundred.' Winter plucked the figure out of nowhere.

'Six *hundred*?' Mackenzie was already on his feet, hunting for glasses. 'Shit, mate, someone was taking the piss. Listen, you need serious financial advice, someone to sort out your affairs.' He grinned, uncapping the bottle. 'Know what I mean?'

Thirteen

Barbara Large lived in a rambling bungalow in a village south of Winchester. Faraday parked his Mondeo and checked the address. Chinook, as far as he knew, was the name of an Arctic wind that scoured the Canadian prairies, melting the snow in winter.

She must have been waiting for him because the front door opened to reveal a tall, thin, elegant figure as soon as he pushed in through the gate. Her handshake was soft, barely a touch. She seemed excited to see him.

'I've got the pot on. Do you drink coffee?'

She led him through to the back of the bungalow. This, she announced, was where she lived, a big sunny room, every working surface littered with opened mail. Faraday stood at the window a moment, glad of the warmth on his face. The square of lawn that ran down to a trellis of roses was begging for a trim. She dismissed it with a regretful shake of her head.

'It's a mess, I'm afraid. This time of year I simply don't have the time.'

The Writers' Conference, she said, was going from strength to strength. Years back, she'd mothered an ailing infant. Now, twenty-five years on, her pride and joy was in the rudest of health.

'Three hundred-plus delegates.' She'd stepped next door into the kitchen. 'Every one of them a potential Tolstoy. Do you take sugar?'

Faraday said no. In less than an hour he was due at headquarters for a session with Willard. She returned with the coffees on a tray, asked him whether he preferred custard creams or ginger snaps. Faraday declined both. He wanted to talk about Mark Duley.

'Strange man,' she said at once. 'I've been thinking a lot about what you said on the phone.'

'Strange how?'

'Intense. Non-stop. *Total* commitment. Don't get me wrong, Mr Faraday. We love total commitment. And we do strange too, and we do intense, plus whatever else it takes to expose yourself on paper. But with Mark there was something else, something that didn't quite fit. Sally has a theory, of course, because that's the way novelists work. She said his glue was falling out. She said he was coming unstuck.'

Sally Spedding was the novelist who'd run the workshop Duley had attended. Barbara had taken the liberty of mentioning Faraday's interest on the phone.

'She's expecting your call, Mr Faraday. I've written down her number. Here.' She pushed a compliments slip towards him, the number scribbled in pencil, then passed him a coffee. 'I've got his prize piece too, the one I mentioned on the phone. You should take it away with you. Give it a good read. The man wrote like an angel. To be frank, he didn't really need us.'

The competition, she said, required entrants to pen the first 500 words of a short story or a novel with a murder theme. Most of the submissions had been all too predictable, wildly violent opening scenes that ticked every box in the *How To* manual. Duley, on the other hand, had opted for something entirely different.

'Like what?'

'Read it, Mr Faraday. I can't possibly do it justice. The man's just got such a vivid imagination. Either that, or he's been there. He was just so *lyrical.*'

'In person?'

'On the page. In person he could be charming. In fact the night he won the prize he was quite the pin-up. We use the student bar after the awards ceremony. We all lost count of the number of drinks he bought.'

Faraday remembered Winter's analysis of Duley's earnings. A thousand pounds a month didn't leave much leeway for heavy rounds at the bar.

'How much do you pay to attend?'

'For the weekend package? The one that Mark bought? Two hundred and twenty-five pounds.' She paused, frowning. 'That was something else. He paid very late. In fact he paid when he turned up on the Friday. And it was in cash. Most unusual.'

Faraday produced his pocketbook and scribbled himself a note. Duley had returned from Margarita, presumably with plenty of money, on 17 May. Over a month later he'd swapped some of it for three busy days with a bunch of fellow scribes.

'You think he might have made any –' Faraday shrugged. '– Special friends?'

'You know what?' Barbara's eyes were shining. 'I asked Sally exactly that same question. She said she thought yes. An older woman in the workshop, very talented, just like Mark. You'd do well to have a conversation, Mr Faraday. Writing can be such a *passionate* business.'

Willard was ten minutes away from leaving for the station when Faraday appeared at his office door. A day at sea had given him the beginnings of a decent tan.

'Summons to the Home Office.' Willard glanced at his watch. 'Another half-day down the khazi.'

He wanted to know the latest on DC Suttle. Faraday told him that the lad was off the ventilator.

'Getting better then?'

'We think so.'

'Thank Christ for that. Now . . . *Coppice*. I talked to Martin Barrie this morning but I'm still not clear where the Scenes of Crime operation at North Shore Road is going to take us.'

'We'll get matches on the stuff recovered from the tunnel, sir. I'm sure of it.'

'And you really think that's down to Mackenzie?'

'I doubt it.'

'Who then?'

'It could well be the lad, Kearns, but even then I'm not convinced he's down for the tunnel. The deeper we dig, the more I'm looking at Duley himself. He got himself involved with Kearns. That we can evidence. I think he may well have helped himself to some of the stake money over in Margarita. That would explain a lot. But what we don't yet know is *why*.'

'Why he took the money?'

'Why he needed it. Duley was getting by. Winter's done the analysis. He was having a run-in with the utility people but he settled most of his bills and had enough left over for some kind of social life. Crossing Kearns meant crossing a lot of other people, stakeholders who'd put money in Kearns' pot, and he'd probably have known that. So why run the risk?'

'You told me he was crazy the other day.'

'Volatile, sir. There's a difference.'

'Volatile, then. Short fuse. Goes off like a firework. These people make poor judgements. That's why they're all bloody lefties. Listen.' He checked his watch again. 'There's something else.'

'Sir?'

'Winter.' Willard had returned to his desk. 'How's he getting on?'

'Fine. He's disappointed we can't nick Mackenzie, but fine. Why do you ask?'

'This.' Willard slipped a photo from a Manila envelope and passed it to Faraday.

Winter was sitting at a restaurant table, the bulk of his body unmistakable. Opposite, facing the camera, was Bazza Mackenzie. The two men appeared to be sharing a joke.

Faraday turned the shot over, recognising the stamp on the back.

'This is a surveillance photo. Covert Ops.'

'You're right.'

'Who commissioned it?'

'I did.'

'Is it recent?'

'Yes. Very.' Willard paused. 'You let Winter off the leash on Saturday. You remember? That was my decision. I told Martin Barrie to action it. Why? Because I was keen to find out what Winter would do with this new-found freedom of his. Turns out the first person he meets is our old friend.'

'Thanks for telling me. Does Mr Barrie know?'

'No, Joe, he doesn't. But that's hardly the point, is it? Why don't you try being a detective? Why don't you ask me *exactly* when this shot was taken?' Faraday just looked at him. Cheap, he thought. And insulting. Willard tapped the photo. 'Saturday, Joe. Just an hour after you were talking to Winter at that apartment of his.' Willard got to his feet, reached for his briefcase. 'You were going to let me have some figures. Be nice to know how much he paid for it, eh?'

Faraday took the country route back to Portsmouth. Beyond the long, busy curl of the M3 the road climbed the chalk upland towards fields golden with standing wheat. There'd be a couple of pheasants, thought Faraday, and maybe skylarks. More important still, he'd give himself a moment or two of peace and quiet, the kind of solitude he needed to marshall his thoughts.

He found a turn-off, the rutted mud packed hard after days of summer heat. Twenty metres along the track, with a fine view of Winchester in the river valley below, he turned off the engine and lowered the window. Willard was plainly doubtful about Winter. He hadn't quite abandoned his plans to make him unpack the POCA legislation and spread the good news force-wide but there were now more pressing issues in the shape of a Major Crimes DC apparently consorting with the enemy.

Before Willard left for the train Faraday had insisted on arguing the toss. Winter was heading the Intelligence Cell, for Chrissakes. There were a million reasons why the man might arrange a meet with the likes of Mackenzie. That was his style. That's the way he'd always played it. Getting in amongst them. Tweaking their tails. Indeed, this very pro-activity was the reason they'd trusted him with the job in the first place.

Faraday defended Winter with a vehemence that took even him by surprise. All the more so because Winter had sworn blind only twelve hours ago that he hadn't had a private word with Bazza for weeks. Faraday closed his eyes a moment, let his head sink back against the headrest. How much rope would you sensibly permit an operator like Winter? And how much trust could you put in a boss who tasked a surveillance team behind your back? Caught between two players, he thought. The one taking pictures of the other.

At length, still angry, he reached for his briefcase. Barbara Large had given him Duley's prize-winning entry. Five hundred words, double-spaced, occupied a page and a half. He began to read, hooked at once by the staccato beat of the prose.

'*You remember the small things*', Duley had written. '*You remember the moment you first saw her, stepping into the meeting from a hard frost. You remember the way her breath clouded in the hot fug of the hall, and then you see the pinkness of her face, and the brightness of her eyes, and the way she drew strangers with her smile. You remember that she made no contribution that night. She sat in the back row. She had a shoulder bag, bright colours, Indian-looking. She'd unbuttoned her coat and folded her scarf and her gloves on the chair beside her and found a couple of quid for the fighting fund when the hat came round. Later, when it was time to go, you stood by the door, stringing out some crap conversation, curious to know what she looked like close-up, how she smelled, whether she'd spare just a little of that smile for you.*

The paragraphs rolled on, film-like, offering further glimpses of this woman. Duley wrote of the play of light on her face when they were riding a bus together. Of a habit she had of cocking her head when a conversation really grabbed her. Of the fall of hair on her bare shoulder, months later, in the warmth of an early spring. These images were stepping stones on a journey they'd shared. The writer was besotted. He treasured every fragment of their time together, every last carefully preserved memory. For reasons he'd doubtless share later, he'd become the archivist of this slowly developing relationship and at the end of the piece came the moment when she took their journey in a new direction. *And you remember the way she first kissed you, sand on her hands after the swim, her body still wet*, – he'd written. Not his decision, Faraday thought, but hers.

Faraday felt in the envelope again, looking for some clue to the story's title. Another page of A4 slipped out. He turned it over. 'Gethsemane,' he read, 'By Mark Duley'.

Faraday felt a stir of excitement, gazing out at the play of wind on the fields around him. Gethsemane?

By the time Winter got to Kingston Crescent, it was nearly midday. Stepping into the Intelligence office, he was relieved to find that Babs had kept all callers at bay. She'd also had word from the hospital that Jimmy Suttle was out of Critical Care.

'I've got the new ward number,' she said.

'Great.'

'Aren't you pleased?'

'Of course I am.' Winter sank into his chair. 'Never touch Bacardi, love. It's the second bottle that does the damage.'

Babs studied him a moment longer, then said she'd taken the liberty of opening his post. Reading quickly through it, Winter didn't blame her. Most of the stuff was routine, inching *Coppice* forward, and Winter was finally left with the one envelope that Babs hadn't touched.

'I thought it might be personal,' she said.

The envelope felt thick. Winter gazed at the HSBC logo on the back. His own bank was NatWest.

He slipped a nail under the flap of the envelope, still perplexed. Inside was a sheaf of bank statements and a compliments slip. He glanced at the name of the account holder. Alan Givens.

'This belongs to *Tartan*.' He put the statements on the desk. 'That's a world record, must be. I only sent them the production order on Friday. Normally takes a week.'

He shut his eyes a moment, gave them a squeeze and a rub, then said yes to Babs' offer of coffee. As she left the office with his favourite Beano mug, Winter's eyes drifted over the first of the statements. It was dated January 2005. On the second of that month Givens had an available balance of £6,782.05. In February, it was broadly the same. Ditto March. Then, suddenly, came a deposit of £190,350. Winter pulled the chair closer to the desk, forcing himself to concentrate. The money had been paid in by Goldstein, Everey and Partners, and Winter nodded to himself, recognising the firm of solicitors who'd been handling probate for Givens' mother's estate. The house had been sold, he told himself. And this must be Givens' share.

He sat back a moment, trying to still the thunder in his head. By the beginning of June, according to the statement Winter had removed from Givens' flat, his account was back down to four figures. He must have shovelled it into a savings account, he thought. Or some kind of bond.

He turned to the May statement, tallying off the

regular payments Givens made: rent, electricity, water, council tax, a PC World insurance premium, an annual subscription to *Digital Photographer*. Then came the withdrawal he'd been expecting: £185,000, on 21 May. He nodded again, hearing Babs' cackle of laughter as she returned down the corridor with the coffee. Then he stiffened, his attention caught by the name scribbled alongside the withdrawal. In a note attached to the production order he'd asked for details on any unusual transactions, and here they were. Not a bank transfer at all. But a personal cheque.

Babs was at the door. Winter couldn't take his eye off the name. Finally, it occurred to him that she was asking about sugar.

'Four,' he said. 'At least.'

Ten minutes later, Winter managed to catch Dawn Ellis before she left the car park. Breathless from the bolt down the back stairs, he leant his bulk against her Peugeot.

'I'm late, Paul. This better be important.'

'Babs says you actioned that interview with the nipper on *Tartan*. The one Ewart says he bought the card off.'

'Dale Cummings?'

'That's him.'

'I talked to his mum. Going through the CPU will take a while to set up. There's a queue for nine-year-olds you wouldn't believe.'

The Child Protection Unit was a specialist team which dealt with stroppy juveniles.

'So what did Mum say?'

'She denied it. *My* Dale? *Nick* anything? You have to be kidding.'

'Form?'

'He's too young for a record but he's on the At-Risk Register and the head at the local primary says he's always bunking off. She also said he's got a thing about setting fire to stuff. When I raised the truanting with Mum, she said the school was crap anyway. They were lucky to see Dale at all.'

'So what do you think?'

'What do *I* think? I think he found the wallet, blew the sixty quid on whatever, and sold the rest on. Just like Karl Ewart said. I suppose we could go looking for the wallet, bosh the house, but what's the point? Ewart'll go down for Suttle. We shouldn't be greedy, should we?'

The mention of Jimmy Suttle put a frown on Winter's face. Dawn said she'd been to the hospital at lunchtime.

'How is he?'

'Much better.'

'Thank Christ for that. What's the ward number?'

'E1. He's playing the modest hero at the moment. The nurses love him.' Dawn reached for her ignition keys. 'Why the interest in Cummings? What's happened?'

'Nothing,' Winter said bleakly. 'Yet.'

A message was waiting for Winter when he stepped back into his office. Babs nodded at the phone.

'Boss wants to see you. Says it's urgent.'

'Faraday?' Winter's heart sank.

'Yes.'

Winter looked down at the bank statements for a moment, then slipped them back into the HSBC envelope and put them in his drawer. Later, he thought. When I can start making some sense of this madness.

Faraday was sitting at his desk, leafing through a pile of messages. He told Winter to shut the door, then waved him into the spare chair.

'This is about Mackenzie,' he said at once.

'Oh yeah?'

Winter crossed his legs, did his best with a smile. He

knows, he thought. Mackenzie's phoned him, or sent a photo, or some other fucking dodge. He knows.

'Yesterday,' Faraday began, 'when Mackenzie came in with his brief. What was all that about?'

'I'm not with you, boss.'

'Bit eager, weren't you? Not your style at all.'

Winter feigned bewilderment. He'd thought it himself at the time – trying to stick it to Mackenzie, trying to land punches when the man was too far out of range – but the resentment, the urge to settle accounts, had been too strong.

'I asked him a couple of questions, boss,' he said at last. 'As you do.'

'No, you didn't. You were all over him. And he was just the same. You were like kids in the playground. So tell me what else has been happening? Before he turned up?'

'I'm not with you, boss.'

'Yes, you are, Paul. That's the whole point. You're with me every step of the way. Either we sort this thing now or –' He shrugged. '– It's going to get extremely unpleasant. We're talking more than Major Crimes here. More than Human Resources finding you some other job. Potentially, if I've got this right, we're talking disciplinary hearings, tribunals, the whole nine yards. That's extreme, I admit, but you're the only guy who can tell me different.' He paused. 'So why don't you start with Mackenzie?'

'What do you want to hear?'

'I want to hear the truth. I want to know exactly when you last saw him alone. I want to know the circumstances, the date, where it happened, the lot. And do yourself a favour, eh? Don't fuck around.'

Winter gazed at him, uncertain now. A lifetime of detective work had taught him the wisdom of giving nothing away. The man who survives, he'd always told himself, is the man who keeps a secret.

And yet Faraday already knew the secret. So what was the point?

'We had a run-in,' he said slowly. 'You're right.'

'About what?'

'Mickey Kearns. That was part of it. Misty too, I suppose. Bazza loses it sometimes. Thinks he owns the bloody city. You know what he's like.'

'Go on.'

Winter looked up, wanting clues, but Faraday's face was a mask.

'They jumped me,' he said woodenly.

'Who?'

'Bunch of Bazza's blokes in Buckland. I'd been to see Donna like you asked and you're right, I should have gone mob-handed. But I didn't . . . ' He let the sentence trail away.

'So what happened?'

Something in Faraday's voice told Winter this was new to him. Shit, he thought.

'Young Donna must have made a call. The blokes that jumped me had a van. We went for a little ride.'

'Who were they?'

'I don't know.'

'How many of them?'

'No idea.'

'Why not?'

'Because . . . ' Winter was certain now. He'd been too hasty. He'd made one supposition too many. Whatever had triggered this sudden interest of Faraday's, it hadn't been a prompt from Mackenzie.

'Because what?' Faraday wanted an answer.

'Because I'd pissed Bazza off.'

'That wasn't my question. I know you'd pissed Bazza off. You just told me that. I'm asking you why you didn't know any of these guys, couldn't even count them.' He stared at Winter, visibly angry. 'Are you going to tell me or do I pick up this phone and make it official?'

The word 'official' put a rueful grin on Winter's face. He'd been kippered. It was a hard thing to admit but it was true. In less time than it takes to boil an egg, Faraday had him backed against the wall. So much for keeping a secret, he thought. In the end, he'd done Mackenzie's work for him.

He stared out of the window, weighing his options. Finally, recognising the size of the hole that yawned before him, he shrugged.

'OK, boss,' he said. 'I'll tell you exactly what happened.'

Faraday listened, inscrutable, as Winter went through it. They'd put a plastic sack over his head, tied him up, stuck him in a van, driven him around for half the night, parked up by the railway line, given him a poke from time to time to keep themselves amused, stripped the clothes off him, taken photos. Then they'd dumped him on top of Portsdown Hill and left him to get on with it. Two o'clock in the morning. Bollock naked. Thank God he'd had a mate he could count on.

Faraday stirred.

'That's abduction,' he said softly. 'Abducting a police officer is a hanging offence. It's not just you, Paul, it's everyone else in the job. You let them do it because you obviously had no choice but afterwards you did fuck all about it. What kind of message does that send?'

Winter nodded. It was the reaction he'd expected, straight out of the manual they kept in the Professional Standards Department. Next, Faraday would doubtless ask for a formal statement. Winter could sense the interminable meetings that lay down the road. They'd end in a disciplinary hearing and the coldest of goodbyes. A big fat pension would have been nice, he thought. And maybe a pat on the back for all those scalps he'd taken.

'I couldn't bear it, boss,' he said simply.

'Couldn't bear what?'

'The wind-ups. The little digs. Blokes laughing behind your back.'

'In the job, you mean?'

'Yeah.'

'And that's why you didn't blow the whistle?'

'Yeah.'

'Even afterwards? Next day?'

'Next day was too late. By next day I had too many questions to answer. Better to let it all blow over.'

'But it wouldn't, would it? Mackenzie's got photos. He's got your mobile. He's got our numbers. And that means he's got you. And you know why? Because he knows you. He knows the kind of bloke you are. He knows how bloody difficult you are, how you play it long, how you piss everyone else off, how you go your own sweet way and end up with a bunch of enemies who should be watching your back.' He frowned. 'Tell me something. Mackenzie has a big pile of chips he needs to cash in. He'll have been in touch by now. Bound to have been.'

'Last night.'

'And he had a proposition, didn't he? Something he wanted you to do?'

'It wasn't that specific.'

'So what happened?'

'We got pissed.'

'Bonding session?'

'Exactly.'

'And how did you feel this morning? Once you realised he'd got you by the balls?'

'No idea, boss. I'll tell you when my head starts working again.'

A smile ghosted across Faraday's face.

'Serves you fucking right.' He stooped to retrieve an envelope from his briefcase. 'Mr Willard gave me this.'

Winter looked at the photo. Bastards, he thought.

'He's saying Saturday afternoon. In the Water Margin.'

'He's right. Mackenzie belled me, wanted a meet. That's when I pissed him off.' He told Faraday what had happened. When he described leaving the restaurant with the tiger prawns, Faraday shook his head.

'Hardly subtle,' he said.

'Bazza isn't into subtle.' Winter was staring out of the window. 'Unless you shout, he doesn't hear a fucking thing.'

Faraday was toying with his pencil. He had some other questions, this time about the Gunwharf apartment, and he made it plain that it was in Winter's interests to answer them.

'How much did you sell the bungalow for?'

'Two seven five.'

'Any outstanding mortgage?'

'Twenty.'

'Savings?'

'Seventeen, give or take.'

'And the apartment?'

'Five fifty.'

'You'd already paid for the operation?'

'Yes.'

'How much?'

'Sixty.'

'So where did the difference come from? Given that you'd shelled out sixty grand for the operation?'

For the first time, Winter knew he had to draw a line. The inference behind Faraday's questions was all too obvious – that Mackenzie or some other scumbag had tided Winter over on the Gunwharf apartment – but Winter resented sharing every last financial detail with his bosses. Even with his record, there came a point when they had to trust him. Otherwise, he might as well spare them the hassle and jack it in himself.

'It's legit, boss. That's all I'm saying.'

'You can prove it?'

'Glad to, if it comes to it.'

'Here? Now?'

'I'm afraid not. Put it down to pride. Say I'm being difficult. It won't surprise them.'

'Who's them?'

'Dunno, boss.' Winter nodded at the surveillance photo. 'Whoever set that up, I suppose.'

There was a long silence. It was like waiting for some kind of death sentence. Winter sat back in his chair, wondering whether it was too late to take up origami. At last, Faraday appeared to have made a decision.

'I'm taking you off *Coppice*, at least for the time being, until we've got Mackenzie well and truly eliminated.' He looked up. 'We'll talk again once I've made some decisions. Concentrate on *Tartan*, will you?'

'The Givens job?'

'Yes.' Faraday offered a thin smile. 'I'm sure there's lots to do.'

Winter returned to his office, chastened. He'd rolled over for Faraday far too easily but he blamed that on the Bacardi. What was worse was the fact that he hadn't a clue what might happen next. Surrendering the initiative, he thought grimly, is becoming a habit.

Babs was about to go into conference with a couple of DCs in the Incident Room. Winter waited until she'd gone, then slid the HSBC envelope from his drawer. He extracted the May statement and studied it carefully to make sure he'd got it completely right. Satisfied, he reached for the phone and dialled a mobile number.

'Jake? That you? It's Paul. You're at work, yeah? Only I need a word.'

Jake Tarrant said he was busy. A traffic jam of bodies and a pile of paperwork he wouldn't believe.

'Sure, son. I'll be fifteen minutes. Put the kettle on.'

The mortuary at St Mary's lay in a gloomy cul-de-sac on the edges of the hospital site. The dead end offered turning space for undertakers' vans and the refuse lorries that called for clinical waste, and security at the cheerless Victorian building had recently been strengthened after a break-in by an alcoholic in search of embalming spirit. Winter pressed the entryphone buzzer, sheltering from a thin rain.

Jake Tarrant was wearing clinical greys, a theatre cap with a tie at the back and a pair of blood-spattered wellington boots. He threw the door open, stepped over a coil of hosepipe, and ushered Winter in. The DC manoeuvred round a plastic-shrouded corpse on a trolley and waited for Tarrant to shut the main door. Beyond the laden trolley, inside the post-mortem room, he could see a bike parked beneath the window. It looked new.

'That yours?' He was following Tarrant into the tiny office.

Tarrant glanced over his shoulder and nodded.

'It's brilliant,' he said. 'Eighteen gears. Titanium frame. All the bells and whistles. Scares me to death just looking at it.'

'Fast, is it?'

'Expensive. Leave it anywhere in this city and you're talking two locks. At least. Tea?'

Winter made himself comfortable in the office. A huge Pompey poster on the wall celebrated last season's 4–1 epic against the Scummers and the side of a big grey filing cabinet had been decorated with an FHM calendar. Miss July, a hefty blonde, left little to the imagination.

'I thought you'd get sick of bodies.' Winter nodded at the calendar. 'Your line of work.'

'Cool, isn't she?' Tarrant was busy trying to find the sugar. 'You should take a look at April. She's black. See the arse on her.'

Winter resisted the temptation. Beneath the window the scabby carpet tiles were covered with what looked like building plans. A ruler, pens, and a pad of yellow Post-its lay beside them.

'What's this then?'

'New mortuary, over at QA. The architects have come up with the shell of the building and we have to decide what we want inside.'

'You moving then?' This was news to Winter.

'Next year. Then you'll get your Home Office PMs back from Winchester. State of the art, mate. Regional showpiece. Computerised locator system. Designer tables. A hundred and eighty fridge spaces. Can't wait.'

'And what about this khazi?' Winter gestured round.

'Storage. Bit like now. All the routine PMs are done up at QA. They're pushed for fridge space at the moment, so we take the overspill. Full house at the moment. Too many people pegging it. Sugar?'

Winter helped himself. 'Thanks for yesterday.' He tipped his mug in salute. 'You were brilliant, son.'

'Pleasure, mate. Sorry about the missus.'

'Not her fault. Christ, who needs some fat old bastard barging in at three in the morning?'

'Exactly what she said. Funny that.'

Tarrant had driven him back to Gunwharf first thing Sunday morning. As Jake'd backed the Fiat off the hardstanding outside the house, Winter had noticed the hint of a face behind the net curtains in the window upstairs.

'I've still got your Pompey top,' he reminded Tarrant. 'I'll put it through the washing machine and drop it off.'

'Whatever.' Tarrant had a mouthful of biscuit. 'Keep it if you want. Little souvenir.'

Winter ducked his head, took a gulp of tea. His headache had gone now and he helped himself to a couple of Jammie Dodgers.

'Listen,' he said. 'I've got a question for you.'

'What's that?'

'This bloke Givens. I've been going through his bank statements. One of the things you do.'

'And?'

'He seems to have bunged you some money.'

'Yeah, I think I mentioned it, didn't I?'

'Not a hundred and eighty-five grand you didn't. What was that about?'

The question hung in the air between them, Winter suddenly aware of the whirr of the extractor fans along the corridor.

Tarrant was looking pained. 'Is this official?' he said. 'Only I'm not quite sure what you're after.'

'I'm after a clue or two about the money, son. You're a bright lad. We're dealing with someone who's gone missing. A hundred and eighty-five grand makes people like me nervous. Motive's a nasty word but I'm sure you know what I mean.'

'*Motive?* Shit. The bloke was a friend of ours.'

'Was?'

'Is. Was. Whatever. That's why he made the loan in the first place.'

'A hundred and eighty-five grand?'

'Yeah.'

'What for?'

'We're thinking of moving house. In fact Rach has got her eye on a property down in Southsea. Better schools for the kids. All that crap.'

Winter nodded, remembering the estate agents' details in the back of the Fiat. Growing family. Hutch of a starter home. Makes sense.

'Was this a long-term loan then? Repayment schedule? Regular standing order? Paperwork? All that?'

'No.'

'Why not?'

'Because we hadn't got round to it. For starters, it was just a whack of money. Tell you the truth, Alan didn't seem fussed about it.'

'A hundred and eighty-five *grand*? And he just gives it away?'

'It wasn't a gift. We'd have done the paperwork in the end, done it kosher. We'd have had to.'

'So what happens now?'

'Dunno.' Tarrant shrugged. 'I suppose that's up to you lot. Last time we talked, you thought someone had done him. In fact you even had a name. Karl Someone.'

'Did you mention that to Rachel?'

'No.'

'Why not?'

'It'd upset her. She really liked Alan.'

'Liked?'

'Likes. As far as she's concerned, he's just gone off for a while.'

'She saw a lot of him? Givens?'

'Yeah, she did. He was mad about photography, took loads of shots of the kids. You see the stuff up the staircase? That was his.'

'So he was round a lot then?'

'Depends what you mean by a lot. Couple of times a week maybe. You should talk to Rach. She felt really sorry for the guy. Thought he was a bit . . . you know . . . lonely. She's big on waifs and strays, Rach. Cats, dogs, people, makes no difference. If it's got a pulse, she'll give it houseroom.'

'And how did you feel?'

'Me? I quite liked the bloke. We weren't, you know, mates but he was all right. Inoffensive. Bit of a loner maybe. But that's not a crime, is it?'

'Not at all.' Winter's gaze had strayed back to the plans on the floor. 'This money, Jake.'

'Yeah?'

'It could be a problem.'

'How?'

'Because it looks odd.'

'You mean suspicious?'

'Yes. This bloke Givens has gone missing. We've got a prime suspect, sure, and he's been silly enough to do a copper so he's going nowhere fast, but he swears blind he never laid a finger on the geezer.'

'Well, he would, wouldn't he?'

'Of course. But you know the way we work. I'm part

269

of a squad here, and there are other people who believe our Mr Ewart when he says he never even met Givens. Which means they're going to go looking further afield.'

'Presuming Alan's dead.'

'Of course. But that's an assumption nasty bastards like us have to make every working day. Think the worst and you're seldom wrong.' He paused, took another gulp of tea, then put the mug to one side. 'Listen, son, I'm here to mark your card, right? All I'm saying is that it might be better to have that money ready to give back. All of it. Whatever happens. You with me?'

'But who do we pay?'

'Givens, if he turns up and if he wants it. Otherwise . . . ' Winter shrugged. 'He's got a solicitor. I happen to have the details. You could do worse than drop him a line, offer the money back. Is that a problem?'

Winter knew at once that it was. Tarrant was shaking his head.

'No can do,' he said. 'The Southsea place I mentioned, Rach is dead set. We're putting our place on the market this week. We're going for a quick sale, one seven five. That's a steal up our way.'

'So why can't you raise a mortgage? Like everyone else?'

'Because I don't earn enough. And no way is Rach going out to work. Not with two young kids.'

'But you told me just now you could convert this money into a mortgage. Pay Givens back monthly. Kosher, you said.'

'Yeah, but he'd see it our way, Mr W., you know what I mean? He'd cut us a bit of slack if things got sticky.'

'So you're telling me you can't pay the money back? Not yet, anyway?'

'That's right.'

'OK.' Winter frowned. 'But if we find a body, there's going to be a problem. You know that, don't you?'

'How come?'

'He'll have an estate, probate, all that. Then you're back in the hands of the solicitors and, believe me, they'll come looking for the cheque.'

'And what happens if Givens has just . . . ' Tarrant shrugged ' . . . disappeared?'

'Then he stays on the radar screen. He's already on the Misper register. Officially, we maintain an interest. Circulate details. Keep looking. After a while, though, it gets to be difficult.'

'So in the end . . . ?'

'In the end, he just stays disappeared. The truth is that people go missing every day of the week. If I told you he'd become a priority, I'm lying.'

Tarrant nodded, saying nothing. At length he asked Winter whether he fancied another biscuit.

Winter shook his head. It was time to go. He stood up, lingering for a moment beside the desk. Then he laid a hand on Tarrant's shoulder and gave it a little squeeze.

'Fingers crossed then, eh? Let's hope this mate of yours turns up in one piece. Either that, or he never turns up at all. Otherwise, my son, you're fucked.'

Fourteen

Tuesday, 19 July 2005, 19.02

Faraday stood on the upper deck of the Gosport ferry as it nosed across the ebbing chop of the harbour. He'd made contact hours earlier with Willard, catching him in the back of a taxi headed for Waterloo. Faraday badly needed another meeting. He'd talked to Winter, he told Willard, and there were important decisions to be made. When Willard said it would have to wait until Thursday at the earliest, Faraday lost his temper. It was Willard's idea to put Winter to the test. The least he could do was give the man some kind of hearing.

In the end, with some reluctance, Willard had agreed they should talk. He had a couple of items he needed to pick up from the boat. He'd drive across to Gosport. If Faraday cared to present himself at the main gate to the Hornet Sailing Club at half past seven, Willard would pick him up and take him down to the clubhouse. If he stopped throwing his toys out of the pram, Willard added, he might even buy Faraday a spot of supper.

The ferry berthed alongside the Gosport pontoon and Faraday joined the surge of late commuters as they jostled to step ashore. The last of the rain had cleared now and there was the promise of a glorious sunset beyond the shadowed tower blocks that dominated the waterfront. Faraday set off along the Millennium Walk that skirted the harbour, enjoying the freshness of the air. This time in the evening, across the water, Pompey was at its best, the sleek billow of the new Spinnaker Tower bone-white against the greys of the dockyard below, the tumble of pubs and houses in nearby Old

Portsmouth glowing in the rich golden light. At moments like this, he thought, there was no finer place to call home.

The former HMS *Hornet* was tucked behind the westerly arm of the harbour entrance. Sheltered on all sides, it had become a haven for a couple of hundred members of the Royal Naval Sailing Association looking for good company and somewhere decent to keep their yachts. Faraday paused on the bridge that overlooked the marina, gazing down at the forest of masts below. Berths like these, so close to the harbour entrance, were gold dust, and membership of Hornet, he knew, was strictly controlled. Quite how Willard had managed to swing it was a mystery.

The new Head of CID met him at the gate. They walked down towards the clubhouse, Willard pausing to point out a neat-looking yacht on a nearby pontoon. It was clearly his pride and joy.

'Moody 27.' He smiled. 'Beautiful manners. Sails like a dream.'

He'd bought a half stake, he said, from a chum of his who was currently holding down an important staff job with C-in-C Fleet on Whale Island. As a serving Commander, Rory naturally had the pick of the best party invites and was nice enough to include his new shipmate when the opportunity presented itself. So for twelve and a half grand, as Willard pointed out, he'd acquired not only his share in *Pipsqueak*, but a whole new raft of well-connected friends.

'They're nice people,' he said. 'Come and see my new club.'

The clubhouse was a low brick and timber building with a fine view of the marina. Willard took Faraday through to the bar and signed him in, exchanging nods and the odd remark with some of the faces around him. Willard's ability to ride the social tide, his unerring instinct for the people who really mattered, had never ceased to amaze Faraday. He'd been coming to this place for no more than a couple of months, he thought. Yet already Willard was treating it like home.

Faraday ordered fish and chips and found a table beneath a line of framed photos featuring a variety of yachts. The bar was crowded, evidently visiting sailors from a club down the coast. Willard elbowed his way through the scrum, deposited two pints on the table. The food would be coming shortly.

'Winter,' he said, settling into a chair beside Faraday. 'Tell me.'

Faraday recounted the conversation he'd had back at Kingston Crescent. Winter, he said, had readily admitted meeting Mackenzie on Saturday afternoon. Mackenzie had warned him off Mickey Kearns, and Winter, in turn, had told him to fuck off.

'He said that?'

'In terms, yes.'

'And you believe him?'

'I do.'

'How come?'

'Because Mackenzie, or people very close to Mackenzie, took it upon themselves to sort Winter out.'

'I'm not with you. How, exactly?'

Faraday told him about Saturday night, about the van, about what happened afterwards.

'That's totally out of order.' Willard hadn't touched his beer. 'Just who do these people think they are?'

'That was Winter's point.'

'So why on earth didn't he do something about it?'

'He did. He talked to me.'

'Two days later? Come on, Joe. This is beyond belief. He's a serving police officer, for God's sake. There are rules here. He can't rewrite them. You call for the cavalry. You sound the alarm. You start making life extremely difficult for the likes of Mr Mackenzie.'

'He had no direct evidence against him. The guys in the van were smart. He saw nothing, heard nothing.'

'Is that what he told you?'

'Yes.'

'And you're really telling me you believe him?'

'Yes.' Faraday nodded. 'But this is where it gets interesting.'

He told Willard about the photos and the missing mobile. Both, in the right hands, were priceless ammunition. And Mackenzie, as it turned out, was the man with the loaded gun.

'He called on Winter last night. For a social chat.'

'I bet he did. He's on a nicking.'

'But why the rush?' Faraday was smiling now. 'Sir?'

Willard's face darkened, the usual cue for an explosion of wrath. For a second or two Faraday feared the worst. Then the Detective Chief Superintendent seemed to relax. He reached for his beer, took a sip, put it down again.

'Go on,' he said. 'I'm listening.'

Faraday took his time. This is important, he told himself. Screw this up and Winter will be looking at his P45.

'We still have a very big interest in Mackenzie, right, sir? Not because of *Coppice*. Not because we necessarily think he might have anything to do with what happened to Duley. But because he is what he is. Not a gram of cocaine comes into this city without Mackenzie's say-so. And he has twenty million quid in the bank to prove it.'

'Go on.'

'You asked me to keep an eye on Winter. The way you see it, the POCA legislation is a stick we can use to beat the likes of Mackenzie. You think Winter might be part of that process.'

'It's possible, yes. Though my senior colleagues are far from keen on the idea. They think Winter belongs on the street. Not poncing around the force trying to spread the word about the Proceeds of Crime Act.'

'They may be right.'

'You think so?'

'Yes, sir. But there may be a better way to bring these people down.'

'I'm not with you.'

'OK, then let me explain. It works like this. Mackenzie's got Winter by the throat. He's humiliated the man and he's got the evidence to prove it. He thinks there's no way Winter's going to risk losing face with the rest of us, and that's a judgement you'd understand. Except it now happens that Mackenzie's wrong.'

Somebody behind the galley counter announced a ticket number. Two plates of fish and chips. Willard didn't take his eyes off Faraday.

'You want to put Winter into play against Mackenzie,' he said slowly.

'Yes, sir.'

'By having him run with the man.'

'Yes, sir.'

'As a kind of double agent.'

'Exactly.'

'Terrific. So who says we can trust him?'

'Who?'

'Our Mr Winter.'

'Me, sir.'

'That's a very big claim, Joe. What makes you so sure?'

He glanced at his ticket, then got up and headed for the bar. Faraday cleared a space on the table for the plates. Willard returned, unloading sachets of tartare sauce from his jacket pocket.

'Well?' He was wrestling with the foil on the tartare sauce.

Faraday speared a chip, popped it in his mouth. Finally, he said that Winter loved the job too much to hazard it. That was their guarantee. That said they were bulletproof.

'But people change, Joe. Especially after all the traumas he's been through.'

'That's true.'

'Which is why I OK'd the deployment to Major Crimes in the first place. So you could keep an eye on him. Remember?'

'Of course, sir.'

'So where are the real guarantees? Only it's more than Winter's head on the block.'

Faraday acknowledged the point. He'd already taken Winter off *Coppice*, an obvious precaution while Mackenzie was still, at least technically, in the frame. Tomorrow, with Barrie's agreement, he intended to remove him from the Intelligence Cell altogether. That way he was denied access to key resources, like the Police National Computer.

'Good point.' Willard nodded his approval. 'So what will you do with him?'

'I'll pair him up with Dawn Ellis. She's steady. That way he'll still be on *Tartan*, which is fair enough because Givens was his Misper from the start.'

'Driving licence?'

'He'll have to depend on Ellis. It shouldn't be a problem.'

'Fine. And in the meantime? As far as Mackenzie is concerned?'

'Winter reports to me. Or Martin Barrie. That would be your call.'

Willard nodded, turning his attention to the plate of food in front of him. Minutes later, most of it had gone. Willard tidied his remaining chips into a neat pile and coated them with sauce.

'This is huge, Joe,' he said at last. 'It's a clever idea, I'll grant you that, but I'll have to sleep on it. It's not just Winter, it's Mackenzie too. He's a clever bastard. One minute he's playing into your hands. The next he bites you on the arse. I'm not going through *Tumbril* again. Not even for you.'

'It's not *Tumbril*, sir, with respect. On *Tumbril* we made the running, or tried to. This time it's Mackenzie's call.'

'Says you.'

'Who else then? Who else makes the running?'

'Winter, of course.' Willard licked a smear of sauce from his finger. 'Which is where we began this conversation.'

Winter sat on his balcony, watching the lights of the Gosport ferry approaching across the harbour. This afternoon's conversation with Faraday had disturbed him more than he cared to admit, not least because he'd let the DI play him so artfully. Not only that, but – in a move that Winter recognised only too well – he appeared to be keeping his knowledge of Winter's little transgressions entirely to himself. It wasn't that he mistrusted Faraday. It wasn't even that he disliked him. On the contrary, he'd begun to develop something close to a healthy respect for the man.

No, it was altogether simpler than that. Buoyed by self-belief, Winter had kept his head above water for decades. Now, that self-belief had gone, stolen first by Mackenzie's little jape, then latterly – for reasons he still couldn't fathom – by Faraday. In front of both men, unaccountably, Winter had lowered his guard. And the results, all too predictably, were extremely ominous.

There still, of course, remained the possibility that Faraday would simply lift the phone and hand the whole affair, the entire shambles, over to Professional Standards. That would undoubtedly make life a great deal simpler for a hard-pressed DI. Winter would be ghosted away, put out to grass pending some kind of disciplinary hearing, and in due course the bureaucracy would wash its hands of him. There might be a paragraph or two in *Frontline*, glossing the facts, and a cheerless round of farewell drinks in the Fratton bar, but that, essentially, would be that. Like so many other washed-up cops, beached by graft, or greed, or a misplaced enthusiasm for breaking the rules, Winter would be left with the dribble of a pension and a terrifying emptiness that nothing else could possibly fill. One week would vanish into the next. He'd start getting interested in the horses or Sudoku. He'd lift the phone to the odd face enquiring about the possibility of a pint or two. He might even find himself saving up the weekly Tesco shop until Friday afternoons, the high spot of this exciting new life of his. The prospect, all too real, filled him with gloom, and he flailed about, looking for some kind of explanation.

Was it really his fault? He thought not. He'd never, for a second, considered throwing in his lot with the likes of Bazza Mackenzie and it hurt him to think that someone up the hierarchy had gone to the trouble of tasking the surveillance boys to keep an eye on him. That, to be frank, was way out of order, and he was still toying with a letter to Willard to nail the bastard who'd taken a step like that. Simple logic, he told himself, would tell anyone with half a brain that getting into bed with Mackenzie was the shortest cut to getting well and truly fucked. He'd seen it happen to countless people in the city. They sniffed the money, spread their legs, and Bazza was only too happy to help himself. But simple logic clearly wasn't enough. Someone had laid treason at Winter's door, and the charge – or the whisper – appeared to have stuck.

So what might he expect in the days to come? That, in essence, was the issue. After the operation in Phoenix, with Maddox still attending to his every need, Winter had kidded himself that close acquaintance with death changed a man, changed his perspectives, his needs, his priorities. But now, faced so abruptly with the loss of the job he loved, he knew that wasn't true. He was still, for better or worse, a detective. He teased out facts. He drew a series of lines between them. He punted his judgement on this pattern or that. And when he knew the bet was safe, the odds stacked overwhelmingly in his favour, he mustered his chips and returned to the table, and when his number came up, as it usually did, there was nothing sweeter than the knowledge of yet more credit in the account he kept against rainy days like this. That was what fuelled him. That was what made him get up in the morning. Take it away, and he wasn't at all sure there'd be anything left.

He got to his feet and peered into the warm darkness, wondering whether to risk a late call to Faraday. He'd doubtless be home by now, tucked up in that house of his beside the water. There was just a little part of Winter that envied the DI's composure, the breadth of his interests outside the job, the way he seemed so armour-clad. He knew, of course, that Faraday was no stranger to life's sterner challenges. Bringing up a deaf-mute kid, essentially on your own, couldn't have been easy. Yet there was a steadiness about the man, a seeming peace of mind that Winter – at times like this – knew he could have done with. Winter thrived on chaos, on mischief, on the splash you made when you lobbed a big, fat rock into the very middle of life's pond. Faraday, on the other hand, preferred silence and a sense of order. With a bird book and a decent pair of binos, thought Winter despairingly, he'd never even dream of *looking* for the rock.

He stepped in from the balcony and wandered through to the bathroom. Minutes later, as he soaped his face, he heard the two-tone trill of his new mobile.

'It's Jake,' said the voice. 'We'd like you to come round.'

Faraday was home late, gone eleven. Upstairs, in his study, he checked his e-mails before turning in. One of them had come from Gabrielle. Faraday had sent her a selection of his own shots from Thailand, with a couple of extras he'd taken locally, and she'd now replied in kind. Chartres, she pointed out, had one of the finest cathedrals in Europe, and she'd attached a series of photos to prove it.

Faraday gazed at the message, wondering what he'd find. The first shots were undeniably impressive, twin spires soaring above the surrounding rooflines, but what took Faraday's eye were the later images Gabrielle had captured inside. He scrolled slowly through them, photo after photo dominated by the glow of the stained-glass windows. Gabrielle had written of the feelings they inspired in her. They were medieval, she said. They celebrated the triumph of truth over darkness, of hope over bewilderment, of the spirit of the stonemasons and carpenters and artists who had devoted their lives to this extraordinary building.

These thoughts were in French, and even with the aid of a dictionary, it took Faraday a while to properly make sense of them. Satisfied with his translation, he took a second look at the photos, concentrating on the windows. She was right. The stained glass had the startling brilliance of fireworks against the night sky. They were, in the exact sense of the word, luminous.

He gazed at one in particular. Square in shape, it pictured Christ on the cross, his pale body pierced by a spear, and he found himself thinking of the garden at Gethsemane, and Judas' soft kiss, and what Duley could possibly have meant by entwining this age-old story of betrayal with the woman he'd so successfully caught in the opening pages of his crime novel. Was this woman of his real? Had she walked into Duley's life they way she'd walked into the meeting that freezing night? Had he too been betrayed?

Faraday didn't know but the bursting radiance of the stained glass fascinated him, and the longer he looked, the more determined he was to see them for real. In one sense, he thought, the cathedral itself was no more than a device for framing these images. Without them, the building would be empty, an orchestra without a score. He tried to put this into French but abandoned the attempt when he realised that even in English he was struggling to voice what he really meant. Instead, remembering the standing invitation to pay her a visit, he decided to say yes.

'*Merci beaucoup de tes photos, surtout les vitrails,*' he tapped. '*Peut-être, il faut que je te visite pour vraiment les apprécier sur place.*'

The lights were on in Tarrant's house when the cab dropped Winter at the end of the cul-de-sac. Jake opened the door to his knock. One glance at his face told Winter that he'd just emerged from a monster row.

'She's in the living room,' he said. 'I said you ought to hear it from the horse's mouth. Went down a bomb, that.'

He stood aside as Winter stepped in and went through to the lounge. Rachel was at one end of the sofa, her feet propped on a low coffee table, watching television. At first, she barely acknowledged Winter's presence. Then, with a snort, she reached for the remote and turned the set off.

'Jake says we'll have to give the money back.'

'What money?'

'The money from Alan.'

'Does he?'

'Yeah, isn't that right?' She was staring up at her husband, daring him to disagree.

'That's what you told me, Mr W.' Tarrant was looking acutely uncomfortable. 'All I did was pass it on.'

'See?' It was Rachel again. 'Well, you're wrong, Mr Winter. What you don't know about is the agreement we've got.'

'Agreement?' This was news to Winter.

'Yeah. When we get the place in Southsea, Alan's coming to live with us. That's the whole point. That's why he gave us the money to begin with.'

'Gave? I thought it was a loan.'

'Yeah, well, loan then. Only it's huge, the new place – huge compared to this, anyway. Four bedrooms, nice bit of garden. Alan came down to see it with me as soon as it came on the market. He can have one of the bedrooms at the back for now but we can probably go up into the roof, do a proper conversion, so he can have his own little place. The way I see it, the arrangement should work a treat.'

'You're telling me you've seen Givens? Recently?'

'No, not for a while, but he'll be back, I know he will.'

'Back from where?'

'God knows.' She paused. 'Anything else you want to know?'

Winter nodded. 'This agreement you've got. Is it in writing?'

'Of course not. Why would we do that?'

'Because . . .' Winter shrugged. He hadn't come here for a family row. Neither was he a solicitor.

Rachel was on her feet now. 'Does that clear it up then? Only it's late.'

She gave Winter a cold stare, then disappeared into the hall. Seconds later, Winter could hear her footsteps overhead, then came the slam of a door.

Tarrant was still standing by the sofa. He tried to raise a smile but nothing could hide his embarrassment.

'I'm sorry, Mr W. She made me.'

'Made you what?'

'Ring you like that. It was out of order. I apologise.'

Winter patted him on the shoulder, reminded him of the call he'd made himself, only a couple of days ago.

'Glad to help out, mate.' He stepped across to the mantelpiece and looked at the photographs tucked beneath the gilt frame of the big mirror. 'Are these Givens'?'

'Yeah. He's taken loads.'

'They're all right. You should be pleased.'

'Rach loves them. She thinks he's a genius.'

'And you?'

'They're snaps, Mr W. But she's right, of course she's right. And kids are only young once, aren't they?' He paused, then offered Winter a drink. 'Beer, Stella, vino, whatever you fancy.'

Winter shook his head.

'I'll ring for a cab, son. Heavy day tomorrow.'

Tarrant said there was no need. He'd run Winter back to Gunwharf. Again Winter said no.

'Why not? It's no trouble. Honest.'

Winter shook his head. The wife looked as though she might need a bit of TLC, he said. The last thing she wanted was her husband running round half the night again.

'You're sure?' Tarrant sounded disappointed, almost plaintive.

'Positive.' Winter was already talking to Aqua. 'Five minutes, max,' he said, pocketing his mobile.

They waited in the living room, talking about the kids again, Winter pushing the conversation along. Jake said they were a handful, difficult age, got on Rach's nerves.

'Not easy, then?'

'Not at all, Mr W. You think, you know, to begin with it's going to be fine, but then kids want everything these days, don't they? DVDs, music, designer gear, the whole deal. And living here doesn't help either. There just isn't the space. Know what I mean?'

'Of course.' Winter had caught the growl of the cab as it pulled up outside. 'It'll get better though, won't it? Once you're down in Southsea?'

He stepped into the hall, aware of Tarrant behind him. 'Mr W. . . . ?' he began.

'Yeah?' Winter was reaching for the door handle.

'It will be OK, won't it?'

Winter looked at him. The cab was at the kerbside. 'What'll be OK?' he asked at last. 'The money?'

Tarrant didn't answer. The cabbie beeped the horn. Winter studied Tarrant a moment longer, then gave him a little pat and stepped into the night.

Fifteen

Dawn Ellis had known Winter for years. A while back, when she'd got herself in deep shit with a predatory ex-Met DC, it had been Winter who'd come to her rescue. He was nearly twice her age, and she knew exactly how manipulative he could be, but she was famous in the bar for her stout defence of his working methods. Winter, she explained, lived in a world of his own. You might not understand the language or much like the way he set about things, but his track record – the villains he'd put away – spoke for itself.

Now she wanted to know more about the bank statement.

'This came in yesterday. Right?'

'Right.'

'And we're talking Jake Tarrant up at St Mary's? The one and the same?'

'Spot on.'

'Has anyone taken this up with him yet?'

'Me.'

'And?'

Winter explained about the loan. They were driving north, heading for St Mary's. At Faraday's insistence, they were now treating Tarrant as a potential suspect. The DI wanted them to start with Givens' line manager, an administrator at the hospital, Deborah Percy. She'd be able to provide a picture of Givens' working day – the people he met, the schedule he kept. Operation *Tartan* had suddenly acquired a new momentum.

'This could be tricky, couldn't it?' Ellis readied herself to overtake a bus, then backed off. 'Knowing Jake the way we do?'

'No alternative, love. Every bloke on the squad knows him. If it wasn't us, it'd be someone else. Exactly the same problem.'

'But what do you think? About Jake?'

'I think what you think. I think he's a good bloke.'

'That doesn't help us though. Does it?'

'No.' Winter shook his head. 'It doesn't.'

Deborah Percy occupied a busy office in the hospital's administration block. She was a plump, friendly forty-something. With the phones going non-stop and a constant stream of interruptions, she suggested they found somewhere else to talk. Winter settled for the canteen.

Ellis found a table at the back of the big hall. Percy returned with a laden tray. Winter had given her a quid for a bacon sandwich, and Ellis turned her head as Winter hosed brown sauce onto the glistening rashers. A committed veggie, she loathed the smell of meat.

Percy was talking about Givens, confirming everything Winter had already learned about the man. He'd been quiet, efficient, kept himself to himself. In the eleven months he'd worked at the hospital, he'd never taken a day's sick leave, and when called upon to fill in for someone he'd never once said no. Which made his sudden disappearance all the more mysterious.

'What did he do, exactly?' Ellis had turned her back on Winter.

'He drove one of the path vans. These are the guys who pick up medical samples around the city. Stuff comes down from the QA, and from GP surgeries. Alan's job was to take them to the microbiology labs across the road here for analysis.'

'Did that involve calls at the mortuary?'

'Yes. We use our mortuary to store bodies after they've been PM'd at QA. Samples taken during post-mortem are often sent down with them. Alan would pick them up.'

'So he'd be a regular caller at the mortuary here?'

'Of course. In fact Jake Tarrant had become a bit of a mate of his.'

'You knew that?'

'Only because Alan once mentioned it. I think he'd got pally with Jake's wife too. He showed me some snaps he'd taken of the kiddies. He was really proud of them.'

Ellis glanced round at Winter. Winter was mopping up the remains of the brown sauce with his bacon sandwich.

'The days before he disappeared . . . did you see him at all?'

'I saw him every day.'

'Was there anything different about him? Anything that struck you? Did he seem tense?'

'Alan was never tense. That was his charm. Mister Laid Back, we called him. It's not rocket science, driving a van, but you'd be amazed at the meal some people make of it. No, from my point of view he was a dream. No dramas. No hassle. Completely on top of it all.' She laughed. 'If I could find a dozen Alans, I'd be out of a job. He was just the kind of bloke you could leave to get on with it. Which is why I'm not being of much use to you.'

Percy had brought a file with her. She leafed through it, looking for anything else they might find of interest. The file was very thin. Ellis wanted to known whether Givens had a car.

'Not to my knowledge.' Percy shook her head. 'He came to work on a bike most days.'

'And he never mentioned a vehicle? Though he obviously had a licence?'

'No. And he never applied for a staff parking permit either.'

Winter at last pushed his plate away. He wanted to

know more about Givens' relationship with Jake Tarrant.

'They were just friends, that's all.'

'Mates?'

'Yes.' She nodded. 'I'd say so. But Jake's that kind of guy, isn't he? I sometimes got the impression most people in this place wouldn't give Alan the time of day but Jake, he—'

'Why not?' It was Ellis this time. 'Why wouldn't they give him the time of day?'

'I don't know.' Percy was being careful now. 'It was the men, really. Not the women.'

'But why? What were they saying?'

'Well . . . ' She looked from one face to the other. Conversations like these didn't belong in the file. 'Like I say, it was the men. They can be very silly sometimes. Cruel too.'

'But what were they saying? What was it about him?'

'I don't know. I honestly don't. He was a loner. He didn't muck in, not like the rest of them. He wasn't one for a fag break outside the bike sheds. Or going down the pub after work on a Friday. He didn't much care for the football either, and that's asking for trouble in this town.'

'Trouble?'

'Nothing serious. You get to know the ones who like to stir it. They're just mouthy. From what little I saw, Alan did the right thing.'

'Like what?'

'He ignored them. Just got on with his job. Like I say, he was a dream.'

'And Jake?'

'Jake makes friends with everyone. You people ought to know that.'

'And Givens responded?'

'Must have done. Otherwise he'd never have taken those shots, would he? The ones of the kiddies he showed me?' She fingered the file, worried now. 'You really think something's happened to him?'

Ellis said she didn't know. Nearly two months was a long time for someone to go missing, especially someone as reliable as Givens seemed to have been. She glanced across at Winter again.

'You went round to his flat, didn't you? Last week?'

Winter nodded. The place had been spotless, he said. The rent was paid; there was food in the fridge, clothes in the wardrobe, absolutely no indication that Givens might have packed a bag and taken himself off somewhere.

'Doesn't that . . . ' Percy shrugged ' . . . sound the alarm bells?'

'Of course it does. That's why we're here.'

'But you've no idea what might have happened to him?'

'Not really. We've followed a couple of leads but, you know . . . ' Winter shot her a grin. 'It's still early days.'

Martin Barrie, to Faraday's surprise, had a temper. He'd just been on the phone to Willard and learned something of what had happened to Winter over the weekend. His thin face was pale with anger.

'I gather Winter got himself lifted on Saturday night.'

'Yes, sir.'

'And we know because he told you so.'

'Yes, sir.'

'Yet you failed to tell me.'

'Indeed, sir.'

'So why was that?'

Faraday ducked his head a moment. In Barrie's position he'd have asked exactly the same question.

'Because I felt obliged to discuss it with Mr Willard first,' he said at last.

'And why's that?'

'Because it seemed to me –' Faraday frowned. '– Extremely sensitive.'

'You didn't trust me?'

'I trust you completely, sir.'

'You thought I might blow Winter out of the water?'

'Yes.'

'Then you're right. That's exactly what I'd have done.' Barrie turned and stared out of the window, his long bony fingers tapping the arm of his chair. Faraday sensed there was a lot more he wanted to say but instead he abruptly changed the subject and asked about DS Brian Imber. Willard, it seemed, was sending him down from Havant to replace Winter in the Intelligence Cell and he'd naturally sold it to Barrie as a major boost to resources.

'What's he like, this Imber?'

'He's excellent, sir. Very experienced. Speaks his mind. No clever games.'

'Thank Christ for that.' He held Faraday's gaze for a long moment, then scribbled himself a note and asked about *Coppice*.

Faraday outlined the day's actions. The broad thrust of the investigation – chiefly the CCTV house calls – was continuing, and enquiries were in hand to locate Mickey Kearns. According to Winter, he was back in Margarita, looking for the local suspected of stitching him up, and his details had been circulated to Immigration to intercept him when he flew home.

'So what's the strength, do you think?'

'Kearns? For the tunnel job? I doubt it. The beating was probably enough. They got what they wanted. They got a name. Why would they want to go any further?'

'And the name was Querida, am I right? As in *Mia Querida*?'

'Yes.'

'So Kearns is off looking for a pet name Duley used

for some girlfriend or other? Is that what you're telling me?' The thought at last put a smile on his face.

'Exactly, sir.'

'Do we know who this girlfriend is?'

'Not yet.'

Faraday reminded him about the absence of letters at Duley's bedsit. On the face of it, given Duley's literary activities, that seemed strange.

'Nothing in his address book?'

'Winter's been through it all now.'

'And?'

'It wasn't much help. Most of the numbers related to work contacts, some people from the bookshop, then there were loads of political activists. These guys knew nothing about his private life but we got a mobile number for Duley off one of them. The TIU billing should be coming through soon.'

'What about the computer you seized. Any news from CCU?'

Faraday shook his head. The Computer Crime Unit at Netley was stretched to breaking point. PCs represented a vital source of evidence but there was currently a three-month waiting list for hard-disk analysis.

'You want me to fast-track it? Put it out to one of the commercial houses? It would cost a fortune but we could maybe wear that.'

Faraday said no. He'd prefer to wait for the billing. And there was something else too. He told Barrie about the Writers' Conference at Winchester. Duley had stayed the whole weekend only a fortnight before his death. He'd written an interesting piece for a competition, got pissed on the Saturday night after the prize-giving and talked some fellow scribe into bed. Faraday himself was about to phone the novelist who'd run the workshop Duley had attended. She'd have this woman's name.

'I'm losing you, Joe. How does this take Duley into the tunnel?'

'I've no idea, sir. Except the whole thing's more complex than it looks.'

'Complex how?'

'We've been thinking some kind of revenge killing. We've been thinking high-profile message to anyone else out there who fancies crossing the likes of Kearns or Mackenzie. I don't think it was that at all, not anymore.'

'Evidence?'

'None.' Faraday smiled at him. 'Yet.'

Barrie nodded, and held his gaze for a moment before scribbling himself another note. Then he returned to *Tartan*, asking whether Winter and Ellis would feel comfortable investigating someone they both knew well.

'They'll be fine, sir,' Faraday reassured him. 'They're both professional. They know the difference between friendship and the job. If there's any kind of case against Tarrant, they'll make it.'

Ellis and Winter lingered outside the mortuary, waiting for someone from Human Resources to accompany them inside. Jake Tarrant, it turned out, was up at QA, attending a meeting about the provision of fridge spaces in the new facility. His assistant, Simon Hoole, had been warned to expect a visit from Major Crimes.

Ellis was musing about the state of Jake's marriage. 'Have you ever met his wife?'

'Yeah.'

'What's she like?'

'Pretty. Two young kids. Pissed off. You know the story.'

'Pissed off enough to be looking for a bit of comfort?'

'Yeah.' Winter nodded. 'Definitely.'

'Like Givens, maybe?'

293

'It's possible. Of course it is. Do I think it happened? Fuck knows.'

'But he may be alive after all. He may be away somewhere, back up in the north, waiting for her. You're telling me she's got a hundred and eighty-five of his money. All she has to do is get in the car and drive off into that bright new future of theirs. One hundred and eighty-five grand's a decent deposit. They could find somewhere nice to settle down. Start all over. No?'

'What about the kids?'

'He loves the kids. He takes pictures of them. He's a natural.'

'And Jake?'

'He gets the house down here. A little something to ease her conscience. I'm telling you, Paul, it works beautifully.'

'But how come he hands over the money in the first place? If they're going to elope together, there'd have been no need. He's got the dosh. She puts the kids in the car and buggers off to join him.'

'It's timing, Paul. He baits the trap with the money. She realises she loves him. And bingo . . . case closed.'

Winter laughed. It was a neat theory. And it would also explain why he hadn't found a camera at Givens' flat. Why hadn't he thought of it himself?

A woman appeared around the corner of the building. She wore a trim grey suit and carried a clipboard. Human Resources.

She introduced herself and shepherded them towards the door. Winter knew the old entry code by heart but the recent break-in had prompted the hospital authorities to fit a replacement lock. Their minder had forgotten her swipe card. Instead, she keyed in the new entry code. Winter watched her. 7713.

Simon Hoole was in the post-mortem room beyond the chilly corridor that housed the fridges, heaving a shrouded body onto one of the examination tables. Bodies occupied the other tables, and there were two more corpses on trolleys beneath the window. He was singing to himself, something cheerful and inane, and there was a dull, bony clunk as he let the head of the parcel fall onto the stainless-steel table. He was unaware of their presence in the front lobby and Winter watched him for a moment, struck by the freedoms he must have. Working here, thought Winter, you'd be well and truly your own boss.

Catching sight of the group by the open door, Hoole wiped his hands on his theatre greys and shuffled towards them. He was huge, a dumpling of a youth, no more than early twenties.

'What's all this?' Winter nodded at the bodies.

'One of the fridge motors is on the blink. I just called the spark. He won't touch a fridge unless it's empty.' He grinned at them. 'You must be the law. The name's Si.'

He led them through to the office. The woman from Human Resources asked Winter if he wanted her to stay. Winter said it wouldn't be necessary.

Ellis took the armchair; Winter stayed on his feet. Hoole's bulk dwarfed the desk.

'What's this about, then?'

Ellis explained that they were investigating the disappearance of one of Hoole's colleagues.

'Givens.' He laughed. 'Has to be.'

'Why do you say that?'

'Because he's not been around, for starters. Used be in here all hours. Not a sight of the geezer, not for weeks. You don't go to Greece for that long, do you? Not on the money we get.'

Winter wanted to know more about these visits of Givens. How come he was here so often?

'Good question, mate. Often asked it myself.'

'And?'

'Dunno, do I? I ain't blaming Jake, don't get me wrong. He did nothing to encourage the bloke because he's not like that, know what I mean?'

'Not like what?'

'Not like bent. Bloke's a woofter. Spot it a mile off. Thought Jake had sunshine coming out of his arse. I used to tell Jake, I used to say for him to keep his back to the wall. Jake, mate, I'd say. Yer little friend's arrived. Brought him a bunch of flowers once, right embarrassment it was.'

'Flowers?' Ellis didn't believe it. 'For Jake?'

'Well, he says they were really for Rach, Jake's missus. She'd done him some favour or other. I can't remember. But me, I *knows* they were for Jake. You can tell, can't you? They get that look, woofters. They got that special smile. Generous, mind. It wasn't just flowers.'

Winter enquired what else Givens used to turn up with. Hoole's stubby fingers picked at a spot on his chin. He was thinking.

'Football gear, magazines and that, because he knew Jake was crazy about the game. And books, like. One time he wanted to take them all to Venice, the whole lot of them, kids and all. So he turned up with all these brochures and a couple of guides, and other stuff for Jake to look at.'

'What did Jake think?'

'He thought it was hilarious.'

'Did he take them home? Show them to his wife?'

'You're joking. That's the last place he fancied going. Venice is woofter heaven, ain't it? All them Italians?'

Ellis ducked her head, wondering how Jake stayed sane in company like this. No wonder he had so many meetings.

Winter wanted to know more. Did Givens have money?

'Loads of it, mate. I heard them talking.'

'And what did they say?'

'It was Givens mostly. He'd inherited a whole stack from somewhere or other, hundreds of thousands of quid. This was early on, when he first arrived, and I don't think Jake believed him. Not that it was any of Jake's business. But Givens was back the next week with this really flash camera he'd bought, state of the art it was, cost a bomb, just to show Jake, like, just to prove it. The bloke was minted.'

'And Jake?'

'Jake couldn't care a toss. He just humoured the geezer. Gave him the odd cuppa. Yeah, and that's another thing.'

'What?'

'The cakes. He started bringing cakes in. Really nice they were, well lovely, fresh cream, strawberry jam, proper icing. When he realised we used to keep them in one of the fridges, he started bringing in them fancy ice cream gateaus too. Set your watch by him, you could. Four on the dot, every afternoon. Me? I wasn't complaining.'

'So where did Rach come into this?'

'Rach? I don't get you, mate.'

'Jake's wife. She and Givens became friends, isn't that right?'

'Oh yeah, yeah, right. Givens got his feet well under the table there. That was the camera again. All them shots of the kids. Right little snapper, he was.'

Ellis pressed for more detail. Hoole's tiny eyes were troubled. The last thing he wanted, he said, was to land Jake in it.

'In what, Simon?'

'In trouble, like.'

'How could you do that?'

'Well . . . ' He was frowning now. 'I just could, that's all.'

'But how?'

He looked at them, saying nothing, his huge face beginning to redden. Winter took a step back and shut the door.

'This is serious, son,' he said. 'And my colleague here just asked you a question.'

'I know.'

'So give her an answer, yeah? And don't fuck us about.'

Hoole nodded, chastened.

'He hated it,' he said at last. 'Jake did.'

'Hated what?'

'Having this bloke around all the time. It wasn't just here. In fact that probably wasn't so bad, not with the cakes and all, but he'd find him back home too, when he got in of an evening, and he'd drop all these hints and stuff, but his missus wasn't having it, so next morning he'd come in with a right mood on him. Bloke was practically kipping with them, the way Jake saw it. Fucking weirdo, Givens. Good fucking riddance, says me.'

'Where's he gone then? Any ideas?'

'Dunno, mate. Venice, I expect. Where he belongs. On his fucking tod.'

'And Jake? How's he been these last few weeks?'

'Brilliant. Absolutely brilliant. Just the way I knew him first.' He frowned again, and his fingers strayed to his chin. 'Shame about them cakes, though.'

Faraday sat at his desk, waiting for the phone call to pick up. He'd checked the number with Barbara Large and she was positive that Sally Spedding was waiting in for his call. She lived in the Midlands. Any closer, and they could have met. Finally, a voice on the line.

Faraday introduced himself. Sally Spedding didn't waste time on small talk; she was up to her eyes marking university dissertations. She could spare him ten minutes or so.

'It's about Mark Duley, am I right?'

'You are.'

'Barbara tells me he's dead.'

'I'm afraid so.'

'Something about a tunnel.'

'Indeed.'

Faraday explained what had happened. There was a long silence.

'I'm not surprised,' she said at last. 'This is going to sound bizarre but I knew from the start he couldn't work out a proper ending.'

'A *what*?'

'A proper ending. I knew Mark for three days but, believe me, that was enough. He was one of those people who *explode* into a room. He was exhausting. He was the same with everyone; I watched him. It was there in everything he did, his body language, the way he talked to people, the way he charmed them, the way he had no respect, you know, for physical *distance*. He had enormous zip, sheer physical energy. That was one of the reasons his writing was so flawed. He had no perspective. He crowded you. He wanted to shut out the daylight. You'd be talking to him, maybe in a classroom, maybe a bar, whatever, and you'd suddenly realise there was nothing else going on around you, just this really intense conversation, just you and him. You'd be flattered to begin with but then you realised he did it with everyone else too. It's the way he related to people. I know it sounds horrible but it's a bit like the dog and the lamp post. He had to mark his territory. He had to take *charge*. Are you with me?'

Faraday had jotted down the odd word. He underlined '*perspective*'. Then his eye went back to the top of the pad.

'I still don't understand "proper ending",' he said slowly.

'It means he had no sense of . . . ' she struggled to frame the thought ' . . . *completion*. The best writers have a sense of wholeness. Their books are no more than metaphors. There's a circularity, a feeling that events are feeding off themselves, pushing a story forward, yet reinforcing something important that's happening underneath. It's a very hard thing to put into words, which I guess is why there are so many

299

crap writers around, but what I think it boils down to is a sense that these people have well and truly got it *together*. They've had a bit of a think about life. They're sure of their bearings. They've got the measure of their own situation, and that means they've got the measure of the raw material that goes into the book. Mark didn't have that. He didn't have it in his writing, in his ideas, in what he wanted to do on the page. And I suspect that means he didn't have it in his life either. To be frank, he was all over the place.'

'A mess?'

'A mess, yes. But more than that. Mark's problem was you couldn't avoid him. And because you couldn't avoid him, you pretty quickly came to the conclusion that he couldn't avoid himself. Like I say, the best writers are ghosts in their own lives. They dwell in the shadows. They watch. They listen. They remember. Mark wasn't like that at all. Sometimes he was a very noisy little puppy. Other moments you had the feeling that he was a bomb about to go off. Oh dear . . . ' She started to giggle. 'The poor man's dead. That sounds awful, doesn't it?'

'Did you like him?'

'Yes, in a way I did.'

'Why?'

'Because he was what he was. That sounds daft, doesn't it, after everything else I've just told you? But the thing about Mark was his honesty. He was a one-role actor. If you didn't happen to like that role, then he had a problem because sure as hell you didn't like him either, but the charm of the man was his absolute lack of interest in, you know, social *camouflage*. These kind of events, you meet so many people who fall over backwards pretending they're someone else. Mark couldn't pretend to save his life. He didn't know how to do it and he didn't see the point. Now that can be a problem if you're planning to write fiction but, one to one, if you're drunk enough, it can work.'

It was Faraday's turn to laugh. He liked this woman. She'd thought hard about Duley and she pulled no punches. He wondered what her own books were like.

'You say drunk,' he said carefully. 'We recovered a photo from the place where he was living. It must have been taken at Winchester during that weekend.'

'Oh God . . . ' She laughed again. 'Am I in it?'

'Describe yourself.'

'Black hair? Roll-neck top? Red skirt? Pendant thing round my neck?'

'That's it. That's you. Front row. It looks like some kind of bar.'

'You're right. It must have been the Saturday night. Mark had pushed the boat out. He'd just picked up one of the prizes and there was no way we weren't going to celebrate. I wouldn't fault him for generosity. Far from it.'

Faraday was tempted to ask how a writer this flawed had collared a prize but thought better of it. Instead, he asked what happened next.

'I'm not with you.'

'After the bar closed.'

'With Mark, you mean?'

'Yes.'

'Ah . . . ' There was a longish silence. 'You're asking me for a name?'

'Yes, please.'

'What did Barbara say?'

'She told me to talk to you.'

'I see. Well, that's a bit tricky, isn't it?'

'The man's dead, Sally.'

'I know.'

Another silence. Just a question of time, Faraday told himself. And patience.

'Is she married, this person?' he enquired at last.

'No. Not to my knowledge.'

'Then what's the problem?'

'I don't know. It just doesn't feel, you know, right.

How about I talk to her and ask her to give you a ring? I'd feel better about it that way, to be honest. Then it's her decision, not mine.'

'That's fine.' Faraday was eyeing the photo again, wondering which of these women Duley had taken to bed. 'Barbara gave me the impression it was someone older than Mark.'

'She'd be right.'

'Taller than him? Grey hair? Strong face?'

'That's unfair.'

'On the contrary. He's got his arm round her. That's what we detectives call a clue.'

She laughed again, then said she had to go. Faraday thanked her for her time and made sure she'd written down his mobile number. Then he bent to the phone again.

'Tell me something, Sally.'

'Go on.'

'Do you think Mark committed suicide?'

'Absolutely not,' she said at once. 'This was a man who did everything for a purpose. There'd have been no point.'

Jimmy Suttle was asleep when Winter and Dawn Ellis turned up at his hospital bedside. Winter commandeered a chair from the other end of the ward and settled down to wait while Ellis departed to find a hot-drinks machine.

To Winter's immense relief, Suttle was clearly on the mend. There was a blush of colour back in his face and someone had given him a decent shave. The only sign that he'd just spent a couple of days in Critical Care was a tiny wisp of adhesive plaster on his arm where one of the drips must have been attached.

Winter looked at him a moment, wondering whether to give him a shake, then thought better of it. On the bedside locker, behind a thicket of get-well cards, he found a recent copy of *FHM* magazine. He was still inspecting a raunchy Brazilian newscaster with an all-over tan when Suttle stirred, yawned and opened one eye.

'All right, son?' Winter abandoned the magazine.

Suttle gazed at him, uncomprehending. 'Paul?'

'Yeah, son. Me.'

'Been here long?'

'Ages, mate. You look shit.'

'Piss off.'

His voice was barely a whisper. Winter grinned at him, then gave his hand a pat.

'Brought you a little present, son. Here . . . '

Winter rummaged in the Tesco bag at his feet. His attempt to gift-wrap a box of fudge put a smile on Suttle's face.

'My favourite,' he managed. 'You must have parted with money for that.'

'Pleasure, son. How do you feel?'

'Crap.'

'Hurt, does it?'

'Yeah.' Suttle had caught sight of the magazine. 'Trude brought me that.'

'Trude? Here?'

'Yeah. She came in at lunchtime.' His tongue flicked out, moistening his lips. 'Nice to see her.'

Winter edged his chair closer, thinking he should spare Suttle further conversation, but when he suggested bringing the visit to an end, Suttle shook his head. He wanted to talk. He was sick of being flat out like this. He shifted his weight in the bed, wincing at a sudden stab of pain.

'Steady, son.' Winter was on his feet.

'It's OK.'

'You sure?'

'Yeah.' Suttle nodded. 'Could you sort these pillows out?'

Winter gently lifted his head then rearranged the pillows. Trude was Misty Gallagher's daughter. A couple of years back she and Suttle had got it on, until a couple of Mackenzie's heavies had given the young DC a beating.

'How is she then? Young Trude?'

'Brilliant.'

'You be careful, son. Don't want to end up in hospital, do we?' He finished with the pillows and eased Suttle's head back. Suttle grunted a thank you, then managed a smile.

'She was talking about you. Says you've been a bad boy with Mist. What's been going on?'

Winter feigned ignorance. Said he hadn't a clue. Suttle didn't believe him.

'Seriously, son, I don't know what she's on about. You know Mist. She gets bored. Has to have something to keep her amused.'

'You've been shagging her?'

'You have to be joking.'

'So you pissed Mackenzie off some other way? Is that it? Only Trude seemed to think it was funny.'

'Yeah? Well you tell her to keep her gossip to herself.'

'It wasn't funny?'

'It never happened.' Winter looked down at him. 'End of story.'

Dawn Ellis returned with two plastic cups. She gave one to Winter.

'It's hot chocolate,' she said. 'I must have pressed the wrong button.' She looked down at Suttle, then kissed him on the forehead. 'How are you?'

Suttle pulled a face. Ellis wanted to know more but he shook his head.

'Tell me about Ewart,' he whispered.

'We've done him for attempted murder.' Ellis sipped at her chocolate. 'And fraud. He'll be looking at twelve to fourteen years. Minimum.'

'And Givens?'

Ellis glanced at Winter, then explained about the

story Ewart was running. A kid from Somerstown had flogged him the debit card. He'd never seen Givens in his life.

'And you believe him?'

'Yes, I do. Ewart says it happened around the end of May. The kid found the wallet in the newsagent next to the offie. That's about a week after Givens didn't turn up for work. The dates fit with the withdrawals from his bank account. Ewart was buying season tickets a day or two later.'

'So . . . ' Suttle was fighting to get the words out. 'We're saying Givens was in Somerstown a week after he went missing? Then disappeared?'

'Yeah.' Winter had abandoned his hot chocolate. 'Either that, or someone deliberately left the wallet. There was cash in it too. Sixty quid. Think about it, son. It's a clever move. That kind of area, it's odds on no one's going to hand the thing in. The cash is easy. Then there's the card. In the end it's going to find its way to someone like Ewart. Ewart figures out some scam to empty Givens' bank account but leaves a trace. We do the necessary and hey . . . '

'You've got a name.' Suttle's eyes were closed now.

'Exactly.'

Ellis was looking impressed. She turned to Winter.

'When did you figure all that out?'

'I didn't, love. It's obvious. If we accept it wasn't Ewart. If we believe all the business with the wallet. Then it has to be deliberate.'

'Unless Givens is still alive.'

'No chance.'

Ellis looked at him a moment. This was turning into a case conference. She glanced round the ward. There were six beds, all occupied.

'You think we should pull the curtain?' She gestured up at the track above the bed. 'Give ourselves a bit of privacy?'

Winter shook his head. His eyes were back on Suttle.

'No point, love. Look . . . ' He lowered his voice. 'The boy's asleep again.'

Minutes later, they left the hospital. Dawn drove down into the city, Winter beside her. A scatter of gulls were fighting for scraps beside the Paulsgrove tip and the last of the sunset was dying over the distant bulk of Portchester Castle as they joined the motorway.

'He's amazing, isn't he? Much better than I'd expected.'

'He's a good lad.' Winter was deep in thought.

'Yeah, but strong too. Has to be, a wound like that. Did you see the size of the knife Ewart had on him?'

Winter didn't answer. Something was bothering him, she knew. In his own good time he might tell her. Or not.

She edged into the outside lane, took the little Peugeot to seventy-five. Ahead, the ivory spike of the Spinnaker Tower flagged her destination. After she dropped Winter off at Gunwharf, she was planning a drink or two with an old schoolfriend who was about to set up an alternative therapy clinic. This woman had substantial financial backing, plus a client list she already served in their own homes. The invitation was there for Dawn to join the new business and lately she'd begun to take it seriously.

'Funny, isn't it?' She was thinking of Jimmy Suttle again. 'Too many bad things happen to good people. Bad things should happen to bad people.'

'Yeah?' Winter wasn't interested.

'You agree, Paul?'

'Whatever, listen . . . computers.'

'What about them?'

'Givens had one. Either a PC or a laptop.'

'How do you know?'

'Because I've got his bank statements. He took out a warranty contract with PC World. Direct debits every month.'

'So?'

'I couldn't find it. Not at the flat. Not when I went through it.' He paused, frowning. 'The camera's missing too. Funny that.'

Sixteen

It was Babs who brought Faraday the letter from Vodafone. It had come in the morning post, the first envelope she'd opened.

'Is this what you're after, boss?'

She laid the trophy on his desk. Billing on Duley's mobile number went back six months and covered nine sheets of paper. Someone at Vodafone had been kind enough to do some basic analysis, identifying numbers which cropped up more than once. The calls to all of them were in single figures with one exception: 07967 633524. This too was a Vodafone number, and the helpful analyst had pre-empted a further enquiry from the Hantspol TIU by supplying caller details. Between 2 February and 12 July, Mark Duley had made 487 calls to a Ms Jenny Mitchell, 25 South Normandy, Old Portsmouth.

Faraday stared at the name, aware of Babs still standing behind him. At length he looked round, grinning.

'Is Winter around?'

'No, boss, not yet.'

'Seen DC Barber at all?'

''Fraid not.'

'OK.' He nodded, tapped the letter. 'Thanks.'

Babs left the office, closing the door behind her. Faraday lifted the phone to Martin Barrie, but a recorded message told him that the Detective Superintendent was in London all day. Still grinning, Faraday contemplated putting in a call to Barrie's mobile but then decided against it. On paper, this was the breakthrough he'd been anticipating for a couple of days – the name, the presence that shadowed everything he'd learned about Duley. He sat back in the chair, hearing Sally Spedding's voice on the phone. *He had no respect for physical distance. He had no perspective. He crowded you. He wanted to shut out the daylight.* Faraday nodded to himself, doing the maths. Four hundred and eighty-seven calls in six months boiled down to an average of three a day. *Crowded* was an understatement.

He went through the billing more carefully, week by week, aware of the way it fluctuated. Duley hadn't called her at all until the last week in February. Over the next month the volume of calls had grown and grown. By April he was calling her five, sometimes six times a day. In early May it fell off for some reason, a couple of daily conversations at the most. Faraday paused, running his finger down the column of entries until he got to 14 May. From Venezuela, over the next three days, Duley had made eight calls. None of them had lasted less than twenty minutes. No wonder he'd needed to help himself to Mickey Kearns' war chest.

With Duley back in the UK, the usual pattern of calls had abruptly changed. Instead of the normal series of lengthy conversations, the billing recorded lots of briefer calls, 32 seconds, 53 seconds, 43 seconds – seven or eight of them a day. This non-stop bombardment smacked to Faraday of desperation. Something had happened between them. Time and time again, Duley was trying to get through to her, trying to talk to her, trying – perhaps – to put his case. But she must have been resolute because, as May crept into June, the barrage of calls slowly fell away. Faraday reached for a pencil, circled the key date when the pattern changed: 18 May.

Then another entry caught his eye. On 28 June Duley had been on the phone to Jenny Mitchell for fifteen minutes. The following morning, at 09.32, he'd called her again. This time the conversation had lasted nearly an hour. After that more calls, much briefer. Then, on 5 July, a longer chat, ten minutes or so. Two days later three attempts – none successful – to coax her into conversation. Finally, on Sunday 10 July, two last calls. The first, again, was brief. The second, at 12.03, was logged at nearly fifty minutes. By early next morning Duley was dead.

Faraday tidied the sheets of paper, wondering whether he wasn't committing the cardinal sin. Every detective learns not to load the bare facts. These were simply phone calls. They might have been in business together. They might have been political junkies, bent on dissecting the day's developments. They might have been discussing the weather. Any of this was possible. Except that every last shred of circumstantial evidence argued otherwise.

In his prize-winning story *Gethsemane* the writer had met the woman in the depths of winter. In real life, according to the Vodafone billing, this relationship had begun on 24 February. From Venezuela, Duley had dispatched a card to his own address. It had been sent to *Mia Querida*, but the day after Duley returned to the UK, something had brought their phone conversations to a close, and – maybe as a direct result – the card had never been picked up. On 26 June, according to the entry in Hantspol's own Records Management System, Duley had been admitted to A & E after a severe beating. Two days later, a little better, he'd been on the phone to her again. Faraday's eye drifted back to the first page of entries. In the *Gethsemane* extract the woman had kissed the writer. Was this the Judas kiss? The sweet taste of betrayal? Had it triggered a passionate affair? With consequences too horrible to contemplate?

The answer, Faraday knew, lay in the hours before

and after Duley's death in the tunnel. He reached for the phone again. Babs answered at once.

'Get onto TIU,' he told her. 'Ask them to chase up Vodafone for historical billings and cell site on the Mitchell number. Tell them it's urgent.' He read her the number, then put the phone down.

By the time Winter got to Kingston Crescent, Faraday had gone. Babs updated him on the Vodafone development and mentioned that Faraday had been looking for him. Winter grunted something about having had to wait in for a plumber and settled behind his desk. A call to PC World, with the details on Givens' direct debit payments, secured a promise to get back with details of the equipment under warranty. The morning's post produced nothing of real interest. He glanced at his watch, wondering whether Dawn Ellis had finished the report she was doing for Faraday about the injuries to Jimmy Suttle. He picked up the phone.

'You ready, love?'

They drove north, through the city. At the mouth of the cul-de-sac that would take them to Tarrant's house, Winter laid a precautionary hand on Ellis' arm.

'I'll take the lead,' he said. 'That OK with you?'

'Whatever.' She shrugged.

Rachel Tarrant was trying to fix the younger kid's high chair when the ring brought her to the front door. She scowled at Winter, ignoring the proffered warrant card.

'He's at work,' she said. 'You're wasting your time.'

'We've come to talk to you, love. This is DC Ellis, a colleague of mine.'

'Talk to me, why?'

'Let us in and I'll tell you.'

She looked at him, uncertain now, then stepped aside. Both kids were in the sitting room, watching television.

'We'll do this in here.' Winter was already in the tiny kitchen. 'It shouldn't take long.'

He nudged the high chair aside with his foot, dislodging a clamp Rachel had fixed to a broken strut at the bottom. Ellis bent to retrieve it.

'Handy round the house, are you?' Rachel was watching her attempts to reattach the clamp.

'Have to be, Mrs Tarrant. Living on my tod.'

'Lucky you.'

'Yeah?' Ellis glanced up at her. 'Haven't got any more glue, have you?'

Rachel passed down a tube of No-Nails. Ellis quickly resealed the joint.

'There,' she said. 'Nipper-proof.'

Winter was debating the chances of coffee. When Rachel didn't offer, he gestured her towards the vacant stool.

'This is about Alan Givens,' he told her. 'There's a couple of things that are troubling us.'

'What's that got to do with me? I thought we'd been through all this.'

'We have. I just need to check on some details.'

'Like what?'

'Like when you last saw Mr Givens.'

'You asked me that the other night.'

'I'm asking you again. Only this time I want you to think a bit harder.'

She looked at him, startled, then leaned back against the kitchen work surface.

'It would have been a while ago,' she said at last. 'A couple of months, nearly. May time.'

'So where is he, do you think?'

'I haven't a clue. I ask Jake the same question.'

'And?'

'He doesn't know either.'

'He's just gone? Disappeared? No warning? No explanation?'

'None.'

312

'Don't you think that's odd?'

'Yes.' She nodded. 'To tell you the truth, I do.'

'So why didn't you do anything about it?'

'I did. I made Jake report it. He told me he'd gone to the management but it turned out they'd already been in touch with you lot.'

Winter nodded. It was true. He'd checked the Misper log a week ago. On 31 May Human Resources had phoned Kingston Crescent. The duty sergeant had sent a couple of uniforms round to the hospital and they, in turn, had checked Givens' premises. They'd taken a note of his mobile number but no one had bothered to apply for billing. Since then, nothing.

'So he disappears at the end of May, leaving you holding his money. Am I right?'

'Yeah.'

'No phone calls? Texts? Postcards?'

'Nothing.'

'Weren't you worried about him?'

'Of course I was. People don't just disappear. Not just like that. Especially not people like Alan.'

'What does that mean, Mrs Tarrant?'

Rachel turned to look at Ellis. She was in the corner of the kitchen, leaning against the door.

'It means he was a bit . . . ' she shrugged ' . . . vulnerable, I suppose. Needy. You know what I mean?'

'No.' Ellis' eyes were cold. 'Tell me.'

'I don't know. It's difficult. He lived alone. He didn't have anyone.'

'You mean he couldn't cope?'

'No, not that. In fact he was very organised, looked after himself, sorted everything out. No, on a practical level he was fine. But that made it even more odd, the way I see it. Alan's a bloke you can set your watch by. He's completely reliable. If he says he's going to do something, he does it. That's a novelty in my house, believe me.'

313

Winter laughed. 'I'll tell him that,' he said. 'Young Jake.'

'Don't bother. He never listens.'

'So Givens . . . ?' Ellis wasn't letting go. 'You think what?'

'I think it's bloody strange. Like I said, one minute he was there, the next he's vanished. No warning. Nothing.'

'So you must have wondered, mustn't you?'

'About what?'

'About what might have happened to him?'

'Of course I did.'

'And what do you think?'

'I . . . ' for the first time, she hesitated ' . . . just don't know.'

There was a silence. Through the thin walls Winter could hear the blare of the TV.

'Some people think he was a bit keen on you, Rachel,' he said at last.

'Alan?' The thought made her laugh. 'Keen on *me*? That way, you mean?'

'Yes. Why's that so funny?'

'Because it's absurd. He needed a mother. Not, you know . . . '

'And does Jake think that?'

'God knows.'

'But say he *did* think that. Givens was round here a lot. Isn't that true?'

'Yes. I wouldn't say a lot, but yes. It's been lovely weather. He'd bring that camera of his, take shots of the kids in the garden. They enjoyed having him here. We all did. That's why we started talking about sharing the Southsea place.'

'And Jake? He was part of that?'

'Of course he was. In fact it was Jake who met him first, through work.'

'Sure. I understand that. But then you and Alan got very –' Winter shrugged '– pally. You spent a lot of time together. Maybe Jake thought all that went a bit too far. And maybe he didn't fancy having a lodger all of a sudden.'

'In Southsea, you mean?' Rachel was getting angry now. 'So how else do you think we're going to get out of this place?'

'I've no idea, love. All I'm saying is that Jake might have had a bit of a problem with Mr Givens. And that quite suddenly Mr Givens isn't around anymore. We're detectives, Rachel. We always think the worst of everyone.'

Rachel held his gaze. It took a while for the implications to sink in.

'You mean Jake . . . ?'

'It's a question, Rachel. A suggestion. That's all.'

'After everything he's done for you?'

'That's irrelevant.'

'But you really think he might have . . . '

'I think it's possible, yes. We deal in facts. Fact one, your Mr Givens isn't around anymore. Fact two, you have most of his money. And then there's something else, isn't there? Jake might not be sad to see the back of him.'

'That's not a fact. That's you talking. Jake's as worried as I am.'

'Really?'

'Yes. And if you knew him, if you *really* knew him, you'd realise he was a pussy cat. That's Jake's problem. He's too nice to people. You ask anyone at work. He's an easy touch. Go and talk to the blokes he plays football with. That five-a-side lot. They think the world of him – good player, good bloke – but you know the one thing they can't believe? Anyone fouls Jake, he just takes it in his stride. Never retaliates. Never loses his cool. Complete pussy cat, like I say. Rolls over for anyone.'

This little speech temporarily silenced Winter. Then

came the sound of a door banging outside, followed by tiny footsteps pattering up and down the hall.

Ellis stirred. Any minute now the kids would be in the kitchen, bringing the interview to an end. In these situations it was sometimes best to go for broke and watch what happened.

'Let's say Alan's gone away somewhere,' she began. 'He likes the kids. The kids like him. You're pissed off here. The pair of you have money.' She smiled. 'That's do-able, isn't it?'

Again, Rachel seemed to have difficulty following the logic. Finally, it dawned on her what Ellis was really saying.

'Wash your mouth out.' Her face had darkened. 'You have to be bloody joking.'

Afterwards, driving back down to Kingston Crescent, Ellis wanted to know what Jake had done for Winter. Winter said he hadn't a clue what she was talking about.

'Back there in the house. She had you down as some kind of special friend of Jake's, a real mate. No?'

'No.' Winter shook his head. 'Jake's a good bloke. She's right. Everyone loves him. Me amongst them.'

'I don't believe you. Something's been going on between you and Tarrant. Am I right or what?'

'You're wrong, love. Women get confused.' He shot her a weary grin. 'It's part of their charm.'

South Normandy was a cul-de-sac of post-war houses tucked into a quiet corner of Old Portsmouth. The last time Faraday had been there was years back, after the death of a wayward fourteen-year-old who'd plunged to her death from a block of flats a mile or so away. On that occasion he'd been dealing with the girl's mother, unlocking a mausoleum of family secrets. Now he wondered whether something similar awaited him.

DC Tracy Barber had come too. They stood in the hot sunshine for a moment or two, inspecting the house at the end. There was a bicycle propped against the front wall of the house. It had a tiny seat on the back and a mini-saddle bolted to the crossbar for a second child.

Faraday hadn't phoned ahead. The value of the next hour or so, he told himself, was the fact that the knock on the door would come as a complete surprise.

The door opened at once. She was Tracy's height, late twenties, maybe a year or two older. She had wonderful hair, a wild perm that framed her face, and when she smiled Faraday knew at once what must have seeded the madness in Duley. She had huge eyes, the softest brown, and the tan suggested she'd made the most of the recent weather.

She was looking at Tracy Barber's warrant card. She seemed to be having difficulty connecting it with the two strangers on her doorstep.

'Police?' she said blankly.

'That's right. You are . . . ?'

'My name's Mitchell. What's this about?'

Barber suggested they all talk inside. Faraday could see two small faces peering round a door at the end of the hall.

Jenny took them into the front room. There were kids' toys all over the floor. One look at her face told Faraday she was very, very frightened.

'This is crazy . . . ' she said.

Barber suggested she sat down. Faraday took the chair by the window. The faces were at the door now. The girl was the older, the boy a year or so younger, both pre-school.

'They've been in the garden.' She apologised for their nakedness. 'This weather, who can blame them.'

The older, she said, was Freya. Milo, her brother, was a saint.

Barber asked whether there was someone handy who could look after them for an hour or so. A neighbour maybe.

She shook her head, alarmed.

'My neighbour's out at the moment. She goes swimming every morning. My mum's got a flat round the corner but she's in Malta. Is this going to take long? Only I promised . . . ' She tailed off.

Faraday tried to reassure her. They were here to ask her about someone who might have been a friend of hers. It formed part of an ongoing enquiry. He was sorry to spring this on her but they worked for the Major Crimes Team, and there was a degree of urgency.

'Major Crimes?'

'Yes.'

'So who is this person?'

'His name's Duley. Mark Duley.'

She nodded, reached for the younger of her children. The boy clambered into her lap. He must have been playing in a flower bed, Faraday thought. His tiny feet had left brown tracks across the carpet.

'You knew Mr Duley?' It was Barber.

'Yes.'

'How well did you know him?'

She was hugging the child now, holding him close. He kicked his feet and arched his back, loving it. His sister grabbed at her mother's skirt, demanding the same kind of attention.

'Mrs Mitchell?'

'I knew him well. If that's what you want to know.'

'How well?'

'I'm not sure I have to answer that question, do I?'

'Of course not. We can continue this conversation at the police station, if you'd prefer. I'm sure you've got a lawyer.'

'A lawyer?' She looked aghast. A sunny day was getting darker by the minute.

'Mrs Mitchell . . . ' Faraday tried to soften the impact of these relentless questions. 'I think it's in all our interests if we're frank with each other. Are you still married?'

'Yes, I am.'

'What's your husband's name?'

'Do I have to tell you?'

'Only if you want to.'

She nodded, extended a hand to her daughter, hauled her up onto the sofa beside her.

'Andy,' she said at last. 'Is he part of this too?'

'Part of what, Mrs Mitchell?'

'Whatever it is you want to know about?'

'I've no idea, at this stage.'

'But you think he might be?'

Faraday refused to answer. Milo was wrestling with one of his mother's earrings, a long silver dangle that looked Indian.

Barber took up the running. 'You'll know that Mark Duley was killed last week.'

'Of course.' She shook her head. 'Dreadful. Terrible. Poor bloody man.'

'How did you find out, as a matter of interest?'

'It was in the papers, on the TV. I can't remember, to be honest. I just knew, that's all.'

'That would be on the Monday?'

'Yes, the Monday, yes.'

'What were you doing on the Sunday? Can you remember?'

Jenny frowned, one hand for Milo, the other for her fretful daughter. At length she said she wasn't sure. Most Sundays they just slobbed out, she said. She took the kids swimming. They all went for a bike ride together, had friends round, other kids, sorted out a barbecue if the weather was nice – just routine stuff, family stuff, the kind of stuff you do with a couple of harum-scarum infants in a seaside city like this. Faraday watched her carefully. Already, he thought, she's saying goodbye to this life of hers. She's been expecting us for days, probably longer. She's not yet ready for the truth, not quite. But she will be.'

Barber wanted to know what her husband did for a living.

'He's a kind of businessman,' she said. 'He calls himself a social entrepreneur.'

'What does that mean?'

'It means he runs a charity. It's called Landfall. It's to do with mental health. Basically it's accommodation and support services. He used to be a social worker.'

'Would you prefer we talked to you together?'

She gave the question some thought.

'Why? Why would you want to?'

'Because you might find it easier.'

She hesitated again, then shook her head. Milo was grabbing for the wooden beads around her throat.

'Just ask what you have to ask,' she said quietly. 'If I can help you, I will.'

Faraday nodded. He understood that Jenny had known nothing about Mark Duley's death until it had appeared in the media. Now he wanted to go back to the relationship she'd had with him.

'How would you describe it?'

'We were friends.'

'How come?'

'We just bumped into each other. It was a while back, during the winter. I was getting angrier and angrier about the Iraq thing. I just felt it was important to do something, not just sit here, reading about it all. And so I went along to a Respect meeting. I'd seen it advertised in the library. Mark was there.'

'And you became –' Faraday smiled. '– Friends?'

'After a bit, yes. I liked the Respect people. They were a nice bunch. They were like me when it came to the war except they were involved. They were *doing* stuff, holding rallies, pushing round leaflets, drawing up petitions. I know it doesn't sound much but when you're a mum all day. That can be pretty attractive, believe me.'

'And Mark?' It was Barber, softer this time.

'He was in there with them. In fact he was on the stop-the-war committee too.'

'And?'

'As I said, we became friends.'

'Good friends?'

'Yes, I'd say so.' She was being careful now, taking her time. She's got her second wind, Faraday thought. She's had a good look at us and decided that the situation isn't quite as hopeless as she'd thought.

'As part of this investigation,' he began, 'we've laid hands on Mark's phone records. He talked to you a lot, didn't he?'

The news startled her. Milo was curled in her lap. She looked down at him for a moment.

'Is that why you're here?' she asked at last. 'Because of the phone calls?'

'Yes.'

'And you want to know –' She frowned. '– Why he phoned me so often?'

'Yes. There's a pattern to his calls. A handful of numbers he phoned reasonably often. That's perfectly normal. We all do it. But there were periods when he was on the phone to you all the time.'

'You're right.'

'So why was that?'

'Because . . . ' Her head went back against the sofa and she closed her eyes. Faraday was watching her fingers. She was winding a curl of her son's blond hair round and round and round.

'Well, Mrs Mitchell?'

Barber's question opened her eyes.

'He was obsessed,' she said softly. 'Totally head over heels.'

'In love, you mean?'

'That's the way he put it, yes.'

'And you?'

'Me?' She was still looking at Barber. 'I was flattered, I admit it. He was very bright, very committed. He *knew* so much. He'd *done* so much. Demos all over Europe. Shit, he even had a criminal record. Affray. I remember him telling me about it. That was a turn-on. For me, at least.'

'You're telling me you had an affair?'

'I'm telling you I found him attractive. Or maybe it was the situation.' She waved her hand gently over the child in her lap. 'I love my kids to death. I'd do anything for them. But just sometimes it can get a bit, you know, claustrophobic. Being with Mark was different. And that's because he made it exciting. He just had so much to say. There wasn't an issue he couldn't explain to me. There'd be something in the paper, some story about ... I don't know ... city academies, or Zimbabwe, or the Trident programme, whatever, and he'd just bring it all to life. Stuff, issues, started to make sense in ways they hadn't before. They weren't just headlines any more. They *mattered*.'

Faraday was thinking hard about the times on the billing. He had them open on his lap now. Jenny couldn't take her eyes off them.

'He'd phone you during the day,' he suggested.

'Of course. We could talk, then.'

'But you met as well? You saw each other?'

'Occasionally, yes. But that could be difficult. I didn't want the kids involved.'

'In what, Mrs Mitchell?'

'In this thing of ours. You make it sound sordid but it wasn't. That was the whole point. It was something *apart* from all this. The last thing I wanted was Mark here – with me, with the kids, with all that.'

'So you met somewhere else?'

She didn't answer. Faraday put the question a different way.

'You say he was obsessed. Obsessives need physical

contact. They need to be close. He'd have suggested places you could meet.'

'Of course.'

'Like his bedsit? The place in Salisbury Road?'

'Yes.'

'Did you go there a lot?'

'For a while, yes. To be honest, I didn't like it.'

'Why not?'

'Why not? Because it made me feel dirty. Mark knew when people wouldn't be around, like the other tenants. He'd try and make it easy for me. He was good that way, kind. But I still felt, you know, *dirty*. I was a married woman. I had a husband, kids, a wonderful life. What was I doing there, creeping up and down those horrible stairs? Trying to make sure nobody set eyes on me? Mark used to tell me to pretend. Make believe I was a secret agent or something. He'd talk about occupied territory all the time. He'd tell me I had to evade the enemy. Some of that was funny, and it could be exciting too, and romantic, but deep down I just knew it was wrong. Wrong was a word he had no time for. He said it was bourgeois.'

'And did you agree?'

'Women can be very feeble-minded sometimes, Mr Faraday. It was easy to agree with Mark, at least it was to begin with, because, you know, he was just all over you.'

All over you. Faraday thought of Sally Spedding again. *He crowded you*, she'd said. *He wanted to shut out the daylight.*

'Tell me something, Mrs Mitchell. Did you ever go swimming together?'

The question took her by surprise.

'Yes,' she said. 'Once. Mark swam a lot. Salisbury Road is near the beach. He did it in all weathers, all seasons. That's the kind of person he was. There wasn't anything he wouldn't confront. I like swimming, too, but not in April.'

'That's when you went in with him?'

'Yes. It was a lovely day, warm. He talked me into it and in the end I said yes. Christ knows why because it was freezing.'

'Did you say yes to everything?'

'I resent that question. Of course I didn't.'

'Let me put it another way, then. Would Mark have had grounds for thinking that you –' Faraday shrugged. '– Were as keen as he was?'

'Was I in love with him, do you mean?'

'Whatever.'

'Then the answer's no. Of course we fucked. He was an attractive man. He had a lovely body. He was good in bed. I loved his mind, his conversation. But not for one moment would he ever have thought that, you know, it was for real.'

'How do you know?'

'Because I told him. Every time it came up, I spelled it out. I'm married, I used to tell him. I've got kids I adore. This is a fairy tale, you and me. It's brilliant for both of us, it does it for both of us, but never *ever* mistake it for real life.'

'He had nobody,' Faraday pointed out.

'You're wrong. He had himself. I've never met anyone so self-sufficient.'

'So why all the phone calls?'

'Because he was in love with me and that was his way of showing it.'

'Do you think he meant it? Believed it?'

'I . . . ' She frowned. 'I don't know. We all kid ourselves sometimes. Mark's problem was that he was bloody good at it.'

'You're saying he'd talked himself into falling in love with you?'

'Yes.'

'Obsessively?'

'Yes.'

'He wrote you letters?'

324

'Yes.'

'Lots of letters?'

'Yes.'

'And he had a name for you, a special name?'

'Yes.'

'What was it?'

'He called me *Querida. Mia Querida.* It's Spanish. It means loved one.' She paused. 'He was always speaking to me in Spanish. He made love in Spanish. If you want the truth, that was a turn-on too.'

Faraday nodded, glanced across at Barber.

'What did you do with the letters?' Barber wanted to know.

'I burned them.'

'When?'

'When things got difficult. Mark had been away. He'd gone to the Caribbean.'

'Do you know why? Why he went to the Caribbean?'

'No, except that he expected to make a lot of money. That was the problem, really. He . . . ' she faltered ' . . . wanted to take me away.'

'Where to?'

'Spain. He said he had friends down there, in Andalucia. He said he could make the kind of money that could buy us a place up in the hills. It was a fantasy.'

'You told him that?'

'Yes. But he didn't believe me. In fact I don't think he even listened.'

'Didn't that bother you?'

'Of course it did. And there was another thing too. There was someone else in Respect who'd, you know, cottoned on. They'd seen what was happening and they were nice enough to . . . I dunno . . . have a word.'

'Daniel George,' Barber said softly.

'You've talked to him?' She looked shocked.

'Of course. And he said absolutely nothing. But he knew, didn't he?'

'Yes.' She nodded. 'He told me to be careful. He knew I was married. He knew Mark could be over the top. The word he used was intense. He thought I might be getting in too deep.'

'And you listened?'

'Of course I did. And in my heart I think I knew Danny was right. Mark never knew where to draw the line. In fact he never knew there was a line to draw. He lived in another world. Like I say, that can be attractive. To begin with.'

'So what happened?'

'Mark came back from Venezuela. He'd been phoning me lots from this island. That was a problem too, because he was hopeless with the time difference.'

'Your husband found out?'

'No, thank God. But it was close, sometimes.'

'No suspicions?'

'No. He's a busy man, Andy. And like most men he sees what he wants to see.' She ducked her head a moment and buried it in her son's tummy. Milo squealed with delight.

'So Mark came back from Venezuela?'

'That's right. And I told him it was all over. Finished.'

'He accepted that?'

'No. But then I knew he wouldn't, not to begin with. He kept phoning and phoning. He just wouldn't take no for an answer. I tried blocking his calls. I even thought of changing mobiles.'

'Why didn't you?'

'Because . . . ' She looked Barber in the eye. 'You want the truth? Because he threatened to come round if I did that.'

'Come round here?'

'Yes. In the evening. When Andy was in. And so I kept the mobile, and I even answered the odd call. He said it was his lifeline. He told me those calls kept him going.'

'Did he threaten suicide at all?' It was Faraday this time.

'No.'

'Never?'

'Not once. Mark wasn't like that. He could be dramatic, of course he could. And Danny was right, he was always intense. But he was never, you know, pathetic.'

Faraday nodded. Duley's calls to Jenny's number had slowly tailed off through June. Then, towards the end of the month, they'd talked again.

'The twenty-eighth of June.' Faraday glanced down at the billing. 'He phoned you. The call lasted fifteen minutes. What was that about?'

'He wanted to meet me. Nothing heavy, he said. Just a chat.'

'And you?'

'I said no. But then he told me he'd got into trouble.'

'What kind of trouble?'

'Physical trouble. He said he'd been beaten up.'

'Who by?'

'He wouldn't say. He just wanted to talk to me about it.'

'And you agreed?'

'Yes.' She nodded. 'Yes, I did. It was difficult. That was the day the Queen came down for the Fleet Review, all that. Andy had fixed for us to watch it all from a friend's yacht. The kids were really excited. I was too. Then in the evening there was this amazing firework display, the Trafalgar celebrations, son et lumière. You may have been there, I don't know.'

Faraday shook his head. 'Go on.'

'Well –' She frowned. '– We were with friends in the evening too, just local mates from Old Portsmouth. They had kids as well. We all went along to the Common. The crowds were huge and I knew I could slip away for half an hour, before it all started, and I knew the kids would be OK because Andy was there. So I told Mark to meet me.'

'Whereabouts?'

'Outside the Queen's Hotel.'

'And?'

'We met.' She shut her eyes again, shaking her head. 'He was a mess. I don't know what I was expecting but he looked awful. His face was swollen, one eye was closed, he'd lost a couple of teeth. I felt really sorry for him.'

'But what did he want?'

'He wanted to take me to Spain.'

'He could do that? He had the money?'

'He said so.'

'And what did you say?'

'I said no.'

'Did he accept that?'

'I . . . ' She ducked her head. 'I don't know. He was just . . . different – not the Mark I knew at all. The old Mark, all that energy, had gone. He just kept looking at me. To be honest, I felt awful about it. I wanted to get back to the kids, to Andy, and time was moving on, but somehow I just couldn't. He was holding my hand. He was like a kid, like a child. He just kept squeezing and squeezing. Then the fireworks started.' She tipped back her head, felt blindly for a box of tissues on the other end of the sofa, blew her nose. 'It was terrible. I was looking at his face in the light from the fireworks. He was staring up at them. And he was crying. Horrible. Just horrible. I couldn't bear it, couldn't bear to see him like that.'

'So what did you do?'

'I stayed with him until the fireworks ended.'

'And then what?'

'I said goodbye.'

She started to cry. Milo wriggled off her lap in alarm.

Freya just stared at her. Tracy Barber was on her feet. More tissues.

'I'm sorry.' Jenny gulped. 'I'm really, really sorry.'

There was a long silence while she slowly composed herself. At length Faraday wanted to know what had happened afterwards. With her husband. With the kids.

Jenny stared at him, her face still shiny with tears.

'I told them I got lost.' She blew her nose and then struggled to her feet. 'In a way I suppose it was true.'

She made them fresh coffee. Faraday could hear her out in the kitchen, putting the kids' minds at rest. Mummy had a little pain. Mummy's better now. When she returned with the tray, she was colder, more distant.

Faraday wanted to know about the calls the following day. Midweek, she said, her husband was at work. Mark had called twice. The first time she'd told him to phone back while she took the kids next door to her neighbour. Then they'd talked.

'For nearly an hour,' Faraday pointed out.

'Really? It felt like even longer. It was a bit of the old Mark again. He wanted to tell me how good we would be together, how he could get it all sorted, how I owed myself a better life.'

'With him.'

'Yes.'

'And he still had the money?'

'Obviously.'

'Did he tell you any more about the beating?'

'Only that some guys had been waiting for him outside the place where he lived. He'd been away for the weekend.'

Faraday nodded. Winchester, he thought, the Writers' Conference.

'And what happened? Did he tell you?'

'Only that they took him off somewhere.'

'No details?'

329

'No, he didn't want to talk about it.'

'And you didn't ask?'

'Of course I did. I'd seen the state of him. It was criminal what those people had done. But he just dismissed it all. He said it was the price he'd had to pay.'

'For what?'

'I never found out. He never told me.'

'But he still had the money?'

'So he said, yes.'

'Did he say how much?'

'No.'

'Enough for a house in Spain, though.'

'Obviously.'

Faraday nodded, made a note. Barber was sipping her coffee.

'How did this call end?' she asked.

'By me saying goodbye. I asked him not to call again. He said he wouldn't.'

'But he did.' Faraday had his finger anchored in the billing. 'Six days later he was in touch again.'

'I know. And the day after, and the day after that.'

'Why?'

'The usual – we could go to Spain, all that. We owed it to each other. I was cruel, I'm afraid. I just put the phone down.'

'And Sunday?' Faraday was still watching her. 'The day he died?'

'That was the last call.'

'Forty-eight minutes.'

'Really? I can't remember. To be truthful, it's all a bit of a blur. I think I was frightened by then, frightened by what had happened to him, frightened by the difference it seemed to have made. I thought he was capable of anything. He was like a stranger. And yet . . . I don't know . . . there was still a bit of me . . . '

'What?'

' . . . that cared for him, I suppose. Maybe that's why

he kept calling. Maybe he recognised it in my voice. To be honest, it was just all such a mess.'

'The call was at midday.'

'That's right. The kids were in the garden.'

'And your husband?'

'He'd gone to drinks with some friends. I didn't fancy it.'

'How did the call end?'

'Like every other call. He seemed to accept it. He said he loved me. He said he'd do anything for me. He promised not to call again. Usual story.'

'Did you believe him?'

'I didn't know what to believe. I was exhausted.'

'And the rest of the day?'

'Andy came back. We put the kids in the buggy, went for a walk. Andy was a bit pissed so he went for a swim to sober up.'

'And that night?'

'We had a meal, as usual. Andy cooked. I put the kids to bed. We might have watched a bit of telly. I honestly can't remember.'

'What then?'

'We went to bed.'

'And?'

'I don't know what you're after. We went to sleep. Like people do.'

'No phone calls?'

'No. Absolutely not.'

'And next day?'

'Next day?' She frowned, reached for her coffee. 'Next day Mark was in the papers, wasn't he?'

Seventeen

'You think she's lying, Joe?'

'At the end, definitely.'

'DC Barber?'

'I agree, sir. We took her by surprise. It was all over her face. She told us far more than she had to, far more than was probably wise, but at the end you realised why.'

'Go on.'

'She wanted to share it with us, the whole story, show that she trusted us. If we believed her, then we'd believe that at the end she'd simply washed her hands of the whole business. She'd made a kind of peace with herself. She'd drawn a line. Whatever he chose to do was his affair. Nothing to do with her.'

Martin Barrie nodded. He was sitting at the head of the conference table flanked by Faraday and Barber. They'd been in his office for the best part of an hour.

'I'm still not clear about the money,' he said at last. 'We're assuming that Duley had his hands in the till in Margarita. And it's also a fair bet that the loss of that money put him in the caravan for the beating. Am I right?'

'Yes.' Faraday nodded. 'She didn't offer any details but she seemed pretty sure he had enough for them to set up in Spain. That's why he kept coming back to her.'

'So he still had the money, and sooner or later Kearns was going to realise that.'

'Kearns was off to Margarita. To look for Señor Querida.'

'Mackenzie then.'

'That's a possibility, certainly, but even if he knew, there's still no way he'd go through the performance in the tunnel. Legs apart? Chained to the track? That smacks of Duley to me. Not Mackenzie.'

'But she's telling us he wasn't suicidal.'

'She's also telling us he'd changed.'

'Changed enough to chain himself to a railway line? Are you serious?'

'I don't know, sir.' Faraday sat back, tossing his pen onto the pad at his elbow. 'We didn't talk to her under caution. None of it's admissible. We can go back and do the whole thing again, and we will, but first I think we need to know a bit more about her circumstances. Specifically, her marriage. By that time Vodaphone may have come up with her billing and cell site. It would be good to be in the driving seat by then.'

Winter had heard of Landfall.

'Bloke called Andy Mitchell,' he said. 'And the woman to talk to is Ellie Holmes.'

Holmes, the last time he'd talked to her, had been holding down a Social Services job. She was good mates with Carol Legge, who'd been so helpful over Emma Cusden, and knew a great deal about the mental health field.

'She's got an axe to grind, like they all have,' he warned Faraday, 'but once you get past all the *Guardian* bollocks, she's good value. Drinks a bit too. Loves all that real-ale shit. Here.' He consulted his address book and reached for a pen.

Faraday pocketed the number. He wanted to know about *Tartan*. Winter said that he and Dawn Ellis had been up to see Jake Tarrant's wife. Like everyone else in the world, she hadn't a clue what had happened to Alan Givens but was keen to find out.

'Dawn thinks he's probably done a runner,' Winter added. 'That's a sweet theory if Tarrant's missus was planning to join him but I can't see any way that's going to happen. Jake obviously drives her barmy but I think she's still there for him.'

'And Jake?'

'Jake . . .' Winter shook his head. 'Jake is a problem. Someone's been in that flat of Givens', someone with a key.'

'How come?'

'Because the camera and the laptop have gone missing. I knew Givens was kitted out because he's paying a warranty. PC World came back to me before lunch. They sold him a brand new Toshiba laptop in May, just after his mum's money came in. Top spec. Twelve hundred quid's worth. The purchase cross-checks with one of his bank statements. So where is the bloody thing? Number one, he's alive and he's still got it. Number two, he's dead and someone's had it off him.'

'But why does that implicate Jake?'

'Because it's a reasonable assumption that the camera and the laptop were at Givens' flat. When I went round there last week, there was no sign of them. Neither was there any evidence of a break-in. Whoever had been in the flat had a key.'

'But that takes us nowhere. If Givens was killed, then someone had his wallet. That would give them an address. They'd also have his flat keys. So why Jake?'

'Because he's the classic prime suspect. He's got a motive because Givens is all over his missus. He's got the opportunity because Givens thinks he's a mate of his. He's also sitting on one hundred and eighty-five grand of the man's money and he doesn't want to give it back. Call me old fashioned but that lot sounds well dodgy.'

'You want to search Tarrant's house? Get Scenes of Crime in? Do it properly?'

'No point. Rachel bosses the house and whatever's happened to Givens, I don't think she's part of it. The mortuary might be a better option, and we need a proper look at Givens' flat as well. I'm not saying anything happened there. I couldn't see any evidence at all. But the landlord's going to want it back so we ought to get in there sharpish.'

'Scenes of Crime?' Faraday asked again.

'No.' Winter shook his head. 'I'll take young Dawn down there. That girl's got a nose like a Labrador. Never fails.'

Ellie Holmes agreed to meet Faraday and Barber for an afternoon pint. She was on leave for a couple of weeks after the busiest winter and spring of her life and at the mention of mental health community initiatives, she welcomed the chance to get one or two things off her chest.

The Dolphin was a favourite haunt of Faraday's, a dark, timbered pub in the middle of Old Portsmouth. He and Barber had been talking for the best part of half an hour before Ellie bustled in. Faraday glanced up to find himself looking at an overweight forty-year-old with greying curly hair, huge rings on her fingers and a fierce sense of social justice. After the briefest of introductions, she gazed down at them. She'd worked in the public sector all her life and was, she announced, prepared to defend to the death the state's right to fuck up. Faraday found her a chair and returned to the table.

'Fuck up what?'

'Everything. Anything. Child protection. Social housing. Secondary school education. Operations for gallstones. Public libraries. Whatever. Just as long as nothing else falls into the laps of those greedy bastards who call themselves businessmen.'

Faraday had a feeling this was the way she opened most conversations. Her indignation, he guessed, was seldom less than gale force. You bent before it or you were doomed.

Barber returned from the bar with fresh drinks. Holmes hadn't finished. 'Another thing.' She reached for the nearest pint. 'Language. You know what we're supposed to call unemployment now? Worklessness. And failure? That comes in as deferred success. What's gone wrong with this fucking country? Anyone prepared to tell me?' She took a swallow or two of beer and wiped her mouth with the back of her hand. Barber was looking amused.

Faraday wanted to know about Andy Mitchell. Holmes leaned towards him, happy to share a lifetime of full-blooded prejudice.

'Young Andy? He used to be a good bloke, a really good bloke, before he got greedy. You want me to tell you a story about that lad? This is way back. I was duty call-out on the drugs team. We got word that some kid on acid had tried to top himself, I forget how. Wrists I think, Stanley knife. The kid was a mess. He was lying there in the Tricorn, howling his eyes out, wanted us to take him up to the top floor and chuck him off. The paramedics had done their best but he was all over the place, kicking and screaming. And you know who calmed him down? Took the edge out of the situation? Andy. Brilliant he was, just brilliant, and it didn't end there either, because later it turned out that the kid was into cocaine as well, big time, and it was Andy who looked after him, bunged him money, got him on a rehab programme, broke all the rules to keep him there when things got sticky, all that. And you know what? He never wanted anyone to know, not a dickey. Embarrassed to hell when I found out.'

'So what happened?'

'The boy got into smack. Died in the end. Fucking shame.'

'I meant Andy.'

'Ah . . . Andy.' She reached for her glass again. 'Like

336

I say, he got greedy. I'd put all the blame on him but strictly speaking that wouldn't be fair. Poor guy's got to make a living just like the rest of us. Problem is, it's too easy these days. This government's in love with the marketplace. You try and turn care provision into a market, and you end up with lots of Andies. These are blokes who got bloodied on the front line. They know how hard the job can be. Some tart from Whitehall turns up with her Powerpoint presentation and a big sack of money, he's not going to say no, is he?'

'But what does he *do*, Ellie?'

'Andy? He runs an outfit called Landfall. It's a lovely idea, it's really elegant. For a lot of money he provides what we call supported housing for a certain group of clients. Now these people are real dross. They're the scrapings. They're what's left over when you've filled all the prisons and what's left of the nuthouses and you've run out of space. We're talking schizos, alcoholics, multi-drug abusers, recidivists, whatever. These people are well and truly *wasted*. Andy puts a roof over their heads. He bungs some graduate a couple of quid to run an anger management course. He sorts out a music workshop. He offers an advocacy and support programme for when they end up in court again. And then he goes back to the office and writes reports for the lady from Whitehall and he's cluey enough to use all the sexy buzzwords. Gobshite like integration, person-centred development, independent living. Andy's brilliant at it because he's clever, and because he knows he's helping the suits out of a fucking great hole.'

'And there's money in it?'

'Big time. Andy's got at least a dozen properties. Some of it is move-on accommodation. Some of them have a live-in warden. The rest of it is looked after by mobile support. That's nerd-speak for someone who belts round in a van wiping their backsides and cashing their giros and trying to make sure they don't get too arsy with each other. From Andy's point of view, it's a

337

piece of piss. Sixteen grand a year'll buy you some spotty graduate with nothing better to do with his life. The van comes out of the auction. Andy? He's coining it. How? Because each of these clients of Andy's comes with a big fat whack of government money. Why? Because it's the likes of Andy that gets the rest of us out of the shit. We pay our taxes and we turn our backs and the Andies of this world take care of all the real garbage. You know what people in the know call Landfall?' She beamed. 'Landfill. That tells you everything.'

'Can't be easy though. Looking after these people.'

'Sure. But that's at the coalface. Andy Mitchell runs the joint. And the joint's big. In fact it's almost an empire. And you know what that makes Andy? That means he's become –' she savoured the description '– a social *entrepreneur*. Sweet, isn't it? And there's little me, still thinking all this stuff must have something to do with the goodness of the human heart. But no. Nowadays you have to square the circle. Social entrepreneurs do the biz but they do it for a profit. You think the voluntary sector is still soft and fluffy? My friend, you'd be wrong.'

Faraday nodded. He was back in Jenny Mitchell's house, trying to chart the journey that this woman must have made. She'd have met Andy in his days on the Pompey front line. She'd have admired his commitment, his patience, his courage. Then, as the years rolled by, she'd have watched his transformation into something else. Instead of jeans and a T-shirt, he'd be wearing a suit. Instead of sharing war stories in the pub about that week's psychopath, he'd be locked away all evening on the PC, writing reports about social capital and collective provision. Holmes was right. Faraday had seen it himself in the police service. On paper it looked wonderful but most of it was the purest bollocks.

338

'You know Andy's wife at all?' It was Barber putting the question.

'Jenny? Sweet child. Heart of gold and naive as fuck. Andy's lucky to have her. Let's hope he knows it.'

'Why do you say that?'

'Because he's a very busy man these days. And some of the company he keeps ... ' She shook her head. 'This is a village when it comes to the movers and shakers. The people who have made it, they tend to stick together. Have you noticed that? Success attracts success. They eat in the same restaurants. Go to the same parties. Take the same fucking holidays for all I know. Now some of these people are legit, or more or less legit. They'd be solicitors, accountants, university people, whatever. Then you get your rich bastards, property developers mainly. Then you get your *really* rich bastards. And most of them are criminals.'

It was a lovely theory, beautifully put. Faraday was laughing.

'So where does Andy Mitchell belong in all this?' Barber wanted to know more.

'Andy's big time now. He's made it. He's up there. He counts these people as friends. Jenny? You tell me. She likes Old Portsmouth, I know she does. There's nice friends for her kids to play with, decent primary when they get to go to school, all that. But I'm not sure she buys the rest of it.'

Faraday nodded, savouring a mouthful of HSB. Duley, he thought, would have been a breath of fresh air. And, for a month or two, perhaps more than that. Maybe, deep down, she misses him.

Ellie Holmes had finished her pint. Barber checked her watch, shot Faraday a look, said she had to go. Faraday nodded, then reached for Ellie's glass.

'Another?' he offered.

She shook her head, waited for Barber to leave. Then she gestured Faraday closer.

339

'I want to be fair to Andy,' she said. 'But there's someone else you really ought to talk to.'

'Who's that?'

'Peter Barnaby. He's a consultant over at St James'. Lovely man.'

St James' was Portsmouth's psychiatric hospital, a rambling Victorian throwback set in acres of grounds on the eastern edge of the city. Faraday passed it every day on his way to work.

Barnaby, Holmes explained, had been a keen supporter of Landfall. Indeed, in the early days, when the organisation had been a twinkle in Andy Mitchell's eye, it was Barnaby who'd turned all that conceptual bollocks into a solid proposal that could pass muster with the funding people.

'Peter's been working with this client group for years. He's seen the same old faces up at St James', the druggies and the dropouts and the guys who can't pass a woman in the street without doing something totally inappropriate. Care provision was hopeless. Therapy was a joke. He knew there had to be a better way and, bless him, he thought Andy was the man to make it happen.'

When Landfall applied for charitable status, she said, it was Barnaby's name on the board of trustees that swung the application. And when Andy Mitchell passed the bucket round for funding, it was Barnaby, once again, who knew which doors to knock on.

'The guy's a leader in his field. If you're talking severe behavioural problems, Barnaby's the man they all listen to. He had a lot riding on Landfall. In a way, it was his baby.'

'Had?'

'Yeah.' Holmes was chewing gum now, and Faraday could smell the spearmint on her breath. 'He resigned from the board a couple of weeks ago.'

'Why?'

'No one really knows. There's lots of gossip but

340

that's standard MO in the voluntary sector. Situation like this, people can't wait to put the boot in. We're talking serious character assassination. Blood all over the fucking carpet.'

'Whose blood?'

'Young Andy's. This is gossip, right? There's talk of embezzlement, care workers helping themselves to client funds. That's pretty small scale but perfectly possible. Some of the people he deals with are completely out to lunch. They wouldn't have a clue what's in their wallet. Then there's the heavier stuff – false invoicing, dodgy maintenance contracts on the properties, work ticketed but not done. Add it all up and you might be looking at five figures. Easily.'

'Has anyone done anything about all this?'

'Not to my knowledge, no, but Peter resigning made a bit of a splash. Even the fucking suits might take notice now.' She laid a hand on Faraday's arm and gave it a little pat. 'That's a nice car young Andy drives. And kids are expensive these days, aren't they?'

An X-reg. Volvo estate was parked outside Givens' flat when Winter and Dawn Ellis arrived. The tailgate was open and Winter could see a stack of cardboard boxes inside. He got out of the Peugeot and bent to inspect the contents of the nearest box, recognising items from Givens' kitchen.

A shadow fell over him.

'Can I help you?'

Winter turned to find himself looking at a tall individual in jeans and a faded check shirt. He had yet another cardboard box in his arms and he bent to lodge it in the back of the Volvo before inspecting Winter's warrant card.

Winter was looking at the new box. More of Givens' stuff.

'And you are?'

'My name's Wilson. I own this property. I'm the landlord.'

'And all this?' Winter nodded at the boxes.

'Belongs to Mr Givens. I'd have been prepared to cut him a little more slack but I understand there isn't much likelihood of him coming back.'

He said he'd been on to Givens' employers at the hospital. Reading between the lines, he'd concluded that the man had gone well and truly missing. Last month's standing order for rent hadn't been paid because his account was evidently empty, and there didn't seem much prospect of payments in future. Rather than let the situation drag on any longer, he'd decided to look for a new tenant.

'So where's that lot going?'

'To the hospital. Apparently a friend of his has volunteered to look after it. A Mr . . . ' He frowned. ' . . . Tarrant?'

Ellis and Winter followed the Volvo to St Mary's. Young Simon was on a half day and Jake Tarrant was by himself in the mortuary. He opened the door when Winter rang the bell, peering into the hot sunshine. Wilson was already piling the cardboard boxes on the tarmac beside the Volvo. The contents of Givens' wardrobe lay heaped on the back seat.

'What's all that?'

'It's Givens' gear.' Winter was laughing. 'This must be novel for you, son, this kind of delivery. It's normally just the body, isn't it?'

Winter and Ellis helped Tarrant carry the boxes into the mortuary. Tarrant told them to use the big post-mortem room for the time being. Ellis, who loathed mortuaries, lodged her box on one of the stainless-steel tables and looked round. On the window side of the room were two sinks for scrubbing up and a litter of surgical instruments awaiting a sort-out. She looked at the scalpels and forceps, the big blunt-ended scissors and a single thin stainless-steel probe. Tarrant joined her, laden with two more boxes.

'What's that?' She pointed at something that looked like a power tool.

'It's a bone saw. We use it for taking the skull off.'

'Nice. And what's this lot doing here?' She was looking at a row of pot plants on the window sill.

'My babies.' Tarrant dumped his boxes. 'This place might be knackered but the air con still works a treat. Seventeen changes of air an hour. The plants love it.'

Winter was at the door with the last of the boxes. The tables were full now, so he left it on the side beside a pile of yellow bags marked DANGER OF INFECTION.

'What happens to those?' Winter was looking at the bags.

'Clinical waste. Goes for incineration.'

'So you still use this place then?'

'Only for fridge storage and the odd bit of tidying up.'

'Tidying up? What's that about?'

'We take bodies from QA after post-mortem. They're shipped down here in packs of ten to make it easier at their end. Mondays are favourite, start of the week. The state of some of them . . . ' He shook his head. 'I'm not saying reconstruction's easy, not after a full post-mortem, but you deserve a bit of dignity, don't you?'

Some of the bodies, he said, still had their eyes open. Same with mouths. Then there was the issue of hair.

'Hair?' Winter was fascinated.

'Yeah. Do it properly, and it should be towel-dried and brushed back. Some of the people we're getting now, they look like they've been left out in the rain.'

'So you tidy them up? Is that what you're saying?'

'Yeah. Of course. Bit of respect.'

'And that happens here?'

'Yeah. Normally it's just a cosmetic thing. Takes no time at all. Though sometimes you get a really shit job from QA so you have to take them to bits and go through the whole reconstruction thing again. That's rare though, to be fair.'

Winter nodded. He'd lost count of the number of times he'd watched Jake Tarrant slice up a body for the Home Office pathologist. His skills were awesome, especially when it came to putting everything back together again.

'You still do that? Hands-on post-mortems?'

'Up at QA.' He nodded. 'Yeah.'

'But not here, obviously.'

'No. Like I say, this place is just a dump bin. Overspill from QA.'

'How many can you take?'

'Thirty-six, max.'

'And it's normally full house?'

'Give or take. At the moment we're looking at thirty-one.'

'Easy though, eh? Not big eaters, are they?'

Ellis, who'd been listening to the conversation, turned away in disgust. Winter and Tarrant exchanged glances. This was no place for a veggie.

Winter wanted to know what happened to the bodies after they'd arrived from QA.

'Why do you want to know?'

'Nosiness, mate. Comes with the job.'

'Sure.' Tarrant shrugged. 'We check with the undertakers. We need to know whether they're down for the crem or for burial. If they start asking about body size we know they're going to the crem.'

'Why's that?'

'Affects the amount of gas they use. Big buggers take a bit of burning. You'd be a nightmare, mate. Take it from me.'

'And you're saying most go for cremation?' Winter ignored the dig.

'Ninety-five per cent. Burial's rare.'

'Embalming?'

344

'Even rarer. And barbaric, says me.'

'So how long do you hang onto the bodies then?'

'A week, maybe longer. Most funerals are organised within a fortnight.'

'So the bodies go from here to the undertakers?'

'That's right. They've got fridges too, obviously, and chapels of rest, all that.'

'So chummy dies. He has a PM. He gets sewn back up. He comes down here. Then the blokes from the undertakers call by and pick him up. Is that the way it goes?'

'Yeah.'

'And the rest is down to them? The viewing of the body? The hearse? Organising the crem? All that?'

'Yeah.' Tarrant nodded, braced for the next question. 'This is worrying, Mr W. Are you sitting an exam or something?'

Winter laughed, clapped him on the shoulder.

'Fat chance, mate. Far too busy. Now then, this lot.' He gave Dawn Ellis a shout. 'Are you fit, love? Only we should make a start.'

Tarrant was staring at the boxes. He looked aghast.

'Make a start on what?' he said.

Faraday was on the phone to Jerry Proctor when one of the Management Assistants appeared at his office door. Something in her face told him it was urgent. He signalled her to wait, bent to the phone. He'd just given Proctor Jenny Mitchell's address. He wanted someone round there sharpish to take a cast of the tyres on her car.

He brought the call to a close. The Management Assistant had someone on the line.

'Who?'

'A lady from Buriton. Her name's Bullen. She says she needs to talk to someone in charge.'

'About *Coppice*?'

'I think so. OK if I transfer the call?'

345

Faraday nodded. When the call came through he was still trying to remember if the name Bullen had figured in the house-to-house reports. He thought not.

'You are Mr . . . ?'

'Faraday. DI Faraday. How can I help you?'

She explained that she'd been away for a while. Got back a couple of days ago. Half the village was talking about what had happened in the tunnel and a neighbour had kept a copy of the newspaper coverage. Last night she'd popped next door for a drink and had gone through the various bits and pieces. After some thought, and another look this morning, she'd concluded that it had to be the same person.

'Who?'

'The man in the tunnel.'

'Of course. But the same as who?'

'Young Mark.' She excused herself for a moment to stifle a cough. 'Mark Duley.'

It took Winter and Ellis most of the afternoon to trawl through Givens' possessions. Tarrant was with them at the start, lurking on the edges of the post-mortem room, inventing little tasks for himself, watering his plants, tidying up stray items, offering to make coffee – any excuse to keep an eye on proceedings. Winter tolerated this covert supervision with the broadest of smiles, sharing discovery after discovery with Tarrant.

Early on, tucked down the side of one of the boxes, Dawn found the brochure for Venice. There wasn't just one of them but three, different companies but all top of the range. She passed it to Winter, who showed it to Tarrant.

'Your oppo Si says Givens wanted to take you all. Is that right?'

'Yeah.' Tarrant nodded.

'Didn't fancy it?'

'Couldn't get the time off.'

'Shame, eh? Especially since he was paying.'

Winter put the brochure to one side without further comment. Minutes later, he found some correspondence tucked into another brochure, this time for a cruise round the Galapagos Islands. The company responsible was answering Givens' request for a quote: two cabins on the Christmas cruise, one for two adults and a couple of kids, the other for a single adult.

Winter called Tarrant across again.

'Was this for you lot as well?'

'That's what he wanted, yeah.'

'What did Rachel think?'

'She wasn't fussed, to be honest. She gets seasick.'

'But he was keen, wasn't he?' Winter's finger found the quote at the bottom of the letter. 'Thirteen grand's a lot to spend on a Christmas present.'

'He had the money.' Tarrant shrugged. 'He thought it might be a nice idea. I told you, Mr W., he was a generous bloke.'

'Yeah but *thirteen grand*? He could have sent a card, couldn't he? Taken you all down the pub?'

'He didn't drink.'

'OK, then. MacD's, Burger King, nice Chinese, whatever. *Thirteen grand*? You're kidding.'

'Not me, mate. Him. His idea. His money. Me? I just kept my head down, got on with the job.'

'And what about the missus? She'd have known by now, wouldn't she?'

'Known what, Mr W.?'

'Known he was minted. A bloke with that kind of money to chuck around obviously had lots more. Was it her idea? The loan for the Southsea place? Or yours?'

'I honestly can't remember. She was always banging on about us having to move. You know what she's like. It was something she'd got in her head. I'm sure she even talked to the bloody postman about it.'

'She'd have mentioned it to Alan then? That new pal of hers?'

'Bound to have done.'

'And told him you couldn't afford it?'

'Something like that.'

'So what was your take on all this? Once it was settled?'

'I'm not with you.'

'Yes, you are. You come home one night and she's got the whole deal wrapped up. They've been to see the house down in Southsea. They're both thrilled to bits. She's even worked out the sleeping arrangements. For a hundred and eighty-five grand, Mr G. gets to kip in a bedroom in the back. Later, if he's a good boy, you might tuck him away in the attic. But whatever happens, you're down for a whole new life. Did you fancy that, mate? Sharing houseroom with Mr Givens?'

'It never got to that.'

'No, it didn't. Fucking good point. And the question, my son, is why not?'

Tarrant had stared at Winter, trying to read the smile on his face, the cheerful bonhomie, trying to work out whether or not he was serious. In the end he'd settled for making another round of coffees rather than give Winter any kind of answer, but while he was out looking for the electric kettle, Ellis too had asked Winter quite what he was up to.

'We've got him on the hop, love,' he said. 'You can call it an interview, if you like. You can call it any fucking thing. But just keep watching his face.'

Minutes later, from another box, Winter disinterred some literature on laptops. Givens, a careful man, had obviously looked at dozens before he'd settled on the Toshiba. After dishing out the coffees, Tarrant had retreated to the shelter of his office. Winter found him in front of his PC, compiling some kind of report.

'This laptop of Givens' . . . ' Winter perched himself on the edge of Tarrant's desk. 'When did he first get it?'

'Haven't a clue, mate.'

'Think. He seems to have shared pretty much everything else with you.'

'No. I knew he had one. But I wouldn't know any details.' He looked up from the screen at last. 'Why do you ask?'

'Because no one seems to be able to lay hands on it. That and the camera.'

'Maybe someone's had it away.'

'Maybe they did.'

'Maybe he's still got it.'

'Yeah? And maybe I'm the man in the moon.'

Winter extended a languid foot. Tarrant heard the door click shut behind him.

'Listen, my old mate.' Winter's voice had sunk to a conspiratorial whisper. 'If there's anything you want to get off your chest, now might be a good time. You're a good bloke. There might be ways out of this.'

Tarrant stared up at him. The rabbit, Winter thought. Caught in the headlights. Full beam.

'Out of what?' he managed at last.

'Out of all this shit you've got yourself into. There's another side to my job, son. It's called sympathy. I know what you've been through – Givens, Rachel, all the nonsense about the house – and believe me, I'd be the last person to blame you.'

'For what?'

'He was a cling-on, wasn't he? He was a pain in the arse, coming round here all hours of the day, dropping in with his cakes and all those lovely photos he kept taking. You were just being friendly to begin with – polite, giving him the time of day – but he took advantage, didn't he? And once he'd met Rachel, you were well and truly fucked. Am I right? Or am I wrong?'

Tarrant shook his head, wouldn't answer. Winter changed tack. He wanted to know whether Tarrant had a key to Givens' flat.

'No, never.'

'Had you ever been up there?'

'Yeah. Once. He had stuff he wanted to show me.'

'On the laptop?'

'Yeah. It was photos, all the photos he'd done with the kids. He wanted me to make a choice, pick shots that I thought Rachel might like. Her birthday was coming up. He wanted to send off for some extra big prints, get them nicely framed, a present, like.'

'And were you comfortable with that?'

'How do you mean?'

'This bloke, this virtual stranger, giving your missus all these presents?'

'It didn't matter what I thought. He'd do it anyway.'

'Not if you told him otherwise he wouldn't.'

'Yeah, but . . . ' Tarrant shrugged.

'Yeah but what? Yeah but you needed the money? The hundred and eighty-five K? Or yeah but you couldn't be arsed because you didn't care a fuck for your marriage in the first place?'

'Piss off, Winter.' Tarrant was outraged. 'Me and Rachel, you mean? Couldn't be arsed? You have to be joking.'

'Do I?'

'Yes, you fucking do. I love that woman. She's a pain in the arse sometimes but we're all guilty of that. She's gorgeous. She's the mother of my kids. She loves me. We can be great together, really great. You think none of that matters? Is that what you're trying to tell me?'

'No, my son. I'm not saying that at all. I'm simply asking the question. And now that you've answered it, I'm a whole lot clearer.'

'What does that mean?' Tarrant was looking alarmed again.

'It means that I had you right in the first place. It means that you're a good bloke. It means there are some things that matter to you, really matter to you. And like every other bugger in your situation, you'd move heaven and earth to make sure they stay yours.' He smiled. 'Am I right?'

Tarrant held Winter's gaze for a long moment, then

he turned back to the PC. He had a report to complete. They got sticky about deadlines up at QA. If he didn't ping this lot across by five at the latest, he'd be bollocked rotten.

'What is it, as a matter of interest?' Winter peered at the screen.

'It's a locator system I've developed. It's for the new mortuary. It's all computer-based.'

'Locator system for what?'

'Bodies, Mr W. We lose track of them sometimes. It might sound odd but it's true.'

'I believe it, son.' Winter touched him lightly on the shoulder. 'Sometimes we have the very same problem.'

Ellis and Winter left the mortuary shortly before five. The trawl through the boxes had confirmed what Winter already knew about Givens, but little else. The man was methodical to the point of obsession. He filed away all his correspondence, all his bills, every last item that might conceivably be important. This paper trail confirmed that he was diligent, self-contained and appeared to have absolutely no friends or relatives worth keeping in touch with. As far as the future was concerned, he had plans for installing broadband as well as building a shelter for his bike round the side of the house.

Once again, presented with evidence like this, Winter could only ask himself what had happened to Givens. These weren't the actions of a man who planned to elope with his mate's wife. Neither did they anticipate any sudden interruption to his solitary, impeccably ordered life. No, Givens had been killed. Of that he was certain.

At lights a mile short of Kingston Crescent, Dawn Ellis joined a lengthy queue of traffic. She'd just asked him about the personal impact of their hours in the mortuary. Winter had been close to death himself. Had the knowledge of all those bodies in the fridge unnerved him? Made him think a bit?

'No, love.' He'd shaken his head. 'Not at all. That's over. Done. Dusted. I was bloody lucky. This is much more interesting.'

'What?'

'This. Jake. Givens.' He smiled. 'Fucking nightmare for the boy. Must be.'

'You think he killed Givens?'

'I know he did. But he's been clever, hasn't he? He must have done it there, must have. He's got the run of the place. He's the keyholder. He can come and go as he pleases. Weekends, evenings, he could kill half the city and no one would be any the the wiser. He could carve up Givens like a turkey, turn him into handy little parcels of meat and gristle, and there'd be no forensic trace. That place must be crawling with DNA. Hundreds of bodies have been through it. Probably thousands. You'd never prove anything. He's home free, isn't he? It's beautiful. The boy's a real star.'

'So where's the body?'

'My point exactly. We haven't got a clue.'

'So we give up?'

'Fuck, no. Of course we don't. We keep looking. It'll happen in the end, I know it will. There are cleverer things in this world than DNA.'

Dawn Ellis nodded, inching forward. At length she told Winter to look in her briefcase.

'There's a letter in there,' she said. 'From Jessops.'

Winter retrieved the letter. It was addressed to Givens. It confirmed dispatch of his latest print order and hoped that he would be pleased with the results. Then, towards the bottom, came an additional paragraph.

You will note that we haven't printed photo #00015620:30774.jpg. It is the policy of this company, in common with standard industry practice, to treat pornographic material under a special protocol. In certain circumstances we have no hesitation in bringing such material to the attention of the appropriate authorities. In this case, given the degree of ambiguity, you will be pleased to know that we have decided against that course of action.

The latter was signed Bernard King, quality controller. Winter looked across at Ellis.

'Well, well . . . ' He was smiling.

Eighteen

It was nearly six before Faraday got out to Buriton. Tracy Barber had been delayed by a phone call from Special Branch. With their interest in Duley, they were curious to know what *Coppice* had unearthed and she'd spent a while briefing them on developments to date. Odds on, she said, they were looking at complications in his private life, though it was still too early to nail down the details.

Now, driving into the village, Faraday was wondering quite what to expect. How come this woman who'd made contact knew Mark Duley in the first place? And, more to the point, what light might she be able to shed on the events that had led him into the tunnel?

The cottage lay up a narrow lane, close to the church. There was an ancient Morris Minor convertible parked outside, with the roof down. The car was in beautiful condition, and Faraday paused beside it. There was a wicker shopping basket in the back, full of apples, and a rug covered in dog hairs.

The dog was the first to the door, a moist-eyed spaniel. A woman stood behind it, shading her eyes against the low slant of the sun. It was hard to judge her age. Late forties? Older? Faraday didn't know. He offered her his warrant card but she waved it away. She'd been expecting him all afternoon. She invited him in.

Faraday introduced Tracy Barber and followed her into the cottage. There was a smell of fresh polish and

354

something with olive oil and garlic was bubbling on the Aga in the big kitchen at the back.

'Do you mind talking in here? Only I've got to keep an eye on supper.'

She was a tall woman, full-bodied, with big hands and a warm smile. She wore a loose cotton dress and wisps of stray hair kept escaping from the scarlet bandanna she wore round her head. Her name was Bullen but she insisted they call her Ollie.

'That's short for Olivia, if you're interested.'

Barber had produced a pocketbook. She checked the date on her watch and made a note.

Faraday confirmed that he was investigating Duley's death in the tunnel. He thanked her in advance for taking the trouble to make the call.

'Major Crimes? Is that an assumption or just the label on your door?'

'Both, I'm afraid.'

'You think something terrible happened to that young man?'

'We know something terrible happened to him. We're just keen to know why.'

'I see.' She nodded. 'Will you take a sherry?'

Faraday said no. He'd appreciate an account of her own relationship with Duley.

'Not me, Inspector, my twin.'

Her twin sister, she said, was called Ginnie. Short for Virginia. She'd been living down in the south of France for a while now, sweet little house in a village miles from anywhere. She scraped a living as an artist but made enough to finance a trip or two back home. She always came in June, and she always stayed here in Buriton.

'With you?'

'Indeed, Inspector. I have a spare bedroom upstairs. Ginnie stays for a month or so, normally. We have a lot of fun together. She can be a hoot when she's in the mood.'

This year, Ginnie had turned up in early June. She wrote as well as painted, and for the first time she'd been bold enough to enrol herself on some kind of course.

'It was a weekend thing,' she explained. 'Friday to Sunday. Sounded terribly intense.'

'Whereabouts?'

'Winchester. It couldn't have been more convenient. Frankly, Ginnie could have slept here on the Friday and Saturday night, just commuted as it were, but she thought there was more value in going the whole hog. She's a bit like that, my sister. It's always all or nothing. No halfway house.'

Faraday nodded. Sally Spedding, he thought. Her workshop.

'She enjoyed the conference?'

'Oh, she did, she did, she enjoyed it very much. In fact she brought a little trophy back.' She smiled. 'Our Mr Duley.'

Faraday was trying to keep track of the chronology. The conference had taken place between 24 and 26 June. On the Sunday afternoon Duley had returned to Portsmouth. Sometime later that day, he'd been swifted away by persons unknown and taken to the caravan in Hayling Island. Early next morning, Monday, he'd been dumped in Cosham. The following evening, bruised and battered, he'd met Jenny Mitchell outside the Queen's Hotel.

'He came here on the Wednesday of that week after the Fleet Review,' Ollie Bullen explained. 'He phoned ahead and Ginnie picked him up at Petersfield station. To be frank, he looked awful. It takes a lot to shock my darling sister, but she couldn't get over the state of him. His face, Inspector, here, here . . . ' Her fingers touched her right cheekbone, her left eye. 'And when Ginnie got his clothes off, upstairs in the bathroom, the bruising was just everywhere. You know, the way bruises go after a while? That livid, yellow colour?'

'Did you ask him what had happened?'

'Of course we did.'

'And what did he say?'

'He said he'd been beaten up the previous week. He wouldn't go into details but it seemed to have something to do with money. Some people down in Portsmouth, business types. In fact one of them lives up this way. He told Ginnie he was going to have it out with the man. I've no idea whether he did.'

'Did he mention a name at all?'

'Yes ... ' she frowned ' ... he did.'

'Does Cleaver ring a bell?'

'Yes.' She nodded. 'Yes, it does. That's funny, isn't it? Ginnie thought he was making it up.'

Faraday reached for his pocketbook, signalling for Barber to take over.

'Did your sister tell you anything about Duley before you met him?' she asked.

'Oh yes, she'd told me plenty. This talented young man who scooped up one of the prizes. This gorgeous young thing who'd swept her off to bed. She was full of it, just full of it. Not him, necessarily, but the fact that it had happened. She's no spring chicken, Ginnie. It did her no end of good.'

'And what did she make of him?'

'Of that, to be frank, I wasn't so certain. She said he was very ... ah ... wrapped up in himself. This is Ginnie talking. You wouldn't appreciate the joke unless you knew her.'

'She's like that too?'

'Completely. Utterly. Always has been. That's one of the reasons she never married, at least that's my theory. And it also explains what she's doing in the Languedoc. Normally, she can't stand other people, has absolutely no time for them. Mark Duley was a very lucky young man. I put it down to booze, myself. That, and the fact that he was so young.'

'So it was a conquest?'

'Indeed. Call it a notch on her belt. Before that Wednesday she had absolutely no interest in ever seeing him again. To tell you the truth, the phone call came as a bit of a shock. It was only the fact that he seemed to be in some kind of trouble that persuaded her to meet him at all. One look at him, of course, and it was all very different. You couldn't just walk away. No one could. Not even Ginnie.'

'You looked after him?' It was Faraday again.

'We did, Inspector. Both of us. Ginnie moved in with me. Mark had the spare room.'

'And how was he?'

'To be honest, at first I thought he was on drugs. He just didn't seem to, you know, *connect*. He'd just sit where you are now, perch himself on the stool, try and get comfortable, and talk. He never stopped. He'd talk morning, noon and night. And it was always the same thing, the same topic. He was like a man with an itch, a scab. He just couldn't leave it alone.'

'Leave what alone?'

'Some girlfriend of his. He never gave her a name. Just "she". Ginnie said he'd been the same in bed, at the conference thing. The poor boy was totally obsessed.'

'He took your sister to bed and talked about this woman of his?'

'Yes. That's exactly what he did. She said it was like listening to the plot of some dreadful novel. He just wittered on and on about her. How she was married. How she had young kids. How she was trapped in a marriage she didn't want anymore. Ginnie didn't care two hoots, of course, not my sister. She knew exactly what she was after, and she got it, more or less, and the rest was just drivel. That's her term, Inspector, not mine.'

'But back here? After he'd . . . settled in?'

'Exactly the same. By the Thursday morning, to be frank, we were beginning to wonder what we'd let ourselves in for. He was *unrelentingly* miserable. Not an easy thing to put up with, not in a tiny cottage like this.'

Faraday nodded. The cuckoo in the nest, he thought.

'Did he go out at all?'

'Yes, and that's another thing. In fact that's why I phoned you in the first place.'

Duley, she explained, had been nervous of going into Petersfield and looking at him you could understand why. But on the Thursday, at Ginnie's suggestion, he'd taken himself off for a little walk.

'Where did he go?'

'Down the lane there to the pond. If you follow the little road round, it leads to the railway. Go under the bridge, and you're up in the forest. There are the most glorious walks, Inspector. I'm up there with the dog most days. Keeps us both fit.'

'And Duley?'

'He ignored the forest, took absolutely no notice of our directions. Instead of going on under the bridge and then following one of the paths into the forest, he turned left. That takes you along beside the embankment. There's a fence of course, but I don't think he took much notice of that.'

'He went up onto the railway line?'

'He did. And then he walked into the tunnel.'

Faraday shifted his weight on the stool. He knew every step of this journey. He'd made it himself, only last week. He'd had it photographed, mapped, plotted – the lot.

'Why the tunnel?' he asked.

'That's exactly what we asked him. He said it was irresistible. I remember the word exactly. Irresistible. He said he stood on that railway track and looked into the darkness, and knew that's where he belonged. Am I wrong, Inspector, or is that not creepy?'

Faraday nodded. Creepy was one word for it. Dramatic was another.

'Did you get a feeling that this was some kind of –' He frowned. '– *performance*?'

'For our benefit, you mean? No. Definitely not. Most of the time he was talking to himself. We needn't have been here. I suppose you'd call it a soliloquy. That place, that thing – the tunnel – just fascinated him.'

'He went back?'

'He spent the night there.'

'The *night*? When?'

'The Thursday. The day after he arrived. We all had supper. We watched a bit of telly. We were about to turn in. And he suddenly announced he was going for a walk. We weren't to worry. He might not be back until daybreak. He said it was just something he had to do. Apparently there are little recesses in there, holes in the tunnel wall where you can keep out of the way of the trains. He called them refuges.'

'Weren't you worried? Concerned on his behalf?'

'Well, yes, in a way. But he seemed so certain that he'd be back that we just assumed he meant it. In any case, Inspector, what else could we have done? We weren't his keepers. We couldn't lock the poor boy up. And of course at that point we hadn't the first idea he'd really be spending the night in the tunnel. I think both Ginnie and I had some vision of him sleeping under the stars. That would have been perfect, of course. *Most* therapeutic.'

Next morning, she said, he was back as promised. He still looked terrible and there was something strange about his eyes.

'Like what?'

'I don't know. I can't describe it. Ginnie thought he looked like something out of a Renaissance painting. I told her she was being fanciful but maybe she had a point. It was almost an *otherworldliness*. Do you know what I mean? There was a light in his eyes. He said he was making a journey. He said that twice, I remember. Then there was the music.'

He'd gone to bed for a couple of hours, she said. They'd both been downstairs when suddenly they heard this music. It was choral music. He'd arrived with one of those Buddha bags and it turned out he'd brought a little mini-CD player.

'What was the music?'

'Bach. The St Matthew Passion. Do you know it at all?'

'Very well. There was a performance down in Portsmouth, over Easter.'

'Excellent. Then you'll know exactly what I'm talking about. It wasn't the whole of the work, not at all, just one part of it. The "Descent from the Cross". You know the bit I mean?'

'Yes.'

'Well, it was that. He just played it and played it, over and over. Drove us mad, to tell you the truth. I've still got the CDs, as a matter of fact. He was kind enough to leave them.'

Faraday nodded. *Gethsemane*, he thought.

'When did he go?'

'He went on the Friday. I know it sounds awful but we'd really had enough by then. Ginnie kept dropping these heavy hints about having to get back to France the following week and in the end I think the message got through. Poor boy. I feel terrible now, just telling you.'

'Did he go by train? Back to Portsmouth?'

'No. That was another thing. The plan was to go by train, but when they both got to Petersfield, he said he couldn't face it.'

'Face what?'

'Another train journey. People looking at him. In the end Ginnie had to drive him back. At least that way she'd know he'd got back safely.' She offered Faraday a weary smile, then shook her head. 'There was something else though, Inspector. And I'd be remiss if I didn't tell you.'

'Go on.'

'When they were in Petersfield, Ginnie and Mark, he made her stop at a hardware store. There's a place called Basset's Ironmongers. It's on Swan Street. He gave her some money and asked her to do him a favour.'

'Buy something?'

'Exactly.'

'What was it?' Faraday knew the answer already.

'A padlock, Inspector. With two keys. He kept one. Ginnie was to hang on to the other one.'

'Why?'

'He didn't say, not specifically. All he wanted to know was when, exactly, she was going back to France. She told him Tuesday, because that was the plan.'

'And when *did* she go back to France?'

'We both went. On the Saturday. The afternoon crossing from Portsmouth. It was a last-minute thing, just something we both decided on.' She turned to the stove and gave the saucepan a stir. 'We were in the Languedoc by Sunday evening, just in time for a late supper. It was a bit of a relief, to tell you the truth. That man was beginning to disturb me.'

Ollie Bullen had kept the key. She'd handed it over to Faraday, sealed in a white envelope, glad to be shot of the thing. Now, driving back to Portsmouth, he wanted Barber's view on exactly where this conversation might take them. One lead was Duley's mention of Chris Cleaver.

'Winter's always been convinced he's tied in with Mackenzie. If Cleaver invested in the Margarita trip, he'd have every reason to want his money back,' Faraday said.

'Which might put him in the caravan.'

'Sure. But what does Duley gain by having it out

with him? He's been beaten half to death as it is. Why risk all that again?'

'Maybe it wasn't Cleaver he was after seeing. Maybe he was going to drop by when only his wife was there. That's Duley's MO, isn't it? Always go for the weaker sex?'

Faraday shot her an approving look. He remembered the note Jimmy Suttle had attached to the forms he and Dawn Ellis had brought back from their house-to-house enquiries. They'd both talked to Mrs Cleaver, and they'd agreed that she knew a great deal more than she was prepared to admit. Maybe Duley really had paid a visit the week before he'd died in the tunnel. And maybe the sight of his battered face had awoken all kinds of anxiety. Either way, Faraday made a mental note to enquire further.

They drove on in silence for a while. Then Faraday started musing about Duley's state of mind during those final few days.

'He was depressed,' Barber said at once.

'Obviously.'

'Partly over Jenny Mitchell. Partly the beating. Nothing was working out, was it? He'd convinced himself they were going off to Spain together. He'd laid hands on the money to make it possible. He'd suffered badly in the process. But still it wasn't going to happen.'

'Sure.' Faraday nodded in agreement. 'But was that really enough to put him in the tunnel?'

'Yes, I think it probably was. But that's not the issue, is it? What we need to know is whether he was alone or not.'

Faraday glanced across at her. He'd been wrestling with the same question since they'd talked to Jenny Mitchell. Everything he'd put together about Duley convinced him that someone else would have been involved. Sally Spedding again. *This is a man who did everything for a purpose.*

'Duley was an actor,' he said softly. 'He needed an audience. That was the shape of the relationship from the start. He performed. He dazzled Jenny Mitchell. She admitted it. He *knew* so much. He'd *done* so much. That was the role he was playing. She lapped it up.'

'An audience of one?' Barber wasn't convinced.

'But that's the whole point. For someone like Duley an audience of one was perfect. Why? Because it gave him sole control. For that period of time before she twigged what he was really like, what he was doing to her, she'd become a kind of mirror. Put yourself in his shoes. She's beautiful. She's a bit of a challenge because she's married. And there she is taking your calls, and listening to you bang on about politics or whatever, and agreeing to secret little meetings, and then getting into bed with you. That's perfect, isn't it? That's the world he created for her. That's the spell he cast. It's the same with every love affair. For a while you lose your bearings.'

'And she did –' Barber nodded. '– Big time.'

'So you agree?'

'Yes, I do. I think there are difficulties, but . . . yes.'

'What difficulties?'

'Jenny Mitchell says she didn't like that bedsit of his. From what I saw of it, I'm not surprised. So where did they meet? Where did they get it on?'

'Her mother's place. Has to be. Her mother's in Malta. She may have been there a while. Jenny would have a key. Perfect.'

'OK. Let's say you're right. Let's say she was knocked out by him for a while. And let's say that when she finally came to and realised how bloody dangerous this man was going to be, she tried to get rid of him. That makes perfect sense to me. That's exactly what you'd do. But then why is she spending fifty minutes on the phone to him the day he dies?'

'I don't know. Maybe she felt sorry for him. You would, wouldn't you? The state of the man?'

'Sure, but *fifty minutes*? When she's trying to draw a line under it all?'

Faraday's mobile began to trill. He reached for the hands-free cradle. It was DS Jerry Proctor. A guy from SOC had finally managed to lay hands on Jenny Mitchell's car. It turned out that she shared an Audi A4 convertible with her husband. He'd been driving it today and had only got back home at seven. One look at the tread pattern on the tyres told Proctor's investigator that there was no match with the casts from the plantation.

Faraday nodded.

'Did the tyres look new?'

'No.'

'And what about the husband?'

'He was quite arsy. Kicked up about it. Talked about lodging a complaint.'

'About what?'

'About you lot.' Proctor laughed. 'Apparently you gave his missus a bit of a grilling.'

'He knew that?'

'Obviously. I get the feeling she'll have a solicitor on hand next time. Good luck though, eh?' He rang off.

Barber had heard every word. She glanced across at Faraday.

'Duley seemed to think the marriage was on the rocks.'

'He might have been right. You don't do what Jenny did without good reason. Not to begin with, anyway.'

'And now?'

'She's got two kids. A house. A life. Like I say, falling in love's a spell. Spells get broken.'

'Do you think Duley knew that?'

'No, I don't. He *was* the spell.'

They drove on in silence. Faraday knew the question that was coming. This thing begins and ends in the tunnel, he thought. Crack that, and *Coppice* might turn into a modest success.

'That Sunday night,' Barber said at last, 'he had to *get* to the tunnel. He's carrying stuff with him – chain, the piece of angle iron, rope. He hadn't got a car. So how did he do it?'

'I don't know.'

'And once he's inside, are we really saying he could strap himself to the line?'

'It's possible. I've been through it a million times. He could have wedged the angle iron under the rail by himself. He could have tied his own ankles to either end. He could have wound the chain round his belly, under the rail, round his belly again, tightened it, put the padlock on. All that's possible. Bizarre but possible. Where it falls down is why? You'd only go through all that if you were making a point. It's performance again. And for that you need an audience.' He frowned. 'Am I wrong?'

At Kingston Crescent Faraday attended to a list of messages, nothing really urgent. Then, at his suggestion, he and Barber went for a curry. He liked one of the smaller restaurants on Albert Road, a balti place he used a great deal. He'd got to know the family who ran it and sometimes bought packets of the rarer spices from them. On a Thursday night it would be quiet.

Barber toyed with the menu for a while, eventually settling for a chicken jalfrezi. Faraday, she sensed, was in the mood for a heart to heart, and *Coppice* was a perfect place to start. The last couple of days, to her relief, his post-holiday gloom had visibly lifted.

'You're enjoying this, aren't you?'

'I'm fascinated by it. Enjoyment's not quite the word. You start out believing one thing, one interpretation, and end up with quite another. Duley did a good job. He made it very hard for us.'

'You think that was his intention?'

'I don't know. There's something that still doesn't make sense. We haven't got a real timeline, not for the hours he was in the tunnel, but you'd have to be completely insane to strap yourself to a rail and simply wait.'

'Maybe that's the way he was.'

'Completely insane?'

'Yes. With some people it's just a little push, isn't it? They're predisposed. They're halfway mad already. Maybe Jenny did it by leaving him. Maybe it was the beating.' She shrugged. 'There but for the grace of God, eh?'

Faraday permitted himself a brief smile. She was right. There were times in his own life, and doubtless hers, when the constant ambush of events became overwhelming. You struggled and you struggled, and then suddenly you gave up. Medics called it the tipping point, the moment when the drowning man stops fighting the ocean, stops regarding it as his enemy. The first chill lungful of water, they said, and then the glad embrace of death.

Glad?

He shook his head. He still didn't believe it. Not trapped in the darkness with nothing but the certainty of mutilation to fill your last hours. There had to be another explanation. Had to be.

'How's Paula?' He changed the subject.

'She's great. Busy as ever. It's manic up there, especially now. She never stops.'

Barber had a long-term relationship with a desk officer in MI6, Paula Adamson. They'd met on some conference or other, a couple of years back, and had been together ever since.

'Doesn't it get frustrating? You down here? Paula up in town?'

'Yes, of course it does.' She smiled at him. 'I could ask you the same question.'

'And I'd give you the same answer. Except you couldn't get a train to Sydney.'

'Couldn't? Past tense?'

''Fraid so.'

'You've binned it?'

'Yep.' Faraday nodded. 'We got together in Thailand, as you know. Hopeless. She'd changed. She wasn't the same person at all.'

'And you?'

'Fair question. Maybe I'd changed as well.'

'Do you miss her?'

'No, I don't. I miss what we had, what I think we had, but the more time goes by, the more I start to wonder. Relationships are odd. The right time, the right place, the right person, and it can be quite magical. The mistake is to confuse it with real life.'

'You never made that jump? Not with anyone?'

'No, I don't think I have, not since I was married, at least.'

'She died, didn't she?'

'Yes. And we were young too. That makes a huge difference. Age is no friend of the romantic.'

'Really? You amaze me.'

'Why?'

'Because that's exactly what you are. A romantic. I can say this because you're safe with me, but I knew it from the start. It's what makes you so unusual as a detective.' She smiled at him. 'You bruise easily, don't you? That's why you read Duley so well.'

Nineteen

Winter brought the photo to Martin Barrie's office like the trophy it was. The Detective Superintendent had convened the meeting at Faraday's prompting, finding space for the entire *Tartan* management team around the conference table. Dawn Ellis was there too, and Winter had the grace to award her the credit for spotting the Jessops letter in the first place.

'Help yourself, gentlemen. Sorry it's in black and white.'

Winter was in his element. After a lengthy conversation on the phone, Jessops had e-mailed down the offending shot from one of Givens' files. Winter had taken a dozen copies of the photo, and now pushed them into the middle of the table.

Martin Barrie was the first to break the silence: 'So what, exactly, does this tell us?'

'It tells us, sir, that Givens wasn't quite as well organised as we thought he was. This one slipped through. Maybe it was finger trouble on the laptop. Maybe he got himself confused between files when he pumped the stuff up the line for printing. The rest of the batch are completely kosher. But a tenner says he's got a stack of others like this.'

Heads bent again around the table. The photo had been taken in Jake Tarrant's back garden. In the colour version Winter had recognised the pattern of the living-room curtains. The two kids were playing in the sunshine. There was a blow-up pool with an inch or two of water. Rachel's daughter was doubled up over the side of the pool. She had her legs spread on the grass and her bum in the air. Her younger brother had tried to mount her. Both kids were naked.

'I don't see it,' Barrie said. 'Am I thick or am I missing something?'

Winter passed him a copy of the letter from Givens' files. He read it quickly, then returned to the photo.

'This is pornographic?' He sounded incredulous.

'Borderline, sir. But that's the point. This is the only one we can find with them in that kind of pose. There were hundreds in the boxes. We went through them all.'

'But these are kids. It's a hot day. They're larking around.' He frowned. 'Aren't they?'

Dave Michaels intervened. He'd seen pictures like this too. And he knew exactly what Winter was driving at. 'It's not the kids, sir. It's the bloke behind the camera. There are numpties out there who'd cream themselves over stuff like this. And maybe Givens was one of them.' He glanced across at Winter. 'Where were the parents?'

'Jake was probably at work. The mum, Rachel, she might have been out. She might have popped next door. She might have gone shopping. She might have been in the bath. I've no idea.'

'You saying she trusted this bloke? Givens?'

'Completely. The pictures he bunged her for the family album were lovely. Nothing like this. As far as she's concerned, he's a thoroughly nice bloke. Trust him with my life. You know the way it goes.'

'So she would have given him free rein? Left him alone with the kids?'

'Without a doubt.'

'That's grooming. That's the way these guys operate,' said Michaels.

'Of course it is.'

Winter gazed at the faces round the table. Faraday

was the next to offer support. 'Tell us about the laptop and the camera, Paul.'

'Of course, boss. Fact is, they've both disappeared. They're high-value items, obviously, but there's no other evidence of robbery.'

'What about Givens' wallet? The cash? The credit card?' It was Barrie again.

'I think they were planted, sir.'

'*Planted?* How does that work?'

Winter was beginning to get irritated. Faraday could see the blood pinking his face.

'You've killed this man Givens,' he said patiently. 'You want to lay a false trail. You want someone to find Givens' wallet and start knocking the shit out of his debit card. What do you do? You prime it with sixty quid's worth of notes and you leave it somewhere evil.'

'Remind me.'

'Somerstown. Some nipper picks it up, nicks the money, does his best with the debit card but ends up selling it. After that, it's in the hands of someone who knows what they're doing. Which is why we spent a week running round after Karl Ewart. Shame Jimmy Suttle can't be here, sir. He'd give you chapter and verse.'

Barrie ignored the sarcasm. He was still looking at the photograph.

'OK,' he said slowly. 'So Givens had wormed his way into Tarrant's family. Is that what we're saying?'

'Yes, sir.'

'And once he was in there –' He tapped the photo. '– he helped himself?'

'Exactly. We talked to Tarrant's oppo, Dawn and I. Givens had a reputation round the hospital. The blokes thought he was bent.'

'That's gossip.'

'Sure. And then we find stuff like that. As I said, sir, that's a photo that slipped through Givens' net.

Normally, he wouldn't dream of printing the dodgy shots. He'd leave them on the hard disk, then view them through the laptop. If he had something really tasty, he could even offer them for sale online.'

'Is there any evidence of that? In his bank statements?'

'No,' Winter admitted. 'And to be honest that's a long shot. Normally, he was very careful. Selling kiddie porn these days isn't easy.'

'OK.' Barrie nodded. 'So what about Tarrant? The father?'

'He found out.'

'How?'

'He told us yesterday that he went round to Givens' place one time. Givens wanted him to look at a whole pile of stuff on the laptop and select some shots for Tarrant's missus. Givens must have left him to it at some point. Maybe he went to the loo, made coffee, whatever. Tarrant is good with computers, knows what he's doing. He'd have had a poke around. Bound to have done. And then . . . ' He spread his hands. ' . . . He's looking at all kinds of dodgy stuff. His kids, remember. In his own bloody backyard.'

'You'll have to evidence this.'

'I can't. Not without the laptop or the camera. That's why they've gone.'

There was a long silence. Then Jerry Proctor had a question: 'You're telling us Givens was definitely down to Tarrant? You're saying Jake killed him?'

'One hundred per cent.'

'That's a shame.' Proctor, with his SOC duties, knew Jake Tarrant well.

'Of course it is, Jerry. We all like him. He's a player. He's a good lad. He makes you laugh. But the story here tells itself, doesn't it? Givens gets himself a job with the hospital. The bloke's a creep. He latches onto Jake. Gets himself befriended by that poor bloody wife of his. Takes shots of the kids she can't fail to love.

Rachel's hammering on to Jake about moving to somewhere bigger but Jake's got a problem because they're skint and he doesn't want a bloody great mortgage round his neck. Then laughing boy reveals he's minted. Not just that, but he's happy to make them a loan. In exchange, of course, for houseroom. By now Jake's discovered that the man is perving after the kids. And a couple of months down the road he's going to be *living* with them. Well? What would *you* do?'

'I'd tell him to fuck off. Then I'd tell the wife.'

'About Givens? But then you've lost the money. And by losing the money, you've lost the new house. There's always a cleverer way, Jerry. Always.'

'OK, so how did he do it?' Proctor had folded his enormous arms.

'Good question. I made some other calls this morning. There's a very helpful bloke up at QA.' He smiled, pulling another rabbit from the hat. 'His name's Carragher and he's in charge of Clinical Waste.'

Afterwards, in the privacy of his own office, Faraday made Winter go through it all again. The *Tartan* meeting had broken up with the glum acknowledgement that Tarrant might well have killed Givens. The real problem, seemingly intractable, lay in proving it.

'OK, boss. You're Jake Tarrant, right? Motivation we've got sorted. All that's left is doing the bloke. Getting him into the mortuary by himself is no problem. The way we're hearing it, they couldn't keep him away. So you choose a time when no one's around, you kill him – bang him on the head, stick him with a blade, whatever – then you pop him on the table, chop him up into neat little pieces, parcel them up, and dump them in the Clinical Waste bin. The butchery's a piece of piss. He'd been doing it for a living for years.'

Faraday nodded.

'And you're telling me this stuff's collected from the skip outside?'

'It's a wheelie bin. It's locked. Tarrant's got the key. Off it goes to be incinerated. As far as I know, it's not checked, opened, nothing. Straight in the furnace and up the chimney. Beautiful. Us lot? We come round six weeks later and there's absolutely fuck all left. Why? Because chummy's a puff of smoke. Like I say, sweet.'

'You need to check all this. The waste chain, link by link, how it works.'

'Of course, boss. I'll get it sorted.'

Faraday was frowning, looking for the holes in Winter's explanation. A human body wasn't a small thing. Seventy kilos of flesh and bone might attract attention. 'Would Tarrant really risk dumping all those parcels at once?'

'I doubt it. If he could keep some in the fridge for later, I expect he would.'

'Who else has access to the fridge?'

'His oppo. Young bloke. Simon someone.'

'Check him out too.'

'Of course.' Winter paused. 'On the other hand, boss, Tarrant might just have taken the risk. He could have emptied the wheelie bin, filled it back up with chummy, saved the other stuff for later or just re-bagged it and taken it to the city tip. If he got the timing right, he could have had all of Givens en route to the incinerator within half a day of killing him.'

Faraday sat back. It sounded plausible enough. As, all too sadly, did Winter's conclusion.

'Without the body, as you say, we're stuffed.'

'That's right, boss. We can haul him in and go over it all, time and again, and God knows he might drop a stitch or two and make it easy for us, but somehow I doubt it.'

'So what do we do?'

'I'm not sure . . . ' Winter was stepping towards the door. 'I'm still working on it.'

*

Faraday's call found Daniel George on a train. He'd spent the night in London and was returning to give his wife a breather at the café. When Faraday asked for ten minutes of his time, he said there was no way. He had to get home from the station, drop some Respect stuff off at the printer's and then get over to Albert Road. Faraday said it wouldn't be a problem. He'd pick him up and run him to the printer's place, then give him a lift back to the café. They could talk on the way. With some reluctance, George agreed.

The train, for once, was early. George shuffled down the steps with his briefcase and eased his lanky frame into the front of Faraday's Mondeo. He was sweating in the midday heat.

'Before we go any further,' he said, 'you should know I've talked to Jenny Mitchell.'

'When?'

'This morning. She phoned me on the mobile.'

'How was she?'

'Bloody upset.'

'I'm not surprised.'

Faraday was trying to spot a break in the traffic. Finally, he darted out in front of an oncoming bus. George wanted to know whether this conversation of theirs was to be on the record.

'You're not under caution, if that's the question.'

'I know that. I'm asking you whether this is strictly for background, like last time.'

'Last time you told me nothing.'

'Exactly.'

'And this time?'

'This time might be different.'

'Why?'

George didn't answer. Faraday was slowing for a roundabout. The printer had premises in Milton. Milton was five minutes away.

'You knew about Jenny and Mark Duley,' Faraday said carefully. 'What else did you know?'

'I knew she was in the shit with him. And I knew she had to get herself out of it.'

'You told her that?'

'Of course.'

'And afterwards? Did you talk to her again about it?'

'I didn't have the chance. She'd abandoned Respect by then and I understood why.'

'Because she didn't want to see Duley?'

'Exactly.' He nodded. 'I like Jenny. She's got a good heart. She worked hard for us. It was a shame she couldn't have stayed longer.'

'Were you surprised then? By her and Duley?'

'Not really. You've met Jenny. She's very attractive. She's vulnerable too. Suggestible. Duley had an eye for that kind of weakness. To be frank, he could be a bit of a control freak.'

'No love lost then? Between you and Duley?'

George was rolling himself a cigarette. Only when he'd lit it did he permit himself the slightest shake of the head.

'We all have our needs, don't we?' he murmured. 'Duley just happened to be needier than the rest of us.'

Needy, Faraday thought. Maybe it was as simple as that. Pure appetite. Unquenchable. The kind of need that could turn into a death sentence.

'When did you last see Duley?'

'The day before he died.'

'Really?' Faraday looked across at him. 'The Saturday, you mean?'

'Yes. He came round to the café. He'd obviously been in the wars. He wanted to borrow my car.'

'Do you know why?'

'I've no idea. I didn't ask and he didn't tell me.'

'How long did he keep it?'

'Longer than I'd anticipated. He said he'd have it back by six. I was going across to Gosport that night.'

'And?'

'He turned up with it gone midnight. Said he'd had a puncture.'

'Was it true?'

'I've no idea. I never checked.'

'What sort of state was he in?'

'Agitated. Definitely.'

'And he didn't say where he'd been?'

'No.'

They were in Milton by now. Faraday followed George's directions to the printer's premises. Until recently it must have been a garage of some kind. There was a Stop-the-War poster nailed to one of the big double doors and the ghostly shape of a large black cat behind the net curtains in the window upstairs.

'I won't be long.' George was fumbling in his briefcase.

Faraday waited at the kerbside, trying to nudge this latest piece of the jigsaw into the puzzle. He could see George in the upstairs window, sorting through sheaf after sheaf of paper. Minutes later, he was back out on the pavement.

They drove back towards Southsea. Only when they were in sight of the café did George break the silence.

'What now?' he wanted to know.

'We soldier on. I'll need to take a statement.'

'I thought you might.' He glanced across. 'Have you finished with Jenny?'

'I doubt it. We need to know exactly what happened on the Sunday. She might be able to help us there.'

Faraday drew the car to a halt. Half a dozen students were chatting in the sunshine outside the cafe. Recognising George, they looked curiously at the bearded figure beside him.

'Tell me something,' Faraday said. 'Duley's dead now. He's gone. What was your real take on him?'

George was already opening the door. The question brought him to a halt.

'There are people in my bit of the wood who are

badly damaged,' he said at last. 'That's why they're drawn to the far left. They're alienated. They're on the run.'

'From what?'

'From us, Mr Faraday. And from themselves.' He reached for his briefcase. 'Does that answer your question?'

Winter treated himself to a cab to St Mary's Hospital. Dawn Ellis had said she'd run him up there but he turned down the offer. He was due a check-up session with one of the consultants, he told her. These guys were always running late and he'd hate to have her hanging round for hours in the car park.

The cab dropped Winter outside the main block. He stepped into the sunshine and followed the road round the administration HQ until he found the cul-de-sac that led to the mortuary. A gleaming hearse was backing carefully towards the doors that opened into the chapel of rest. Tarrant's assistant, Simon Hoole, signalled the driver to stop, then spotted Winter.

'You after Jake?'

'Yeah.'

'He's up at QA all day. I'll be with you in a minute.'

Winter wandered across to the main entrance where 7713 on the keypad took him into the lobby. It was cooler in here, and there was a sharp chemical smell gusting in from the post-mortem room. He hesitated a moment, looking at the row of battered fridge doors, knowing how easy it must have been for Tarrant to dispose of the body. Winter had never had much time for theories about the perfect murder but for once he was prepared to make an exception. All you need in life, he thought, is the right job.

The office door was open. Jake must have been in first thing because Winter recognised his Pompey sports bag abandoned on the armchair. He shifted the bag and sat down. From outside came the purr of the departing hearse. Then Simon's bulk filled the door-way.

'What can I do you for, Mr Winter? Only Jake's not back until late. One of them big management meetings. Me? I'd be bored to fuck.'

'What time's he back then?'

'Round six,' he said. 'Then he's off to five-a-side. Big night tonight. Three wins and they're top of the league.'

'Who's "they"?'

'Southsea Town.'

'Where's that then?'

'On past Fratton. Down round the Pier. Big place with a beach.'

'I meant where are they *playing*, son.'

'Soccer City, over at Fareham.' He grinned down at Winter. 'Fancy it, do you?'

Tracy Barber brought Faraday the news about the padlock. Outside Enquiries had despatched a DC to the ironmongers in Petersfield. The manager had confirmed they sold identical padlocks, but the woman who might have served Ginnie Bullen only worked at weekends. Once he'd had the chance to check his till receipts for 9 July, he'd get back. Odds on, he thought it was probably one of theirs.

'That's a yes, then.' Faraday was smiling. 'And what about the return visit to Mrs Cleaver's place?'

Barber smiled. She'd pressed Outside Enquiries to add it to their list of actions but the team were still swamped with follow-ups on the CCTV checks so in the end she'd driven out to the Cleavers' place herself.

'And?'

'You were right. Duley turned up on the Thursday afternoon.'

'What did he say?'

'Not much. Apparently he never got past the front gate. He rang the entryphone and then just stared up at the camera. When she wanted to know what he was after, he just lifted his T-shirt and told her to take a good look, and then ask herself what else her husband did for kicks.'

'And that was it?'

'Yes.'

'Very dramatic.'

'Quite. And effective too. If we're talking MO, it fits Duley like a glove. She said it scared her half to death.'

'And her husband?'

'Apparently she never told him.'

'Why not?'

'She wouldn't say. From where I'm sitting, she couldn't cope with an honest answer. The place is a dream. It must have cost the earth. Maybe she's better off not knowing where the money came from.' Barber glanced at her watch. 'Are we still OK for St James'?'

They drove east across the city. St James' Hospital was ten minutes away. Faraday had phoned ahead for an appointment with the psychiatrist, Peter Barnaby, and he'd agreed to meet them at two. Faraday parked on the tree-lined avenue that swept up to the imposing entrance. A couple of patients were sitting on a nearby bench, back to back, staring into nowhere.

Barnaby occupied a big sunny office on the ground floor. He was a tall, slightly rumpled figure in corduroy trousers and a denim shirt. His auburn curls were beginning to recede but his eyes were bright behind a pair of thick-lensed glasses. He waved them into the chairs in front of his desk.

'I'm completely in the dark,' he said. 'Tell me what you're after.'

Faraday's attention had been caught by a photo balanced precariously on a line of books behind the desk. It showed Barnaby at sea at the helm of a sizeable yacht. There was a woman with him, grinning at the camera, together with a couple of kids. Looking at the photo, Faraday was reminded at once of Willard. Nearly three days, he thought. And not a single call about Winter.

'Do you sail at all?' Barnaby had noticed Faraday's interest.

'No. I'm afraid not.'

'You should. Everyone should. It's God's therapy.' He gestured at the mountain of correspondence on his desk. 'To tell you the truth, I'm not sure I could get by without it.'

Faraday explained briefly about Major Crimes' interest in Mark Duley's death. They'd been working on the enquiry for nearly a fortnight now and one of the leads that had been thrown up related to Landfall.

'Good Lord.' Barnaby seemed surprised. 'Why's that?'

'It seems there may have been a link between Duley and a woman called Jenny Mitchell. Do you know Jenny at all?'

'Very well. I'm godfather to one of her children. Young Milo.'

'I see. And were you aware of any . . . ah . . . link between them?'

'What precisely do you mean by "link", Mr Faraday?'

'Relationship.'

'I see.' He turned in his chair, rubbed his face, gazed briefly out of the window. 'This is tricky,' he said at last. 'I'm not sure I'm in a position to help you.'

'No?'

'No. These things are personal. Someone confides in you, you're obliged to offer them a measure of . . . ah . . . discretion.'

'She's not a patient of yours, Mr Barnaby.'

'Indeed not. But she's a friend, and a very dear one. To be frank, the last thing I'm going to do is discuss her private life. Not at least without her permission. Does that sound terribly unhelpful?'

His smile had real warmth. You'd tell this man anything, Faraday thought, if he was asking the questions.

'You mentioned Landfall.' Barnaby was sitting back in his chair now, his hands linked behind his head. 'Care to tell me why?'

'Of course. My understanding is that Jenny may have some involvement. Is that the case?'

'She used to do the books in the early days, yes. Now?' He shrugged. 'Andy has a full-time accountant. He's got no option. It's a big organisation, turns over a lot of money. The audit obligations are terrifying. Jenny's got kids to bring up and a life of her own.'

'But she maintains some kind of interest?'

'She'd have to. She can't avoid it. She lives with the man who runs it. He might come home at night but looking after an organisation like that is a twenty-four-hour job. I'm sure there are days when Jenny wishes she'd never heard of Landfall. But that, I'm afraid, comes with the territory.'

'I'm not sure I understand. You're telling me she *is* involved?'

'Only on the margins. My point is this: Andy's chosen probably the toughest client group in the country. These are folk in whom you people will have a professional interest. A lot of them are recidivists. The only thing they know how to do is break the law, and believe me they're not very good at that. The rest are in various stages of disrepair. It's either drugs or alcohol, or some form of chronic mental illness. They have no homes, no prospects, nothing they can call their own. From my own point of view I have nothing but admiration for –' He broke off. 'Do you know Andy, by the way?'

'No.'

'He's an impressive individual. I can't think of anyone else in this city who could have taken Landfall to where it is now.'

'It's flourishing?'

'More than that. It's irreplaceable. If Landfall went down the tubes tomorrow you'd have to invent its twin sister the following day. In my view, that's the true measure of Andy's achievement. He's built it up from nothing, literally a couple of lines on a sheet of paper, and five years later people are queueing round the block to ask him how he did it. It's true.' He nodded at the pile of correspondence. 'I've got letters here from Social Services departments up and down the country. One came in this morning. Walsall. The man wants to come and shake Andy by the hand, sit at his feet, *learn*.'

'I understand you recently resigned from the board. Is that true?'

'Yes, it is. Why did I do it? Frankly, because I had no option. I had some small part in setting Landfall up. That was five years ago. But it was always my intention to step back and leave them to it once the thing was well and truly up and running. They don't need me anymore, Mr Faraday, and to be honest with you I need the time it buys me. In fact if I don't get a grip on the rest of my life, I'll probably go pop. That's my wife's phrase, by the way, not mine.' The smile again, even warmer.

'There are rumours . . . ' Faraday began.

'About Landfall?'

'Yes.'

'Of course there are. Rumours, gossip, scuttlebutt – it all comes with the territory. And you know something rather sad? The more successful you are, the uglier – the more vicious – the rumours. People hate success in this country. I've never understood why, but it's true. Do something difficult, make it *work*, build yourself a bit of a reputation, and there are people who can't wait to see you fall flat on your face. If anyone's going to go pop, it should be Andy. But he's stronger than that, thank God.'

'It must be a pressure though.'

'Of course it is, of course it is. And pressure doesn't stop there either. I'm not sure how much you know about social provision, Mr Faraday, but the truth is it's turned into a bit of a nightmare. The government, to be crude, want shot of it. They want to hand it over to the marketplace. They want to freeload on the back of motivated young men like Andy. There's nothing necessarily *wrong* with that if only they had the courage of their convictions. But they don't. They meddle, and they micromanage, and they get up to all kinds of tiresome nonsense, and it's people like Andy who end up as the meat in a particularly loathsome sandwich. He makes a profit, of course he does, but given the pressures he's under I sometimes wonder why he simply doesn't jack it in.'

'Maybe he enjoys it.'

'Maybe he does.'

'And maybe –' Faraday shrugged. '– It pays well.'

'Indeed. And are we saying that Andy should be ashamed about that? The kind of people he has to deal with? The kind of challenges he has to face?'

'From the government, you mean?'

'Yes, and the umpteen other folk with fingers in his pie. Local authorities. Probation. Social Services. Development agencies. The benefits people. You lot.' He laughed. 'Just talking to you like this puts it all into perspective. If anyone deserves a bit of peace and quiet, a bit of *support*, it's Andy Mitchell.'

Faraday nodded. It was a telling word. Was he talking about the small army of naysayers out there? People with an axe to grind like Ellie Holmes? Or was it a subtler reference to someone rather closer to home?

'Do you see a lot of them?' he asked.

'Of who?'

'Andy and Jenny?'

'Socially, yes, when we all find the time. In fact we were afloat with them just a couple of weeks ago, when the Queen came down for the Fleet Review. We had a seat in the front stalls. Apart from a drop or two of rain, it was a wonderful day.'

'And they're happy, do you think?'

'Very happy. Under the circumstances.'

'What does that mean?'

'It means, alas, that this little chat of ours has to come to an end. Nothing personal but time is pushing on. I have a committee meeting at three, another at four, and I'm addressing a bunch of students at the university at half past five. That's a full hour on my feet and I haven't even *thought* about what I'm going to be telling them.'

'Do you have a mobile, by any chance? In case I have to call you again?'

'Of course. Here.' He extracted a card from his wallet and slid it across the desk. 'So, if you don't mind . . . ' He got to his feet and offered them a farewell handshake. 'This time of day, the patients tend to wander around a bit. Be careful when you're driving out.'

Barber voiced it first. They'd left the hospital and were approaching the busy junction at the end of the road.

'He's loyal, isn't he?'

'Very. You've got to admire it. Whatever Mitchell's been up to, the last man who's going to blow the whistle is Barnaby.'

'You think they're in the shit?'

'Definitely. You don't part company with something you've created without good cause.'

'What about all his other commitments?'

'That's bullshit. People like Barnaby thrive on a full diary.'

'What then?'

'I've no idea, except that it must be serious. Maybe Mitchell doesn't listen to him anymore. Maybe he's gone his own sweet way. It's happened before.'

'And Jenny?'

'I'd say he's very fond of her. And I'd hazard a guess that he's become a kind of father figure. Just as well, really . . . ' he offered Barber a thin smile ' . . . under the circumstances.'

Twenty

Soccer City was a gleaming silver shed on an industrial estate off the motorway to the north of Fareham. Winter, who'd never been here in his life before, eyed it from the back of the taxi. The driver, a Spurs fan, had a couple of nippers who turned out in one of the Pompey youth leagues.

'What's the form then?' Winter wanted to know. 'You can just go in and watch?'

'No problem. There's a bar inside and loads of tellies if you're after decent football. You want me to come and pick you up afterwards?'

'No mate.' Winter was sorting out the fare. 'I'm OK for a lift back.'

'You're sure?'

'Positive.' He smiled. 'Thanks.'

Winter crossed the car park and pushed into the reception area, glad to be out of the heat. Through the big floor-to-ceiling windows, he could see the playing area. There were two pitches, side by side. Beyond them lay Fun City, a paradise of bouncy castles, ball pits and slides for the younger kids. The place felt like a warehouse on a retail estate, a big cavernous space echoing to the shouts of the players. Games had already begun on both pitches, and Winter watched through the glass for a minute or two, conscious of the thunder of feet on the carpeted floor.

There was a small bar overlooking one of the pitches. Winter bought a pint of Stella and made himself comfortable at a table with a good view of the play. Jake Tarrant's team was kitted out in green, Tarrant himself commanding the midfield. Winter had never bothered much with football but it was obvious even to him that Southsea Town had the measure of the blokes in scarlet and gold.

By the time Winter returned to the bar for a refill, Southsea Town had won their second game. By now a dozen or so supporters had gathered, girlfriends and wives, and a voice on the tannoy announced that Southsea were just a game away from going top of the league. Winter still wasn't clear whether this gave them the championship but the Stella was slipping down nicely and he kept his eyes on Tarrant as the referee blew for the start of the next game.

For someone looking at a possible life sentence, thought Winter, Tarrant appeared to be remarkably focused. He played football like he conducted a conversation in the bar, quick-witted, deft, full of spark and energy, and Winter watched as he closed down attack after attack, anticipating moves, intercepting passes, then stroking the ball forward for one of his teammates to blast it into the net. By half time, they were 5–1 up, but Tarrant was still going from player to player, a word here, a pat there, keeping them concentrated, taking no chances.

The second half kicked off, and the opposition scored an early goal. Then came two more and the pulse of the game changed. The greens were falling back now, their lead reduced to a single goal, and it was Tarrant who was rallying the defence, screaming for cover when an opposition winger broke loose, then stretching a leg and deflecting the shot with the Southsea keeper well beaten. With two minutes to go the score was 5–5. At this rate, thought Winter, they'll be taking the bus home. But then a loose ball fell to Southsea's only black player. He dummied the defender, laid it off to Tarrant, took the return pass, and squirted it into the bottom left-hand corner. The spectators erupted. The whistle blew for full time. Even Winter was on his feet.

Forty minutes later he spotted Tarrant as he pushed out of the building and headed for his car. His mates were with him. Back in Pompey, they'd be meeting at a pub called the Apsley. Going top clearly called for a pint or two.

'Jake, mate.'

Tarrant stopped in his tracks, amazed.

'What are you doing here?'

'Away support.'

'You *watched* it? I thought you hated football.'

'I do. Just thought I'd show a bit of solidarity.' He nodded across the car park at Tarrant's Fiat. 'Any chance of a lift back?'

Tarrant hesitated a moment. His mates were eyeing Winter with some interest.

'They think I'm your dad.' Winter patted him on the shoulder. 'We should have a drink or two. My shout.'

They drove back to Portsmouth. Tarrant, keen to rejoin his mates, asked how long this drink of theirs was going to last. Winter was non-committal. They had a lot to discuss and it was maybe in Jake's interests to forget about the football for an hour or two. Unless, of course, an evening on the piss was more important.

'More important than what, Mr W.?'

'That would be telling, son. Just trust me, eh?'

At Winter's suggestion, they went to a Gales pub up the road from the hospital. A table in the corner at the back gave them privacy and Winter returned to the bar. Tarrant, taking it easy, asked for a half but Winter ignored him. Champions, he said, drank pints. End of story.

Back at the table, Winter settled in, lifting his glass and toasting the final score.

'Touch and go,' he said. 'Another evening like that and I might start taking football seriously.'

'You enjoyed it?'

'Yeah.' He nodded. 'I did. You're good, aren't you? You read the game, just like all those twats I work with say you're supposed to. Where did you pick all that up? Take lessons, did you? Or were you born a genius?'

Tarrant gave him a look, not quite sure how to take this. His hair was still wet from the shower and there was colour in his face. In the end he touched glasses with Winter, accepted the compliment. He loved the game, he said. Always had. His own dad had been semi-pro with Aldershot and some of the old man's talent must have rubbed off. Fitness was a bit of a problem, and he'd be wise to knock the fags on the head, but football had always been a bit like riding a bike. Once you'd cracked it, figured out how the game ticked, then there were a million little labour-saving tricks you could learn.

'That big geezer? Played for the reds in the first game tonight? He was a fucking handy bloke, good with both feet, but you know how you cope with that? You nick the ball off him a couple of times, then tell him to try harder. Mind games, see? Never fails.'

'Rach says you're a puppy. Never retaliate.'

'She's right. That's another thing. You watch the mouthy blokes, most of them haven't got a clue. All they want is a fight. That's always easier than playing football.' He laughed, tickled by the thought, took another swallow of beer. 'You want to come and watch us when the proper season starts, eleven-a-side. That'd be good. We could make you our mascot. Mr W.'s boys. Courtesy of the Old Bill. Fancy that?'

Winter said he'd give it a thought. They were settling in nicely. He bought two more beers.

'Here's to August then.' He raised his glass. 'Is that when it kicks off?'

'Yeah. Can't wait. Play to our strengths, no one'll be able to live with us. You know what they say? If you've chalked twenty-one points on the board by Christmas, you're home and dry.' He laughed again. 'Twenty-one points is seven wins. Piece of piss.'

'Here's hoping then, eh? To Christmas.'

Winter raised his glass again. Tarrant's grin was fading.

'Christmas?'

'Yeah. Let's just hope you're still around to see it.'

'I'm not with you.'

Winter put his glass back on the table and gestured him closer. Time for a change of tack.

'I've got people on my back, son, you wouldn't believe. Powerful people. Senior coppers. They've looked at the evidence and they've made up their minds. The way they see it, you're dead in the water. The only mystery is why they haven't nicked you already.'

'For what?'

'Doing Givens.'

'Oh yeah? How's that? Got a body, have they? Proof?'

'No, they haven't, but that's a detail. Mine's a nasty little gang. You've seen the way they work. You know they never bloody give up. I tell you this for free, son. They think you're taking the piss. And they don't like it.' He leaned forward, patted Tarrant on the knee. 'You want some advice, son? Get a babysitter lined up. Someone the kids like. Someone you can trust.'

'Why would I do that?'

'Because they're likely to pull you in. Maybe Rachel, too. And once that happens you won't be seeing daylight for at least a couple of days.'

'Yeah?' Tarrant was worried now. The euphoria, the memory of the evening's goals, had gone. 'So where are you in all this?'

'Me? I'm part of the gang too. But I'm something else, son, as well. I'm your mate. And you know why? Because you helped me out, big time.' He nodded, patted him on the arm. 'Listen, no bullshit, I admire the life you've got together – Rachel, the kids, even that weird job of yours. I admire the way you're matey with people, the way you give them the time of day, even nonces like Givens. Yeah.' He nodded. 'Even him. That says a lot about you, son. In my book it says you're a gentleman as well as a player, and how many people can you say that about these days, eh?' He leaned back a moment, the proud father, took a swallow of beer. Then he was back again, his face close to Tarrant's. 'But there's something else too. I never really bought the stuff about the money, about Givens giving your missus one. The rest of my little gang, like I say, think that's enough. In fact they think it's more than enough. Paul, they tell me, you're off the fucking planet. We've got the bloke banged to rights. Number one, he's sitting on a hundred and eighty-five grand of Givens' money. Number two, Givens is shagging his wife. How many other reasons does a bloke need to give someone a good hiding? They've got a point, son, of course they have, but me, I know different. Why? Three reasons. One, because I know he forced that money on you. Two, I know he couldn't get it up for Rachel if he tried. Yeah? Am I being fair?'

'Yeah.' Tarrant couldn't take his eyes off Winter. 'You are. So what's number three?'

'This, son.'

Winter glanced round, then felt inside his jacket. Tarrant spread the sheet of A4 paper Winter produced on the table.

'That's my kids,' he said softly. 'Where did you get this?'

'Doesn't matter.'

'Yes, it fucking does.' He glanced up. 'Have you got the rest too?'

It was nearly ten by the time they left the pub. Tarrant was pissed. At Winter's insistence, they walked the half-mile to the hospital.

'Left, Mr W.,' he said when they reached the roundabout by the main entrance. 'Big place, can't miss it.'

Winter steered him through the maze of buildings to the mortuary.

'Seven seven one three,' he muttered, puzzled by the fact that Winter had already opened the door.

Inside, Winter kicked the door shut with his heel. He could hear the whirr of the fridges in the chilly darkness.

'The lights, son.'

The lights came on. Tarrant was fighting to keep his balance. He weaved towards the open office door, then had second thoughts, heading instead for the fridge room.

'Bottom drawer,' he muttered.

Winter went into the office. Under a phone book, in the bottom drawer, he found half a bottle of vodka. He took the cap off and gave it a precautionary sniff. This was no place to trust clear liquids.

Tarrant was back. 'You want a mug? Glass? Whatever?'

Winter shook his head, offering the bottle. Tarrant took it, swallowed a mouthful, blinked.

'What's that then?' Winter was looking at something in Tarrant's other hand. It looked like an envelope.

'It's for you, Mr W.'

Winter took the envelope. The CD inside was cold to the touch.

'Where did you get this?'

'Fridge four.' Tarrant grinned at him. 'My lucky number.' He nodded at the PC. 'Go on. Help yourself.'

Winter shook his head, surrendered the seat at the desk.

'You do it, son.'

Tarrant sank heavily into the chair, lodging the vodka bottle between his thighs. He turned the PC on and slipped the disc into the CD drive. Winter accepted a slurp or two from the bottle, standing over the screen, watching.

At last the screen cleared. Jake reached for the mouse.

'Enjoy,' he muttered.

The first image showed the same two kids, naked again, lying on their backs on a patch of grass. Both had their legs scissored open, tiny fingers pointing at their genitals. It was hard to be sure from this angle, but Winter fancied they were both in fits of giggles. Uncle Alan, he thought. And his funny little games.

Tarrant was slumped in the chair, his eyes half closed. He clicked on through the photos, cursing this pose, dwelling briefly on that, telling Winter that Rach had trusted this man, left him to it, gone off down the fucking shops to get something nice for their lunch.

'Something tasty, eh? As if that nonce needed it. Look at that.'

He'd paused on a shot of Tarrant's daughter. Givens must have found a length of string from somewhere. He'd tied it round her tiny waist and then raided the washing line for a couple of handkerchiefs. The handkerchiefs were pegged to the string, one either side of her belly button, leaving a slim panel of naked flesh at the front. Once again, she was grinning fit to bust. All this attention. All these fun and games.

'How sick is that?' Tarrant was shaking his head.

The shots went on. After a dozen or so Winter lost count. There was no ambiguity in these poses. Had any of this stuff found its way to Jessops, Givens would have been arrested.

'Where did you get all this?'

'Cunt's flat.'

'When?'

Tarrant shook his head, refusing to answer, then clicked another image onto the screen. His son, this time, gazing at his stiff little willy.

'Am I imagining things,' he said softly, 'or did my nipper need a bit of help?'

'Disgusting.' Winter was still waiting for an answer.

'Yeah, and this one, look.'

The boy again, bent over this time, arse to camera.

'You getting the picture, Mr W.? Only you guys would call this evidence, wouldn't you?'

'Yeah, too fucking right.'

Winter manoeuvred his bulk between Tarrant and the screen, then sat on the edge of the desk.

'You must have had some clue that Givens was doing all this,' he began.

'Clue?' Tarrant was slurring now. 'Of course I did. You just had to look at the nonce. Camera? Bloke like Givens? My kids at his mercy? You're the detective, Mr W.; you tell me.'

'But you'd need proof, wouldn't you? You'd need to be sure?'

'Of what?' Tarrant was trying to peer round Winter's bulk.

'Of what he was doing. Listen to me, son. This is important. Think. Tell me. You suspected Givens. You knew in your water what he was up to. But you had to be sure.' He leaned down, his face very close to Tarrant's. 'So you went round his flat, right?'

'Yeah.'

'And you got him to show you the decent shots, right? The OK stuff?'

'Decent? Fucking right. Fucking well decent. Yeah. Janet and fucking John. What a joke.'

'And while he was out of the room, you had a look through the rest. Right?'

Tarrant was trying to focus. At length he started laughing again.

'Wrong,' he said. 'I went through the laptop but couldn't find anything so I went through his drawers, didn't I? Found one of them little tiny picture card things, for his camera, all wrapped up in cling film.

Easy, mush. Straight in the pocket. Wanted to know, didn't I? Wanted to know what kind of party he'd really been having, the nonce.'

'He'd been looking at this stuff through his camera?'

'Must have been. All on one card, they were.'

'And you accessed the card through another camera?'

'Yeah.'

'Whose camera?'

'Mine.'

'Did Rach know?'

'Never. Still doesn't.'

Winter shifted his bulk on the desk, relaxed a little. Tarrant's chin was on his chest.

'So where's Givens' camera now?' Winter murmured.

'Binned it, didn't I? Dropped it in the fucking harbour.'

'And his laptop?'

'That too. Return ticket on the Gosport ferry. Best couple of quid I ever spent.'

'Why? If there were no shots on the laptop?'

'Cos . . .' He frowned, trying to remember. 'Cos I wanted it to look like some scrote had done a job on that flat of his. Same with the wallet. Leave it somewhere tasty and it's gone in seconds.' He grinned to himself. 'That poxy newsagent's place in Somerstown. Cool, eh?'

'OK.' Winter nodded, trying to sort out the timeline in his head. 'And all this was afterwards?'

'After what? After all them cream cakes? After all them nonce trips to fucking Venice?'

Winter steadied himself on the desk. He knew he was running out of time. Tarrant was beginning to talk nonsense. Any minute now, he'd call it a day. He bent closer.

'You found the camera card. You knew what he'd been up to. I want to believe you sorted him out, son.'

Winter stared down at him, the anxious father, the trusted mate. 'I want to know you did what any decent dad would do . . . Yeah?'

Tarrant gazed up, then nodded. His eyes were moist.

'Late on a Monday,' he said softly. 'Piece of piss.'

'Here?'

'There.' Tarrant gestured vaguely over his shoulder, in the direction of the post-mortem room. 'Told him I was working overtime. Needed help.' He smiled at the memory. 'Help, fuck. He was the one needing fucking help.'

'What about your mate?'

'Mate?'

'Simon. Your oppo.'

'Oh.' He grinned. 'Fatboy. On leave. Fortnight in Ibiza. Lucky bastard.'

'So how did you do it?'

Something in Winter's voice, just an edge of over-eagerness, brought Tarrant to a halt. He peered up, his eyes half closed.

'Why?' he mumbled. 'Why do you want to know all this stuff?'

'Because I'm here to help you, son. Because otherwise you're gonna be in deep, deep shit.'

'Yeah? Why's that?'

'I told you back in the pub. Because mates of mine want to put you away.'

'And you?'

'Me? I'm the only one who can stop them.'

'Yeah?' Winter knew he wanted to believe him. He bent closer again.

'You have to trust me, son. I want you to know I understand. Any bloke would, any dad. What Givens was up to was evil. The bloke was vermin. Thank God you had the bottle to sort him out.'

Tarrant gazed up at him, nodding.

'Yeah,' he said softly. 'Too fucking right.'

'So what happened?'

There was a long silence. Winter edged his body sideways on the desk, watching Tarrant as his eyes found the image on the screen.

'I whacked him, didn't I? Under the ear, just round the back here.' His fingers touched the soft skin behind his right ear. 'Bloke went down like the squinny he was. Beautiful shot. Beautiful, beautiful shot.'

'What with?'

'Rounders bat. Belonged to Rach. She was saving it for when the kids get older.'

'Where is it now?'

'I burned it.'

Winter stirred on the desk. A Monday evening, he thought. The door locked. Plenty of daylight left. And all the usual tools to hand.

'He was dead by this time?'

'No.'

'So what did you do next?'

Tarrant was frowning now, confused.

'What is it with you, Mr W.? What do you really want?'

'I want to know how you did the rest of it.'

'Why?'

'Because it matters. Just trust me, son. Trust me.'

'Yeah, but . . . ?'

'Listen, son.' Winter was close again. 'You helped me out, big time. I appreciate that. You'll never know how much, but it's true. Where I've been this last year or so, it makes you think. Most of my life I've been a loner, a *real* fucking loner, but now it's different. Mates are important. So is Rach. So are your kids. You love 'em, don't you?'

'Yeah, to death.'

'Well then.' Winter's hand found Tarrant's shoulder. 'Trust me. Either we get you out of this or you're history. You understand that?'

'Who's "we"?'

'You and me, Jake. You and me.'

398

'And you mean it?'

'I do. If you want to stay with your missus, your kids, all that, then you have to give this a shot. Otherwise, son . . . '

'Otherwise what?'

'I can't help you.'

'Fuck.'

'Exactly.'

Tarrant shook his head as if something had come loose inside. This conversation had definitely taken a turn for the worse. He stared up at Winter.

'You mean that? About Rach and the kids?'

'Yeah.'

'And you really need to know the rest?'

'Yeah. Starting with what happened after you whacked him. It's the only way, son. Either you tell me, either you get it off your chest, or someone's going to come knocking at your door. And this time it won't be me. Right?'

'Right.' Tarrant nodded, swallowed hard.

'So how did you kill him?'

Tarrant stared at the screen, lost for words.

'I put a cushion on his face,' he mumbled at last. 'And then I sat on it.'

'Did that do it?'

'Yeah. Big time.'

'And afterwards?'

'I got him up on one of the tables.'

'Was that hard?'

'Not really. Not if you know what you're doing.'

'Good lad.' Winter gave his shoulder another little squeeze, coaxing the story out. He wanted to know what Jake had done next. Every little detail.

'Why?'

'Because it matters, son. For all of us.'

Tarrant closed his eyes. For a moment Winter thought he'd gone to sleep but then he stirred.

'I stripped him first,' he said at last. 'Little runt he

399

was. Pathetic. Nothing to him. Then . . . ' He frowned. 'You start at the bottom. Take the feet off. Here . . . right?' His hand crabbed down his jeans until it got to the ankle. 'Then this bit, lower leg . . . Split the tibia and the fibia. Going too fast, am I?'

'You're doing good, son. Good.'

'Yeah?'

'Yeah.' Winter had begun to relax. 'Thigh next, was it?'

'Yeah. Bone saw. Strip the muscle. Big scalpel. Then . . . ' His hands were working slowly up his own body, ' . . . the pelvis. Bone saw again. Then slice the arse off him. And his guts too. Water, you need water. Lots of water. Down the drain.'

Winter nodded. The yellow hose pipe, he thought. And bits of Givens' insides washing down towards the metal sluice beneath the table. Tarrant was staring up at him, lost.

'Lungs? Did I do the lungs yet?'

'No, son, you didn't.'

'Deflate them,' he said. 'Remember that. Get the air out of them. Otherwise it's a fucking nightmare.'

'Deflate them how?'

'Knife.' One hand jabbed towards Winter. 'Sssssshhhh . . . '

He began to yawn. He's bored, Winter thought. He's relived this so often, it's sending him to sleep.

'Arms?' he suggested.

'Yeah.' Tarrant touched his own arms. 'Top and bottom. Then this lot.'

'What lot?'

Tarrant reached forward, fingered Winter lightly on the chin.

'This lot. Knife section through the ligaments. Jaw comes off easy. Then the face tissue. Beautiful. Then three cranial cuts, right?'

His hands were back on his own skull, tracing the

lines, one like the brim of a hat, another over the top, forehead to nape, the third laterally, ear to ear.

'Four sections. Fits a treat.'

'Fits a treat where?'

'Here, mush.' Tarrant patted his own chest.

'Inside, you mean?'

'Yeah, course. Where else?'

Winter stared at him, working it through, putting it together, sequencing the actions, imagining the remains of Givens neatly heaped on the cold metal, awaiting disposal. Then, finally, he had it. Tarrant was right. It was truly beautiful.

'OK.' Winter grinned down at him. 'You bagged the bits up.'

'Yeah.'

'Yellow bags?'

'Red. Always red.'

'OK. That left you with how many bags?'

'Ten. Wasn't much to the cunt.'

'And how many bodies did you have in the fridge?'

'Ten. Monday, see?' Tarrant was enjoying himself now. 'Fresh delivery from QA.'

'So each of the bags went into one of the bodies? Was that it?'

'Yeah.' He nodded. 'You slide 'em out of the fridge. Unpick the stitches. Bung a bit of Givens in, one bagful each. Zip 'em up again. Ten minutes max. Easy as you like.'

'And afterwards?'

'Afterwards?'

'What else did you have to do?' Winter was back in the post-mortem room, trying to imagine the scene. 'It's tidying up time, mate. There are bits of him all over the fucking place. Little bits.'

'Hose.' Tarrant was frowning again. 'You hose it all down. Just like normal.'

'And his clothes?'

'Burn 'em.'

'Where? When?'

'Can't remember. Must have been later.'

'OK.' Winter nodded. 'And the bodies? In the fridge?'

'Cremmed.'

'No one looks inside?'

'Fucking no way. You think I'm stupid?'

'But what if they did?'

'Wouldn't matter.'

'Why not?'

'You use red bags anyway. After PMs.'

'Brilliant.'

'Yeah. Say it again, Mr W.'

'Brilliant.'

'Now get off that fucking desk.'

'Why?'

'Why d'you think?' He struggled upright in the chair, one hand wrapped round the vodka bottle, then pushed Winter out of the way. A single image hung on the PC, the two naked kids entwined round each other, the boy trying to avoid his sister's kiss. 'There, Mr W.' He took a last mouthful of vodka. 'You blame me?'

Winter accepted the bottle, emptied it, wiped his mouth.

'No, son.' His voice was soft. 'I don't.'

Minutes later, with Tarrant slumped in the chair, Winter stepped out into the lobby. The register was on a shelf by the door. Givens, he knew, had first gone missing on Tuesday 24 May, although the police hadn't been contacted until nearly ten days later. He opened the register, and leafed back through weeks of entries. On Monday 23 May, someone had recorded the details of ten bodies, shipped down from the Queen Alexandra Hospital. Beside each name was a series of details – sex, age, date of death, post-mortem details, accompanying property – and the signature of the funeral director who'd assumed responsibility for the body on collection.

Winter gazed at the list for a moment or two then returned to the office. Tarrant was sound asleep, curled in the chair. Winter found a sheet of paper and a pen. Moments later, beside the register, he began to copy the list of names.

Twenty-one

Faraday awoke to a perfect summer's morning. For at least a minute he resisted the temptation to anticipate the day's events, to pick up the threads from *Coppice* and ask himself where all yesterday's conversations might lead. Ollie Bullen, Daniel George, Peter Barnaby, it didn't matter. All he could feel was the warmth of the sun on his face through the open window and the splash of a mallard or a cormorant as it landed on the water beyond the towpath. High tide, he thought to himself. And the promise of a hot, hot day to come.

At length, yawning, he padded through to his study. A couple of e-mails had come in overnight. One was from J-J. 'This place is UNBELIEVABLE,' he'd written. 'Everything's fallen apart except the PEOPLE. I'm staying with Gennady. He's got a sister in a wheelchair and three dogs. One of the dogs is called GEORGE and Gennady says it's because he's stupid and comes from TEXAS. Cool or what?'

The e-mail went on, tiny fragments of J-J's latest adventure, pearls strung together on a string of breathless e-prose. At the end he said he thought he'd be in Moscow for a month yet because there was a problem with getting paid and if you left the place too soon there was no way you'd ever see the money. It was news to Faraday that the Russians were responsible for his son's salary but he imagined that there must be some deal involved. Either way, he seemed to be having the time of his life.

The other e-mail was from Gabrielle. She said she

was getting towards the end of her book. She'd worked harder than she'd ever worked in her life, chiefly because she couldn't wait to get out of France and back to the Far East, but she was thinking of taking a couple of weeks off and wondered whether Faraday might like to join her. She had the camper and the dog and she'd be heading pretty much wherever she pleased. The first draft of the book should be finished, she wrote, '*vers la fin d'août*'. September, she promised, would be perfect. Rural France empty. The weather still hot. No one around. '*Ça te dit?*'

Faraday winced. Willard was insisting that Barrie drive both *Coppice* and *Tartan* full throttle through the second consecutive weekend. September was five weeks away. The prospect of a fortnight in the depths of France sounded hopelessly remote.

Faraday was at his desk by half eight, the window open, his jacket on the back of the chair. It was Babs, once again, who brought him the good news.

'The TIU e-mailed it through, boss.' She was carrying a sheaf of paper. 'I printed it off.'

She gave him the message from the Telephone Intelligence Unit. It came in two parts, both of them courtesy of Vodaphone. The first couple of pages dealt with recent calls on Jenny Mitchell's mobile. The rest supplied cell site information, as requested, on calls made on Sunday 10 and Monday 11 July.

Faraday thanked her and spread the sheets on his desk. The key to this enquiry, he knew, were the hours immediately before and after the moment when the train entered the Buriton Tunnel. On the Sunday morning Duley had made two calls to Jenny's phone, one brief, the other lasting nearly forty minutes. Faraday checked the times of the calls, then tallied them against Jenny's own billing. Duley had hung up at 12.48. After that she'd made no calls until 21.43, when she'd dialled an 02392 number. The conversation had lasted no more than two minutes. At 23.48 another call to the same number, again brief. Then, at 02.58, a third call. This time the conversation had gone on for eight minutes. The same Pompey number.

Faraday turned to the cell site data. Each call had registered on three cell sites, and by a process of triangulation Vodaphone were able to locate, with various degrees of accuracy, where the caller had been when the call was placed. Mobiles used in cities or towns offered the best fix. In the countryside, with cell sites much bigger, the point of origination was harder to nail down.

The first two calls, according to Vodaphone, had come from the Pembroke Park area of Southsea. Faraday glanced at his big wall map of the city. Pembroke Park was a semi-gated mix of houses and apartments on a biggish site half a mile from the seafront. The address offered an unusual degree of peace and quiet and many of the householders had chosen to retire there.

Faraday brooded, trying to work out what Jenny Mitchell would have been doing in Pembroke Park. Then he remembered her mother. Maybe she lived there. Maybe she had an apartment or a house. Maybe she was still in Malta. And maybe Jenny had a key.

He nodded to himself, turned to the last call, felt himself stiffen at the desk. At 02.58 Jenny had phoned that same Portsmouth number – but this time the call had come from somewhere else. According to the Vodaphone data, her approximate location had been Chalton.

Faraday scribbled down the Pompey number and left his office. Winter, he knew, had an Ordnance Survey map pinned to his wall. Babs was sitting at her desk when Faraday burst in.

'Chalton?' he queried.

Babs got up. She'd already located the village. She took Faraday across to the map, indicated a village

406

north-east of Horndean. Half a mile away ran the railway line.

'I just rang Jerry Proctor to check.' Babs was grinning. 'If you drive south from the tunnel on the country roads, Chalton is the first place you start getting a decent signal.'

Faraday gazed at the map a second or two longer. The one confirmed sighting of a car that night had come around 02.50, two miles north of Chalton. If you were Jenny Mitchell and you were driving south, Chalton was the first place from which you could make a mobile call.

Faraday sank into Winter's chair. At the Netley control room they kept a reverse phone book that tallied subscriber information against any landline number. Faraday read the number that Jenny had dialled three times and waited while the desk operator accessed the database. The woman was back within seconds.

'Mr and Mrs Andy Mitchell,' she said. 'South Normandy, Old Portsmouth.'

Faraday thanked her and hung up.

'Where's Winter?' he asked.

Babs shrugged.

'Dunno, boss. Should be in any minute.'

Winter had never had much love for crematoriums. The last time he'd been here, to the Portchester Crem, was five years ago, a blustery autumn day with rain in the air and a thin drizzle of friends and relatives who'd gathered to say goodbye to Joannie, his wife. After the brief service Winter had done the rounds, shaken hands, tried to fix names to faces, accepted whispered consolations from people he'd barely seen in his life, praying all the time that the conveyor belt of cremations – the long queue of hearses stretching down to the main road – would crank into action and drive these well-meaning folk back to their cars.

He'd fixed for a modest wake at a local Beefeater – half a dozen bottles of wine and three big plates of sandwiches fighting for their lives under tightly stretched cling film – but everyone was driving or teetotal, and hours later he'd ended up by himself in a wasteland of squirly carpet, determined to finish the last bottle of Riesling. Driving back that evening, he'd passed the crem again, up on the slopes of the hill overlooking Portchester, and he'd shuddered. When my time comes, he'd said to himself, I'll just crawl away somewhere private, where no one will ever find me, and call it a day.

That, of course, was never an option. He understood that now, after America. He understood how illness removes all privacy, all control, and leaves you in the hands of someone else. Like it or not, you'd probably end up in some chimney or other, a puff of ragged smoke on the wind, and in his grimmer moments he'd occasionally imagine his poor dead wife, looking down, shaking her head at the folly of a man who thought he could beat the system. You ended up where you ended up, he decided. And the only consolation was the fact that you probably knew fuck all about it.

Cheered by the thought, he told the cabbie to drop him outside the crematorium and then walked across the car park to the manager's office. For once, he'd phoned ahead for an appointment. The manager, curious to know what interest CID could possibly have in ten cremations in the middle of May, had wanted to enquire further but Winter had cut him off.

'Just being nosy,' he'd said. 'Comes with the job.'

Now the manager was sitting behind his desk. Dark suit, crisp white shirt, black tie. Winter had been expecting someone older. This blond youth looked barely in his twenties.

Winter showed him his warrant card. The manager examined it carefully.

'What's it take to get in the police these days?'

Winter laughed. 'Bored, are you?'

'Yeah. Seen one funeral, you've seen them all.'

'Bit like us, then. Half the blokes I work with are dead from the neck up. Your kind of experience, you'd walk into the job. Listen, I've got some names for you. I just need to know if they've been through here.'

The manager asked for the list. Winter shook his head.

'You'll never read my writing,' he said. 'I'll just read out the names.'

'Suit yourself.' He bent to a drawer and produced a big ledger. 'When are we talking?'

'A two-week period after the seventeenth of May.'

'OK.'

Winter began to read through the names. Day by day, the manager checked them off. The first cremation had taken place on Friday 20th. Two more on the Saturday. Another on Monday 23rd. Three on the 25th. One on the 27th. And a ninth on the 28th. After that, nothing.

'You want me to go on a week?'

'OK.'

'And that last name again?'

'Reid. Herbert Reid.'

The manager began to turn the pages. Finally, he shook his head.

'I went right through to the eighteenth of June,' he said. 'No can do, mate.'

'You're sure?'

'Certain.'

'You think he might have gone somewhere else?'

'It's possible, certainly. Where did this bloke come from?'

Winter consulted his notes.

'Pompey,' he said at last. 'Milton address.'

'He might have gone to the crem in Southampton. Or Chichester. Or anywhere really. Depends on the family. Most come here but not everyone. Who did the honours?'

'You what?'

'The undertakers.'

'Ah . . . ' Winter glanced down again. 'Barrell's.'

'Easy.' The manager was smiling. 'Talk to Sue. She's a good girl. Say Trev sends his love.'

'Got a number, have you?'

'Yeah.' He nodded, the smile wider. 'I have.'

Winter made the call on his mobile from the car park. When the number answered, he asked for Sue. After a while a cheerful voice enquired whether she could help. Winter introduced himself, mentioned Trevor's name.

'You want me to call by?' he asked. 'Show you the warrant card?'

'That's OK. I'll blame Trev if you're having me on.'

'Right. There's a bloke you did called Herbert Reid. Back in May. I need to know what happened to him.'

'Happened to him?'

'Where he got – you know – cremmed.'

He spelled the name. She wrote it down.

'How urgent is this?' she asked. 'Only I'm snowed under just now and I'm supposed to have Saturday afternoon off.'

'Whenever, love.' Winter smothered a yawn. 'As long as it's today.'

After a brief conference with Martin Barrie, Faraday phoned Jerry Proctor. The Scenes of Crime DS was at home. He agreed to drive down to meet Faraday at Kingston Crescent.

'You'll need the tyre casts from the plantation,' Faraday told him. 'We've got a copy in the exhibits cupboard but no one seems to have the key just now.'

'I'll bring a copy down. You want the footprints as well?'

'Please.'

Faraday was in the car park when Proctor arrived. He slipped into the passenger seat, reached for the belt.

'Where are we going?'

'Pembroke Park, first. Then Old Portsmouth.'

They took the dual carriageway into the city centre. At midday, weekend shopping traffic was heavy. Proctor wanted to know what was going on.

'We've got a lady friend for Duley,' Faraday said. 'Blame Vodaphone.'

They drove to Pembroke Park, turning in at the main entrance. Faraday was looking for a particular block of flats, Lingfield Court.

'The vehicle's a beige Toyota.' He read out the registration number.

'How come?'

'We pinged it on the CCTV trawl. It was logged coming back into Pompey at 03.19. The house-to-house guys have tried twice so far but there's never been anyone at home. It's registered to a Mrs Milne. Flat 45.'

'Maybe she's away.'

'We think she's been on holiday for a while. It's the car we're after.'

Proctor had found the parking space that belonged to the flats. Amongst the scatter of vehicles there was no sign of a beige Toyota. Garages in a line along one side of the tarmac were locked.

'It's in one of those. Bet your life.'

Faraday told Proctor to drive on. They were heading for South Normandy. 'It's off Warblington Street,' he said.

Minutes later, Faraday was emerging from the car. Jenny's bike was propped outside the house, just like last time. Her front door was open, as were most of the windows. It was very hot.

Faraday and Proctor made their way up the cul-de-sac. Faraday pressed the bell. The kitchen door was open at the end of the hall and he could hear the yelp of kids. They're in the garden, he thought. With their mum.

He was right. Jenny at last appeared. Barefoot on the wooden floor, she was winding a sarong around her bikini. Recognising Faraday, she did her best to muster a smile.

'Hi.'

Faraday nodded, introduced Jerry Proctor.

'He's a DS,' he explained, 'from Scenes of Crime.'

She stared at Proctor for a moment, and Faraday glimpsed the fear in her eyes. Then she forced another smile.

'Do you want to come in? Only this is a bit public, isn't it?' She gestured helplessly round at the rest of the close.

Faraday and Proctor followed her into the kitchen. She needed to keep an eye on the kids, she explained. They weren't great around water. Faraday could see Freya and Milo out in the back garden, taking it in turns to hose each other down.

Faraday asked about Jenny's mother. He understood she lived close by.

'That's true. She's got a flat in Pembroke Park. Do you want to talk to her? Only she's still in Malta.'

'I see. Does she have a car?'

'Yes.'

'What sort of car?'

'It's ... ' Jenny frowned. ' ... Beige.'

'Make?'

'Japanese thing.'

'Do you ever drive it?'

'All the time. In fact it's parked outside, just along the road.'

Proctor shot Faraday a look. 'Do you have the keys?'

'Of course. What's this about, Inspector?'

Faraday wouldn't say. Jenny fetched the keys.

'You can't miss it,' she said. 'Two kiddie seats in the back.'

Faraday and Proctor left the house. The Toyota was parked across the road. Proctor knelt at the kerbside, checking the tyre tread against the photo of the cast. Faraday, meanwhile, had unlocked the driver's door and was sitting behind the wheel. An audio cassette box caught his eye. It was down in the footwell on the passenger side, empty. He picked it up, turned it over. In red ink, on the card insert, someone had scrawled a single letter. Q.

Proctor appeared beside the driver's window. He was squatting on the pavement, his face level with Faraday. Faraday wound the window down.

'Looks identical.' Proctor nodded down towards the tyre. 'Can't be sure, of course, but I'd say ninety-five per cent.'

Faraday nodded, reaching for the radio/cassette in the dashboard. A cassette was already loaded. He pressed play, waited a moment or two, adjusted the volume. Then came strings, a clarinet, and finally a bass voice. The rise and fall of the music was unmistakable and Faraday sat back, knowing that *Coppice* was about to turn an important corner.

'What's that?' Proctor was still beside the open window.

'St Matthew Passion.' Faraday closed his eyes. '"The Descent from the Cross".'

Back at the house Faraday had a last request. Jenny had got herself changed. Her legs were tanned below the white shorts, and the pink T-shirt drew an admiring nod from Proctor.

'Do you have a pair of trainers at all?'

'Several.' Jenny nodded at a wicker basket beside the front door. 'Take your pick.'

'Nike. Size seven.' It was Proctor.

Faraday began to rummage in the basket. Then he felt the lightest touch on his arm. It was Jenny. She was kneeling beside him.

'Are these the ones you want?' She sounded suddenly exhausted.

Faraday gave the trainers to Proctor, who began to explain that it would be necessary to take them away, but she cut him short. She was still looking at Faraday.

'Listen,' she said. 'We need to talk.'

'You're right.'

'Only I don't want to do it here.'

'Of course not.'

'Where then?'

'I'm afraid it'll have to be at the Bridewell.'

'The where?'

'The Bridewell. It's at the central police station. We have an interview suite there. There's a process, Mrs Mitchell. It's the way we like to do things.'

'You're arresting me?' She was staring at him.

'Only if we have to.'

'What about the kids?'

'You need to make arrangements.'

'Now?'

'I'm afraid so.' Faraday offered her a thin smile. 'And you may be with us for a while.'

It was early afternoon before DC Dawn Ellis finally caught up with Winter. He was in the kitchen at Major Crimes, trying to prise the top off a new tin of Happy Shopper instant coffee.

'Where have you been?' Ellis demanded.

'Out and about.'

'Where though? I tried phoning last night. You were on divert. All night.'

'That's right.' Winter was looking at the bent spoon. 'I had a date with a friend. Why the drama?'

'You asked me to sort out the Clinical Waste arrangements at St Mary's. You remember?'

'Yeah.'

'I just needed to know how far you wanted me to go.

414

It's complicated, believe me. I could get old chasing all those yellow bloody bags.'

'Coffee?' Winter gestured at the open tin.

They talked in Winter's office. Babs had popped out for a delayed lunch break. Ellis made herself comfortable behind the empty desk.

The waste from the mortuary, she explained, was collected on demand. When the bin was full, Jake or Simon would call the Clinical Waste department and a van would turn up to cart the contents away.

'Where does it go?'

'There's a waste compound on site. It's on the western edge of the hospital.'

'Is it fenced? Locked?'

'Both. Then a lorry arrives. The contract's with a firm called Whiterose. They've got incinerators all over. Stuff from Pompey goes to Bournemouth. This is state of the art, Paul. Once it gets to the incinerator, there's an automated tipping system so no one's going to interfere. And you know what? All the energy created goes straight into the national grid.'

Winter rocked back in his chair. The thought of Givens finally being of some use clearly amused him.

'Brilliant,' he said. 'So let's say Jake did it that way. Where are the risks?'

'The weather, for starters. The pick-ups are daily but if it was really hot and those parcels were lying around until – say – late afternoon, you might know about it.'

'He could double-bag the contents. Are they airtight, these things?'

'Apparently.'

'Easy then. What else?'

'Foxes. Vermin.'

'You told me the compound was fenced.'

'It is. I'm just trying to pick holes. Foxes are bloody clever.'

'You're telling me it happens?'

'No. I'm telling you it might. And if it might, then Jake would be crazy to take the risk.'

'Yeah. Right. But if you chop someone up like that, you're crazy anyway, aren't you?' Winter was frowning. 'So you talked to these people? Whiterose?'

'Of course.'

'And did you mention the time window? Mid-May? When Givens disappeared?'

'Yeah. It was just business as usual as far as they were concerned. Daily pick-ups, stuff straight into the incinerator, nothing dramatic.'

'There you are then.' Winter pushed his chair back and put his feet on the desk. 'Givens binned. No DNA. No witnesses. No one any the wiser. You know what we're looking at here? The perfect murder.'

'But we don't even know the guy's dead, Paul.'

'Exactly.' Winter was beaming now. 'My point exactly.'

Twenty-two

It was late afternoon before Faraday was ready to interview Jenny Mitchell. He and Proctor had stayed at the house while she phoned for a friend to come round and look after the kids. Changed into jeans and a loose top, she explained that she'd volunteered her help on a police enquiry. There were yoghurts in the fridge, spaghetti hoops in the larder and oven chips in the deep freeze. If Andy turned up before she was back, he wasn't to worry. Everything, she assured her friend, was under control.

At the Bridewell Faraday left Jenny with the Custody Sergeant. She wasn't under arrest and at this stage didn't need fingerprinting. Jenny's appearance at the police station coincided with the arrival of a couple of Buckland slappers, detained in Commercial Road on shoplifting charges. They were both drunk, and both on first-name terms with one of the uniformed PCs charged with booking them in. Before Faraday left for Kingston Crescent, he glimpsed Jenny's face as she watched the girls mugging for their favourite cop. This was a slice of Pompey life for which she was plainly unprepared, and Faraday began to wonder just how much of her husband's work she'd really shared.

At Kingston Crescent Faraday sought out Martin Barrie. He briefed the Detective Superintendent on the day's developments and explained why he intended to tackle the forthcoming interview himself. He and Tracy Barber had the best working knowledge of this particular line of enquiry. Jenny Mitchell had volunteered herself for interview and Faraday anticipated few problems in establishing her role in the events of the Sunday night. Billing evidence linked her to Duley earlier in the day. The tyre casts and footprints put them in the plantation by the railway line. CCTV had caught her return to Portsmouth in her mother's car. En route, she'd found the time to phone home, presumably her husband. The question she had to answer couldn't be more straightforward: what, exactly, had happened?

Barrie was intrigued. A gangland revenge killing seemed to have turned into some kind of bizarre suicide pact. Was that a fair assumption?

Faraday cautioned against easy conclusions. Nothing in *Coppice*, he said, had been straightforward. Even this late in the day, he had a sense that they might be in for a surprise.

Tracy Barber was waiting in Faraday's office.

'How's she taking all this?' she asked.

'Surprisingly well. She's probably thought of nothing else since the bloody man died and I just get the sense that she needs to get the whole thing over.'

'Bloody man?' Barber was amused.

They drove down to the Bridewell. On Faraday's advice, Jenny had asked for legal representation. For some reason she was reluctant to phone her family solicitor so the Custody Sergeant had put a call in to Michelle Brinton.

Faraday found her in an office along the corridor. She was deep in the small ads section of the *News*.

'Duty again?'

''Fraid so.' She folded the paper. 'I'm after a mountain bike. Any ideas?'

Faraday shook his head. When he checked whether she'd yet had a chance to talk to Jenny, Michelle nodded.

'Nice woman. Bit of a change after Karl bloody Ewart.'

'She explained our interest?'

'Yes.' She held Faraday's eyes for a moment or two. 'Bit of a pickle, isn't it?'

Jenny was waiting in the interview suite, her chair positioned to catch the late-afternoon sunshine flooding through the high window. She looked composed, her eyes closed, her arms folded. She might have been waiting to sit an exam, Faraday thought, pushing in through the door.

The preliminaries were over in minutes. Faraday cued the audio and video recorders, read the caution, introduced those present, and established the time. He and Tracy Barber sat on one side of the table, Michelle Brinton and Jenny on the other.

'I want to take you back to the Sunday before last,' Faraday began. 'Sunday the tenth. Can we establish first that you knew Mark Duley well?'

'Yes, I did.'

'How would you describe the relationship?'

'We were lovers. Briefly.'

Faraday coaxed more details. Jenny began to falter. We've been through all this, she said, last time.

'That's right. But this is under caution, Mrs Mitchell. And that means we can use it in court.'

'*Court?*'

Faraday pressed her again for more detail on her affair with Duley. He needed to know that Duley had become infatuated with this new woman in his life.

'I prefer "obsessed". He wanted all of me, all of the time. That's why I knew it couldn't go on.'

'Did he accept that?'

'No.'

'How do you know?'

'He phoned me. Endlessly. I'd tell him not to, beg him not to, but he never listened. It got very . . . ' she frowned ' . . . difficult.'

'For you?' Faraday sensed something new here.

'For us all. He was threatening to come to the house,

cause a scene, have it out with my husband. He seemed to think I belonged to him, to Mark. He had no time for marriage. That was something else that was bourgeois.'

'This was after he came back from Venezuela?'

'Yes. He had money by now. There was no reason why we couldn't go to Spain, just me and him. I kept pointing out I had kids but it didn't seem to matter to him. This was bigger than kids, he'd say.'

'This?' It was Tracy Barber.

'Us. The affair. What we had.'

'Where did these conversations take place?'

'On the phone . . . ' She faltered. ' . . . Mainly.'

'Where else?'

There was a moment or two of silence. Michelle glanced enquiringly at her client but Jenny shook her head. She seemed to have made some kind of inner decision. She'd do it herself. Her way.

'At my mother's place,' she said at last.

'You used to meet there before Mark went to Venezuela?'

'Yes.'

'And you still got together there afterwards?'

'Yes. Not as much but . . . yes.'

'And talked?'

'Yes.' She nodded. 'And made love sometimes.'

'Why? If you didn't want this thing to carry on?'

'Because . . . ' She shrugged. 'Because my marriage wasn't so great. Because I still fancied him, not just physically I suppose but in other ways too. He was a comfort. He knew what to say, which buttons to press. You could say I needed him.'

'And he, you?'

'Definitely.'

Barber made herself a note, then glanced at Faraday. Faraday wanted to establish the timeline here.

'You told us a couple of days ago that you finished it

with Mark after Venezuela,' he said. 'You're now saying that's not true?'

'No, it was later.'

'How much later?'

'A couple of weeks, around the middle of June. I'd been trying to stop him phoning and by that time he'd started making threats. He'd shout, sometimes, really rant. I couldn't bear that. It was completely irrational. He was like a child, a spoiled kid. He wanted total control. If he couldn't have it his way, he'd make trouble.'

'So you ended it?'

'Yes.'

'How?'

'We were at the flat, my mum's place. Andy wanted to take me to Paris. It was supposed to be a surprise but I knew he'd got these cheap tickets on the ferry because I'd found a copy of the offer he'd filled in, and then I poked round a bit more and I found the hotel booking. That was nice. I felt guilty as hell but it was still nice.'

'So you ended it with Mark?'

'I had to. There was just no way I could go off with Andy like that and just ... ' She shrugged. ' ... Pretend. It had to end. I knew it did.'

'So you told him? Mark?'

'I did. I'd been to Salisbury Road that day. I still had the key to his room. I knew he wouldn't be there because he was always in Buckland on a Wednesday morning. Some local history thing.'

'And what did you do?'

'The place was horrible, really, you know, smelly. I don't think he'd changed the sheets for weeks. In fact I know he hadn't. So I opened the window and tried to tidy up a bit and then I just went round picking up everything that was mine, little knick-knacks, presents I'd given him, the odd letter, a couple of books of poetry, some music, photos. I took it all. I wanted to draw a line. I wanted him to know it was well and truly over. He came back that afternoon, saw what I'd done.'

'And?'

'He went crazy – phoned me, just wouldn't accept it. He said we were made for each other, that he couldn't live without me, all that tosh. Then he said . . . ' She swallowed hard, looked away.

'Said what?'

'He said I'd be the death of him.'

'Did you believe him?'

'No. That was typical Mark. He'd just crank it up and crank it up, totally over the top. As I think I said before, that can be a turn-on. After a while though it's just . . . a pain in the arse. It's the kid thing again. Maybe he was spoiled rotten as a child. Maybe that was it. Anyway, the point was he just wouldn't accept it.'

'Did you go to Paris?'

'No, in the end Andy had to cancel. Something to do with work. To be honest, I was so strung out by then I was quite relieved.'

'Strung out why?'

'Because Mark was being such a bastard. He'd drop notes in during the day, sometimes in the middle of the night. Andy started wondering why it was always me who got up first.'

'Did he ever come round and knock at the door? When you were both in?'

'No, but it was worse than that in a way. He'd have left one of his middle-of-the-night notes, and I'd be down there in the morning, tearing it up, getting rid of it, and then I'd look out of the window in the front, and there he was, just across the close, looking at me. It was creepy, mad, horrible.'

'And Andy?' The question came from Barber. 'Be honest.'

Jenny looked at her for a long moment. Then she nodded. 'He knew.'

422

'You're sure about that?'

'Positive. Andy's a cluey guy. He notices stuff. He's no angel himself, and that had been a problem as well, but he knew something was up. You can sense it, can't you? It's an atmosphere. It's the normal things you don't do. You don't touch anymore. You don't laugh, joke around. I think even the kids were aware of it in the end.'

'You're telling me Andy had been having an affair as well?'

'Earlier, yes.'

'And you knew?'

'I found out, yes.'

'When?'

'Round the end of last year. Just before Christmas. I came across a letter.'

'From the woman?'

'From Andy. He'd forgotten to post it. It was a long letter. There wasn't much I didn't know by the end of it.'

'And?'

'I confronted him, of course I did. That was the worst bit, really. He didn't even bother to deny it. He just said yes. I asked him whether she mattered to him, and he said no. He said she was a great fuck and they laughed a lot but it wasn't love so I wasn't to get upset. That hurt too. I'd have settled for a great fuck and a few laughs, believe me.'

'And then Mark Duley came along.'

'Yes.'

'After Christmas.'

'Yes. Andy and I had the worst Christmas I can remember. It was like living in a tomb. It was horrible. Mark was exactly what I needed, exactly what every woman needed. I could have bottled him and made my fortune. Shame I didn't, really. It might have saved everyone a great deal of trouble.' She gestured round –

the bars on the window, the video cameras bolted to the wall, the soft whirr of the audio cassettes.

Faraday sat back, reflective. The path to Sunday 10 July was slowly becoming clearer.

'So Duley was a kind of punishment? For Andy stepping out of line? Is that what you're saying?'

'No.' She shook her head. 'Mark was a reward. For little me. For surviving. And I grabbed it, in both hands, believe me. Mark made it easy. I told myself it was a mind fuck. It was like a wising-up course but most of it happened to take place in bed. He was my teacher. He was doing me *good*. If life owed me anything, then it owed me Mark. He had loads of dope, good dope. He made me feel . . . ' She frowned. ' . . . *me* again. I wasn't just a mother. I wasn't some disaster of a wife who didn't know how to laugh anymore. I was getting it on, ideas-wise, and I was raunchy as hell.' She turned to Barber. 'You know what I mean? When you can't get enough of pleasing someone? No wonder the poor man turned into a headcase. I shagged him witless.'

'Until you stopped.'

'Yes. And then, as I say, it got tricky.'

'So *why* did you stop? If it had all been so great?'

'Because I think I'd had enough. In fact I knew I'd had enough. And because there has to be more to a relationship in the end than . . . shagging.'

'Mark didn't accept you finishing it?'

'Never.'

'And you were worried about Andy?'

'Yes. To begin with, I think Andy just turned a blind eye. Like it was my turn. But then it was obviously getting serious, whoever this guy was, and it was at that point that he started dropping hints about the kids.'

'What kind of hints?'

'Just casual stuff. Like how they needed a stable background, mum and dad, all that. Then he'd start coming home with all these stories about people he knew, couples who were calling it a day, and how their kids ended up in a real mess. He was sending a message, trying to frighten me.'

'Trying to keep you?'

'Yes. Trying to keep all of us really, all of us together. Then came the night of the fireworks on the Common, and Mark getting himself beaten up, all that, and to be honest I just lost it. I didn't know what to do. I mean I'd screwed up big time, *truly* big time, and I was just . . . all over the place.'

'Like Mark.'

'Yeah.' She nodded. 'I suppose.'

Faraday nodded, sitting back in the chair. They'd been talking for nearly half an hour. It felt like minutes. Barber stirred.

'We're in July by now. Am I right?'

'Yes.'

'Andy's feeling threatened, Mark's spooking you, you're starting to worry about losing your kids, your family . . . yes?'

'Yes.'

'So what did you do?'

'I went to see a friend of ours, a good friend. In fact he's Milo's godfather.'

Faraday ducked his head, hid a smile. He'd been starting to wonder when Peter Barnaby was going to make an appearance. Barber wanted to know more.

'He's a psychiatrist, this friend of ours. He knows about madness. I thought he'd be a good person to talk to.'

'About?'

'Mark. I told him everything, or more or less everything.'

'And?'

'He was brilliant. God knows what he thought really but he was nice enough to say he understood.'

'And did he offer advice? Based on what you told him?'

'Yes. He said that Mark's behaviour sounded like a form of personality disorder. That was his description. He used the word "narcissism". He said Mark could be one of those people who need to be in total control. That's why he had so few friends. That's why he was so *busy* all the time. And he said something else too. He said that with all these people there was a really fine line between operating perfectly OK, between seeming perfectly normal, and being totally off the planet.'

'You mean mad?'

'Yes.'

'And you? What did you think?'

'Me? I could only agree. I was living with it every day. The phone calls. The notes through the door. The hanging around first thing in the morning. That was why I'd come to see him. I needed advice.'

'And he offered it?'

'Yes.' She nodded. 'He did. He dug out a copy of some act or other. Mental Health Act? I can't remember. Anyway, the point was that under this act Mark could be arrested if he was doing something that would either harm himself or members of the public, and that after the arrest he could be assessed and sectioned. That meant going to hospital. For his own good.'

'In a locked ward,' Barber pointed out. 'Section 136.'

'That's it.'

'Until he got better.'

'Exactly.'

'And stopped bothering you.'

'Yes.'

Barber glanced at Faraday. Over to you.

'Let's talk about Sunday.' Faraday had folded his arms. 'Mark phoned you around midday. You talked for nearly an hour. Yes?'

'That's right. He wanted to meet me that night.'

'Did he say why?'

426

'Yes. That's when I realised that he probably *was* mad.'

'How come?'

'He said he wanted to have a last supper. That was his exact phrase. Last supper.'

'In the religious sense, you mean?'

'I presumed so, yes. That was the implication, certainly. He said I'd crucified him, betrayed him.'

'How?'

'With a kiss.'

'Did that make any sense?'

'None.'

'But you agreed to meet him?'

'Yes, I did. He wanted to come to my mum's flat. He said he'd cook, bring the wine, everything.'

'And Andy?'

'I told him I was meeting a girlfriend.'

'Did he believe you?'

'No.'

'So what happened?'

'I got to the flat first, just like always. It was around nine o'clock. Quite late. I watched TV for a bit, just waiting. Then Mark turned up. I knew he'd been smoking. I could see it straightaway. But he was very subdued, very quiet, not what I expected at all. On the phone he'd been full on, just like the old Mark, but something must have happened, God knows what . . . '

'You had something to eat?'

'Yes. He'd brought two bananas.'

'Just that?'

'Yes. He didn't say why. He just gave me one, took a mouthful of the other and threw it in the bin. Then he did something quite odd. He walked to the window and just stood there for ages, staring out. When I asked what he was up to, he wouldn't say. Then he turned round. There were tears streaming down his face. He was really choked up. I felt sorry for him. I put my arms round him, gave him a hug, tried to make it better, but all he wanted to talk about was the music.'

'Music?'

'There was music out there. He wanted me to share it with him, listen to it, understand it. He said we were lucky. He said that only a handful of people had ever heard the music. And that handful included us.'

'What did you say?'

'I lied. I said I could hear it too.'

'And could you?'

'No.'

She nodded, a moment frozen in time. Outside, in the street, the blare of an ambulance siren.

Barber wanted to know what happened next.

'He asked me to go to bed with him. He didn't want to make love or anything. Just to be held.'

'And did you?'

'Yes. We stayed in bed until late, maybe midnight.'

'Did you phone anyone?'

'Yes. I phoned Andy. I'd talked to him already, earlier. I just said things were going on a bit and that he shouldn't wait up for me. I'd be back later.'

'What did he say?'

'He just grunted.'

'What then?'

'We got up. My mum's car was outside. Mark told me to drive out of the city.'

'Did he tell you where?'

'No. He just said he wanted me to do him one last favour.'

'*Last* favour?'

'That's the way he put it. One last favour. Then we'd be quits. I hadn't a clue what he was talking about but I was starting, you know, to wonder whether this might not be my chance. I mean, he was behaving *really* oddly. I just didn't know what to expect. Maybe this was what Peter meant by madness.'

'Peter?'

'Our psychiatrist friend. The one who told me about the Mental Health Act. I just thought ... ' She shrugged. 'I just thought it was worth a try.'

'So off you went?'

'Yes. We went out on the motorway, then north towards London. There's a turn-off before you get to Petersfield. You go down into all the little lanes, then you get to a village. Buriton. There's a crossroads. We went right. I remember the hill. We went up and up, trees everywhere, absolutely no one around.'

'And Mark?'

'Said nothing. Just gave me directions.'

'He'd been there before?'

'Must have done. After a bit we got to a really narrow track that went down into a wood. I carried on driving, then just before the end we got bogged in a marshy piece of ground, and we had to get out and push the car back out. It took a bit of effort but we managed it.' She paused, fingering the edge of the table. 'It was then that I realised we were beside the railway line. It was a moonlit night. The track was down a little embankment. Mark said we had to climb over the fence, walk a bit.'

'And you?'

'I just went along with him.'

Faraday reached for his pen, scribbled himself a note: *I just went along with him.* Back in February this would have served as a perfect description of their fledgling relationship. Six months later nothing had changed.

Jenny was describing the walk now, the pair of them stumbling along the trackside, keeping well clear of the live rail.

Barber interrupted: 'Did you have any idea where you were going?'

'None.'

'Weren't you ... curious? Anxious? Frightened?'

'Of course I was. I kept asking him what was going on. He just begged me to trust him.'

'Begged?'

'Yes, like I say, I'd never seen him like this before.'

After about half an hour, she said, they were approaching the tunnel.

'I could see it in the moonlight, just this big black hole. I really didn't want to go in. I told him that.'

'So what happened?'

'He had a torch. He said there wasn't a problem. He'd done the checks and everything. There wouldn't be a train through for hours. All we were doing was going maybe a hundred metres in. It wouldn't take long, he said. Then I could go.'

'So you went in.'

'Yes. I was terrified. I hated it.'

'And what did you find?'

'About a hundred metres in, exactly as he'd said, there was this stuff tucked into a kind of hole in the wall. I didn't know what it was to begin with. Then he started dragging it all out. There was some chain and some rope, and this long piece of iron. He went down on his hands and knees by the rail. As soon as you get into the tunnel, the live rail switches to the other side of the track, so there wasn't, you know, any real *danger* . . . ' She broke off, looking down at her hands.

'Did you ask him what he was up to?'

'Of course I did.'

'And?'

'All he would say was that he'd been up here yesterday, borrowed someone's car, made sure that everything was *ready*. I said ready for what but he wouldn't answer me. I was holding the torch by this point. Mark was down on his hands and knees, digging away at the stones under the rail until he could slide this iron thing in. Then he got up and made me shine the torch on where he was standing.'

'Why?'

'He wanted to strip, take his shoes off, all his clothes, everything. He just piled them by the side of the track. Then he wanted me to kiss him.'

'And did you?'

'Yes. He was crying again by this time. Then he got down and lay on the rail with his ankles on either end of the iron thing. He told me to tie him up like that.'

'And did you?'

Jenny's head came up again. For a long moment she stared at Barber. Then she nodded.

'Yes,' she said softly. 'I did.'

'Why?'

'Because I'd twigged what he was up to, what he was doing. It was a kind of accusation. He wanted me to see what I'd done to him, where it had taken him. We'd been so happy, he seemed to be saying. And now this.'

'And you?'

'I thought he was mad. I thought he'd finally lost it. And more important than that, I knew I could get him put away.'

'Sectioned?'

'Yes. He told me the first train through was at five in the morning. It was only two fifteen, two thirty, something like that. I had loads of time, *loads* of time. I could get people into the tunnel – you lot, the ambulance, the fire brigade. I could get the current switched off. I could do it all. He'd obviously gone bonkers and here was the evidence.'

After the rope, she said, he'd asked her to wind the chain around his middle. That had taken some time, trying to thread the chain beneath the rail, but she'd done it in the end.

'And the padlock?' It was Faraday.

'That went on last. He did it himself. Shit . . . ' She shook her head, shuddered.

'What happened?'

'He snapped it shut, then held up the key. I'd still got the torch. I could see his face. He was grinning at me, dangling this key, telling me how much he loved me, how much I meant to him, how good we could have been. He was like a wonky radio. Someone had suddenly tuned him in. He'd suddenly come to life again. He was the old Mark. He started laughing. It was horrible, everything echoing in the tunnel. Then he stopped, just like that. He was staring into the torch. Dead silence. *Dead* silence. Then he threw the key away. I heard it. I heard it tinkling in the darkness, over beyond the live rail. It was like some really scary movie. Shit . . . '

She broke off, covering her face. Michelle fumbled for a tissue, couldn't find one, then wrapped an encircling arm around her client's heaving shoulders. Faraday leaned forward with a word of explanation for the tape machines, then called for a break. Everything fits, he thought. Even the location of the key they'd found on the other side of the tracks.

Jenny was looking at him. 'Don't,' she said. 'I need to finish this.'

'You're sure?'

She nodded. Faraday cued the tape machines again, announced the time, gestured for Jenny to carry on. A tiny frown clouded her face as she settled herself. Then she described stumbling back along the track in the darkness with Duley's torch. As soon as she was out in the fresh air, she'd tried to make a call on her mobile but she couldn't get a signal. The car must have been a kilometre away at least. She ran and ran, looking for the gate in the fence. Finally, she found it. She tried again with the mobile. Nothing. She got in the car, praying that it didn't bog in again, drove out of the wood. At the top of the track she turned left, heading south, towards the glow of the city. By the time she got a signal, she'd decided to phone her husband first and not the emergency services.

Faraday wanted to know why.

'Because . . . ' Her face was wet with tears. 'I wanted to explain.'

'And what did you say?'

'I told him everything. I told him Mark was in the tunnel. I told him he was tied to the line. I told him he was mad. I told him we could get him off our backs, that it was all over, that everything would be fine again. I said there wasn't a shrink in the country who wouldn't lock him up and throw the key away.'

'And Andy?'

'Andy said I was hysterical. He told me to come home. He said not to call anyone. If I did, he said I'd never see the kids again.'

'And you?'

'I –' She gulped. '– Believed him. I knew I had to get home. It wasn't even three. I had a couple of hours at least. What does it take to stop a train? A phone call.'

She drove back to Portsmouth. When she got home Andy was still up.

'He said he'd known about Mark all along. He said he thought it would just burn itself out but lately he'd realised that wasn't going to happen. He said the man was crazy. And he said Peter Barnaby was wrong.'

'Like how?'

'Like Mark would definitely be sectioned but that he'd be out again before long. And then everything would kick off, just like before. Andy knows about this stuff. He deals with these people all the time. I'm telling you, he *knows*.'

'What else did he say?'

'He told me I was in the shit because of what I'd done. I'd already helped someone try to commit suicide. I'd go to court for that, maybe go to prison.'

'You believed him?'

'Yes. Then I asked him what we were going to do. I remember he was looking at me. Then he shook his head. Nothing, he said.'

'*Nothing?*'

'Nothing. I told him Mark would die and he just nodded. Then he said it was up to me. If I wanted a life, if I wanted my kids, if I wanted us to start all over, get it together, be friends again, try really hard, then we had the chance. But if Mark was still around, if they got him out of that tunnel, then it was all over.'

'He said that?'

'Yes.'

'And you?'

'I just ... I just ... ' She shook her head again, covered her face with her hands. 'I just ... oh Christ ... oh God ... help me ... help me please ... '

Barber moved to stop the tape but Faraday caught her eye and shook his head. There was a moment of total silence. Then, for the last time, Jenny's head came up.

'You're right,' she said. 'I killed that man.'

Faraday organised the meeting in Barrie's office. Barber was there, and the two DSs from the Incident Room, and Jerry Proctor appeared seconds before Barrie made a start, asking Faraday to summarise developments.

For the time being, Faraday explained, Jenny Mitchell had been arrested on suspicion of aiding another to commit suicide. After discussions with the Crown Prosecution Service, a formal charge would doubtless follow but the immediate priority was a decision over her husband. Andy Mitchell, on his wife's evidence, had played a key part in Duley's death.

Barrie wanted to know more about Jenny Mitchell. 'Why didn't she tell us earlier? Get it off her chest?'

'Because her husband told her she'd be complicit. He'd spelled out the probability of a criminal charge. He'd told her she'd be looking at a heavy sentence. She'd be lucky to see her kids grow up.'

'She's right.' He nodded. 'Assisting suicide carries fourteen years. So how come she coughs it all now?'

'Because she knows the marriage won't work. Regardless.'

'She blames herself for that?'

'Partly. I think she's horrified, too, by what happened that night with Andy. She'd never seen that in him. She'd never believed he could be so . . . ' Faraday shrugged. ' . . . Ruthless.'

'But she went along with it.'

'She did, sir.'

'So what does that make her?'

'Guilty. Which is why she opened up. There wasn't a problem. She just gave it to us. All we had to do was listen.'

'Sure. I understand that. But why now?'

'Because we turned up. And because . . . ' Faraday broke off, not knowing quite how much weight to put on the other factor.

'There's something else?' Barrie was getting impatient.

'Yes, sir. She told me she got a little parcel a couple of days ago. It had been sent to the wrong address. Turned up late.'

'What was it?'

'An audio cassette. Duley must have posted it on the Sunday, before he turned up at her mum's flat. There was a piece of Bach on it. Part of the St Matthew Passion. She says she's been playing it ever since.'

'And so . . . ?'

Faraday gazed at him a moment, then shrugged, gesturing round.

'And so here we are, sir.' He smiled thinly. 'Case closed.'

Winter was tucked up at home in Blake House when his mobile rang. It took him several seconds to place the voice. The woman from the undertakers, he thought.

'Sue,' he said. 'You've got some news for me.'

435

'I have. It's about your Mr Reid.'

She talked for perhaps a minute. Winter reached for a pen, scribbled himself a note on the back of the *Daily Telegraph*. By the time he concluded the call, he was out in the kitchen, hunting for the Scotch. He poured himself three fingers, caught his image in the big mirror back in the living room, raised the glass in a toast, then stepped out onto the balcony. A group of partygoers were locked together in a riotous conga, weaving along the promenade beside the harbour. He beamed down at them, gave them a little wave. Then he got his mobile out again, thumbed one of the stored numbers. It answered almost at once.

'Jake, son?' he said cheerfully. 'We need another meet.'

Twenty-three

Jake Tarrant was already at the cemetery. Winter spotted the red Fiat from the back of his cab and told the driver to pull up alongside. Tarrant was sitting behind the wheel, absorbed in the sports pages of the *News of the World*. Only when Winter tapped on the window did he bother looking up.

After days of glorious weather, it was pouring with rain. Tarrant wound down the window.

'Morning,' he said.

'Are you going to let me in or what?'

'Depends.' His gaze held Winter's for a couple of seconds, then a grin creased his face and he leaned over and released the lock on the other door.

Winter settled his bulk in the passenger seat. Rain was dripping off his nose. Tarrant studied him for a moment or two, then turned down the radio.

'What's this about? Only this is supposed to be my day off.'

Winter didn't answer. An elderly woman was shuffling towards them from the bus stop. She was carrying a jam jar with a small posy of flowers. She turned in at the cemetery gates and made her way down towards the gloomy neo-Gothic chapel that dominated the acres of surrounding graves. Winter had always hated this place. On days like today, under a leaden grey sky, it was the perfect embodiment of everything he found depressing. The puddled drive. The lines of crumbling gravestones. The sodden turf. The dripping trees. Even the crem, thought Winter, would be better than this.

'I've been thinking, son,' he said at last.

'Yeah?'

'Yeah. You remember what you told me the other night? Our little chat? About Givens?'

Tarrant nodded. 'I was pissed,' he said.

'Of course you were, son.' Winter patted him on the knee. 'That's why I took you seriously. Made a few enquiries. Like you do.'

'I'm not with you.'

'The bodies in the fridge. The ones you popped bits of Givens into. You remember all that?'

Tarrant didn't answer. He folded the paper and reached for the ignition key.

'What are you doing, son?'

'I'm going home. I don't have to listen to this shit.'

'No?'

'No.' He looked across at Winter. 'I don't know what you're up to but, if you want the truth, I'm not really interested anymore. You play games, Mr W. You're a clever bloke. You make me laugh sometimes. If you want to arrest me, help yourself. I'll deny everything. Otherwise –' He shrugged. '– Fuck off.'

'Who said anything about arresting you?'

'No one. But why else would you be here? Come for a chat, have you?' He nodded at the paper. 'Politics, is it? Cricket?'

Winter laughed. He wanted them both to take a little walk.

'Where?'

'Into there.' Winter nodded at the cemetery gates.

'Why?'

'Come with me and you'll find out.'

Tarrant had an umbrella in the back of the car. With some reluctance, he opened it, sheltering Winter as they made their way into the cemetery. Beyond the chapel, Winter could see the old woman, bent over a headstone. She must be drenched, he thought, stuck out in the rain like that.

At the end of the drive, past the chapel, the scatter of headstones began to thin. Finally, close to the encircling stone wall, they found evidence of recent digging. Winter stepped off the path and poked at a smear of yellow earth with the toe of his shoe.

'Apparently they let everything settle before they bother with a headstone. Takes months.' He turned to Tarrant. 'I never knew that. Did you?'

'Yeah.' Tarrant was staring at the oblong of turf that marked the new grave. 'Who's in there, then?'

'Bloke called Herbert Reid. One of your lot.'

'He was down for the crem.'

'I know, son. But it seems there was a bit of a domestic about the funeral arrangements. His son and daughter wanted the crem but his missus wasn't having it. When she found out, she went potty, phoned the undertaker, insisted her husband deserved better. Apparently it took a month to sort out. His missus won.'

'And he's in there?'

'As of the week before last. And not just him, son, eh?' Winter grinned at him. He'd abandoned the shelter of the umbrella by now and was standing in the rain, his face tilted up, oblivious to the spreading dark stain on his shirt.

Tarrant said nothing, staring at the unmarked grave.

'You're taking the piss, aren't you?' he muttered at last. 'This is Mr W.'s idea of a joke.'

'No, son. It's not.'

'What do you want then? Money?'

'You haven't got any money.'

'Yes, we have. We've got a hundred and eighty-five grand.'

'That's not your money. That's Givens'.'

'You can have half of it.'

'I don't want half of it. I don't want any of it.' Winter was looking hurt. 'Do you think I'm that cheap? That easy?'

'What then? What *do* you want?'

'Nothing, really. Except to point out that you got it wrong. People think we're stupid sometimes, thick. Fact is, old son, we're not.' He nodded down at the muddied turf. 'It would take us an hour or so to have Herbert Reid out of there. Then another two days for a result on the DNA inside. Red bag, wasn't it? I wonder which bit of Givens would blow it for you? Just think about it, eh? And don't ever take us for fucking granted.'

Winter turned on his heel and began to walk back towards the gates. Tarrant watched him for a moment, undecided, then set off in pursuit. Winter had got to the chapel by the time he caught up.

'You can have all the money,' he said. 'Every fucking penny.'

'Thanks.'

'I mean it.'

'I'm sure you do.' Winter stopped. 'From anyone else that would be seriously out of order. You, son?' He patted him on the shoulder. 'I'll do you a favour and put it down to inexperience. There are some seriously nasty people in this city. You're not one of them.'

He started to walk again. This time, Tarrant let him go.

Faraday found Willard waiting for him in Martin Barrie's office. The Detective Superintendent had called a special meeting of the *Coppice* management team for eleven o'clock and senior detectives were already drifting down the corridor outside.

'Result, Joe.' Willard was looking pleased. 'It's been a lot of resource to throw at a suicide but it sends a message, doesn't it?'

Faraday wasn't quite sure what Willard meant. They'd picked up Andy Mitchell at half past seven in Old Portsmouth, given him half an hour to sort out cover for the kids. Tracy Barber, who had been one of

440

the arresting DCs, had told Faraday of the little faces at the window as their father walked away towards the squad car at the end of the close. The Family Liaison Officer would have been round there by now, but there was going to be a big hole to fill in the months to come. Two more kids without a home, he thought. Two more recruits to Pompey's army of bewildered nippers.

'Well, Joe?' Willard was still waiting for an answer.

'I don't know, sir.' Faraday was aware of Martin Barrie watching him. 'We did what we did. I'm not sure "result" is a word that anyone should be proud of.'

'You think we missed something?' It was Willard's turn to be puzzled.

'Not at all. I think we did OK. It's what happens next, isn't it?'

This wasn't at all the conversation that Willard had been planning to have. He stepped closer to Faraday.

'It's about consequences, Joe. Everything you do has consequences. You know it. I know it. Those nice Mitchells know it. Strap someone to a railway line and leave him for dead, and one day there'll be a knock at your door. We're in the justice business, aren't we? Or have I got that wrong?'

'Not at all, sir. Two kids without parents? Some bloke in pieces in the Buriton Tunnel?' He nodded. 'Definite result.'

The meeting began shortly afterwards. Barrie called on Faraday to summarise the state of play. Andy Mitchell, he said, had called his solicitor to Central and was digging in for the first of the interviews. After his wife's resigned compliance, Faraday was anticipating a spirited defence. The only direct evidence against him was Jenny's statement, and in Faraday's experience, given the circumstances, Mitchell might well decide to deny everything. His wife, he'd claim, had entangled herself with a lunatic. The only way she could keep the lid on the affair was by helping the bastard to his death. Afterwards, with luck, there'd be no evidence of her involvement.

Heads nodded round the table. Mitchell, it was noted, had retained Bazza Mackenzie's solicitor, Nelly Tien. She'd doubtless find a way of turning events to her client's advantage. By the time Jenny Mitchell had confessed, it would have been too late to save Mark Duley. Mitchell had stayed silent ever since in a heroic attempt to keep his family together. Not a murderer at all, predicted Faraday, but a hard-working father, committed to helping society's cast-offs, trapped into a lie by his faithless wife.

The tabloid potential of the eventual court case brought a contribution from Willard. For the last ten days he'd been fending off media interest in the case, feeding the Media Relations Department a series of bland press statements about promising lines of enquiry and unceasing effort. Now, before the media storm broke, he wanted to be quite certain that *Coppice* was reporter-proof.

It was Martin Barrie, this time, who asked for clarification. What did Willard mean, exactly?

'I need to know we've got our ducks lined up. The last thing I want happening is some smart-arse journalist digging around and finding material we've overlooked.' He glared round the table, then settled on Faraday. 'Does that make sense, Joe?'

'Perfectly, sir.'

'You can give me an assurance?'

Faraday thought about the question. In this company he didn't want to give any hostages to fortune.

'Forensically, there's nothing we haven't done.' He gestured at the *Coppice* file, open on the table in front of him. 'We spent a couple of days in the tunnel. We boshed Duley's room, we did the caravan, in fact we pretty much spent every penny we could lay hands on. Right, Jerry?'

Jerry Proctor nodded. 'Right, boss.'

'In terms of other lines of enquiry, we obviously chased a lead or two, eliminated names, but that's standard MO.'

'What about this Mickey Kearns?'

'He's yet to reappear. There's an all-ports watch for him.'

'And when he does?'

'He'll have some questions to answer.'

'About Duley?'

'Yes, sir. And about the money he's alleged to have lost.'

'And Mackenzie?'

'No evidence, sir.'

'So he's home free? Again?'

'I'm afraid so.'

Willard nodded.

'Go on,' he said. 'I'm still listening.'

Faraday was reviewing the last couple of weeks in his head. The broad thrust of events that had taken Duley into the tunnel was, he thought, clear. He'd fallen hopelessly in love, wrecked a number of lives and ended up under a train. Jenny Mitchell, by her own admission, had been complicit in his death and would now have to face the consequences. There was, though, one tiny bit of the jigsaw for which Faraday couldn't find a place.

'There might be an issue with the spare key,' he said slowly.

'What key?'

'The spare key to the padlock. Duley bought it in Petersfield a couple of days before he died. And he made a point of leaving it with the woman who'd been looking after him.'

Faraday explained about Ginnie Bullen from the Writers' Conference. Her sister's cottage, he pointed out, was a mile up the road from the tunnel. Duley knew that because he'd first discovered the tunnel when he was staying there.

'Where does this woman live?'

'In the south of France. She came over for the conference but she was back home again by the time Duley died.'

'So what's your point, Joe?'

'I'm not sure, sir, not yet. Just that the spare key might represent ... ' He tapped the *Coppice* file. ' ... Another line of enquiry.'

'Really?' Willard was smiling now. 'Fancy it, do you? Couple of days in the sunshine?'

The meeting went on. Martin Barrie complimented his team on a good job well done and said it had been a pleasure to see how open-minded they'd remained in the face of evidence which might, presented to a different bunch of guys, have led the enquiry into choppier waters. There were smiles around the table, a recognition that the items seized from Mackenzie's Hayling Island property hadn't, after all, derailed *Coppice*.

Faraday's assumption was that Duley had driven out there on the Saturday, in the car he'd borrowed from Daniel George, and picked up the items he'd need for the tunnel. He may well, said Faraday, have wanted evidence to point in a certain direction. Since he was evidently going to the trouble of killing himself, he might as well exact a little revenge for the beating he'd taken in the caravan.

'Which direction?' It was Willard again.

'Kearns. Plus whoever else. As far as Duley knew, these guys owned the place.'

'And he assumed we'd trace this material?'

'Yes, sir.' Faraday nodded, weary now. 'And it turned out he was right.'

The question provoked another nod of approval from Martin Barrie. The Detective Superintendent wasn't in the business of singling out individuals for special praise but he wanted people to know that Faraday had been driving two enquiries at the same time. In their very different ways, he said, both *Coppice* and *Tartan* had demanded total focus, total concentration.

Even Willard had the grace to agree. He was on the point of adding his own round of applause for Faraday's efforts when the door opened. Heads turned. It was Winter. There were blotches of rain on his shirt and his hair was plastered against the pinkness of his scalp.

'Sorry I'm late.' He was out of breath. 'Got held up.'

The Detective Superintendent waved him to a chair at the end of the table. His mention of *Tartan* had come at a fortuitous moment. For the time being, until they all knew the outcome of the interviews with Mitchell, there was nothing more to say about *Coppice*. Winter had been taking a lead role in the hunt for clues about Givens' disappearance. Now was a good time for the DC to share his latest thoughts with the Head of CID.

'My pleasure.' Winter gazed at Willard. 'What would you like to know, sir?'

Willard understood that Jake Tarrant had become the prime suspect.

'They knew each other well. Am I right?'

'Yes, sir.'

'And this Mr Givens was on close terms with Tarrant's wife. Yes? And on top of that, a hundred and eighty-five thousand of Givens' money would tell most of us that he had . . . ah . . . another compelling reason to kill the man. Am I getting warm?'

'Without a doubt, sir.'

'So when might we start thinking of an arrest strategy?'

Winter gave the question some thought. At length he frowned.

'It's really a question of evidence, isn't it? You're right about motive. And you'd be right about opportunity as well. Tarrant does death for a living. We all know that. But we haven't got a body. And without a body I doubt we've got a case. Pull him in by all means. But a tenner says he'll deny everything. The bloke's disappeared. He's gone. He's history. Tarrant's no fool. Assuming he did Givens, he'd have thought the thing through. My money's on the waste process.'

At Barrie's prompting, he described the hospital's procedure for disposing of Clinical Waste. Willard was watching him carefully.

'They used to have an incinerator of their own at the hospital,' he pointed out.

'Shut, sir. Everything goes through Whiterose.'

'And they had a random sampling policy. One bag in twenty. Just in case.'

'Everything's automated now. Time is money.' He smiled. 'You know the way it goes.'

'So you're telling me Tarrant's off the hook?'

'I'm saying we haven't got any evidence. Nothing to chuck at him.'

'So we kick it into touch? Pretend Givens is still alive?'

'I don't know, sir. That's a policy decision. Like I said, time is money.'

'But what's your feeling? Deep down?'

'Here and now? Hand on heart, sir, we don't even know whether the bloody man's dead or not.'

'But the overwhelming evidence, surely . . . ?'

'Of course, sir. Dead right. But you ask me for proof . . . ' He shrugged. 'There isn't any.'

At lunchtime, Faraday ducked out of the back entrance and hurried to his car. The wind had got up now, blowing the rain in flurries round the corners of the building. Willard had asked for a private meeting, just Faraday and Winter, at three fifteen. On the phone Peter Barnaby had cautiously agreed to a spot of lunch in a pub a couple of minutes away from the hospital.

The weather, alas, had made him cancel his plans for a day at sea.

The Oyster Catcher lay at the end of Locksway Road. Sepia prints of Victorian fishermen lined the wood-panelled bar and there were glimpses of Langstone Harbour through the windows at the front. Faraday knew this area intimately. His own house was barely half a mile away.

Peter Barnaby was soaked by the time he arrived. He'd driven across the city from his Southsea home but his umbrella, blown inside out by a sudden gust of wind, had been useless for the dash from the car. Now he sat at the table, dripping rain onto the floor, while Faraday collected a pint of Guinness from the bar.

'I might as well be at sea,' he told Faraday on his return. 'This is like most weekends without the fun.'

Faraday apologised for making so sudden a hole in his precious Sunday. Barnaby said he was pleased to be here. Just kidding. He swallowed a mouthful of Guinness, then looked up.

'This about Jenny? Am I right?'

Faraday nodded. 'We arrested her last night,' he said. 'After she gave us a full statement.' Briefly, he explained Jenny's role in Duley's death. 'She'll be up for assisting suicide, I'm afraid. That's a serious charge, as I'm sure you know.'

'Christ.' Barnaby looked shocked. 'That'll crucify her.'

Barnaby's choice of verb stopped Faraday in his tracks.

'Crucify?'

'Of course. Those kids mean everything to her. She'll go down?'

'Almost certainly. We haven't charged her yet, not until we've had an account from Andy. We arrested him this morning.'

'Bloody hell.' Barnaby's hand found his glass. 'You blokes don't hang around, do you?'

'I'm afraid not.' He paused, looking for ways of softening the appalling news. 'After we've charged Jenny, she'll go before the magistrates. There'll be every possibility of bail. She may be home for a while before she faces trial.'

'And Andy?'

'It depends how he plays it. To be frank, her fate's in his hands. If he denies everything, his own part in it all, he could hang her out to dry. Assisting suicide could put her away for a fair time.'

'Terrible.' Barnaby shook his head. 'Those poor bloody kids.'

'You're right.' He hesitated again. 'There's another reason I wanted to see you. When we interviewed her yesterday, Jenny said she'd talked to you about Duley.'

'That's true. She wanted advice.'

'What did you tell her? We should be doing this officially, of course, a proper statement and we will –' Faraday's gesture bridged the gap between them '– but for now maybe you'd just tell me informally.'

'Of course.'

Barnaby explained that Jenny had rung him up the week before Duley had died. She'd asked to meet him and he'd taken her to lunch in a pub in Old Portsmouth.

'How was she?'

'Very upset. And, listening to her, I could understand why. It's her own fault, of course, and she was the first to accept that, but she told me she just felt helpless. She'd never suspected anyone could turn out like this Duley character.'

'She told you about him?'

'In some detail. The more she said, the more it made sense. This is classic stalker behaviour. It's obsessive. And it can be deeply disturbing. Jen had got to the stage where she'd run out of options. Hence, I suppose, her call to me.'

'I gather you told her about Section 136.'

448

'That's right. To be frank, it was a pretty small port in a pretty big storm but I think it gave her some comfort. That's what she said, at any rate.'

'And you based this advice on what she told you? About Duley?'

'Oh no.' He shook his head. 'I met the man.'

'You *met* him?'

'Yes. Actually, I insisted. Second-hand diagnosis is poor clinical practice. Wherever possible, there's nothing like the real thing.'

'How did you fix it?' Faraday was fascinated.

'I phoned him up. Jen gave me his mobile number. I explained who I was and asked for half an hour of his time. He said yes straightaway. He came to the hospital. To my office, as a matter of fact.'

'And how was he?'

'A great deal saner than I'd been led to expect, but that was no surprise, really. These people can be brilliant actors. He sat there and he said his piece, and it all made perfect sense. At least from his point of view.'

'What did he say?'

'He said that he and Jen were a couple, a perfect match. He said he loved her and there wasn't anything he wouldn't do to prove it. Evidently he'd got himself in some kind of trouble. Someone had certainly had a swing or two.'

'*There wasn't anything he wouldn't do to prove it*? He said that?'

'Yes, that's exactly what he said.' Barnaby studied Faraday a moment. 'You're thinking suicide, aren't you?'

'Yes.'

'You'd be wrong. In my judgement, that was the last thing on his mind. It was pretty plain to me that he still had hopes, assumptions even, about Jen. These people always do. Life's open-ended for them. Anything's always possible. That's why suicide is a dead end.

That's why they wouldn't even contemplate it. They always assume things will work out. Why? Because they *should* do. Because they *must*. It's not like you and me. It's not a question of acknowledging someone else's rights in the matter, someone else's wishes, someone else's territory. These people recognise no boundaries. It's a question of the imperative, of what they *need*. Life owed him Jenny Mitchell. And he'd move heaven and earth to make that happen.'

Faraday nodded. Sally Spedding had said something very similar. Andy, too.

'Her husband was right then? Whatever happened, Duley would always be around?'

'Is that what Andy said?'

'According to her, yes. He said Section 136 and the rest of it wouldn't work. Getting rid of Duley, if Jenny was serious, meant exactly that.'

'Then he *is* right. You know about Section 136. You guys could have arrested him, detained him, but then what? After seventy-two hours we have to start making some serious decisions. We can treat a sectioned patient on the basis of second opinions but there are regular review periods and appeal procedures and all sorts. Could I give Jen an assurance that we could lock Duley away for ever? Of course I couldn't. And I hope to God she didn't go away thinking otherwise.'

Faraday nodded. In the absence of meeting Duley himself, he sensed this was the closest he was going to get. He thought again of Jenny, alone in a holding cell in the Bridewell, and of her kids, wondering when on earth they were going to see their mother again.

'So where does the blame lie?' he said at last.

'That sounds like a philosophical question.'

'It is. It's exactly that. Pretend I'm not a copper for a moment. Pretend I'm interested in cause and effect, in what makes people do what they do – that's your field, isn't it?'

'Yes. It is. And to let you into a small secret, it's

imprecise as hell. There's nothing hard and fast about it. It's not like physical medicine. There's no wiring diagram, no maintenance manual. Human behaviour's a movable feast. You must know that. I suppose that's what makes our jobs so fascinating.'

'Was Jenny greedy?'

'That's a moral judgement.'

'No, it's not. It's a question.'

'But you're *inviting* a moral judgement.'

'OK.' Faraday smiled at him. 'Then take a deep breath and give me an answer. You've seen lots of her. You sense what makes her tick. You care about her. You'd *know*.'

Barnaby acknowledged the logic of Faraday's argument with the slightest tilt of his head. He gazed out of the window for a moment or two, thinking. At length, he turned back to Faraday.

'Yes, of course she was greedy,' he said. 'And stupid. And headstrong. And deeply, deeply selfish. All that. But what's done is done. Did she anticipate any of this? I doubt it very much. She needed to find someone. She'd had problems of her own. She wanted someone to talk to. I suspect she told you about all that.'

Faraday nodded. 'So it was just bad luck? That this someone happened to be Duley?'

'Yes, in a way it was. They're rare, these people.'

'Was it some kind of judgement then? On her own . . .' Faraday frowned ' . . . recklessness?'

'Recklessness? I think I prefer naivety. Jenny's someone who always thinks the best of people.'

'That's naive?'

'Very.' He smiled. 'Detective Inspector.'

Willard was late for the meeting. In his office Faraday had been bringing Winter up to date with developments on *Coppice*. Tracy Barber had phoned from the Bridewell with news of the interview with Andy Mitchell. As expected, he was denying everything.

'She's fucked then.' Winter was gazing out at the rain. 'So much for happy families.'

'We'll have another go. It's not over yet.'

'Sure, but what else have you got to put to him? It's his word against hers.'

'A jury might not see it that way.'

'That's pissing in the wind, boss. You know it is. That's a stand-up confession she's given you. A decent brief should be able to do something in the way of mitigation but if she's looking to hubby to share the blame, it ain't going to happen. Given what you've told me, you've got nothing on him. I doubt he'll even go to court. This is a domestic with bells on. Take Duley out of the equation, it wouldn't have got past the front desk. Families fall apart every day of the week. Give it a couple of years and there won't be any marriages left in this country.'

The door opened. Willard said he had fifteen minutes. Winter was about to surrender his chair but Willard waved away the offer. He closed the door, turned his attention to Faraday.

'You've done well, Joe.' He grunted. 'I don't want you getting the wrong idea.'

'About what?'

'*Coppice*. It was a nice piece of work. I meant to tell you in there –' He jabbed a thumb in the direction of Barrie's office. '– But to be honest you were pissing me off.'

'Why's that?'

'Because sometimes you let it get to you, don't you? That's not our job, Joe. We collect the evidence. We sort it. We put it in neat piles. We try and make sure it's lawyer-proof. And then we hand it over to the CPS. There's no bonus in second-guessing any of that. There are no fucking medals for compassion. Society's a shit heap, at least the bit we tend to see. Always was, always will be. And if it ever cleans itself up, then we're all out of a job. Fair enough?'

452

Faraday looked him in the eye, said nothing. Winter was next in the firing line.

'Mackenzie, DC Winter.'

'What about him?'

'The next time he lifts you off the street, bloody well do something about it, right? Give me a ring. *Tell* me. It doesn't matter what he's done to you. I don't care a toss whether every fucker in this city knows what you look like with your clothes off. That's not the point. You think he humiliated you, right?'

'Right.'

'Well, you're wrong. He didn't humiliate you. He humiliated every single one of us. Why? Because you let him get away with it. Because you didn't lift the phone. Because you never *told* anyone.'

'I told Mr Faraday here.'

'Sure. You did. But that's because he was clever enough to chisel it out of you. You're a decent copper, Winter. We might even owe you from time to time. But never, *ever*, think you're fireproof. Why? Because you're not.' He paused, towering over them both. 'As it happens though, you might have given us an opportunity.'

'Really?'

The speed of Winter's response put the beginnings of a smile on Willard's face.

'Has Mackenzie been back to you again? The last day or so?'

'No.'

'Is that the truth? Because if it isn't, I'll fucking have you.'

'It's the truth.'

'Do you expect him to come back?'

'Yeah.' Winter nodded. 'In the end, he's bound to.'

'Good.' Willard paused. 'That new apartment of yours. The one in Gunwharf. DI Faraday tells me you paid five hundred and fifty grand for it.'

'That's right.'

'While you only got two hundred and seventy-five for your previous place.'

'Correct.'

'And you had other expenses, medical expenses, yes?'

'Yes, sir. Sixty grand.'

'Plus a mortgage to pay off?'

'A small one, twenty grand.'

'So . . . ' Willard frowned, doing the arithmetic. 'I make that about three hundred and fifty grand short. Where did you get that kind of money?'

Winter exchanged looks with Faraday. Willard had never seen any point in not meeting life head on but this was bluntness on an industrial scale. Winter had rights here. And he wasn't about to be turned over.

'What's any of this got to do with you, sir?'

'Because I'm your boss. And because I have something in mind that needs me to be very, very sure about you.'

'You think I'm bent?'

'I think you've got certain talents. I think you play games with the truth. I hope to God – for all our sakes – that you do it for the right reasons. But I'm not sure.'

'And all this financial stuff will make a difference?'

'It'll help, certainly. Any detective of mine owing three hundred and fifty grand could be a problem. Does that sound reasonable?'

Winter nodded, thoughtful. Then he started talking about last year. He'd developed a tumour. It had become, in the most literal sense of the word, a pain. They'd done tests. Taken scans. Identified the problem. He'd been up and down to QA like a yo-yo, and every time he'd made that journey, another little bit of him had died.

'I'm talking belief.' He looked Willard in the eye. 'You believe you're going to make it through. You believe the karma fairy's on your side. But then you start to wonder.'

Those were black days, he said. He wasn't a pessimistic bloke, never had been, but he was starting to get into trouble. Not with the job. He was way past that. But with himself.

'Belief, again,' he said. 'Belief in me.'

Faraday was spellbound. He'd heard this story before but he'd never seen Winter so passionate, and so angry. Even Willard resisted the temptation to look at his watch.

'So?' He queried.

'There was a woman I'd met. Her name was Maddox.'

Willard nodded. He'd heard about her. A looker.

'Right. And a friend. A mate. She stuck with me. She looked after me. She got me through.'

He told Willard about the search for a neurosurgeon, for someone prepared to take a risk or two, and he explained where Maddox's ceaseless enquiries had led.

'Phoenix, Arizona,' he said softly. 'She was there for the duration. Never left me. Not once.'

Afterwards, he'd come home to convalesce. Maddox had gone down to South America. But they were still in touch.

'I had to move. I had to get out of the bungalow. There was nothing left for me there. It was driving me bonkers. Gunwharf was favourite. The buzz. The views. The people. It was perfect, just perfect, and the longer I looked the more I knew I had to have the best seat in the house. There was a top-floor apartment in Blake House just come on the market. Problem was, I hadn't got the money.'

Willard nodded. 'And?'

'I talked to Maddox. Phoned her.'

'She had that kind of money?'

'Yeah.' Winter nodded. 'She's a rich kid. Plus she had a flat in Rose Tower, Southsea seafront. I sold the flat on her behalf, cut her in fifty-fifty on the Gunwharf place.'

'So she co-owns it?' Willard was frowning now.

'Yeah. It's all in the paperwork. She's got half. With the mortgage I raised, I've got the other half.'

'And you're still . . . ' Willard hunted for the word. ' . . . Together?'

'Christ no. I've no idea who's she shagging now but it certainly isn't me.'

'So . . . I don't understand.'

'You don't understand what, sir?'

'You're telling me she has half your property, half your life? That means she can come back any time, pull the rug from under, send you back to bungalow land, doesn't it?'

'Of course.'

'And that doesn't bother you?'

'Not at all.'

'Putting yourself at the mercy of someone else? Making yourself a hostage to fortune?'

'Christ no. We're all hostages to fortune. Every minute of the fucking day.'

'We are?'

Winter contemplated the question for a long moment. Then he smiled at Willard.

'When you've been where I've been,' he said softly, 'that's a really silly question.'

It was a rebuke. All three men knew it. Willard looked at his watch for a moment. Winter hadn't taken his eyes off him.

'You mentioned something about an opportunity . . . sir.'

'I did?'

'Yes. What did that mean, exactly?'

'I'm not sure I'm in a position to tell you. Not yet, anyway.'

Willard glanced at Faraday. Faraday was looking out of the window. Winter hadn't finished.

'Is it about Mackenzie? All the nonsense in the van? All those pictures he's got? Only I'm thinking you might need to mark my card about where we go from here . . . ' He smiled. ' . . . Sir.'

Afterwards

September 2005

Faraday left for France in early September. He'd taken his remaining two week's annual leave, extended by a further three days in lieu of overtime, leaving Martin Barrie to wrap up Operation *Coppice*. Jenny Mitchell had been granted bail pending her appearance at the Crown Court, indicted with assisting another to commit suicide. Her husband, finally released without charge, had moved out of the marital home and was rumoured to be living with a social worker in Southsea. The kids, according to Peter Barnaby, were showing signs of serious disturbance.

As for *Tartan*, Karl Ewart was on remand awaiting trial on charges of attempted murder and fraud. Jake Tarrant had been pulled in for a lengthy formal interview but had denied any knowledge of Givens after his disappearance and as a result Willard had accepted Barrie's recommendation that little was to be gained by throwing more resources at the enquiry. The files, marked NFA, had been dispatched for storage. NFA meant No Further Action.

Now, standing on the upper deck of the P&O ferry as it slipped past the Spinnaker Tower, Faraday couldn't remember a time when he had been more relieved to be leaving the city. Even the shiny new glass elevator, the tower's crowning glory, was reporting malfunction after malfunction. Nothing, Faraday thought, seemed to work anymore.

From Le Havre, in mid-afternoon, he drove south, across the green billow of the Pays d'Auge. By early evening he could see the twin towers of Chartres Cathedral, burnished by the soft golden light of the approaching sunset. Gabrielle had given him directions to a street in one of the newer parts of the city. Her apartment was on the top floor of a three-storey block with views of a volleyball pitch in a tree-shaded park. She had a scruffy dog called Meo and a modest living space devoted almost exclusively to the storage of books. She'd prepared a bouillabaisse and insisted on opening a bottle of Montrachet that her mother had given her years ago. Faraday, surprised and flattered by the warmth of her welcome, found himself talking about the events of the last three months. It was nearly dawn before he collapsed into the bed she'd prepared for him on the floor in the main room.

Faraday awoke to find the dog licking his bare feet. That afternoon, Gabrielle took him to the cathedral. He stood in the vaulted emptiness of the nave, dwarfed by the immensity of the building, and sensed at once what she'd meant in her e-mails about the explosions of medieval light trapped in the stained-glass windows. These figures glowed. They were luminous. They were a fire at which he could warm the aching chill in his soul. An organist was playing a Bach cantata. Faraday sat in a pew beside one of the enormous stone pillars and thought about the darkness that was Duley.

That night he took Gabrielle to a restaurant in the old quarter of the city. Afterwards, they walked back through a maze of steep cobbled streets, still talking. The days to come, Faraday was beginning to suspect, would be a conversation without end, ungovernable, intense, spiked with sudden moments of surprise and delight.

They shared a passion for Leffe Blonde, for lengthy tramps through the rain and for Hector Berlioz. They both read the left-wing press, and found themselves talking incessantly about the West, about the traps that affluence left in its wake, about the simmering discontent in the rougher parts of cities on both sides of the Channel.

Faraday explained about Somerstown and Portsea, and kids who preferred to take their chances living rough rather than submit to another night at home. Gabrielle recounted a week in the *banlieux* to the north-east of Paris, a brutal reminder, she said, of the gulfs that were opening up in French society. Parched after months of nothing but *Coppice* and *Tartan*, Faraday lapped greedily at each new conversation. This wasn't Thailand; this was something far richer, and far more complex.

The next day, in Gabrielle's ancient camper, they headed south. The country roads were empty. Staying on a campsite near Montbard, they hired bikes and cycled miles along the Canal de Bourgogne. The weather was glorious, the afternoon heat softened by a breeze that stirred the waterside trees. Further south, they camped by a lake in the Auxois, and Faraday spent the afternoon on the deserted gravel beach, watching Gabrielle swimming from buoy to buoy, an effortless crawl that she sustained for the best part of an hour. Afterwards, lying beside him on the towel, she fingered a pattern across his chest and kissed him softly when he pointed out a flight of ducks disappearing towards the far end of the lake.

'*Je t'aime depuis le début*,' she murmured. '*Ça te va?*'

A week later, after a wet interlude trekking across the limestone battlements of the Cevennes, they plunged into the Languedoc. Faraday had an address for Ginnie Bullen from her twin sister. Find a town called Lamalou-les-Bains, she'd said. Drive further west along the valley of the Orb. Look for a suspension bridge across the river to the left. Another couple of miles and you'll find a village called Vieussan. The woman at the post office knows Ginnie well. She'll take you the rest of the way.

Ginnie Bullen, it turned out, lived at the far end of the village, in a plain, two-storey stone-built house perched on the edge of the cliff that hung over the river. At the back of the house, sheltered from the wind that howled down the valley, was a small walled garden.

The villager summoned by the postmistress did the introductions. Ginnie Bullen looked more weathered than the face Faraday remembered from the photo. Her greying hair was savagely cut. She had dark eyes, almost black, deeply set in a bony face. She was wearing a filthy T-shirt and a torn pair of jeans, and there was fresh soil on her hands.

'You know Ollie? Poor you.' She barked with laughter, wiping her hands on a tea towel, inviting them in.

The house felt cool after the heat and dust of the street. The flagstoned room where she lived was at the back. Through the open doors Faraday could see rows of carefully tended vegetables. Huge heads of lettuce. Plump courgettes. Tomatoes at bursting point.

Already, Ginnie was gossiping to Gabrielle about the area, about the years she'd spent here, about her neighbours in the village, and as the conversation quickened Faraday caught the flattened accents of the Midi. Her French, delivered at machine-gun speed, was fluent. She talked with her hands, too, matching Gabrielle gesture for gesture, pulling a face at some memory or other, abrupt, sardonic, slightly baleful. This woman has rooted here, he thought, like a vine. She's tough. She draws whatever sustenance she requires from the sunshine and the stony soil. She needs nobody.

She produced a plastic cask of red wine, and found some bread and cheese in the big antique wardrobe she seemed to use as a larder. Then she shooed them out into the garden, rustled up a couple of battered ornamental chairs, spread a rug at their feet. The sun was beginning to dip now, towards a ridge of mountains in the west, and Faraday could hear the distant growl of a tractor.

'They're bringing in the *vendange*.' Ginnie was hacking at the loaf. 'Everyone's pissed by eight.'

Faraday at last got round to explaining the reason for his visit. He'd been working on a major investigation. There were one or two loose ends he still needed to tie up.

'You really are a cop? How wonderful.' Ginnie was pouring herself another glass of wine. 'Should I get myself a lawyer? Only there's a divine young *avocat* with a weekend place near here.'

Faraday thought that wouldn't be necessary. He began to talk about the body in the tunnel. Ginnie interrupted.

'You mean Duley,' she said stonily.

'How did you know?'

'Ollie wrote and told me when she got home. Come to think of it, she mentioned you too. You made quite an impact from what I can understand.'

Ginnie said something to Gabrielle in French. Gabrielle began to laugh. Faraday reached for his glass. The wine was truly foul.

'What else did Ollie tell you?'

'She said the village had been overrun with policemen. She also said there hadn't been any trains for a couple of days, which I take to be a bit of a blessing. She was over here at the time, of course, Ollie. She told me the village was still full of gossip when she got back. Funny that, isn't it? How it takes bad news to really bring *les Anglais* out of themselves?' She laughed, plunging a fork into a corner of cheese.

Faraday wanted to know more about Duley.

'You had a relationship,' he suggested carefully.

'I took him to bed. Once. There's a difference.'

'But he came to see you afterwards. In Buriton.'

'He did, more's the pity. Pathetic bundle that he

462

was.' She dismissed the memory with a toss of her head. Sometimes you got these things wrong. '*Tant pis.*'

'Wrong, how?'

'You want me to make you a list? He was self-obsessed. He was boring. He could talk of nothing but himself and his own wretched situation. And on top of that I'm afraid he was hopeless in bed. It was probably the booze but in the end he fell asleep on me.'

Gabrielle was smiling again. Faraday sensed she liked this woman.

'Tell me about the tunnel.'

'Nothing to tell, really. The poor lamb was desperate to make us understand how unhappy he was. The tunnel was just another way of putting it. He went up there for effect. He slept in there to shock us. It was pure melodrama. With someone like that, you need a great deal of patience. I'm afraid I had none. That's why Ollie and I left early to come back here. I couldn't stand another minute of the man.'

Faraday nodded, then helped himself to a chunk of bread.

'I understand you bought him a padlock.'

'Yes.'

'Did he tell you why he wanted it?'

'Yes. He had some half-baked idea about tying himself up. He said he had a point to make. To be frank, I hadn't a clue what he was talking about.'

'Did you tell your sister about this?'

'God, no. I felt guilty enough about the boy as it was, having him around all the time like that. The last thing Ollie needed was anything else on her plate.'

'How many keys came with the padlock?'

'Two. He kept one. I had the other.'

'Why was that?'

'He wanted me to untie him, unlock him, whatever.'

'When?'

'Sunday night. In the tunnel. At four in the morning. On the dot.'

'He *said* that?'

'Word for word. And then he made me swear I'd do it. We were sitting in the car in Southsea by this time, outside his flat. That was the Friday. I'd had to run him back from Buriton. The poor lamb refused to get out until I gave him an answer.'

'And what did you say?'

'I said yes. He was talking nonsense, obviously.'

'But he wasn't, was he?'

'No, as it turned out, he wasn't.'

'And you left the next day? On the Saturday?'

'That's right, that's what we decided, Ollie and I, spur of the moment thing, once I got back to the cottage ... though he couldn't have known that, *le pauvre*. He was still assuming we'd be off on the Tuesday.' She laughed again, a toss of the head.

Faraday gazed at her. In the end, he thought, it was simple. Sally Spedding had been right; Peter Barnaby too. Duley had never meant to kill himself. The tunnel had been a performance, a tableau, conceived and mounted for Jenny's benefit. This was how much she'd meant. These were the lengths to which she'd driven him. He'd taken it for granted, of course, that she'd summon help. But just in case that didn't happen, he'd come up with a fallback – someone he'd trust with a spare key, someone he thought he'd impressed, someone who thought he mattered, someone who'd turn up in the darkness and set him free. The plan must have seemed foolproof. Except that Ginnie Bullen had better things to do. And Andy Mitchell wanted him dead.

'Mad,' Faraday said softly.

Ginnie caught the word, shook her head, reached for the bottle.

'Rubbish.' She snorted. 'Madness is interesting. Duley was a child.' She shaded her eyes against the dying sun, looking for Gabrielle. '*Encore du rouge, ma petite?*'

If you have enjoyed

ONE UNDER

Don't miss

THE PRICE OF DARKNESS

Graham Hurley's latest novel featuring
DI Joe Faraday

Coming soon in Orion hardback

Price £9.99
ISBN 978-0-7528-6884-4

Prelude

Monday 4 September 2006. Cambados, Spain

Uncomfortable in the heat, Winter followed the funeral cortège as it wound up the narrow path towards the cemetery. From here, high on the rocky hillside, he could sense what had drawn the dead man to Cambados. Not simply the lure of Colombian cocaine, delivered wholesale across the Atlantic. Not just the prospect of ever-swelling profits as he helped the laughing powder towards the exploding UK market-place. But the chance to settle somewhere remote, somewhere real, to make a life for himself among these tough, nut-brown Galician peasants.

The cortège came to a halt beside the ruins of the Santa Marina church while the priest fumbled with the gate of the tiny cemetery. Winter paused, glad to catch his breath. The view was sensational. Immediately below, a tumble of houses crowding towards the waterfront. Further out, beyond the estuary, the aching blueness of the open sea.

Last night, after an emotional tour of his brother's favourite bars, Bazza had ended up locked in an embrace with Mark's girlfriend's mother. Her name was Teresa. She was a plump, handsome woman who walked with the aid of a stick and, as far as Winter understood, the funeral arrangements had been entirely her doing.

The priest had accepted her assurances that Mark had been a practising Catholic. The friends he'd made had secured a plot in the cemetery. God had doubtless

467

had a hand in the jet-ski accident, and Mark's death doubtless served some greater purpose, but the only thing she understood just now was that her daughter's life would never be the same. Bebe had been only months away from becoming Mark's wife. There would have been children, lots of children. God gives, and God takes away, she'd muttered, burying her face in a fold of Bazza's linen jacket.

The mourners began to shuffle upward again, and Winter caught a whiff of something sweet, carried on the wind. Beside him, still hungover, was a lifelong friend of Bazza's, a survivor from the glory days of the eighties. The last time Winter had seen him was in court, a couple of years back. He'd been up on a supply charge, coupled with accusations of GBH, and had walked free after a key witness had changed his mind about giving evidence. Last night, by barely ten, he'd been legless.

'What's that, mush?' He had his nose in the air.

'Incense.' Winter paused again, mopping his face. 'Gets rid of bad smells.'

Late evening, the same day, Winter was drinking alone at a table outside a bar on the waterfront. The bar belonged to Teresa. According to Bazza, she'd won it as part of a divorce settlement from her husband, an ex-pro footballer, and for old times' sake it was still called the *Bar del Portero* – the keeper's bar. Winter had been here a lot over the last couple of days, enjoying the swirl of fishermen and high-season tourists, conscious of the black-draped photos of Mark amongst the gallery of faces from the goalie's past.

Tonight, though, was different. Bazza and his entourage had disappeared to a restaurant and, to be honest Winter was glad of an hour or two on his own.

The first he knew about company was a hand on his shoulder, the lightest touch. He looked up to find a tall, slim Latino helping himself to the other chair. He was

468

older than he looked. He had the hands of a man in his forties, and there were threads of grey in his plaited hair. The white T-shirt carried a faded image of Jimi Hendrix.

'You're a cop,' he said.

'Yeah?'

'*Si.*'

'Who says?'

'Me. I know cops. I know cops all my life. You tell me it's not true?'

'I'm telling you nothing. Except it's none of your fucking business.'

There was a long silence. The Latino produced a mobile and checked for messages. Then he returned the mobile to his jeans pocket, tipped his head back against the chair, and stared up into the night sky.

'We're wasting time, you and me. Señor Winter. I know who you are. I know where you come from. I know . . .' He shrugged, leaving the sentence unfinished.

Winter leaned forward, irritated, pushing his glass to one side.

'So why bother checking? Why all this drama?'

'Because we need to talk.'

'About what?'

'About you.'

'Yeah?'

'*Si* . . . You want to tell me what you're doing here? In Cambados?'

'Not especially.'

'You're a friend of Señor Mackenzie.'

'That's right.'

'And you've come over because of his brother.'

'Yeah.'

'Because you and Señor Mackenzie are . . .' He frowned. ' . . . Friends.'

'Spot on, son. Bazza and me go back a while. And it happens you're right. I am a cop. Or was. I'm also a mate of Bazza's. A family friend. Here to support the lad. Here to help. Here to do my bit.'

'But cops never stop being cops. And that could be a problem.'

'Yeah?'

'*Si.*' His gaze had settled on Winter's face. 'I have a question for you, Mr Winter. It's a very simple question. As it happens, I know about your friends, about Señor Mackenzie, and I know about you. This man is a cop, I tell them. It's all over his face, the way he talks, the way he moves, his eyes, who he watches, how he watches, everything. Sure, they tell me. The man's a cop. And a good cop. A good cop turned bad. But clever. Useful. Me? I tell them they're crazy. *Loco.* And wrong, too. Why? Because, like I say, cops never stop being cops. Never. *Nunca.* Not here, in Spain. Not in my country. Not in yours. *Nunca.* Whatever they say. *Nunca.*'

'And the question?'

'Tell me why you're really here.'

'You'd never believe me.'

'I might.'

'OK. And if you don't?'

'It will be bad, very bad. For you. And maybe for us also.'

'How bad is very bad?'

'The worst.' He smiled. '*Lo peor.*'

Winter took his time digesting the news. Bazza had pointed out this man twice in the last couple of days, once pissed, once sober. His name was Riquelme, though everyone seemed to called him Rikki. He was Colombian. He was said to hold court in a four-star hotel along the coast. Not a gram of cocaine came into Cambados without his say-so.

Rikki was still waiting for an answer to his question. Winter swallowed a mouthful of lukewarm lager and glanced at his watch. Conversations like this he didn't need.

'I'm fifty in a year or two . . .' He looked up . . . 'And

you know the present I've always promised myself? Retirement. No more fannying around. No more working my arse off for people trying to stitch me up. No more chasing brain-dead junkies around. But you know something about my line of work? It doesn't pay. Not the kind of money I'm going to need. So what do I do? I look for someone who might take me seriously for once. And for someone who might understand what I'm really worth. Happens I've found that someone. And that someone, just now, needs a bit of support. *Comprende?*'

Winter waited for some kind of response. The Colombian studied him for a moment or two, then produced a thin cheroot.

'Bullshit,' he said softly.

One

There are no post-mortem clues for last impressions. Was this body on the slab really asleep when it happened? Was he dreaming? Or did some faint scrape jolt him into wakefulness? Did he half discern a strange shape – mysterious, uninvited, inexplicable – beside the bedroom door? Did he hear the lightest of breaths? A footfall on the carpet? Was he aware of a looming shadow in the darkness? And maybe the soft rustle of clothing as an arm was slowly raised beside the bed?

Faraday, watching the pathologist lift the glistening brain from the cup-like remnants of the shattered skull, could only wonder. Soon, he thought, they'll be developing a test for all this, some kind of clever biochemical method for reproducing a man's last thoughts imprinted before the neurones shut down for ever. The process would doubtless be both lengthy and expensive but days later investigators would find themselves looking at a multicoloured printout, admissible in court, a digital snapshot of this man's final seconds of life. What had gone on inside his brain. What he'd seen. What he'd felt. The green line for apprehension. The red for disbelief. The black one, the thickest, for terror.

Looking up, the pathologist caught Faraday's eye. Earlier, before peeling back the face, he'd indicated the powder burns on the pale skin of the man's forehead. Now he pointed out the pulpy blancmange of the frontal tissue, pinked with blood and tiny fragments of bone where the bullet had tumbled into the deep brain, destroying everything in its path.

'Single shot.' He murmured, reaching for the scalpel, 'Unusual, eh?'

It was. Driving back to the Major Crimes suite at Kingston Crescent, Faraday pondered the investigative consequences of the pathologist's remark. The post-mortem he'd just attended was a coda to the day's events, a painstaking dismemberment of flesh, bone and connective tissue that normally yielded a modest helping of clues. Killings were usually ill-planned, spontaneous explosions of violence, sparked by rage or alcohol, or a simple desire to get even, and that kind of retribution left a telltale spoor of all too familiar wounds. In this case, though, it had been evident from the start that the Major Crime Team were dealing with something very different.

A single bullet at point-blank range was the mark of a professional hit, a calling card rarely left at Pompey scenes of crime. The news had found its way to the duty D/C at Major Crimes at 07:56. An agency cleaner, failing to raise the tenant at a leased house in Port Solent, had let herself in. In the master bedroom lay the body of the man she knew as Mr Mallinder. At first she'd assumed he'd overslept. Only when she saw the blood on the sheet beneath his head did she take a proper look at his face. She'd never seen an entry wound before and the statement she'd volunteered that afternoon had recorded the faintest disappointment. So small. So neat. So different to what you might have expected.

Faraday had driven up from the Bargemaster's House, pushing north against the incoming rush-hour traffic, summoned by the Duty D/S at Kingston Crescent. Port Solent was a marina development tucked into the topmost corner of Portsmouth Harbour. No. 97 Bryher Island was an end unit in a tightly packed close of executive houses, and uniforms had taped off the scene within minutes of their arrival. By the time Faraday added his ageing Mondeo to the line of cars in the central parking bay, an investigator from Scenes of Crime was already sorting out a pile of silver boxes from the back of his van.

'Beautiful job.' He nodded towards the open front door. 'Nice to have a bit of quality for once.'

Back at Kingston Crescent, early evening by now, the car park was beginning to empty. Faraday slotted his Mondeo into a bay beside the rear entrance and spent a moment or two leafing through the post-mortem notes he'd left on the passenger seat. Amongst them was a reminder to phone home and tell Gabrielle that their planned expedition to the Farlington bird reserve would have to wait.

He peered out through the open window. After another glorious September day, it was still warm, the air thick with midges. Shame, he thought. There would have been swallows everywhere, a manic scribble of scimitar wings overhead, and later a chance for Gabrielle to pit her camera skills against a classic Pompey sunset.

He took the stairs two at a time, with a steely resolution that lasted until the first landing. A minute or so later, still out of breath, he put his head round the door of the office that housed the Intelligence Cell. D/C Jimmy Suttle occupied one of the three desks.

'So what've you got for me?'

Suttle abandoned a packet of crisps, wiped his fingers on the chair, and reached for a notepad. Still on light duties after a serious run-in with a Southsea drug dealer, the young D/C had surprised even himself with his talent for coaxing some kind of picture from a multitude of databases and carefully placed phone calls.

'You want the story so far?'

'Yeah.'

'The guy was a property developer. Jonathan Daniel

Mallinder. The firm's called Benskin, Mallinder. His oppo's name is Stephen Daniel Benskin. They work out of a suite of offices in Croydon. The stuff they do is mostly residential, town-centre developments, mainly in the south. I talked to the FIU and belled a couple of contacts they gave me. Seems that the blokes themselves, Benskin and Mallinder, are a bit of a legend in the business. Came from nowhere but put together some really shrewd deals. Class operators. Staked out some territory of their own. Real respect.'

Faraday nodded. The Financial Investigation Unit was an obvious port of call in a case like this.

'You've talked to Benskin?'

'Yeah, this morning. I assumed the news would have got through but it turned out it hadn't. The bloke couldn't believe it. He was sitting in Heathrow waiting for a flight to Barcelona. He'll come straight back after the meeting and says he'll be down here first thing tomorrow.'

Suttle glanced up, his finger anchored in the pencilled scribble on his notepad. According to Benskin, he said, Mallinder had been shuttling down to Portsmouth for a while in a bid to sort out a major project. Lately, he'd been staying over for nights on end. Hence the three-month lease on the house in Port Solent.

'Project?'

'The Tipner site. You know when you come in on the motorway? The greyhound stadium? The scrapyard? All that? The land's zoned for development. It's complicated as hell but it seems that our Mr Mallinder had become a player. There was nothing signed and sealed but it seems that he was keen to have the whole lot off the people who own it. Benskin says that Mallinder was looking for a result before Christmas.'

Faraday sank into the chair across the desk. Tipner was a muddle of terraced houses, light industrial sites and acres of scrapyard littered with the bones of dismembered military kit. The spur motorway straddled the scrapyard and on the harbour side, for years, incoming motorists had enjoyed a fine view of a rusting submarine alongside the tiny quay. The sight had often brought a smile to Faraday's face. It buttonholed you. It made no apologies for the mess. It was chaotic, deeply martial and spoke of the perpetual struggle to make money out of half-forgotten wars. As an introduction to the rest of the city, it couldn't have been more perfect.

'What are they going to do with the site?'

'Develop it. There's a kind of plan already. Basically, we're talking offices, a bit of retail, plus a load of apartments. That's where the real money is. Secured parking, poncy kitchen, balcony you can sit out on, nice view of Portchester Castle, three hundred grand a shot, easy.' Suttle glanced up. 'That's according to an estate agent mate of mine. Put in a couple of hundred units and you're looking at serious money. No wonder Mallinder was up for it.'

'What else have you got on him?'

'Married, Wimbledon address, two kids, both school age.'

'Anyone been in contact with the wife yet? Apart from the local uniforms?'

'Me, boss. She's coming down tomorrow with Benskin first thing. Jessie's going to find somewhere up near Port Solent for her to use as a base. The scene won't be released for a while yet.'

'Jessie's FLO?'

'Yeah.'

Jessie Williams was a long-serving D/C, new to major crimes, with a smile that could warm an entire room. As Family Liaison Officer, she'd be doing her best to buffer Mallinder's widow from the pressures of the coming days.

Faraday sat back in the chair, turning his gaze towards the window. Try as he might, he couldn't rid his mind of the sight of Mallinder's brain, lying in a

476

shiny stainless-steel bowl, swimming in a thin broth of pinkish fluids. How many enemies might a man like this have acquired? Who had he upset?

'Form?'

'Nothing to get excited about. Got himself involved with a traffic stop a couple of months back. Some kind of dodgy manoeuvre on the A3 running north towards Petersfield. The woollies let him off with a caution.'

'But nothing on PNC?'

'Zilch.'

'Shame.'

The Police National Computer listed all known offenders. A conviction for fraud or money laundering would have been nice, thought Faraday. In these situations you were always looking for short cuts, the first hints of debts unsettled, just a single tiny straw poking out through the toppling haystack of a man's life.

'Timeline?'

'He came down from London yesterday morning. His wife said he left after breakfast. His diary had a couple of meetings in the afternoon, one with a council bloke, the other with a planning consultant. That last meeting went on a bit and they had a drink afterwards.'

'Where?'

'Gunwharf.' Suttle named a pub, the Customs House. 'The guy he was with says Mallinder was on good form. In fact this guy would have stayed for a meal with him but he had to get home.'

'So Mallinder ate alone? At the Customs House?'

'As far as we know, though the girl at the food bar couldn't put a face to the card slip. His next-door neighbour in Port Solent says he was back at the house around half nine. It all seems to fit.'

'And he was alone then?'

'No idea. She just heard the car pull in.'

'Did she say anything else? Anything . . .' Faraday frowned ' . . . about regular visitors, for instance?'

'Yeah. Seems Mallinder had a girlfriend.'

'Description?'

'Asian girl. Medium height. On the young side. Nicely dressed. Called by three or four times that the woman knew about, mostly around ten. Stayed an hour or so, then left.' Suttle was grinning. Not rocket science, is it?'

'A tom?'

'Has to be. The guy's married. He has kids, a career, a reputation, all that bollocks. Plus he's probably minted. A proper relationship, a girlfriend, she'd probably have stayed the night. No . . .' He shook his head. 'A tenner says Mallinder was buying it. Makes every kind of sense.'

'She came by car?'

'On foot, according to their neighbour. Need we enquire further?'

Faraday nodded. Suttle was probably right. Currently Port Solent supported two escort agencies, both catering for the higher end of the market. For someone in Mallinder's position company was a phone call away.

'We've actioned it?'

'Tomorrow, first thing. We didn't get to the neighbour until close of play. She works at IBM. Gets home at five thirty. The description's pretty detailed. Piece of piss, boss. Should be.'

'Excellent. What have we got in the way of seizures?'

'Just a laptop and a digital camera. Plus Mallinder's briefcase. There's an address book in the briefcase and some paperwork, but according to Benskin most of the real stuff will be on the laptop. Bloke came over from Netley to sort it out.'

Faraday nodded. In evidential terms, PCs and laptops needed careful handling. The process was time-consuming and the Hi-Tech Unit was overwhelmed with jobs. The last time he'd checked, there was a three-month wait for hard-disk analysis.

'We may need to fast-track it,' he said. 'Is there anything else?'

Suttle shook his head, then bent to his notepad to make sure. Faraday was on his feet, tidying his own notes, when there came a knock at the door. It opened to reveal a woman in her early thirties. She was wearing jeans and a pair of battered Reeboks. A rumpled off-white linen jacket hung loosely over a bleached pink T-shirt and the tan suggested a recent vacation. She was looking at Faraday. Lightly freckled face. A hint of caution in the green eyes.

'D/C Suttle?'

Faraday shook his head, nodded at the figure behind the desk. Suttle clearly hadn't a clue who this woman was.

''D/I Hamilton.' She smiled. 'Gina. We talked on the phone.'

'Yeah, of course we did.' Suttle pushed his chair back and shook the outstretched hand. 'Shit, I'm sorry. This is D/I Faraday.'

Faraday, too, recognised the name. Gina Hamilton was a Devon and Cornwall Detective Inspector attached to the Major Crime Incident Team at Exeter. A long-term drugs inquiry had brought her to Portsmouth, though Faraday was vague about the details. A phone call from HQ earlier in the week had asked him to sort out a D/C to give Hamilton whatever assistance she required, and Jimmy Suttle – still largely office-bound – had been the first name in the frame.

Suttle was indicating the spare chair across the desk. In a couple of minutes he'd be through for the day. She could use the phone, read the paper, whatever. Then, if she fancied it, he'd take her to the bar upstairs for a drink. Hamilton was watching him, amused.

'A phone would be good,' she said.